LET'S HOPE FOR THE BEST

LET'S
HOPE
FOR THE
BEST

CAROLINA SETTERWALL

TRANSLATED BY ELIZABETH CLARK WESSEL

Little, Brown and Company

New York   Boston   London

First North American Edition: July 2019

Let's Hope for the Best was originally published in Sweden by Albert Bonniers Förlag as *Låt oss hoppas på det bästa*: March 2018.

The Hachette Speakers Bureau provides a wide range of authors for speaking events. To find out more, go to hachettespeakersbureau.com or call (866) 376-6591.

ISBN 978-0-316-48962-1
LCCN 2018962442

10 9 8 7 6 5 4 3 2 1

LSC-C

Printed in the United States of America

This book is dedicated to:

Ivan, for keeping me busy since February 2014 and whose sole existence brings me endless worry and daily laughter. Thank you for showing me how to love unconditionally. Don't you ever dare move out or turn your back on me in any way whatsoever. No pressure.

My friends and family. Thanks for sticking with me even though my grief sometimes makes me an egocentric pain in the ass. Good karma will reward you in the end. I hope. Because you sure deserve it.

All the people who told me to write and to keep writing. Maybe it was something you just said to encourage me, give me something to do during all those dark nights. It doesn't matter. It changed my life. Thank you.

LET'S HOPE FOR THE BEST

PROLOGUE

May 2014

I'M NURSING ON the sofa when your email arrives. Nowadays this is all I do. I nurse, then sit as still as I possibly can while holding a sleeping baby, terrified to wake him, terrified he might start screaming again. Then I nurse again, sit very still again, attempt to put the now sleeping baby down so I can take a shower or eat, I fail, I go back to the sofa, I nurse. Day in, day out. Ivan is three months old on the day your email arrives. You're back at work. I have no idea which freelance job you're at since you rarely tell me about them. An advertising production company or some freelance commercial director has probably hired you for your technical skills. You say your job is so boring that I wouldn't even want to hear how you spend your days. I used to insist you tell me anyway, but not anymore. I let you decide if you want to tell me about your job, or not.

As for me, I breastfeed. On your way home every day, you text me and ask what you should pick up for dinner. You take care of most things around the house now. You work, buy groceries, cook, clean, and play with our cat, who's been neglected since Ivan arrived. You've stopped exercising for the time being. I nurse and nurse. And then, on a Thursday in early May, just after one o'clock in the afternoon, I receive an email from you.

From: Aksel
To: Carolina
May 8, 2014, 13:05
Subject: If I die

Good to know if I croak.

My computer password is: ivan2014
There's a detailed list in Documents/If I die.rtf

Let's hope for the best!

/Aksel

I read the email three times in a row. At first I can't make sense of it, then I read it again and start to feel worried. After the third reading, my worry morphs into annoyance. This is so like you. No one is as blunt, as unsentimental, as compulsively realistic as you are. You, with your bone-dry emails and text messages. You, with your never-ending backups of your computer and phone. You, with your constantly changing passwords, combinations of upper- and lowercase letters, numbers, and special characters. You, who don't want to be buried when you die, just scattered to the wind somewhere no one would feel obliged to visit with flowers and candles. No one but you would send an email like this, in the middle of the day, from work, to his girlfriend at home nursing on the sofa. But you did.

I don't respond. Instead, I ask you about it that evening at the dinner table. "What's the deal with this?" I say, and you tell me, just as I knew you would, "It was a whim, and besides, a person can never be too careful." It's stuff I should know just in case something happens. We leave it at that. We never mention the email again.

2009–2014

October 2014

IT'S A SUNDAY in October. We're both tired and not particularly kind to each other. I've hardly slept; Ivan was at my breast for the whole of yet another night. I still haven't mastered the trick of falling asleep between feedings, and now that Ivan is eight months old the future doesn't look particularly bright on that front. So I'm always tired. Today I'm also annoyed and feeling sorry for myself. You're stressed out and trying to finish some project. You still haven't told your clients that next week you're going on parental leave half-time. We argue about that a lot. I want you to lighten your workload so you'll have the time—and energy—for our life, our child, our world. You don't want to. Or you say that you want to but you can't. Free-lancing doesn't work like that, you tell me. You've worked hard to build your clientele, and if you disappear for six months, they'll find someone new. Replace you. You're tired too. When you relax, your face looks sad. You don't have the energy to even think about your imminent paternity leave, mornings with Ivan followed by a full day of work. I'm stressed too. Grumpy. Anxious. This isn't what I imagined family life would be like. You tell me I knew what I was getting into when I chose to have a child with you. I tell you I was hoping things would be different. We don't want to make each other sad, but lately that seems almost impossible. Still, we keep trying.

Three weeks ago we moved, a move we had no time for, but which we pushed through anyway. We packed at night during the brief periods when Ivan was sleeping by himself. We packed in silence, avoiding any conversations that might cause pain or end in an argument. We moved the same way.

9

We've almost unpacked everything now. Today we have to take a break because our car has started acting up. We're going to drive out to your parents' house and have your dad take a look at it. We load Ivan into the car seat in the back, you climb in next to him, and I drive. I can't help pointing out for the hundredth time in a cheery tone of voice that's fooling nobody how handy it would be if you had a driver's license too. You clench your jaw and tell me you'll get to it soon. I don't ask when because I don't have the energy to argue today. I already feel guilty just mentioning it. We both fall silent. Ivan is in a good mood, and you keep him that way by distracting him with funny sounds and toys. I find it hard to drive when Ivan cries, and no one makes him laugh like you do. Listening to the two of you playing in the back as we get closer and closer to your parents' house, I think: I love my little family. Things are just a bit tough for us right now.

At your parents' place, you work on the car with your dad while I drink tea with your mom. She interrogates me, discreetly and respectfully, about how things are going for us. I answer, less discreetly but still respectfully, that life's a lot to handle right now. We don't get much sleep, and you're stressed out. The move was rough, and Ivan's having nightmares. He wants to breastfeed all night. "We don't even have time to think about how we feel right now," I say, which is a lie.

Your older brother pulls into the driveway. His visit is unexpected, and through the kitchen window I see how surprised you both are to see each other. You laugh as you hug each other. He thumps you on your back. You are engulfed by his arms. He's always been much bigger than you. Shorter, but wider and stronger. You light up, laughing at something he says, as the two of you head into the house. Your step is quick on the stairs.

10

You're in a hurry to get to the kitchen and show off Ivan. Your big brother has met Ivan only once before. Not for lack of interest, but everyone's just been so busy lately. Your brother coos over Ivan, says he's gotten so big, that he looks just like you. He calls you "little bro." He slurps down his coffee in large gulps. You drink a glass of Coke. Then you both go back out to the car, and I follow with Ivan strapped to my waist in his carrier. I take out my phone and snap a picture of all three of you standing by the car, trying to figure out what's wrong with the wipers, not yet able to fix them. In the picture, your backs are toward the camera; one of you is scratching his head. You are two brothers and a father who will never again meet in this life, but nobody knows that yet.

April 2009

I'm headed to a former schoolhouse on the island of Adelsö. Friends of mine have rented it and transformed the old building into a summer paradise. They always throw amazing parties. They invite hundreds of people, tickets go fast, and the lucky ones end up with a seat on a chartered bus before it sells out. Inside the school's pine-scented assembly hall, with its high ceilings and creaky floors, there's cheap wine and beer for sale. The hosts are musicians and creative types, so there are usually live performances by bands I like. This is the fourth or fifth time I've been to one of these parties, and I'm pumped.

I'm thirty, and my love life is a mess. I just broke up with a guy from the north of Sweden a few days ago. For a moment I thought he might be the one, but a short affair was enough to realize I was wrong. I reacted in my usual way. I twisted myself out of the whole thing through writing, blasted off an email telling him it wasn't his fault, it's me, I'm not in the right place in my life right now. I don't know why I always find it so hard to reject people. The thought of hurting someone gives me tremendous anxiety. I imagine them destroyed for days or weeks, their self-esteem damaged, their will to live gone. Ending a relationship makes me feel so guilty—even when I need to in order not to continue with something that makes me anxious—that often I've stayed much longer than I should. Since I've made a promise to both myself and my therapist to break that pattern, these days I end things more quickly than before. But I still have just as much anxiety. It's always been like this. And now it's happened again.

It went fairly well this time. Probably because we'd been seeing each other for only a few weeks and maybe because he wasn't particularly into me either. In fact, the breakup went so smoothly that he decided to keep his ticket to this party, which I'd insisted he buy, and attend anyway. With a friend. As a friend.

I feel self-conscious when I see him on the bus but say hello and hug him. Pretend everything is normal. Like I don't have a hint of guilt. I'm just a liberated woman who happens to know what she wants in her life. The truth, of course, is that I have no idea what I want. I haven't for a long time. A vague desire to stop messing around and find the right person hasn't proved sufficient to actually make things right. My love life has been messy for a few years now. But the Northerner doesn't need to know that. We're not going to spend our lives together anyway. And on the bus, with every glass of wine I drink and every mile I put between myself and Stockholm, I feel better. After all, things are pretty much as they should be.

I dance and dance, and my feet never want to stop moving. My throat never wants to stop swallowing wine. I climb up into a deep window casement in the old school's assembly hall and dance all by myself, enjoying the feeling of being unreachable, people's eyes on me. I'm notorious among my friends for climbing up onto furniture or bars or chairs or speakers or stages or window frames in order to dance. Preferably by myself. It's sort of a tradition. So I do it again tonight. I switch between the dance floor, the window, and bellowing with my friends who are spinning records. I go outside to pee in the woods when the line to the bathroom is too long. Every now and then I see the Northerner in the crowd, and every time he stares straight back at me. He nods a greeting, but his eyes are sad. My friend starts calling him Sad Puppy Eyes. I laugh. We're being mean, but I don't care. I'm going to dance and get drunk, and everything is as it should be.

And then, suddenly, there you are. I've never seen you before. You couldn't have been on the same bus as me. Your friend, an acquaintance of mine, says he wants to introduce me to somebody who "loves" me. And suddenly you are standing there. A grin on your face. Tall and lanky with a smile like a horizontal triangle. A cowboy's smile in an old movie. Crooked and twisted and wide and genuine. It covers your whole face. I can't help thinking you'd make a really good cartoon, the kind that makes you happy when you look at it. You're wearing a hoodie. I have to bend my neck back to look up at you. You didn't hear the words our mutual acquaintance used to introduce you, but I get the feeling it doesn't matter. You don't look like someone who would care anyway.

I have a bad habit of taking command when I'm drunk. As a kind of protection against the possibility of rejection, I take the opportunity immediately when it reveals itself, and this evening that opportunity is you. I have decided that I think you're attractive. Tall and crooked and then there's that smile. Your eyes are huge. You really would be so fun to draw. I take you by the hand, you don't protest when I do so, and I drag you outside. It's still light. It can't be later than nine. But who cares about mundane things right now? Not me and not you. In the light, I notice your eyes are almost absurdly blue. I am going to ask you if you're wearing contacts. But not yet.

Outside in the yard there's a hot dog stand set up inside what was once a pigsty. We get in line. You keep a firm grip on my hand. You look like you'd kiss me with the slightest encouragement. I hold back. I ask how old you are. You say twenty-eight. I'm relieved; I thought you were much younger. I ask what you do for work. You say media. I'm preparing to analyze your reaction when I tell you I work in the music industry, with big concerts, but you don't ask. You don't seem to care about my age or my job. You look like you want to make out with me. Your smile is infectious, and I decide that's enough. Enough for me to lead you away from the hot dog line and out toward the back of the school. We make our way to a birch tree standing in a small meadow. I peed somewhere in the vicinity about an hour ago. The bass line is thumping from the dance floor in the building behind us. I kiss you. Or maybe you kiss me.

I kiss you, you kiss me, your hands cup my face, and I love it. I love the way you kiss, and I love your hands, and I love how tall you are, and I love that crazy crooked mouth that never stops grinning, even when we're making out. We neck like teenagers, you pressing yourself against me, me pressed against the birch tree, the back of my shirt covered with bits of bark. If I were more gracefully built, I would lift myself from the ground and

14

wrap my legs around you, but that's not what happens. Instead, we end up pinned against each other and the birch tree like two overeager fourteen-year-olds.

I tell you we can keep doing this later, but not inside, not around all those people. I tell you there's a man inside who is sad, and I'm not sure if I'm telling you this to brag or to seem thoughtful or because I actually am thoughtful. Everything is blurry now, driven by impulse. For the rest of the evening we alternate between dancing with our friends and running out to the birch tree to make out. These sessions become more intense as the night goes on. At one point we exchange phone numbers to make it simpler to set up our meetings by the birch tree.

At one o'clock the party ends, and two buses transport us all back to Stockholm again. The two of us make sure to sit in the front row of the bus that Sad Puppy Eyes is not on, and so I give myself full permission to kiss you passionately in the darkness. People are screaming drunkenly in the back. Between kisses, you make me listen to AC/DC in one of your earbuds. I say I'm not a fan, and then ever so casually mention that I worked with the band a few times. The information doesn't seem to impress you. You say, "Listen here. Listen to this," and then you kiss me again. You lift me up and park me across your knees. I love being lifted by you, and I love sitting on your lap. Finally, astride you.

When the bus arrives an hour later, I have a red rash from your stubble on my chin and cheeks. It's been so long since I made out with anyone like this. We get off the bus, and you want to go home with me. I won't allow it. You ask again and get another no. You suggest I go home with you instead. "Come on," you say. "I just want to sleep next to you." "No," I say. "I'm sleeping alone tonight." I suppose I want to seem like the kind of person who doesn't have sex on the first night. If we were to go home together, that's definitely what would happen. I don't want that to happen. I do want that to happen. But more than that, I want there to be a next time for us. We say goodbye, and I see your head bumping along to the music as your back disappears down Folkungagatan. Before I fall asleep, I get a text message from you. You tell me I'm hot and that you want to see me again.

October 2014

I wake up next to Ivan at six thirty in the morning. We actually got a good night's sleep. Well, everything is relative, but good by our standards. Ivan—soon nine months old and sleeping in his own room since the move three weeks ago—is having night terrors. I still breastfeed between three and six times a night. I mostly end up sleeping on a mattress on the floor of his room, even though the plan was that you and I would finally spend our nights together again. Yesterday evening, after trying to comfort Ivan from ten to eleven, then nursing for what seemed like forever, while you sat in the kitchen working, finally I just texted you from the bed. I wrote that I'd have to stay with Ivan again, and you answered with a simple "Okay" and "Good night." Not long after that, I heard you moving between the bedroom and the living room. You turned off all the lights, brushed your teeth, and went to bed.

I didn't fall asleep right away. Instead, I googled "night terrors in infants" and read the official Swedish health recommendations and posts in a bunch of online parents' forums. After reading more and pondering whether or not Ivan could

16

be suffering from something that's more common in older children, I felt quite convinced. Ivan is having night terrors; that's why he's inconsolable. It almost always happens about an hour after he falls asleep for the night, which fits the descriptions online. I took a screenshot of one of them and texted it to you with this: "I think Ivan's having night terrors. Check this out." You didn't answer. Your bedroom was quiet. I assumed you'd fallen asleep, or maybe you were just reading and didn't feel like answering. I fell asleep shortly after that.

I wake up almost rested. The cat hasn't been whining outside Ivan's room as she sometimes does, and Ivan only needed to breastfeed two times after his outburst just before midnight. He's in a good mood, ready to crawl out of our temporary bed on the floor, aiming for the door and an adventure in the rest of the apartment. I lift him up, tell him it's time to go wake up Daddy. When I open the door, the cat's waiting for us and allows us to pet her. She too seems newly awake. We all head toward your room.

I put Ivan down on the bed so he can crawl over to you, be the first thing you see when you open your eyes. I say, "Good morning, Daddy," in that tone I use when I'm speaking to Ivan but directing my words toward another adult. Mostly to you. Ivan takes aim for your head, but before he can really get going I notice that something's wrong. The way you're lying is unusual. Crooked and bent, in the fetal position, your face pressed against the pillow. There's also something odd about your skin. It's paler than usual. Lifeless.

I don't want to touch your ankle, which is sticking out from under the blanket near where I'm standing, but I do anyway. It's cold. Pale. Stiff against my fingers. There's no blood flowing inside. You're not there anymore. You're dead. I just know that now.

17

*　　*　　*

My reflexes take over. I lift up Ivan and hold him in one arm while my brain shuts down all emotion and I start to act rationally, more rationally than I have ever acted before. I call the emergency services number, and when a woman answers, it all flows out in a single breath: what's happened, my name, your name, where we live, what our door code is. "Come quick," I say. "Right now. I can't stay here anymore." Ivan stretches for the bed, and I hold him tightly, a little too tightly, against my hip.

The woman on the phone asks me to slow down and check your neck for a pulse. I tell her there's no point, but I obey her and do so anyway. With Ivan on one hip and the phone balanced between my shoulder and my ear, I run my hand along your neck. It's cold. Lifeless. Again, I tell the woman it's no use, there's no pulse, there's no one there, you're no longer alive.

I don't know why I do it, but I grab your shoulder. I turn your body over, even though I know you're dead. You're heavy, and I almost lose my balance and fall onto you as I turn your face upward. Your left cheek has an imprint from the fabric of your pillow, and your skin is a pale yellow. One of your eyes, the one that was on the pillow, is slightly open. Your blue eye is no longer as blue as it used to be. Now it's gray, and it will never see our son or me again. I let go of your shoulder when I see the open eye. Your body falls back into the same position I just dislodged it from. You're as dead as a person can be, and I can't stay in this room another second.

I tell that to the woman on the phone, and then I hang up. I wrap a blanket around Ivan and put him in his baby carrier, then drape a sweater around my shoulders. I lock the cat in the bathroom, put her food and water in there with her before I go. I know that the next person who enters this apartment won't be me, and I don't want her to escape.

I go out the front door. Take the elevator down to the ground level, go out into the courtyard, and sit down on a bench. Waiting for the ambulance. The sun is just starting to rise.

It takes at least a half hour for them to arrive. I'm lying. It only takes a few minutes, but it feels like a half hour. Our neighbors pass by us on their way to work or to drop their kids off at school, and they glance over at us where I sit in my pajamas with Ivan in his carrier and a blanket. Nobody says a word. One neighbor turns their eyes away. Another nods a greeting first. I nod back. I realize I need to call someone. I don't know who. I call your big brother. The ambulance arrives.

May 2009

"I'll never be unfaithful," you say, staring at me from less than a foot away in bed. I wonder if you mean to me specifically or if you're just sharing a general moral principle. It's unclear. A common occurrence with you. You tell me something, no frills, a deceptively simple statement that leaves me full of questions I don't yet dare to ask you. I find it enthralling. You're different and I like you. A lot.

We're both lying naked in bed in your sparsely furnished apartment on Långholmsgatan in the Hornstull area of Stockholm. It's suffocatingly hot inside, with windows on just one side of your apartment. There's no air circulation. There are also no curtains for shade, and the sun beats down inside almost all day. But we're at your place because this is where you like to be.

And I'm not picky. We spend quite a lot of time here now. In your apartment, in your bed, naked.

The day after our first meeting, we ended up here after another party, which we also spent entangled, this time under a blanket, on a sofa, at an outdoor bar. It felt impossible to put it off anymore—apparently twenty-four hours was enough for me to prove whatever I was trying to prove, and obviously it was long enough for you too. Now we're lying here, and you tell me you'll never be unfaithful. I mumble an "Oh, good" and think about all the times I've been unfaithful. I find it hard to return the promise, but I like the way you think. It says something about you. I've known you for two weeks now. I want to know everything about you, but I hold back. I try not to ask more questions about you than you ask me. And you don't ask much. So I return the favor.

The first time I saw your apartment I asked if you'd just moved in. You have almost no furniture. An empty hallway, a living room with only a sofa, a TV, and a small desk in one corner. On the desk, your work computer and some Post-its with small notes written on them. Your handwriting is beautiful, the letters tiny. Even the capital letters are small. I didn't know it yet, but the names on those Post-its belong to various production companies you work for. "Backup Callboy" says one. "Fix Annelie's email" says another. "Server Camp David" stands on a third. One Post-it reads only "NEVER AGAIN." When I asked you what it meant, you told me it was a reminder never to take on so much work again. You told me you almost had a breakdown last year. You had to work around the clock and lost a lot of weight. You never want to do that to yourself again. I told you I could relate, mentioned that my job requires a lot of late nights. And to that you shrugged and answered, "Well then, just quit," as if it were the easiest thing in the world. As if my job didn't impress you at all. I think I fell even more in love with you then.

In your bedroom: a bed and a bench press. Nothing else. No rugs, no curtains, nothing on the walls except a print of a sky-scraper with a single cloud hanging in the sky beside it.

You didn't seem to understand why I asked if you'd just moved in. You told me you'd lived here for eight years. According to you, this was the perfect amount of possessions. You hinted that you'd grown up surrounded by a lot of stuff and didn't want that for yourself. Collections, knickknacks, dust—it makes you nervous. I thought maybe you had taken it to an extreme. And did you actually use that bench press regularly? I thought you were an oddball. It made you even more interesting to me.

But for the time being, all we need is your bed. This is where we spend our evenings, our nights, our mornings, and a good portion of our weekends. When we're hungry, we go out to eat, and when we go out, we take long walks. You keep your arm around me, and I love how tall you are. I like the feel of your arm around my waist, and secretly I hope we'll run into people we know as we stroll along Årstaviken, between Skanstull, where I live, and Hornstull, where you live. I want to be seen with you. I want my friends and acquaintances to run into us. "Oh, who was that?" I want them to whisper afterward. "What a cute couple," I like to imagine them saying. "What a tall, beautiful person," I want them to think. I'm proud to belong to you, and even though we haven't talked about it yet, that's how I feel. I belong to you.

We've met basically every other day since that first night, and when we don't meet, we keep in close contact via chat and text message. I've learned several things about you already. You don't like talking on the phone. You're like two different people in text and in person. When you write, you sound almost harsh, go straight to the point, and that's it. But in person, you're warm, thoughtful, funny, physical, and always on the verge of laughter. You like kissing and holding hands, even when we're not in bed. And, yes, you wear contact lenses. They intensify those clear blue eyes. You can't see much without them. When you're home at night, you take out your contacts and put on a pair of glasses, which you hate but I love. They're lopsided like your smile. Everything's a little lopsided on you. Everything's beautiful.

When we say goodbye in the mornings, we rarely make detailed plans to meet again. "Talk to you soon," you say, and I'm not brave enough to ask you exactly what that means. You never ask me about my plans, and I feel intrusive when I tell you about them. I'm fascinated by your double nature. You are complicated, paradoxical, absent and present at the same time. You are so close and far away by turns. I think about you almost constantly. I long to hear from you and find each hour I must wait excruciating.

But I do hear from you. I always end up hearing from you. If I just wait a few hours, you come back. I'm starting to learn your patterns. I'm starting to figure out how to exist in your world. I'm in love with you. It took me two weeks or two days—it's hard to say which.

October 2014

The ambulance has arrived, and a kind EMT has been up in our apartment for a few minutes. He comes back down now. Ivan

22

and I are still on a bench in the entrance hall when the EMT tells me I was right, my partner is dead. He also tells me, "If it's any comfort, he didn't die in pain. It seems to have happened peacefully, in his sleep." It's no comfort.

The EMT wants me to come back up to the apartment. I know I should do it, I know I should at least go up and change Ivan's diaper, but I can't move. I never want to go up there again.

I called your brother, and your brother called your parents. I also called my stepmother, and everyone is on their way now, racing from wherever they'd started a seemingly normal Monday morning. I tell the EMT that I want to sit here until someone I know arrives. He says that's okay. Tells me a police officer is on the way and emphasizes that this is standard procedure when a young person dies suddenly. I shouldn't feel like I'm a suspect or that anyone believes there's been a crime. This is just what they have to do. He says more, but I've stopped listening, because a neighbor is coming down the stairs and into the hall. The neighbor has her child with her, and the child stares at us. I'm in my pajamas, Ivan is in his carrier, the EMT is wearing a loud neon-yellow vest with a dark green overall underneath. The child seems curious about us and asks his mother who we are, what happened, what's our name. I don't respond. Nor does the mother. The EMT is silent as well. The neighbor hurries out, picks up the child, hushes his questions, and exits quickly onto the street. I stare down at the gray concrete floor. I feel like I no longer have a home.

The police arrive at the same time as your brother. I don't know how he has the strength, but somehow he succeeds in taking command of the situation. He leads me up into the apartment with a tight hold around my shoulders. I keep repeating myself: "I refuse to enter the bedroom ever again." He tells me I don't have to. I can stay in the kitchen. The police are there, and they need to ask me a few quick questions.

In the kitchen, the police have started going through our medicine cabinet. I hear one say to the other that it's impossible to know where to start. She looks at my over-the-counter American sleeping pills and asks whom they belong to. I say they're mine and feel ashamed for picking up so many random pills over the years. I've collected all these American pills and almost never taken any of them. Still, every time I traveled to New York I brought a new box home. It sounds insane when I try to explain it to the police. It sounds like something only a crazy person would do. The police just nod and continue sorting through medications while asking me if I'd noticed anything different about you lately. I say no. She asks why we have prescription sleeping pills. I tell them they were prescribed to me so I could sleep after being up with Ivan for so many nights in a row. I explain how he nurses constantly and has night terrors, and I've been having a hard time sleeping in between. I ask her to open the package so she can see that I haven't taken a single one—not a single pill will be missing. It's important to me that she sees I haven't taken any. As she opens up the package, I'm suddenly afraid. What if it's empty? What if you took your own life? It's the first time that thought occurs to me. It feels like her fingers move in slow motion as she opens the small cardboard box with a red warning triangle on the side. The pill bottle is full.

The police officer writes everything down and pours pill bottle after pill bottle out onto the kitchen table. I ask her when they'll be done. Her voice softens, and she says, "Soon. We just have to finish this first. It's standard procedure."

Now my stepmother enters the kitchen. She threw herself

into the car and sped down from Uppsala as soon as she got my call, about an hour ago. She's been a woman of action for as long as I've known her, almost thirty years. When she embraces me next to the kitchen table and the police, I start to cry for the first time. She cries too. I wriggle out of her arms and say, "Ivan needs breakfast and a new diaper, and I haven't managed to do any of it yet." She understands and starts to do what needs to be done, helps me with what I need the most right now. As she lifts Ivan out of my arms, I realize how tightly I've been holding on to him around his carrier, and I'm at a loss for what to do with my hands now that he's no longer in front of me. I feel sick. My stepmother hushes a now crying Ivan, changes him into a dry diaper, plays with him on the part of the dining table not covered by random medicine, and tells me my mother is on her way too. As I move to the sofa in the living room, I hear Ivan laughing, and from the corner of my eye I see my stepmother squeeze pass a police officer to get to a jar of baby food in the fridge. Now that Ivan is taken care of, I try to relax and collect my thoughts. It's impossible. I will never go into that bedroom again, I think. Never, never. Other than that, my mind is blank.

May 2009

It's your birthday tomorrow and you don't want to talk about it. According to you, birthdays are meaningless, and I should absolutely not buy you a gift. Birthdays give you anxiety; they remind you that time is passing, and you haven't accomplished anything particular lately. Birthdays for you are just a painful reminder of your shortcomings. I ask you what shortcomings you're referring to, but that makes you uncomfortable.

Obviously you don't want to continue this conversation. You tell me you've been working with the same stuff, living in the same place, doing the same things for way too many years now. I think, but don't say, that you're weird. Most people's lives are like that. They still celebrate their birthdays. And besides, now you've met me. We're almost a couple. That's a new thing, that's a big deal, right? I wonder why you don't think of it that way.

We've been seeing each other for almost four weeks now, and it weighs on me that I don't know what to give you for your birthday. It doesn't feel right to start out a relationship by not exchanging birthday presents. I decide that I have to get you something. What do I get for a person who doesn't like things, but who just happens to be the best thing that's happened to me for at least a decade? It's hard to strike the right balance, so I search for clues, what you might like, or be missing, or need. Something just right.

Your apartment offers no clues. You obviously enjoy living simply. I wouldn't dare give you art. Nor furniture—that seems too significant after just a few weeks together. Maybe something for your kitchen? So impersonal. Here, here I am with my love and a...frying pan. That won't cut it. I consider buying you clothes, but you seem picky and would probably return them if I chose wrong. Which I then couldn't help but take personally. Your wardrobe is almost as simple as your apartment. During our time together you've switched between three checkered shirts, a few white T-shirts, a dark blue hoodie, and maybe three different pairs of jeans. It often occurs to me that you have fantastic legs for jeans. You've got the hottest jeans legs I've ever seen. I wonder why you're not a jeans model with legs like that. I stop myself. I decide to wait on buying clothes until I know you a bit better.

I peep into your medicine cabinet and see, unsurprisingly, that it's basically empty. Except for a cologne bottle, which is practically full. Your shampoo and soaps aren't fancy. I linger in your bathroom. You spend a lot of time here.

You love to shower, and you shower several times a day. Tell me you think more clearly in the shower, can solve work problems and other, more existential problems as well. "Shower time," you'll say, and two seconds later you've disappeared into the bathroom and left me sitting or lying in the bed or on the sofa, my body still shaped to fit yours. You've never invited me to join you, and I haven't wanted to intrude. Once I peeked through the bathroom door and saw you there, naked with your back to me, your long, perfect legs and buttocks facing me, the shower stream directed at your chest and your eyes fastened on the white tiled wall. You didn't see me, and I quietly snuck back to my languishing on the sofa. Flipped through a book or looked at my phone so as not to appear too desperate for you to come back. Now I wonder if maybe you'd like a shower curtain. Or some expensive, luxurious soap. I reject these ideas quickly, judging them all worthless.

When your birthday arrives, it's a Thursday and a long weekend, Ascension Day, which is a holiday. We wake up from an alcohol-fueled night, our bodies entwined as usual, with yesterday's clothes in a wrinkled heap on the floor at the foot of the bed. Yesterday was one of our first times going out together, and when I wake up, I go through all the people who have seen us together now. I'm so proud to belong to you, to be the woman that you, a self-described lone wolf, have chosen to put your arm around in public. The one you kiss, the one you laugh with. I believe there's a glow around us. We're both long and lanky, more striking than classically beautiful. I imagine we stand out in a crowd, and it delights me to think so.

You're still asleep when I sneak into your kitchen, make some sandwiches, and pour a glass of juice. I can't find a tray and realize that would have made a good gift. Instead, I bought you a baking pan. Once you told me you make an amazing apple cake and that I'd faint the day you make it for me. I couldn't come up with anything better. I bought you a paperback, a humorous book about useful things you should've learned in junior high but probably forgot, and a baking pan. I'm embarrassed by my presents, but there they stand next to a glass of orange juice and two sandwiches. I do my best to push down my embarrassment, take a deep breath, head into the bedroom, and start singing.

October 2014

The police have left, and the EMT has passed the baton, meaning us, over to a coroner, who's here to ascertain cause of death. At least I think that's his task. I can only absorb fragments of sentences. Words fly around my head, and no matter how hard I try to listen, they don't penetrate. But now a doctor is here. He's gone into your room and will examine your body to see when, and why, you died.

Your mom, dad, big brother, and nephew are with us now. My stepmother is with Ivan, close by and constantly ready to step in if I need her. She also cries now and then. She lost my dad when my little sister was the same age as Ivan, so being around us reminds her of her own loss, what it was like. Despite that, or maybe because of it, she's efficient and practical now. She does what needs doing most. Focuses on Ivan. On what

28

will make things easier. She plays with him, keeps him fed and dry, brings him to me when he needs to nurse, takes him back when he's done. Continues her quiet work.

Your father breaks down now and then with a howl, a kind of bottomless cry. In between, he can't stop talking. His voice takes over the rooms. He walks around, sits down, stands up, walks on, all the time trying to make sense of things. I want to tune out both him and his voice. "It doesn't make sense," he says over and over again. "Completely incomprehensible," he says. I want silence. Your mom is silent. Her eyes aren't present. Nor are mine. I focus my eyes on various points in the room, but none of it means anything to me. Nothing registers. Your brother has taken on the role of leader and protector. He holds me, talks to me in whispering tones that don't grate on my ears, makes sure I drink water. And now the doctor is coming out of your bedroom, our bedroom. I want to vomit, absolutely don't want to hear what he has to say. I whisper to your brother that I won't go into the bedroom. I know the doctor is going to say I should.

The doctor does say so. He sits down beside me and speaks slowly. Like he's talking to a child or a deaf person, or to someone who's incapable of understanding; he articulates every word, and I realize he's trying to penetrate the fog around me. He's done this many times before.

"Carolina, listen to me, and I'll tell you what I can about what happened. Are you following me now? You can ask me any questions you want, and I will try to respond so that you understand. Aksel died in his sleep late last night, probably just a few hours before you went into the room. I can't right now say for sure why he died. His body won't tell me that yet. It might have been his heart. We're going to need to do some tests to determine cause of death. But, Carolina, listen now. He died painlessly. You hear me? He didn't suffer. It happened in his sleep. He was sleeping just like he slept every night. It's important that you listen to me now. After some time passes you'll be glad to know this, once everything sinks in. He died painlessly, probably never woke up. And I want you to understand, Carolina, that it would have made no difference if you were in the room when it happened. You could not have saved him. When a heart stops like Aksel's did, there's nothing we can do, even if the patient is in a hospital when it happens. Even then it's not certain you can save someone with this type of cardiac arrest. I can't tell you today why his heart stopped, but sometimes hearts just do. It's called acute cardiac arrest. It doesn't look like he suffered. And you could not have done anything to change the situation, not if you were next to him or if you called the ambulance earlier. Soon a car will come here to transport Aksel's body to a postmortem examination center in Solna, and it's not going to be an easy thing to see. I think you should all leave here for a while. In Solna the doctors will autopsy his body and do tests to determine the precise cause of death. You'll get the name of someone to contact with the police, someone you can call and ask questions. I understand this is a lot to take in right now. But before we move Aksel's body, I want you to go into the bedroom and say goodbye. It usually feels—"

No.

No.

No.

I can't.

I've been pulled out of my passive fog in my struggle to listen as closely as I can to what the doctor's saying. Now he's come to the moment I feared. I don't want to go in there. I don't need to. "I can't handle it," I say. I did that when my dad died, and I did that when my grandmother died, but I don't have the strength now. It's impossible.

I break down. I'm shaking while I sob, and a stream of snot and saliva flows down onto your big brother's shirt, and he hugs me hard. I disappear into his arms and never want to leave them again. "You can do this," he whispers into my ear, and probably there's snot in there too, but he keeps on whispering and holding me tight. "We'll do it together," he says. "Let's do it. This is important."

I don't know how long we stand there. But somehow your parents, my stepmother, and Ivan have already been in to see you now. They surround us where we stand, circling us in a clumsy hug that almost suffocates me. I can't get any air. Their arms are all around me, and I can't breathe. They tell me it's okay, that you looked peaceful, and it will be okay.

I give up. I have to get out of that hug, breathe again, and I won't get out of here without going in to you one last time. Your big brother holds on tightly to me, and we go in, together, for one last goodbye. As we step over the threshold, I squeeze my eyes shut.

May 2009

We've been out walking all day. Right after lunch you told me this was the best birthday you can remember. In Tantolunden Park we had a picnic, and you held my hand. You discovered that I bite my nails. You looked at them, the part of my body I find most embarrassing, the part that betrays my nervousness and lack of self-control, but you didn't seem disgusted. You examined them, kissed them, stroked the blunt edges of my short nails, and after a while you stated without judgment that I have a guitarist's fingers. My heart pounded in shame, and I could feel myself turning red. I hate when anyone looks closely at my fingers, but this was you, and it had to be done. My intention is to make my fingers and thereby myself a permanent fixture in your life. In fact, I want my fingers to be in contact with your body at all times from now on.

In the afternoon your mood changes suddenly. I can't figure out what happened. You've stopped laughing at my jokes, and you seem to stare blankly into the air more often. Your side of our conversation flags. You seem to be mulling something over. You've stopped caring where we walk. I do my best to appear easygoing, talk more, make more jokes, but you're no longer present. In an effort to take control of the situation and the rest of the day, I suggest we have dinner and drinks at the outdoor restaurant part of a nightclub we both like. I think you're going to like the band playing there tonight. I start telling you about the singer's amazing voice, comparing it to Neil Young's, sharing moving anecdotes from the singer's private life. You look at me, present again, and interrupt.

"If it's okay with you, I think I'd rather go home and be alone tonight," you say.

"Yes, of course, totally okay, definitely," I say. A little too enthusiastically. I don't mean it.

Then everything happens fast. The evening is settled. We've decided to spend it apart so why not start now, appears to be your attitude. You seem relieved. When we get to the corner of your street, you give me a quick kiss on the cheek, then I watch your back and your long, perfect legs heading home fast. I watch you put your earbuds in and pull your hoodie over your head as you go. I imagine your steps as lighter now. Even your back looks happy. I stand watching you, ready to wave if you turn around. But you don't. Your silhouette disappears down the street, and when you're small enough to be obscured by the other pedestrians, I turn around too. I have no idea what just happened, and I wonder when I'll hear from you again.

I go out to celebrate your birthday without you. Meet some friends at the restaurant I'd suggested, but my mind is on you all night. My good mood has been destroyed. I can't have a good time anymore without you by my side. And now you're home. At least I think you are. You seemed happy to be going home, glad to get away from me. I won't hear from you until tomorrow—I just know it. It hurts.

October 2014

I pat you on the cheek. It doesn't feel like you. It's a body, your body, lying in that bed, but you're not there anymore. The doctor seems to have smoothed out your skin tone; maybe he put some powder on your cheeks. Your eyes are closed now, and your entire body is under the covers. No foot sticks out at the end of the bed. You lie there, dead, and I know that the point of this is to make my last memory of you be nice, peaceful. I also know that will never happen. You're just a body now. A body that a doctor staged to give us an opportunity to say goodbye.

You don't look like you anymore. You look like every other dead person I've ever seen. You look like my dad and my grandmother did. Smooth and still. Touched up, cold, pale, and...not present. Before I even opened my eyes, as your brother led me to the bed, I knew you would look like this.

33

And I know this isn't how I'll remember your death. I've already seen you dead. When it was only you, me, and Ivan.

I miss how you looked earlier this morning. I miss your wrinkled cheek, your half-open eye, your cold ankle, and the strange way you lay against the pillow. I miss you as you appeared then. I miss the last view I had of you that was private, the last moment that was just us.

I pat your cheek again and whisper goodbye. Disconnected, I watch myself doing it and feel ashamed I'm not weeping more. Your big brother is crying now, for the first time since he got here, tears streaming down his cheeks. He stifles his sobs as he talks to you, but his voice remains thick. He bends down toward you. "Goodbye, little bro," he says. Kisses you on the forehead. "My little brother," he whispers. Gently hugs you without lifting up the blanket or moving your arms. He buries his face in the pillow next to yours. "My sweet brother," I hear from the pillow.

I turn my eyes away, feel like I'm in the way, an unintentional intruder on an intimate moment. I want us to leave now. I knew I would feel this way. I did it out of a sense of duty. Now it's done. Your brother strokes your cheek one last time. We leave the room, and that's the last time I see you.

June 2009

We walk across a meadow and pass by a horse paddock. It feels like we're out in the country, but we've only taken a bus for eighteen minutes from downtown. You're taking me to your childhood home, and you tell me enthusiastically about every little grassy spot, every ditch, and every hill we pass by. "A creepy old man lived in that house when we were little," you tell me and point to a shack on a hillside. "I fell asleep there once on my way home from a party," you say, pointing to the side of a road next to a deep ditch. On the other side of the ditch is a horse paddock. I stop, hop across the ditch, go up to the electric fence, and try to attract the attention of one of the horses inside. None approach. It's early June, and the grass in their paddock is a brilliant green. Not a single lonely horse sees any reason to get near the electric fence where I stand calling to them. I'm disappointed. It would have been so nice to pet a horse's muzzle, catch my breath a bit, and drag out our last moment of being alone together today. I'm about to meet your parents for the first time, and I'm a bit nervous.

I was surprised when you asked me to come along with you. We haven't been seeing each other that long. As far as I know, you've yet to call yourself my boyfriend. Nor have you called me your girlfriend. I'm someone you're "hanging out with," as far as I know. You "like" me. Nevertheless, you wanted to take me along to your parents, introduce me to them. It puzzles me. I'm having trouble calculating your investment in this. You're stingy with labels, but you want me to meet your parents right away. The numbers don't add up. I can't make out where I stand with you. I suspect all this is only making me fall more deeply in love with you.

You don't talk much about your parents. Declared early on that you didn't have a traumatic childhood, and there simply wasn't much to say about it. I thought, involuntarily, that generally people who say stuff like that have the worst childhoods. I myself suffered a whole slew of childhood upheavals and traumas. My parents divorced when I was eight, and it crushed me when my mom moved out of our house and into a nearby apartment. My dad fell in love with the mother of my pen pal when I was nine, and that crushed me too. In a new family arrangement, we left Stockholm and moved to a farm in Västmanland when I was twelve. I grew apart from my mom during my teens. My dad was diagnosed with cancer when I was seventeen. A year later he died. Not without a hint of pride, I describe my childhood as a buffet of trauma when someone asks. I wear each one like a little jewel and wonder why you don't do so too. Could it really be that you don't have any of your own?

Since then I've tried to get you to open up. Where are you from? Who are your parents? Have they really lived together since they were teenagers, raising a family of four children with twenty-four years between the first and last? How did you rebel as a teenager? Did you do anything? How did you spend your free time? Who were you in grade school, junior high, high school? Who's your favorite sibling and why? Who broke your heart for the first time? Who raised you, where do you come from, what did you talk about at the dinner table? How did you become who you are?

By being in your physical vicinity more and more, I have, over the last few weeks, come to the conclusion that you're closest to your mother. You seem to talk on the phone often, almost every day. Your tone is often curt, almost rude during these calls. You tell her to quit smoking. Sometimes you interrupt her, say, "Hurry up and get to the point." Sometimes you make it sound like she's interrupting you, even when you were the one who called her. I've heard you call her up, snap at her, and finish the call within a minute. But you always end the conversation with "Love you" before you hang up. Sometimes you call her back immediately after you hang up and tell her you're sorry for being a grump. The whole thing puzzles me. I'm very curious about your parents. Now I'm about to meet them, and for some reason I'd like to delay that moment as long as possible.

After fifteen minutes of walking, we arrive. We turn off a small forest road, and there stands a small, boxy brown house, surrounded by a large garden. The house itself is a bit run-down, with stains on the siding and moss growing on the roof tiles. A gravel path leads up to the house, grass on either side. On one side of the yard stand some apple trees; on the other, a huge raspberry patch, the largest I've ever seen. I count five rows, each ten meters long, and the bushes are taller than you. They have to be at least two meters high. You let go of my hand and enter the raspberry patch to examine it up close. I stand next to you, saying "Oh" and "Wow." That's when your father arrives.

With bushy hair, a crooked nose, crooked glasses, stained work clothes, dirt beneath his nails, and a deep voice that is in no way reminiscent of your soft tenor, he looks exactly like what he is: a shop teacher. His bright blue eyes meet mine directly, don't shy away. He's full of curiosity, and he stretches out his hand. His grip is strong. My hand feels like a child's in his. The handshake hurts a bit. He holds on for a long time. I try to squeeze back, but it's no use. My hand is folded inside his.

Your dad welcomes me and then turns to you, where you stand in the raspberry patch looking at this year's bushes. He gives us an impromptu monologue on this year's expected harvest. "You can see our raspberry patch from Google Earth," your dad informs me with pride. He continues telling us about the raspberries. About how winter and spring weather affects the crop. How he fertilizes the bushes. How in a bad year the raspberries only last through winter, and I should know that out here they eat raspberries with pancakes for breakfast every day of the week. Your dad asks me if you told me you ate raspberries for breakfast every day of your entire upbringing. I verify that you have, eager to support your father's pride in his enormous raspberry bushes. Your dad chuckles happily, chatters on. "We had to get an extra freezer in the workshop just for the raspberries," he says. "There are no better raspberries than ours," he boasts. "Soon you'll get to taste them yourself," he promises.

We stand there for a while. Your dad's enthusiasm and volubility make me feel safe. He likes to talk. I like to listen, take things in. The dynamic suits me perfectly. Your dad is open and warm, almost childlike. When you tease him, he laughs at himself. I think: This won't be a problem. And I understand where you got your frankness, your generous ability never to cushion the truth, to always speak straightforwardly, even if it stings.

Our guided tour of the bushes ends when you interrupt your dad, tell him it's time to go in. Your dad asks me if I drink coffee, and I see in his eager eyes this is an important question for him. When I answer "Of course," he shines like the sun. "Finally somebody around here wants to drink coffee with me," he says and then takes me under the arm, and we head together toward the house.

October 2014

It's not yet noon, but it feels like I've been awake for a lifetime. It's quarter past eleven, and the coroner just told us to leave the apartment to avoid seeing them take your body away, drive off with it toward the place where they'll autopsy you. They need to determine cause of death. Verify that you died from natural causes. Or what is considered natural in this context. I'm not exactly sure. But I understand that you are now the subject of a police investigation, which is apparently automatically triggered when someone young dies suddenly and inexplicably. It's just standard procedure intended to protect the deceased and their relatives. They have to be sure. It may take months. Maybe I'm part of the investigation too? Maybe I'm the primary suspect? I don't know. I don't understand. And I can't bear to think anymore about it.

Slowly we start to fumble our way through the apartment, your mom, dad, big brother, and me. Trying to decide where to go. Unable to think beyond the next few hours, we agree to gather at your brother's house, a fifteen-minute drive from here. The next question is how to get there. Are your brother and father capable of driving right now? Do Ivan and I dare to ride along with one of them? What alternative do I have? Taking a train or bus feels overwhelming. I start packing a bag.

Ivan's diapers. Some jars of baby food. A change of clothes for me, and one for Ivan. I have no idea where I'll sleep tonight. My mind is slow and gets stuck easily. I end up staring emptily into space as I move between each room. Except the bedroom, which I avoid. Ivan is still babbling with my stepmother as she makes calls to arrange for a car seat, having realized she'll need one from now on. She's never needed to mull things over before doing them. Two of my friends are already on their way to a large gas station to buy one for her. I hear snippets of phone calls and conversations addressed directly to me but can't quite put it all together. I feel stressed by the fact that they'll be arriving in the hall at any moment to pick up your body. I don't want to see them, or the coroner's van, so I do my best to hurry.

June 2009

Your mother is beautiful and seems much more reserved than your eccentric dad. Like both you and your father, she has bright blue eyes that light up her face. I wonder if that's what the two of them first saw in each other as teenagers. Two sets of shining blue eyes that met in the beginning of the sixties. It's a nice image to ponder.

Your mother has high cheekbones, red lips, raven-black hair gathered on top of her head, and long, dark red nails. Her body is slim, more suited to a woman of my age than a mother of four on the verge of retirement. She's wearing a black dress and a long, dark gray cardigan. She's really very elegant. I feel like a bum next to her. Compared to your dad, she seems like a self-contained, dignified, and reticent observer. She examines me in return, more discreetly than your father, and I'm forced out of my role as the passive visitor doing all the observing. I want to impress her. Prove to her how capable I am. And what I'm capable of. For example, being worthy of her son.

Something about the mood in the kitchen—your dad putters around making coffee, your mother converses with us politely, and you pace restlessly between the table and the fridge—tells me this might be the first time you've brought a girlfriend home for a visit. Or somebody you're "hanging out with," to use your language. Everyone is tiptoeing around the situation, and especially around me. Sometimes there's an awkward silence, and one person rushes to fill it (usually your dad) and then someone else with the same intention (usually your mom) almost immediately interrupts them. "Go ahead." "No, you go ahead." "No, you. I had nothing important to say." Laughter.

We leave the kitchen for a tour of the house, during which

I'm apprised of the entire story of how you moved here when you were six or seven years old. Before that your family lived in a commune in a wonderful house on a lake. But sometime in the eighties the local municipality wanted the house and land back, and you were given this place in exchange. You had to make do. Your dad emphasizes that it's nothing compared to the commune, nothing compared to the huge house by the water, but this is where you've stayed. And things have been pretty good here.

Hundreds of potted plants obscure the windows, like a jungle. In the living room, the bookshelves are so stuffed the walls look like they're made of books. Six cats meander nonchalantly through the rooms, jumping on and off the furniture, lounging on the sofa, using the kitchen window to go outside. Your parents go through each cat's name and personality, and though I know it's hopeless, I do my best to memorize them all. They adore their cats—that much is clear—and talk about their personalities as if they were children.

And they also love, if the walls are anything to judge by, their books. I run my eyes along the shelves and find an impressive array of subjects. There are novels, mysteries, historical memoirs, political books, biographies, and my favorite genre: psychology. There are so many books about psychology. Probably because your mother is a therapist. I start flipping through one of them, and your father disappears into the kitchen to make more coffee. You follow him. I can hear the two of you talking about politics. Something about Per Albin Hansson and *folkhemmet*. "*Volksgemeinschaft*," your dad exclaims, drowning out the kettle in the kitchen, and I hear fragments of you two moving on to a discussion of the National Socialist German Workers' Party. I've noticed you're interested in politics and history, and it makes me feel uneducated and stupid, so I always change the subject when we're alone. Now you and your dad are debating in the kitchen. I stay with the psychology books for a while longer.

Your mother lingers on with me. We start to talk about the book I'm holding. She asks me if the subject interests me, and I tell her it does. Admit that I dream of becoming a psychologist someday. She nods, interested, and asks me what I'm working with now. I give her a brief summary of my professional history, tell her about my years at a bookstore, my short stint in the film industry, the writing I've done for magazines, and how I'm now working with concert production in the music industry. She asks me what that entails, and I say, "Late nights and long hours. I can't see myself growing old in this job." The minute I say it, I realize it's true. The two of us are already sharing confidences. We loop around to where the conversation started, and I ask her about her work in psychiatry. She tells me. The conversation flows more easily when you're not in the room. We find our own rhythm. She's a good listener and a deliberate story-teller, and soon she's interrogating me about how we met. I get the feeling she already knows the answer to her question, but I tell her anyway. About the party, about our mutual friends, and how long we've been seeing each other. Your mother listens, nods. I wonder if she approves of me. It feels like she might.

At the dinner table a few hours later, your dad does something he'll do many times over the coming years, throws out a half-formed, not quite thought through question. It seems to pop out of his mouth at the very moment it occurs to him. Half question, half unintentional insult. "So, Carro—can we call you Carro by the way? What do you really see in our... weird son? A blunt loner like him, he can't be very easy to live with. I mean, you must see something."

An abrupt silence falls across the dinner table. Your mother laughs to smooth over this far too direct question. She glances at you. I do too. But you don't seem to think it's particularly strange. You keep eating, your eyes on your plate, your salad, french fries, and the entrecôte your dad grilled on the balcony. I realize you're all waiting on me, and I decide to answer the question as bluntly as it was asked. That seems simplest. I meet your dad's eyes.

"He's the best person I've ever met."

Silence again. One second, maybe two. I start to feel embarrassed by my words. I haven't spoken so sincerely to you yet, we haven't shown each other that kind of affection, and now I've done it in front of your parents. I feel myself turning red. I don't dare look at you, so I keep staring at your dad, who nods now, apparently satisfied by my response. You don't meet my eyes, but I see you smile at your plate. My words seem to have made you happy.

We keep eating. The conversation turns to the subject of the sixties and seventies, and for the first but far from last time, I hear the story of how your parents met, about the spirit of the times and their own parents, about demonstrations and the elm trees in Kungsträdgården, and hilarious anecdotes from their years in the commune. It's a fun story. They've lived a long and eventful life. Your dad tells most of it, but your mom breaks in with corrections and additions. I listen and enjoy their story. I can relax now that the spotlight's not on me. Any further interrogation of me or my intentions toward you doesn't seem to be on the menu tonight. Also, no deeper questions about who I am and what my story is. Soon enough, we say our goodbyes and head back to the bus.

By the time we do, I feel fairly certain I've won them over.

I felt it when they hugged me goodbye in the hallway and told us to come visit again soon. I could see it in your mom's eyes when I said what I saw in you, and your dad wants to make plans for a summer trip together in a few weeks. I'm almost sure your parents are on my team now, on team you and me, and I relish it. Our numbers are growing. Soon we'll be a tiny army. Soon you'll be the only one left with any doubts. But surely I can convince you.

October 2014

At your brother's house, something snaps for many of us. We take turns breaking down. I have my first crying fit at the kitchen table. I can't stop myself from sobbing loudly, like a child, and I tell the whole group gathered there—your little brother has joined us, along with my mom and two of my best friends—what a terrible person and girlfriend I've been lately. I'm sure I was the one who killed you. It's my fault—if not directly, then at least indirectly—that you died. Your heart couldn't handle the stress of a life lived with me. I never stopped pushing you forward at a pace you didn't feel comfortable with. You tried to show me how exhausted you were, several times. I kept pushing. Your heart burst because I made it burst. Literally. Everything is my fault. I can never forgive myself. I've killed a human being. I've killed Ivan's father. Ivan will grow up without two parents now. Everything is my fault.

Your dad interrupts me, drowning me out, telling me, "Stop, just stop, Carro. You can't think like that. You're the best thing that ever happened to our son, and even if it's hard to understand right now, we knew our son for thirty-four years, so sorry,

44

but we know what we're talking about. We saw how he blossomed with you, Carro. He was happy with you. So that's that. There's nothing more to say. You made Aksel live, and you and Ivan gave his life meaning. Stop this," your dad says again, and his voice breaks. It's his turn to break down. I fall silent. Suddenly my head aches. My hair is greasy, and my face has a shiny layer of tears and sweat on it. I say I want a shower, but somehow I failed to bring my own change of clothes with me. Your brother's wife helps me upstairs, gives me a pair of socks and a towel. Tells me to lie in their bed and rest for a while after I'm done. They'll take care of Ivan. "Ivan's just fine," she promises me. I realize I haven't thought of Ivan for a while now. Where is he? How's he doing? Where's my stepmother?

I find them in the living room. Ivan is crawling around on the floor, and she's sitting next to him. I ask when he last ate. My memory of this day is fuzzy. She reminds me I breastfed just before we left the apartment. We estimate that was a couple of hours ago. I take Ivan in my arms and feed him. He eats greedily. I stare at his little cheeks as he sucks down my milk. It hasn't dried up yet, but maybe it will over the next week. I've heard that's a common reaction to shock and trauma. My stepmother's milk disappeared the day my dad died. I can't stand looking at Ivan anymore. His innocent face. His tiny ears, exact copies of yours. He has no idea of the significance of what happened to him today. No clue that this event will change his life forever. He's unaware that he'll grow up without a father and probably, most likely, that it's his mother's fault. He eats and smacks his lips, and his hand clutches at my shirt, which is balled up in my armpit. I can tell I smell like sweat.

I have to get out of here. I stop breastfeeding abruptly, leave the room, start crying again. My stepmother takes over, keeps

doing what she's been doing all day, protecting Ivan. I go up
the stairs of your brother's house. Pictures of his family line the
walls. One is of you. You're seven or eight years old. It's in black
and white. You're laughing at the camera. I turn my eyes away,
can't take any more. Need to sleep.

June 2009

Your distance has started to bother me. We've been seeing each
other for two months, and you never seem to want to make
plans with me. You protect your alone time fiercely, tell me you
need it. You've been vague about your midsummer plans and
say maybe we'll figure something out. Maybe. I haven't made
any midsummer plans. I want to be with you. But today you've
changed your mind. It's raining, and you don't want to do anything at all. You say you have some work to finish and that you
just want to be alone, at home.

I'm furious with you right now, and I need to pour out my
anger at you in person. So I demand to see you. You're at home
and I have no plans, anyway. "We have to talk," I say. You say,
"Sure. Come over," and on the bus between our apartments I
start trying to figure out what to say. You didn't really do anything wrong. Is my anger just a trick my brain is playing so I
can find a reason to get close to you, penetrate more deeply into
your sphere? Is this fury, or is it something else? I don't know,
and now the bus is here. It all feels increasingly embarrassing.

By the time I ring your doorbell, I'm no longer angry. I have
to make an effort not to coo like a dove when you hug me and
lead me into the living room, hold my hand on the sofa. You ask
what I wanted to talk about, and my heart starts to pound. Well,

this is weird. I take a deep breath and try to be brave. I try to tell you I want to meet more often, that I find your way of distancing yourself and shutting me out periodically hard to handle. You listen and nod and say you understand what I mean, but you are who you are. You've always been like this. You really like me, you say, and that reawakens my irritation. Why do you use the word "like"? I think, but don't ask. What kind of adult says they "like" someone? Why do you only "like" me? Why aren't you head over heels in love, like I am?

Not brave enough to criticize your word choice, I fall silent. Pretend to understand, nod when you speak, because the stakes suddenly seem so high. The conversation ends up stilted, blunt, short, and when I leave you for a party a few blocks away, I try to convince myself it went well. Our first serious conversation. I could almost call it our first argument, if I wanted to be generous. Even though we didn't quarrel. Even though I was barely angry. But it went well, I think. I told you what I felt and who I am, and you, you... said stop.

Late at night you text me to say I'm welcome to sleep at your place, and even though I want to be proud, say thanks but no thanks, I can't. I come running every time you call, and you, you never call enough.

October 2014

I ended up at my stepmother's place in Uppsala at the end of the day. That's where I am now. Reunited with Ivan, lying in the dark on a borrowed double bed, unable to sleep. It could be eight or midnight. I have no idea.

I've been told that my friends and my brother are in our

apartment. They're taking care of what needs taking care of there. Spending time with our lonely cat. The cat is another factor I haven't had the energy to think about, but she keeps popping into my thoughts in the darkness. How can I take care of both Ivan and a cat now? How will I manage? How will I even take care of myself?

At our apartment in Enskede, they're rearranging the furniture and, at my request, throwing away the bed. I wasn't brave enough to ask if it had been stained by your death, by urine or a bowel movement, but I've read somewhere that at the moment of death a person evacuates on themselves, so I'm having it carted away. Better safe than sorry. I asked them to throw away the bed and everything that was on it when you died: the bedding, linens, and pillows. I never want to see any of it again. My friends went to a department store and bought new textiles. They texted to let me know they were cleaning the whole place, fixing it up so that it will feel a little homier when we return. Whenever that is. I don't know when next I'll go home. I don't even know where my home is.

In the dark next to Ivan, I pick up my phone for the first time in hours. There are hundreds of text messages that I'm too exhausted to open, but I can see from the first few words that most of them are the same. They're teeming with every kind of heart emoji. Earlier in the day I sent out a few text messages, which received varied responses. Some of my friends, probably in shock, replied, "You're kidding, right?" Whereupon I, at first, made the effort to answer, "No." Some replies filled the whole screen with words, statements about their love for me and promises to always be there for me and Ivan. Some of the messages included attempts at comfort and assurances that I'll make it through this. I have what it takes to survive, and I don't have to do it alone if I don't want to. Somewhere around lunchtime I stopped reading. Word spread quickly, and from the amount of unread messages, I'd say there's nobody left to tell. Friends of mine from preschool have contacted me. Old acquaintances. Your colleagues, my colleagues, people I partied with years ago. Even the names of a few people I slept with back in my single years flicker by. Bad news apparently travels fast.

I click out of the message app and stare for a moment at the screen. The blue light shines so brightly I'm afraid it will wake up Ivan next to me. I don't know what to do. I feel sick. There's a pressure in my throat, and my heart is racing. The phone's icons seem threatening; behind each one hides a wave of reactions I don't have it in me to confront. I don't want to talk to anyone. I regret telling anyone at all.

November 2009

One day last summer you texted me and asked if I wanted to go to Iceland with you. "There's a music festival in Reykjavik in November. Your friend is playing. Might be fun," you wrote. When I read the text the first time, I made a rough estimate: the trip was four months away, indicating you expected to be together with me for at least that long. It made me so happy I started to jump up and down. I called you and said, "Yes, of course I want to go. So awesome." You also sounded enthusiastic, told me you'd book the flights and hotel.

After I got off the phone with you, I was so excited I couldn't stop myself from researching both plane tickets and hotels in Reykjavik. I was in Gothenburg on a work trip at the time, and technically, I should have been working—plus you'd offered to take care of the arrangements and maybe had looked forward to doing so. But in my enthusiasm, I couldn't help myself.

Traveling to Iceland on our first trip as a couple—how unique, I mused. Cool. No bland beach trip for us. We're going to Iceland, to a festival. Maybe we'll rent a car, climb a mountain, soak in some hot springs, visit some waterfalls, ride some tiny horses. It's so perfect, it's *so us*.

Within half an hour I was sending you links to the best flights and the perfect hotel—I'd already compared all the prices and departure times and got a tip on accommodations from an Icelandic friend. I wrote, "Here's everything you need. No need to research. I've double-checked it all. Go ahead and book. I'll transfer money to you soon."

You answered, "Oh, okay," and I chose to interpret that as an "Oh, how happy, thankful, and impressed I am that you made the arrangements yourself" rather than "Oh, I was looking forward to this task, but okay, you've already done it all. Oh well."

Now we're at Arlanda Airport, sitting with your friends who are playing at the festival. They booked the same flight as us. I was in a great mood when we left Stockholm this morning, but it's started to falter. I feel left out. You've known each other for twenty years, and you have an endless supply of things to reminisce about. Nobody looks at me. Nobody asks me anything. You never include me in the conversation or give me any context for your inside jokes. I'm increasingly silent. You're all drinking beer.

I stare at my expensive orange juice. We have another half hour until we board. It's ten in the morning. You talk and laugh. You're having fun. You look happy. When you're with your friends, your happiness is palpable. You tease them, and they enjoy it. You take up space in a way that you don't with my friends. This troubles me, but I can't yet put my finger on why.

Instead, I stare at your beer. It worries me too. You have less beer left in your glass than your friends do. It's almost empty, despite the fact that you just ordered it. Your gulps seem twice as big as your friends'. They're laughing at a joke you just made, a re-creation of yet another scene from your past that I'm not a part of and don't actually find funny. When I try to laugh along, it sounds artificial and is drowned out by the real laughter of your friends. You raise your glass to your mouth and now, now the beer is gone. I feel uncomfortable. I haven't yet told you that I have problems with alcohol in relation to the people I love. You still don't know that behind my party girl facade, I'm tightly wound, a person who counts beers and gulps, who gets worried and wants to go home if I feel like I'm losing control. That ungainly fact about myself is something I keep close to my chest. That part of my trauma is something I haven't told you yet.

Twenty-five minutes until the gate opens. My brain works fast when it comes to alcohol and has for as long as I can remember. I make some calculations: Will you order more beer on the plane? Will you order another beer now, before we even go to our gate? Can I tell that you've been drinking? Is your speech slurred? Will you be drunk before we land in Iceland? I feel my stomach knotting up. I try to talk some sense into myself: Don't mess this up. Don't be that person. Don't put your old issues onto this. Loosen up. I decide a good offense is the best defense. I ask you if you want another beer before we board, say I might have a glass of wine. Your friends seem impressed. They look at the time, point out that the gate is opening in twenty minutes. "We'll make it," I say, laughing, trying to appear relaxed. "Who wants another round? My treat."

By the time we board the plane a half hour later, I've knocked back a glass of expensive and sour white wine, and my head is buzzing. I try to convince myself that we're going to have an amazing vacation if I just stop being so uptight. The plane lifts off, and when the flight attendant comes down the aisle with her cart, we order wine and beer and whiskey. After all, we're on vacation.

October 2014

I'm in the car on my way home from Uppsala. Ivan has fallen asleep in his car seat, and I am forever thankful to him for that. I don't really know how to be a mother right now. I don't feel present when he cries, can't figure out how to comfort him. All I seem to be able to do is nurse. And then I hand him back to my stepmother.

Ivan has cried unusually little over the past twenty-four hours. I wonder why. He's far too young to understand the ramifications of what's happened. But maybe he senses the seriousness of the moment? Maybe he feels so secure with his grandmother at his side that he doesn't need to cry? He's always liked being with her. She's always been a safe person for him. Ever since she ran into our hospital room, hopped into the bed where I sat, sore and exhausted from giving birth, and took him in her arms, her eyes filled with tears, she's loved him. She calls him her Little Prince. I don't love the nickname, but I let her use it anyway. Her love for Ivan is important to him. And to me. Perhaps more important now than ever.

I dread the day when she'll have to go home again, back to her own life. I wish we could live together permanently from now on and that she could take care of Ivan during the days. At least until I figure out how to stand up again, make my head and body start to function again. For now, everything's shut down. My thoughts flow sluggishly and never reach any conclusions.

My stepmother is driving. We don't speak, and I stare out the window, trying not to think. My phone is vibrating almost continuously in my pocket. I receive several text messages a minute. I've glanced through most of them but haven't felt like answering. I've decided to write an auto-response: "Thank you for your concern. I'll be in touch later," a heart emoji at the end. I think I might ask someone to send them all. Probably later tonight.

At home in Enskede, my brother and sister-in-law are waiting for me. They, along with a few of my closest friends, have cleaned and rearranged the apartment. They've removed your coats from the entry hall, put away your shoes, hid the book you had on your nightstand, and made the new bed with new sheets. They accidentally bought the exact same sheets as the ones we had before, the ones you died on twenty-four hours ago. I overheard my brother discussing this with my stepmother over the phone, and I told them it was fine, it didn't matter. The sheets can be identical. It makes no difference.

But I want to put away your clothes tonight. Put them into bags and boxes and move them up to the attic. I can't stand being around them when I'm home. Every second of this existence already seems to scream your absence. I don't need any more reminders. I have plenty. It's enough with the apartment itself. The walls were also yours. The sofa was yours and mine, ours. The knives in the kitchen were bought and sharpened by you. The doors were ours. We bought the nozzle for the shower just last week. The standing closet belonged to both of us. Your clothes hung on the left side, mine on the right. Now yours have to be packed away. I don't know if I'm able to do it myself, but I'll make sure it gets done. These objects have to go immediately.

When we pull into the parking lot, our big ugly apartment building filling my field of vision, I think of the neighbors who passed by us yesterday morning while we waited for the ambulance. I wonder how many of them put two and two together. I wonder if any of them saw your body being carted away in the afternoon. If any of them shared the elevator with the men—I imagine they were men—who picked up your body. I wonder what they put you in, how they packed you up. I imagine black trash bags. A pair of bare feet sticking out. I feel sick. I think about how tall you were. How did they fit you into the elevator? Images from yesterday play in a loop in my head again, restaged by my imagination as if it were a gruesome theater. I'm disgusted, shaken, but I don't move a muscle. The car's parked, and my stepmother is unbuckling Ivan, chatting with him while he wakes up. He smiles at her, happy to be with her as usual.

I climb out of the car, and together we head toward the front door. Pass by the bench we sat on yesterday. Pass by the mailboxes. All I can think now is that I don't want to run into any neighbors, don't want to meet anyone's eyes. Please just let us get to the apartment without running into anyone. If we can manage that, we can manage anything.

December 2009

It's been almost six months since I confronted you and said, "Just so you know, we're a couple now, you and me. I'm your girlfriend. You're my boyfriend. Everyone knows it, so you might as well know it too."

I said it half in jest but also half seriously. We were in a backstage area at a festival in Dalarna. It was late and dark. Maybe eleven, maybe twelve. We were both far from sober. We were sitting on a lawn with some friends, drinking beer from plastic bottles, and suddenly you stood up, called for our friends' attention, and said you had an announcement to make. "We're together, me and Carro," you declared officially. Our friends looked questioningly first at you, then at me, then at you again. Somebody laughed. Someone said yes, with a question mark after it. Yes? Tell us something we don't know. You said it again, almost savoring the words, seemed to think they felt pretty good on your tongue after all. You sat down again. Kissed me. Called me your girlfriend. Fell silent, seemed to be considering something. Added: "But I'm always going to want to spend Christmas at my parents. Just so you know. I don't want that to be an issue. I will never want to be anywhere else on Christmas. That's just how it is."

Now it's Christmas Eve, and last night you headed to your parents in a lighthearted mood. You've told me all about your family traditions, which aren't so different from most Swedish families', except you haven't exchanged gifts since you and your three siblings reached adulthood. Everything else sounds familiar. On the evening before Christmas Eve, you bake saffron buns. Your mother decorates a tree your dad stole or borrowed or got hold of in some way—I'm fuzzy on the details—from the woods around the house. You cook a ham, and later that night you eat some of it along with some smoked lamb and drink Christmas beers. You sleep on the sofa in the living room, end up with more than one cat on your legs. Your dad goes to bed first. Your mom stays up very late, as usual—she stays up until the witching hour. On Christmas Eve morning, you all eat pancakes with raspberries from the latest harvest. At some point in the morning your little brother arrives. Then you all make more food, consume it, then sit around and talk and play games all evening. After that it's Christmas Day. Same story except with a visit from your big brother's family, your parents' good friends, and your aunt. On Boxing Day you go back to the city again. That's the schedule. I've learned that Christmas, no matter how simply you celebrate, is an important holiday for you.

As for me, I haven't really enjoyed Christmas for a long time now. After my parents divorced, back in the eighties, and after my dad died from cancer, in the nineties, Christmas started to feel like a lot of incomplete families and endless stops to tick off in just a few days. One day for my mom and my little brother. One day for my mom's relatives. One day for my stepmother, little sister, stepsister and her children. One day with my dad's family. And now, starting this year, one day for your family. It's not exactly relaxing. But I don't want to appear ungrateful, so I'm doing my best to seem merry. Your dad picks me up at the bus stop on Christmas Day. We both radiate holiday cheer, though I suspect his mood is more genuine.

In the evening we play Monopoly and you win, crushing me slowly and with great pleasure. At one point I even hiss at you, "Shut up," quietly so your mother won't hear. You're an extremely bad winner, the kind who can't stop twisting the knife once you've stuck it into your opponent. Whereas I'm an extremely bad loser, and I hate Monopoly. No game is more humiliating to lose. It takes hours. When I again tell you to shut up, this time loud enough for your mother to hear, you start laughing and grab my hand from across the table. I'm so angry I push your hand away but feel embarrassed in front of your mother, so I take it again and force out a laugh that's supposed to sound cute but sounds more like a witch's wheeze.

By the time we go to bed that night, I've started to get over my defeat, and you've stopped twisting the knife. I ask you in a whisper if you think your mom judges me for snapping at you. You tell me to forget all about it. She probably thought it was funny and that you deserved it. I decide to stop thinking about it, and we say good night to each other in the darkness. I kiss you, and the kiss becomes making out, and then we have sex, and then we sleep, and when we wake up, it's Boxing Day, and soon the holidays will be over. Finally.

October 2014

When I open the door to the apartment, it smells like coffee, and my brother, my beloved brother and best friend, greets me with open arms. I disappear into his embrace, eyes closed, crying, wheezing, dripping with snot. I don't want to leave. But I force myself to. Behind him stands his wife and behind her one of my best friends. They all hug me, speaking to me in soft voices, trying not to upset me, wanting only to give comfort but not sure exactly how. I feel sick. Like I might throw up. My brother puts a cup of coffee in my hand. Points to the kitchen, and the fresh bread, cheese, sweets, and buns laid out on the table. My stomach is in knots. I have to look away, so instead I look at our home, just my home and Ivan's from now on.

The apartment is sparkling clean. The floors shine. Everything is put away, and there's no trace of you in the hall—your coat, hats, shoes. The team, working on the apartment since yesterday, cleared it all away. I know they packed your clothes into boxes and put them in our closet, waiting for directions from me. I don't know what to do with them. I just want the clothes out of my sight. I start a sentence and trail off. Say something about storing them temporarily. My brother nods and starts to carry boxes up to the attic before I even have time to look into the closet. And as for me, I suddenly want to see the room where you died.

I start to move in that direction. The door is ajar, and light floods into the hall. The sun must be beating onto the balcony right now. I want to go in but don't dare. I want to face it, try to reclaim it in some way. The image of your body in the bed, your ankle peeking from under the cover, starts flashing before my eyes. My heart starts to pound in unison. I step inside. Twenty-four hours ago you were still here. Now the lack of your presence echoes in the emptiness.

The room looks different. It's been refurnished. The new bed stands against a different wall. In the old place there's an armchair with a reading lamp and a new rug underneath it. There's a blanket folded over its arm. There are also new curtains on the windows. It's the same room, but not. It moves me to think of how hard they must have worked, these people who love me, who want to make life more bearable for me again. I start to weep in gratitude. And because you died in here, just hours ago.

I feel I must start sleeping here. I have to begin tonight. This room belongs to me and Ivan now, and we have to make it work. We just have to.

July 2010

We've been seeing each other for over a year now. After leaving the music industry, I have a new job in publishing. I rarely work nights or weekends, and we hang out almost every day. Just the way I like it. Just the way I hope you like it too.

It took three months for you to agree to call me your girl-friend or call yourself my boyfriend. Still, you don't say either very often. You don't like the labels. You persist in saying you "like" me when you express your affection, but I've gotten used to that by now. I've decided it means what I want it to mean. You're just stingier with words than most people.

Now I'm your girlfriend, and you're my boyfriend. We go out often to pubs and bars and clubs and concerts. I know what you order at restaurants—steak and fries or meatballs with mashed potatoes and lingonberry jam—and I know what music you like to put on when you want to pump yourself up. I know you have nightmares when you sleep un-der too-warm blankets, and I've learned which buses to take out to your parents' house. I know what makes you laugh, what movies you like, how you prefer to spend your week-ends, what shows we both like to watch. I know we rarely agree on whether a movie is good or bad, and I've learned that you mean it when you tell me it's okay to go out or do things with my friends without you. I know how you smell when you wake up, and you've learned to make yourself scarce when I have PMS. We do most things as a couple now, and our life together feels both safe and simple. I'm amazed at how uncomplicated a close relationship can be, and I'm so glad I pushed past your defenses when we were first together. You seem happy about it too, even if you don't say so. I have

59

to guess sometimes, but I'm getting good at guessing. Not everything needs to be said out loud.

Over the summer we go to a stream of music festivals. This is our second summer together. We often hang out with friends. We meet up with my friends more often than yours. I have more of them, and I spend more time with them than you do with yours. And you're not stingy. You think most things are fun. You don't mind tagging along. We have a good time when we go out. Laughing at the same jokes. And even better: you laugh at mine. Generously and wholeheartedly, you burst out laughing when I make a joke, and I love you for it. It never bothers you that I take up so much space. You're never jealous or possessive when we're out. My exes don't worry you. You like to watch me dance, though you almost never dance. And you're comfortable beside me. You put your hand on my hip in a natural way as we move side by side. I am hopelessly in love with you. I am in love with every inch of your lanky, loose-limbed body. I think you're beautiful from every angle and at every moment of the day.

Sometimes we fight because I think you get too drunk. Ironically, this usually happens when I've been drinking too, which of course undermines my authority. On nights when I'm downing one glass of wine after another, I watch you most closely. I get jealous and worried. Think you're standing and talking too close to other women. I notice you slurring your words or losing control, and I hint ever more obviously that you should take it easy on the beers. I bring you back a glass of water from the bar when I've been sent to buy another round. And you, you start thinking I'm tedious and controlling, tell me I need to learn to relax. You say you don't like the looks I give you when you're ordering a beer. Or when you drink it too fast. I try to leave you alone, but it's hard. I learned early how to count; I do it without thinking. First, I count, then I throw you looks, and then I give you hints. And in the end, we fight. More than once this summer we've had to go home from a party because we're arguing. It's not a big problem, but it's becoming a pattern. I recognize it from my past relationships, and I know I'm mostly at fault, but I can't help it. I can't stop being on guard about this once I've started. And unfortunately, I've started.

When we're sober, we try to talk through our conflicts. I explain that all this stems from my childhood. It's difficult to turn off the counting and nagging. And I don't like how your personality changes by the end of the night. You say you understand, you don't like getting too drunk either, so it's fine, but you gently point out that everyone's personality changes when they drink. Even mine. "Yes, but still," I protest. "I get it," you say. And then we make up. We don't want to argue over something silly, so we focus instead on enjoying our Sunday afternoon pizza. And we spend our weekdays in harmony. Then the weekend rolls around, we go out, you get drunk, I watch you, give you meaningful looks, make it harder and harder for you to be around me. Again. But that's the only cloud in our sky for now.

Today we were at a concert at Stockholm's Stadion arena. We danced, shouted, and drank and eventually ended up at an outdoor bar with some friends. The drinks are still flowing. You break off your conversation, look at me, and say in an almost solemn voice: "You know what? I'm in love with you." You look so pleased with yourself. Proud. As if you're giving me a present.

Your comment stops me in my tracks. I don't know what to say. My first thought is that I hope our friends didn't hear. It was so obvious you were saying it for the first time. I fumble for a reply. "Oh, how nice. Thank you," I say at last. Give you a quick peck on the mouth and again: "How nice, so nice." I don't know if I mean it, but I don't want to detract from your moment, so I pretend to be overpowered and grateful for this gift of words. We've been dating for fifteen months now. Seeing each other almost every day. I've been in love with you since the very beginning. Undoubtedly, utterly, and officially in love with you. You, on the other hand, fell in love with me tonight. I wish it didn't feel like an insult, but it does. Either insult or proof of my inadequacy—I'm not sure which.

In a taxi on our way home it occurs to me for the first time that we don't move at the same speed. The pace is off. You just told me you love me for the first time, and this is the first time I have that thought. When we get home, you want to have sex, but I say I'm too tired. I lie with my back to you, pretending to sleep. You hold me, your body a spoon around mine, and soon you're breathing heavy and even.

October 2014

I can't sleep. My body doesn't know how. After an evening that somehow ended up relatively comforting—the perfect amount of friends and family preparing dinner and cleaning up after it—I'm alone, shivering even though I have two thick blankets on top of me. The room is dark. Ivan is sensitive to light and sound, so I'm trying to move as little as possible. Sometimes the rustling of the covers is enough to wake him. He just fell asleep for the second time tonight after a long session of breastfeeding and a diaper change. The room next to ours, where my stepmother and little sister are sleeping, is silent. My brother and sister-in-law went home around ten o'clock. Promised to be back by breakfast. Tomorrow night my mom will take my stepmother's place. That's the extent of the plans that I'm aware of.

The flowers have started to pour in. I've probably received ten bouquets today, though I haven't counted. They're scattered around the apartment. I don't have enough vases for them, so we've switched to water pitchers, and soon I'll have to bring out the mop bucket. Your colleagues send flowers. Your friends send flowers. My friends send flowers. Colleagues, former colleagues, close friends, and acquaintances. When the phone rings from an unknown number, I've figured out that someone is trying to get into the building, via a stubborn intercom system, to deliver flowers. I don't have the energy to answer. Someone else does for me, and after another minute or two a new bouquet arrives at the door. Many come from a flower shop just a few hundred meters away, others from farther out in the suburbs or from inside the city. Each one arrives with a card bearing loving greetings of various lengths. My brother puts the cards in a folder. My friend has started a rolling schedule for family and friends to take turns being with me over the next few weeks. Earlier tonight, I felt moved and safe, almost confident. I don't have to do this on my own, I thought. I'm not alone. It takes a village to raise a child, and that's what we are, a village. If this village is big enough, I thought, maybe we can do this.

But then came the night. The apartment fell silent. And now I'm here, not at all confident. My body shivers, Ivan is asleep, and I don't know what to do with myself. Don't know what's happening. Don't know how to make this night pass. Should I wake someone up? Should I cry in somebody's arms? I don't know. I don't want to cry. I want to sleep. I want Ivan to sleep. I don't even know what I'd say if I woke someone up. I stay where I am. Something presses down on my chest, my joints tremble, my heart races, and I think, This, this is what true agony feels like. Now I know.

October 2010

One day I got fed up with living at two addresses, so I called a broker, and everything happened quickly after that. A month later, my apartment was sold, the papers were signed, and a vanload of my stuff will be headed to your place this afternoon. I've packed unsentimentally, in accordance with my attitude toward possessions in recent years. I cleaned out or discarded everything with the exception of some diaries and photo albums. I've thrown away, recycled, or donated the bulk of my stuff. You've cleared space for me in your closet, in your still spartan apartment. Moving into your place feels strangely undramatic, like a practical step or a stopover toward the real move, which we'll do later. Soon. When you're ready. You've been busy with work in recent months. You don't have time to think about the future right now. So we're starting with this.

Tonight when we come home there will be no need to remember where we put the groceries or which bathroom your contact solution is in. There will be no more arguments about where to sleep, no statistics wielded to support who should get to sleep in their own bed. From now on we'll be living in the same place. And soon, but not yet, we're planning to get our own place together. Until then, I'll live with you. It's the simplest solution. I'm not that hung up on the details.

You're in bad shape this morning, and I'm not much better. Yesterday we celebrated a friend's thirtieth birthday and partied most of the night. I have some vague memories of an argument on the way home, a fight near the 7-Eleven on the corner of my street, but we woke up and couldn't remember what it was about, so we let it go. Now we're trying our best to focus on the move, but it's tough. We're weak. We need to eat before carrying any boxes. We go to a café and order some brunch. Our conversation is stilted, and neither of us seems particularly excited about the move.

While we eat we talk about the party and gossip about our friends. Who was the drunkest, who made out, who didn't show up, who was newly single and flirty. It bothers you that all my friends have identical politics and respond aggressively to being questioned, that you can never have a respectful disagreement with any of them. You say that there's a consensus among my circle and that consensus is dangerous. I've heard this hundreds of times now. I'm not interested in discussing it again. I change the subject as smoothly as I can in my hungover condition. You let it slide. You laugh while I re-create a conversation from yesterday. Listen patiently and seem interested in my overly detailed retelling of a trivial detail. I exaggerate and make pointed comments to amuse you. You laugh at me and don't question the truth of my story. You're kind to me, and I love you for it. Tonight we'll start living together—not for real but not pretend either. That suits us pretty well. At least that's what I tell myself.

October 2014

My premonition that the flower deliveries were just getting started turned out to be true. Around ten o'clock this morning the door downstairs started ringing again. Our unreliable buzzer meant countless trips down five flights of stairs. The flowers and cards kept pouring in. As for me, I never did go to sleep last night and climbed out of bed this morning in terrible shape.

I spent the night thinking about the moment of your death. I kept turning it over in my head: How did it happen? What did it look like? Why did I not wake up? Why didn't the cat react and wake us up? It must have been very quiet, I thought. But you were lying in such a strange position. As if you'd convulsed, leaned forward, fallen to your side with your head pressed into the pillow. Why did you do that? Was it a cramp? Were you in pain?

I'd like to think it happened so quickly, calmly, that a moment never came when you realized, Now, now I'm dying. The thought of you alone at the moment of your death is so unbearable that I have to convince myself you were asleep, that it happened without your knowledge. I wish I'd been next to you, that you could have held my hand. I wish I had been with you. At the same time: the thought of it fills me with fear. How would I have reacted? Would I have tried to save you and failed? Would I have tried to give you CPR while Ivan was crying next to us? Would I have been successful? Imagine if I'd failed. How would I ever have moved on from that?

In the small hours of the second night, it was important to me that you never knew you were dying. I wished there was something I could do, someone I could pay, to guarantee that fact. I thought you never knowing made it a little more bearable. If that was the case, I might be able to survive this. If you didn't have to lie there and die alone. I wondered if your autopsy would tell me anything and when we'd get the results. Didn't the doctor say it could take months? How could it take months?

The second night inched forward. Hours passed, my thoughts ground on, then dawn came and my agony decreased somewhat. Soon a new day, soon light, soon company, soon help with Ivan would hold me upright again. Just one day, one minute at a time. And all that other stuff they say.

July 2011

We've been living together for nine months now, still in your sparsely furnished apartment with its tiny kitchen, and I think I'm about to sweat to death. Just drain away. There's a heat wave in Stockholm. Unrelenting sunshine and oppressive heat all day, then suffocating nights and sticky bodies. The headlines on the tabloids scream in capital letters about the KILLER HEAT and SIBERIAN HEAT WAVE. Social media is filled with vacation updates. People swimming, reading books; children splashing on the shore, orange floaties on their tiny upper arms; adults reclining in sun chairs and lounging in hammocks. People boasting about the books they're reading, and cold glasses of wine sweating in the heat. It's that kind of summer. Nothing strange about it. I just don't like it.

We didn't manage to get out of town this summer. Our loose plans never materialized, and now we're forced to sweat our way through the Siberian heat wave. I hate it. I want clouds, shade, just a little cold front, but nothing arrives. The days stay hot. The nights too. I take my frustrations out on you and your apartment.

"How can an apartment be this *hot?* It shouldn't be possible," I complain in the evenings. You sigh, get up from your desk, where you were trying to work. You try to mitigate the heat, mostly because you can't stand listening to me complain anymore. I've been on repeat for several weeks now. You open all the windows, and immediately we hear the noise from Långholmsgatan, like we're sitting in the middle of a traffic jam. I grimace in discontent but don't dare complain out loud anymore. You stick a thick book into the mail slot in the front door, step out into the hall, and open the door to a small balcony just off the landing. You're trying to get a draft going. It doesn't work. You see my scrunched-up brows and read the self-pity they betray. You give me a look that says "What do you want me to do? I can't do more than this. Calm down. Leave it alone."

I'm quiet, but I haven't stopped complaining inside. The apartment isn't getting any cooler. This place is wrong for us. It's ugly. With terrible wallpaper. A kitchen that's too small to cook in. In my self-pity, I ignore the fact that I don't cook no matter what size the kitchen is. Still, this place is wrong. We need to move soon. To a better apartment, where a person can breathe at night. A place that belongs to both of us. Not something that's yours, that I moved into. That is what we had decided at the start, so why didn't it happen? Why are we still here?

But I know why, and so do you. My dislike of your apartment is about something else, something we can't bear to talk about very often, something you try to address by getting a draft flowing in here.

Behind my complaints there's an increasing restlessness, a desire to move somewhere new, do something new, share a project, be a team. Behind your sighs there's a discord, because you don't want what I want. You prefer to stay where we are, at least for a while, maybe a long while.

It's this issue of speed again, of pacing.

When we do occasionally talk about it, you shift uncomfortably in your chair, your eyes won't meet mine, and you try to end the conversation as soon as possible. You say pleadingly: "Soon, but not right now. Now isn't a good time. I have so much work, I can't even think about a move. Life's pretty good here after all, isn't it?" I say, "No, no it isn't. This apartment isn't ours, and it's terrible in a hundred ways. It's hot. The bed hurts my back. We're on a loud, busy street. Our upstairs neighbors are lunatics. The downstairs neighbor too. We can't even cook in the kitchen."

You already know what I think of your apartment. You've heard it way too many times. Suddenly, I realize that and break off. Feeling guilty. Ashamed to be criticizing the place you've called home for ten years, which you've never hated or thought was the worst apartment in the whole city. I'm ashamed of my temper, how unreasonable, stubborn, and selfish I can be. I tell myself: It's not okay. I don't want to be like this. You haven't done anything to deserve this. I have to stop. Immediately. I have to be nice. Stop nagging. Be patient.

So we stop talking about apartments. We make up and agree to buy a new bed next weekend. Besides my guilty conscience, everything feels fine for a few days, until I can't stand it, and the whole cycle starts all over again.

October 2014

On the third day, I get out of bed with no memory of sleep and ask myself how long a body can go on like this before it becomes dangerous. It reminds me of the days after I gave birth, how I spent four nights in a row watching Ivan, awake, panicked, full of adrenaline. Maybe this is the same thing. Just a different type of adrenaline. Another kind of panic.

At dawn I decide to get rid of the cat. After yet another night of her wandering around the apartment crying out into the silence for you, it's clear this isn't going to work. I don't have it in me to care for her, Ivan, and myself. I have to give something up. It has to be the cat. Your cat.

It starts as a thought, which leads to a decision, which leads to texting an acquaintance, which leads to a yes. My acquaintance can take care of our cat, at least for now, while things are so tough. Maybe longer. She's picking her up tonight.

The visits from my friends never end. They come four at a time, tightly scheduled by a friend whose project managerial skills are coming in handy, and they stay for no longer than forty-five minutes at a time. In between, breaks are scheduled so I can rest. But I never succeed at resting. I'm allowed to say the moment I want the visits to end, whenever I'm too tired. My friend will immediately cancel the next visit. They tell me there's nothing wrong with that, but so far I've let each group come. One after another, four by four.

On one level there's something comforting about the constant stream of friends. We hug and cry and talk, and soon I'll have accomplished my first meeting with all of them. The first feels like the heaviest. I try to visualize a future when I'm no longer a victim, when no one cocks their head to the side as they talk to me, when no one needs to be extra gentle, but I can't see that far ahead, so I stop the thought experiment and return to my meetings with my friends.

But these visits, these conversations, the words I repeat over and over, and my friends' reactions to those words, serve another function. They correct me every time I touch upon those thoughts I can barely stand to share, that this is my fault. Every time I bring up how we don't know why you died, that your heart probably gave out, that there's no way to know how long you were sick, they interrupt me. When I bring up my belief that I pushed you too hard, never let you rest, always drove us forward, and maybe that's one reason you died, they distract me. At least for a moment. "You couldn't know," they say, hugging me. "You have to treat the living on the living's terms," says another, and the thought stays with me. I have to remember that. I treated you as one of the living, on the living's terms. Can I really be to blame for what ended up happening? Am I, at least in part, the reason Ivan is now fatherless? I don't know. But my friends won't have it, and the hours pass even on this day.

When evening comes, I've told the story of how I found you dead in our bedroom so many times that I've started using the same wording. And every time I tell it, it seems further away. Like something I made up rather than an exact reproduction from memory. I don't know if it's my exhaustion or if the words themselves have that effect, but it almost doesn't feel like a memory anymore. I'm just reciting a story. I repeat the doctor's words as if they were my own.

Finally, the last of my friends head home just before dinnertime, and only the core group remains. Soon we'll put one more day to bed. I look forward to sleeping tonight.

March 2012

We don't do much on the weekends, you and me. We rarely make any plans and usually spend our weekends close to where we live, which is still your apartment. Sometimes we take long walks. Sometimes we meet friends for brunch. Sometimes we drink beer or wine with friends. Sometimes we go to a dinner party at one of our friends' homes. We rarely invite them to our place. Because of the kitchen. And the apartment. It's not exactly suited to dinner parties.

On Sunday mornings I go to a horseback riding school in Enskede, and you often accompany me to the stable. Not because you think it's fun but because I nag you into going. You freeze in the bleachers while I take my lesson, and when I look over at you, you're focused on the bright display screen of your telephone. Things are stressful for you at work—lots of nights and weekends. Whereas I spend my weeknights watching dumb reality television and chatting with my friends.

It snowed in Stockholm during the night, and the temperature dropped to below freezing. I convinced both you and a friend to come with me to the stable today, and then, just for fun, to an open house for an apartment for sale in the suburb of Gamla Enskede. We'll get coffee at Gamla Enskede Bakery afterward. The apartment is in a building I've noticed many times, and the small two-bedroom costs basically the same as what I sold my inner-city studio for. I haven't really been planning to move to the suburbs, not even to Gamla Enskede, but I'm strangely drawn to that building. I want to see the apartment, get a feel for it, try to figure out why the same apartment in the inner city would cost twice as much, and most of all discover what's hidden behind those bright orange walls. The mansard-roofed building sits on the busy street Nynäsvägen, and on the other side lies a neighborhood of single-family houses. The wooden houses, no two alike, line winding streets, and the small paths that lead to their front doors are surrounded on either side by lush gardens full of fruit trees, hammocks, and wooden decks. Then come the English row houses, which, after riding school on Sundays, I often walk by and wonder about. How wonderful that such an area even exists. Imagine growing up here. Life here seems so harmonious. There could be no misery here, I've thought, ignoring how naive that thought is. Here the neighbors must be good friends with each other, saying hello over the hedges, lending each other sugar and milk, and leaving boxes of apples on the sidewalks with notes that read: "Help yourself!"

As soon as I step into the apartment, I realize it was a mistake to come to the open house. There are creaky wooden floors and interesting angles. Long hallways, deep windows, and two small bathrooms. A newly renovated kitchen with preserved original classic cabinets. As I walk down the hall from the living room to the bedroom, which sits facing a small meadow and Gamla Enskede's charming houses, I realize I have to live here. I have no other choice. I have to sleep in this bedroom. This has to be my view when I say good night, and when I wake up in the morning. That meadow has to be mine. This apartment has to be mine. It has to be ours. This is where we'll start over, you and me.

I go to the living room and find you and my friend bent over the deep window, talking to the broker about the traffic noise on Nynäsvägen. My friend, who works professionally with live music, quickly shoots down the broker and his half-baked answers about what decibel levels can be considered a nuisance. The broker fumbles for words and promises to get back to my friend the following day, takes her business card. As for me, I stare at you, trying to figure out if you too feel a special connection to this apartment. Your expression reveals nothing. I decide to move slowly, not tell you right away what I felt in the bedroom. I think it would benefit both of us if I approach the future, our future in this apartment, at a cautious pace, let you get used to the idea before I spring it on you. Still, I know there's not much time to waste. The bidding will probably start tomorrow.

We sit at the charming little bakery next to the orange building I'm already calling "our house" in my head and flip through the prospectus while we make fun of how ignorant the broker was. Laughing at his obvious lie about the couple "from Gothenburg" ready to "put down cash tomorrow." Also, his answers to my friend's questions about noise levels were clumsy and ignorant. He was so intent on a quick sell, it seems likely he'd be willing to go down on the price.

Finally, I ask you, as nonchalantly as I can, what you thought of the apartment. "It was nice," you say. I ask you if you could imagine yourself living there, and you say, "Sure, maybe. There's nothing wrong with it." I wait as long as I can to tell you how I feel, but when I do, you fall silent. I tell you I can afford to buy it on my own, that I really want this apartment, that I think it's perfect for us, and if you don't have any arguments against it, then I'll put a bid in tomorrow.

You stare down into your cup. I'm pretty sure you're not thrilled by how things are turning out this afternoon. At the same time, I'm absolutely convinced that this apartment will bring such a positive change to our lives that it's worth it, all the things you experience as stressful and negative right now. I can already see us spending our evenings walking through those narrow, winding streets of wooden houses. I can see us buying a small car and taking trips to the country on the weekends. I can see us making food in that big, open kitchen and inviting our friends over for soup and freshly baked bread. I can see you using the extra bedroom as an office, a place where you can do your work in peace and quiet. Inside those walls our future is transformed from something cramped, sweaty, and salmon-pink into something beautiful—almost a fairy tale. This is what will happen in Enskede. You just don't know it yet.

The next day I call my bank, and then I offer the clumsy broker two hundred thousand kronor less than the asking price if he'll sign the papers tonight. He says he has to check with the seller, calls me back five minutes later with a yes, and I go to the apartment after work. I sign a number of documents, take another tour, make sure it still feels right, and that's that. Now I own our dream home, and we can move in whenever we want. It was empty and newly renovated when we bought it. Or when I bought it, to be precise. But I think you'll soon want to own it too and will offer to pay for half. I think it's just a matter of time before you arrive at the same conclusion as me. This will solve itself. Now we have more important things to take care of. Packing, renting a truck, and borrowing a car, for example. Asking our friends to help us move. Signing up for electricity and internet service. Starting to look for a used car to buy. Deep inside I still have a gnawing feeling that I sprang this on you too quickly, but I don't have time to deal with that right now. We've got a move to make, a life to live.

October 2014

Night again. I'm still counting the minutes and hours since the moment you died. The doctor said "around dawn," and I've decided that means five o'clock. In three hours it will have been four days. In three hours and three days it will have been a week. I want it to have been a week. I want it to have been six months. I want it to have been one year. I long so desperately for a time, a day, when it isn't so fresh anymore. A day when I've figured out how to keep living, how to keep taking care of Ivan, when life feels normal rather than like a sad, sick joke.

I still haven't slept since you died. Ivan will only sleep, probably because of the turmoil of the past few days, when he's in direct contact with my body. Maybe that's his way of dealing with the sudden absence of both you and me during the days. I'm there for him during the day, and yet not. My stepmother feeds him and changes his diaper. I hold him in my arms, nurse him. I try to play with him. When I take walks with my friends, I wear him in his baby carrier. I put my coat around both of us. He giggles and laughs. But I need breaks often. Then my stepmother steps in again. At night it's just us, and he nurses almost the whole time. If I try to sneak away from him, he wakes up and cries, will only go back to sleep when my breast is between his lips again. As for me, I don't sleep. It's Thursday now, or Friday, depending on how you count.

Just like last night, and the night before that, my thoughts rush continually. But unlike the first night, they're more logical. I don't get stuck in a loop as often, don't freeze up in the same way as the first day. But I never reach any final conclusions. My thoughts race by, one after another, and end up all over the place. Many of them end in exclamation marks. You died! You died! I can't believe you died! You just died! Suddenly you were dead! Dead!

I suspect it's the adrenaline I feel pumping through my body. Heart palpitations are replaced by nausea and pain in the upper part of my chest. It's hard to take a deep breath. My body, which seems to be telling me to run, keeps bumping up against my brain, which has no idea where to go. I don't know where to go. I can't seem to grasp the situation. So I stay where I am, in the darkness next to Ivan. My mind full of exclamation marks.

On the third night alone, my thoughts are all about Ivan. His future. My future. Our future. Where should we live? How will I be able to work full time while raising a baby on my own? Can I afford to work part time? Should I move to a smaller apartment? Should I get a nanny? Could I afford that if I cut out everything else, everything I used to spend money on? Should I move to Uppsala to live near my stepmother and mother? And if I did, would I commute to Stockholm or quit my job? Would I be able to make friends there? Or should I stay close to my friends but farther from what little family I have? What kind of childhood is Ivan going to have? How can I make it a good one under these terrible conditions? How will I manage to heal enough to protect his childhood from unprocessed grief and trauma? I line up the course of events in my head, trying to sort it all out.

And I make lists. I make lists of the last time we did or said various things. I think about our last argument. I think about our last vacation. Our last time in the car. Our last dinner. I think about my last text message and wonder why you never answered me. The fact that I was left hanging in our text message chain hurts me in a way I can't explain. I haven't deleted our text message chain, but soon I will. I just know it. For now, it sits there with me alone at the end, no answer from you.

I think of our last words to each other the night before you died. I can't remember if we kissed when we said good night. That haunts me. When was our last kiss? Why can't I remember it? Why did I take it for granted? I wonder what your last thoughts were before you fell asleep, and if you were unhappy. I wonder again if you woke up just before you died. Were you in pain?

In the darkness, my eyes are drawn to the place in the room where our bed used to stand. Where your ankle stuck out. Where your face lay on the pillow. Your eye half open. I wonder if it's really a good idea that I'm lying here, in this bedroom, when we have another one. We could stay in Ivan's bedroom. I could move back there. But that feels like losing. Like a defeat. Like if I can't take back this room, I can't take back my life. I decide to decide tomorrow. I can take one more night without sleep. I managed to go five days in a row after Ivan was born. The clock ticks toward five. Soon it will be four whole days. Soon the sun will rise.

Another thought keeps circling. Contempt whispers inside me. A stern voice tells me I'm to blame. I've made my bed, and now I need to lie in it. In my misery, in this room that echoes with death and guilt. It's only fair. This is my fault. Maybe I'll spend the rest of my life atoning for my sins. Ivan will never have a father again. I ran him over again and again, and in the end he couldn't take any more. I caused this. Now I have to stay in it. I have no choice but to stay in it.

April 2012

It's Tuesday and your stomach is bothering you, a lot. You're having cramps, and you can't keep anything down, have no appetite. Unable to work, you just lie on the sofa. Running back and forth to the toilet. Your cheeks are pale. We've been living in our new apartment for less than a week, and you've felt shitty the whole time. I'm worried about you. Ask you to go see a doctor. We're supposed to go to Tokyo in a few days. What if you don't feel well enough? What if it's something dangerous? At first you wanted to wait it out, but now you're ready to go to the doctor. I figure out where our new neighborhood doctor's office is and what their drop-in hours are. Send you there right after a breakfast you can't keep down. Wander restlessly around the apartment after you leave.

My worry about your stomach and your general state of health has put a damper on the mood at home. I haven't felt any of the joy I expected to once we were finally moved in. Mostly, it's been stressful. The subway doesn't run as often as I thought. I've stood on the platform in a suburb I don't yet know freezing and wondering how I ended up here. Add your stomach problems to that. You gritted your way through the move, carting box after box up three flights of stairs, working in dogged and effective silence. By the time I bought pizza and beer for the friends who helped us move, you couldn't eat or drink. You had to go to the bedroom and lie down. Didn't come out again for the rest of the evening except to go to the bathroom. It grew uncomfortable, so I sent our guests home and started unpacking alone. That was five days ago.

After several hours, you text me. The doctor sent you to the hospital, where they did tests while you waited in your own room. You fell asleep on a cot and just woke up. The tests came back. It isn't bacterial. The doctor's theory is stress-related gastritis. His prescription: rest, wait, eat carefully, be kind to your stomach, buy over-the-counter medicines for an upset stomach, and come back if you don't get better within two weeks.

I text back and ask you if you're up for a trip to Tokyo with your stomach like this. You respond immediately, "Definitely. We're going." Maybe you'll feel better by then. You write that you're looking forward to getting away, that things have been so stressful lately, and you want to hop on a plane and fly halfway around the world with me. You make a joke about how all those Japanese bidets and toilets are perfect for this. You end your text with words you rarely say: "I love you."

When I get your text, all my uneasiness evaporates. I can't wait to get away with you either. We're going to Japan! Our future has just begun. We're the best couple. I love you so much. There's nobody better than you.

"Come home now so I can take care of you," I text, then pull out my big suitcase and start packing.

October 2014

"Stand clear of the closing doors." I hear them closing, but my eyes are glued to the gray-speckled floor of the train. Ivan's head is in the center of my field of vision, peeking out from the baby carrier strapped to my waist. His head bobbles around as he chases every sound with his eyes. As for me, I stare at the floor. And at my child. I squeeze his little feet, encased in a pair of thick socks my mom knitted for him. His feet calm me, keeping my hands occupied with his frenetic bouncing and squirming in his carrier.

This is the first time I've left our block since I came home after your death. My mom and my brother are on the subway with us, and our destination is the Farsta mall. I feel every eye in this half-filled subway car is on me. We'll soon be there, just a little longer. Just stops at Tallkrogen, Gubbängen, Hökarängen.

Ivan laughs in delight as my brother plays peekaboo with him. Minutes tick by slowly. It feels like the subway is rolling in slow motion.

I'm on my way to meet a psychologist, the same one who helped me after Ivan spent every night of his first six weeks screaming with colic and I realized I was turning out to be a more neurotic parent than I'd expected. The psychologist is my age, and I think she's wonderful. She's helped me so much already. My hope is that she'll help me again.

One of my friends, the same one who made the rolling visitors' schedule, called her the day you died. Asked her, since she's an expert on the connection between young children and their parents, what we should do now. They discussed what kind of emergency help would be best for me and concluded that the easiest thing would be for me to return to her, even though we'd recently completed my therapy. She's cleared her schedule and will see me today. She'd told my friend it was important that I come in as soon as I could. She said she could keep seeing me if that's what I want and for as long as I like.

I like her best of all the psychologists I've met with. She talks more than most do. Tells me when she disagrees with me and laughs at my jokes. She helped me through that first shaky half year of parenting Ivan, through my issues with hearing him cry, my inability to comfort him, my impulse to hand over responsibility to someone else, to some other adult more worthy of the task than me. She helped me see how unique my baby was and what a capable parent I could be. I've made a lot of progress since I started seeing her, and I trust her. If anyone can help me make sense of my thoughts now, it will be her.

There at last. I hand over the stroller and my now sleeping baby to my mom and brother outside the door to the office building. They hug me and say, "See you soon. Good luck." I mumble something, a thank-you. Gently pat Ivan's cheek. The tip of his nose is red from the autumn chill.

I've felt relatively shut down over the last few days. I've had only short episodes of crying, always when I knew Ivan was asleep and wouldn't see or hear me. On the second day, I cried in the shower. Tried to whisper your name and apologize. It was difficult in the beginning. I saw myself from the outside, and it filled me with embarrassment and self-hate. A hollowed-out body, a square gray face with huge bags under the eyes, a naked woman in the shower whispering the name of someone who's no longer there. My voice was coarse even though it was barely audible, and it felt like it echoed in the bathroom. It sounded silly, not beautiful, and I sincerely hoped that none of my scheduled helping hands were anywhere close by to hear it.

"I'm sorry, Aksel. Sorry it turned out like this. Sorry for who I became at the end of our relationship. Sorry that we lost each other. Sorry that I lost you. Sorry I couldn't make you happy. Sorry I didn't say 'I love you' more often. I'm sorry if you felt unappreciated. I'm sorry if I made you feel worthless. I'm sorry that I stressed you out. I'm sorry that I wanted to be in charge. I'm sorry that I was never able to wait for you. I'm sorry it didn't turn out like you wanted it to. I'm sorry that I nagged. I'm sorry that you died. Sorry, sorry, sorry, sorry, sorry, sorry, sorry, sorry, sorry, sorry."

For what must have been a quarter of an hour I stood there begging you for your forgiveness. Even though it was pointless—I'll never receive it or know if I need it. Still, the words made me cry and cry and cry. The whispers were replaced by real sobs that brought on real tears and escalated into a real cry, for the first time since the day you passed away. I didn't feel relieved or cleansed afterward but felt it was probably good to cry. Good that I took the opportunity to do it during Ivan's morning nap.

My psychologist comes out and fetches me in the waiting room, takes me to her office. She stands opposite me and says she's not sure she'll be able to get through our conversation without crying and apologizes in advance. She steps closer to me, puts her arms around me, and I smell her perfume while she hugs me for a long time. It occurs to me that she's much shorter than I am, and I wonder if it's okay for a psychologist to hug a patient on special occasions. I also recognize the shampoo she uses, but then I stop thinking completely and allow myself to cry without restraint on her shoulder.

"This is so fucked up. It's just so fucked up. What should I do? What's going to happen? It's so fucked up," I sob. My psychologist also cries and says, "Yes, it is. It is fucked up. And brutal and unfair and incomprehensible."

The appointment is supposed to be forty-five minutes, but it goes on for an hour. Words I didn't know I had inside me pour out, and she listens and hands me tissue after tissue. Like my friends, she refuses to accept my theory that I'm to blame, at least in part. "You couldn't know," she says. "It would have happened anyway," she says. I don't answer but think that she can't know either. She knows as little as me, so why is she so sure I'm not to blame? Why is everyone so sure about that? It's not logical. We should at least be open to the possibility that I killed you. I stressed you and pushed you until you couldn't take it.

My psychologist doesn't agree. Instead, she tells me that she'll be here for me. I can see her as often as I like, and she'll give me her direct number. I can call and leave a message, and she'll call me back as soon as she is able. She writes her phone number on her business card, and I realize one doesn't usually get a psychologist's direct number, a shortcut past the receptionist. She also tells me that we can meet without Ivan in the beginning, if that's what I prefer. That's also not normal, since she's a child psychologist who specializes in the very young. "I'll be here for you through this," she says, and it makes me cry even more, this time with relief. I know I need her, and I hate that I do. I don't want to need any more people. I want to take care of myself. I have to learn to get by on my own. In the end that's what I have to learn, how to be alone.

During the last part of our meeting, I'm struck by a sudden feeling of defiance. I decide to become the best person to ever work through loss. I'm going to shine at this. Turn over every stone so as not to push anything away, get through my grief quickly and effectively, find a life that works. I just have to. I have to succeed at this. Not for my sake, but for Ivan's. It's my last gift to you, now when everything else is gone, now when I've destroyed almost everything. A competitive streak rears up inside me. Then I'm very tired. Maybe it's the tears. Or that I haven't slept for almost four days. The hour is over, and my psychologist has to ask me to leave. We book a new time next week. We don't hug when we say goodbye.

When I meet my mom, brother, and Ivan outside the same door I entered an hour ago, I can't stop thinking about how the psychologist told me several times that I was still in shock. I'm belatedly offended by her words, which make me feel like a failure, like a slow and sluggish person who's not working as fast as I'd hoped I would through this. I don't want to be in shock. I want to go to the next stage. Whatever that is.

I decide to read about the stages of grief so I can be in another one by my next appointment. Either the next stage or the one after that. I just have to find out what they are first.

On our way home, I tell my mom and brother that tomorrow we'll be making another excursion. We'll go to the library. I'm going to check out every book they have on dealing with grief. I'll read them, learn all there is to learn. I'm going to study my way out of this crisis. There's no other way to do this. I'll have to deal with the guilt later.

I notice my mom and brother exchanging glances when they think I'm not looking. My brother nods to my mother and they seem to agree not to say anything. With that, the decision is made—tomorrow we'll go on an excursion. The second one since you died.

July 2012

It's our first summer in Enskede, and compared to last summer, it's wonderful. A sort of quiet contentment has settled over our lives. We rarely fight. We laugh a lot. Our sex life is more satisfying than it's been in a long time. We handle our differences with compromise instead of touchiness or suppressed anger or passive-aggressive barbs. I can't exactly put my finger on why, but my guess is that it has something to do with the move. In both a practical and an emotional sense.

This year we're living in an apartment with a good draft, where the bedroom stays cool even in the middle of a heat wave. This year we have a parking spot behind our apartment building and a small car to take us on short trips. This year we managed to make some summer plans—sailing, visiting friends at their summer cottages, going to beaches near Stockholm that would be inaccessible without a car. You had a good spring and earned a lot. I have my vacation pay. We don't worry about money. We go to restaurants, stay at hotels in nearby cities, stay home between trips watching movies, reading books, relaxing. You've started jogging in the evenings. You head out on a run and come back with rosy cheeks, your T-shirt soaked with sweat, show me on an app how far you ran today. You're proud you've started running. I'm proud of you for running. As for me, I don't run, but I'm happy with my life anyway. This is what summer is supposed to be. Just like this.

In fact, we have such a lovely life right now that lately I've started to imagine there's room for one more. I want us to get a pet together. Preferably a dog, but a cat would work too. As long as the cat has a doglike personality. For you, a dog is out of the question. You don't like them, and you've made it clear you would never help me take care of a dog. If I get a dog, it's my responsibility. I gave up that idea, at least for now, but I still sneak in the mention of a cat now and then. You say you can imagine having a cat. Eventually. Sometime in the future. I think this future could arrive fairly soon. Maybe even this autumn.

Sometimes in the evenings we amuse ourselves by talking about what life would be like with a cat. We both agree about where the litter box would go, and you don't seem to mind the thought of having a cat in your lap when you work from home. I've been researching breeds online, and I'm fairly sure I've found the one we're looking for. I show you some pictures, and even though your first reaction is that they're ugly—too little hair and oversized ears—you seem a bit amused, maybe even tempted, by the thought of adding a pet to our harmonious life in Enskede.

So I take the bold step of contacting some breeders. When

you're out jogging, I send them emails. I ask them about the breed's temperament. If they prefer to live alone or with another cat as their companion. Eventually I throw in a question about any litters being available in the next few months. I can't quite stop myself, since we're already in contact. Most of the breeders answer no, they don't have any kittens on the way, or if they do, they're already reserved; most have a waiting list.

But then I stumble across a breeder in the small town of Malå in the far north of Sweden. She has a new litter of kittens, and one has not yet been sold. A white female kitten that will be ready for delivery in twelve weeks. The breeder sends two pictures of the kitten and one of its mother. My stomach flutters as I flip back and forth between the pictures. At that moment the front door opens, and you come home from your run. I close my computer and meet you in the hall. I look at your running app and praise you for getting faster. You go and take a shower. I return to the bedroom and my computer.

After reading the email and looking at the pictures a few more times, I call out to you. "Aksel, come here! Look at this!" You enter the room, your hair still wet from the shower, and stare at me where I lie on the bed with my computer open on my stomach. "Look at this kitten," I say. I show you the picture. "That's cute. Why are we looking at it?" you ask. "It's available," I say. "We could buy it. It costs only seven thousand kronor, which is a thousand kronor cheaper than any of the others I've found of this breed."

As gently as I can, I ask if maybe we should take this opportunity. She won't be ready for twelve weeks, and I could fly up north and pick her up. It would be no problem. I promise. First you look at me, then at the picture on my computer, then back at me. You seem caught by surprise, like you hadn't expected our cat fantasies to turn into reality quite so quickly. Your face is still flushed from your run. Your chest is a patchy red. I wipe away a few drops of water from your shoulder. You look at the screen again. I'm ready for you to say no, let's wait a little bit, think this through for a while longer. Instinctively, I'm already preparing my arguments for why this is a good idea. Twelve weeks is a long time, I'm ready to tell you. It will be wonderful, I'm going to promise you. You look at the screen, then you look at me. Searchingly. Is she serious? I imagine you thinking. Then something changes in your eyes. I can't quite interpret it. Are you about to sigh? Get angry? Say I can never just leave things as they are, no matter how good?

But instead you start to smile. First your eyes, then your mouth, then your whole face. "Sure," you say, "let's do it. Let's get that kitten. I'm in. But I'm not going to fly up north and pick it up. You'll have to do that. Do we have a deal?"

Do we have a deal? We have such a perfect deal I can't imagine anyone has ever had a better one. I start jumping on the bed, squealing like a teenager at a concert, throw myself at you and kiss you all over your rosy face. This summer will go down in history as the century's best.

She arrived in time for my birthday, the white Devon Rex kitten whose household nickname would soon end up being Pea. Since then she's become a member of the family, and I adore her, even though she's made it clear who her favorite human is: you. It's already become a part of our daily routine to discuss who's going to "play with the cat" for a half hour before we go to bed. Playing with her means we'll have a good night's sleep. If we don't, we can count on being woken up before dawn; our cat has proven to be as unscrupulous as she is verbal. Suddenly, our little family consists of more than just the two of us. I think it does us good. The cat has become a daily topic of conversation, a subject we both can discuss endlessly. Your love for the cat is unmistakable. She makes you laugh, and you play with her for hours as the weeks go by and the autumn turns to winter. You text me reports with pictures and videos several times a day. All of which are a welcome break during my days at the office. As soon as the clock strikes five, I hurry home to be with both of you.

November 2014

Monday morning. Today it's been a week. My body commemorated that milestone by finally falling asleep last night. When I woke up, I had no memory of the last few hours. I didn't remember breastfeeding or waking up from Ivan crying, no thoughts and no dreams. That should be a good sign. When I woke up, it was five o'clock, and I knew immediately: now, now it's been a week. Exactly a week. Perhaps to the minute. From now on I'll count the weeks rather than the days. Weeks will turn into months and months into years. Somewhere along the way, this existence will start to feel normal. Someday each breath will stop hurting, will stop feeling like an effort I'm not sure I'm capable of. That's not where we are now. Now we are at one week. It's not much, but it's not nothing either.

In the room next to mine, my mom, who was here over the weekend, has been replaced by my stepmother and my little sister. My friends and family have taken over every task they can for me with quiet concentration. Together and without much discussion, they've become my artificial lungs, heart, legs, and arms. They handle all the paperwork, the schedule, the mail, the meetings, the buying and making of food. I don't know the last time I cleared a dish. Or emptied a dishwasher. Or hung up laundry. Cooked dinner. Made coffee. Everything happens as if by itself.

The only thing I have to do is keep breathing and keep trying to make it through these days. And be there for Ivan. I know I'm lucky. I don't know how I would have made it otherwise. It's as if I have just enough energy to be somewhat normal with Ivan, and when he's resting, I spend my time crying or talking or thinking. With all the life support this network gives me, somehow my days are able to go on. Maybe because I'm never alone. Perhaps because I'm able to take breaks, hand Ivan to his grandmother and sit down at the kitchen table and stare into space. Maybe because life with a nine-month-old baby doesn't give a person much choice.

Oblivious to the tragedy that will shape his life, he fills up diaper after diaper. He crawls and stumbles. Cries and then is happy again. Laughs and plays, splashes in the bath and tries out new sounds. Learns to stand up against the sofa, falls down and sulks, puts his little fist onto the table and starts over again. His life continues and my life revolves around him. He is the basis of my routines. Sometimes he even makes me laugh in a way that's not artificial.

The magnitude of what happened is starting to sink in. In the books I borrowed from the library about trauma and crisis management, I've read all about the stages of grief. Still stubbornly focused on getting through the shock as quickly as possible, I've studied it, noted that after shock comes reaction. Then it's time for processing. Finally, reorientation. I've read about the later phases with great interest. It's hopeful to read about what happens later. I want to get there as quickly as possible. My goal is the fourth stage. Unfortunately, the books give me little hope that I can move fast. It seems to take at least a year to get to the fourth stage. Or even longer. Some crisis management books have noted that sometimes grief is postponed because we don't have the capacity to deal with it right away. I hope that won't happen to me. I try to feel as much as I can, as much as I'm able, in hopes that it will help me in the long run.

At the same time, now and then a new feeling arrives. One that will probably become more prominent as all this settles in. A voice that is ever more audible inside me. A complaining, dissatisfied, whiny voice that despite all the angels around me, despite all the help and love I receive, wants to tell them: Thanks, but no thanks. I only want to do this with *you,* and the rest of you can go home. Thank you for coming. It was very kind, but it's no longer necessary. I just want you to come home again. I have no interest in learning to live without you. I think I'll pass. If you'd just come back, if I could just wake up from this bizarre dream, then I could make everything right again. You'll see. I promise to never stress you out again. I'll let you sleep more. I'll never complain about your pace. You can be whomever you want and need to be. Give me more time, and I'll do it right. I know I could. I know I can.

Instead, in just a few hours I'm meeting your parents at a funeral home nearby to plan your funeral. A friend booked the meeting for us. My brother is going to take Ivan for a walk while I'm there. And my friend will come with me for moral support. Everything's been planned meticulously.

Still, I can't even imagine how I'll shower and get dressed in time. How I'll be able to leave the apartment and walk ten minutes to the funeral home. The task seems overwhelming. I can't even make breakfast for myself anymore. All I can do is sit and stare at Ivan, play with him, breastfeed him. I try my best to avoid everything else, say it will have to wait until I have more energy, but today I just don't think that's possible. The meeting starts in two hours.

January 2013

No matter how hard I try, my restlessness, my fierce need for change and progress, wins out against every rational argument I make to myself to take it slow, wait a bit, live in the moment, and rest. After a period of calm, it's as if I'm helpless to resist my impulse to tear things down, to provoke, to wrench us from where we stand, shake us until we collide and stumble, just to see where we'll land. I don't understand this about myself. I'm not sure I even like it about myself. Nevertheless, it happens over and over again.

Sometimes it feels like we're in complete agreement only when we travel. Which probably explains why we've traveled together so much. Since that first trip to Iceland, we've gone to the US, Japan, European beaches, spent weekends in capital cities and summers on Österlen, the Swedish west coast, and Norrbotten. When we're away from our everyday lives, we disconnect and live in a sort of state of exception. We read books in the evenings, drink beer and wine at dinner, spend money, make cooperative compromises between excursions (which I propose) and relaxation (which you prefer). We almost always have a trip planned for the near future. And we have enjoyed them, looked forward to them, relished planning them together, and when we get home, our relationship feels stronger for a while. Then we book something new.

Most recently, we got home from two weeks in Zanzibar. We're tan and sweaty and jet-lagged, and I realize I'm bored. I don't want to travel anymore for a while. I feel done with this. This can't be our only challenge in life, the only thing that gives us joy. There has to be something more. We have to find that something more. I feel it in every cell of my body. A premonition about what's coming, that I'm going to make trouble again, knock things down with such force I'll barely realize it before it's a fact. Something I've been pushing away for the past year can no longer be ignored. There is something we have to talk about.

We've approached the subject before but never come to any conclusion or agreement. Time has passed. Months have turned into years. I haven't been clear with you, you haven't been up for it, and having the whole conversation from start to finish has seemed too painful to fully broach. It's felt a bit like a marriage proposal—what do you do if the one you love says no? I haven't been ready to pay that price. Not until now.

This year I turn thirty-five, and I want a child. I know that. For a long time I maintained that I didn't, a few years ago I would have said I didn't know, then for a while I pretended there was no hurry, but now none of that works anymore. I want a child, and if you don't want to have one with me, or at least try, I think I'm going to need to leave you. We have to talk about it. I've been carrying it around too long, and no matter how much I don't want to burden you, you're part of this equation, and it has to be dealt with.

The truth is that I've already thought through four alternatives. Only one of them involves breaking up. The other three include me having a baby, and in only one are you the biological father. I feel extremely smart and farsighted. The alternatives are as follows:

1. You and I stay together, start trying to have a baby.
2. You and I stay together, and I have a child with my gay friends who have expressed a desire to have children with a womb-bearing friend. You're not the biological father of the child, thus skipping the lifelong responsibility, but can stay with me as long as you want (and I hope it will be a long time).
3. You and I stay together, and I go to Denmark to be inseminated at a clinic that allows a single person to be inseminated, unlike Sweden in 2013. You won't be the biological father. See above regarding lifelong responsibility.
4. You and I break up because you don't want to have any kids with me or even in your life. You'd rather break up than have a child with me.

I think I've been responsible and smart, open to so many options that we should be able to find one that feels feasible to both of us. So when this conversation begins, at the end of January, I'm so much further along than you in my planning. I have my solutions written down on a piece of paper that I bring with me to our first serious conversation on the matter.

I go through it all without any frills, because I've learned that's the best way to communicate with you. I present the solutions to the problem of me wanting children while you're not sure if or especially when you want them. After I've presented my options, I ask you if you want to add anything. You stare at the numbered list on my piece of paper in confusion. I can see already that you're not quite at the same place I am. You definitely haven't realized how generous I'm being with my alternatives. Accustomed now to our straightforward style of communication, I haven't sugarcoated anything, didn't start the conversation with how much I love you or what an amazing father I know you will be. I just threw down the paper and pointed to the alternatives. Went through them as pedagogically as possible. Waited in silence while you wrinkled your forehead and stared at the paper with a pained expression on your face.

You don't seem charmed. On the contrary, you seem very uncomfortable. All my alternatives make you anxious, and the alternative you prefer—stay together and wait a few more years before we deal with the baby question—doesn't work for me. I refuse to even put it on the list. I don't trust you anymore when you say "Maybe later." Your "Maybe later" always ends up with me making a decision without you, then getting you to come along via ultimatum. This time I'm not sure how much time I have to wait, even if I wanted to. I don't know how long my body will be able to conceive. I don't even know if it can right now. I haven't been on birth control for the years we've been together, and we haven't always been careful. I can't take the chance of waiting any longer. It's impossible. We're at an impasse.

Our first conversation ends in tears. I cry because I'm angry with you, and you cry for the same reason. Neither of us wants to compromise, so we decide to table the question and return to it, soon. I'm disappointed, but I haven't given up. We schedule a time to talk about it in one week. We take a break from negotiations. Return to where we were before, what we know how to do, what doesn't feel as destructive as the conversation we just had.

The early spring is filled with many difficult conversations. They're so hard we can't stand to have them very often. About once a week we try to find the time and energy to sit down and make each other angry, sad, or disappointed. I'm disappointed with you because you don't dare believe in us. I'm angry with myself because it's always been like this between us, and I've just let time pass by. I'm tired of always having to force change upon us, tired of how anything unpredictable provokes such resistance from you. And as for you, you're tired of me pushing you, never letting you rest, never being satisfied with things as they are. You say I always need to get my way. You feel stressed because you're not sure you're ready to be a father, when you haven't even decided how you want to live your own life. How could you be somebody's parent when that's the case? You say you're afraid you won't have the energy, that you'll be too exhausted. You say it has nothing to do with how much you love me, but I find that hard to believe. Something deep inside tells me that if you loved me enough you'd take the risk. I tell you I think it would do you good not to have a choice. You're not particularly keen on not having a choice. And so it goes, on and on.

Our negotiations are not beautiful. They're not romantic, never interrupted by an embrace or a sweet hug to comfort the one who's crying. Neither of us ever leaves the kitchen table feeling good.

I can see I'm hurting you and our relationship by not dropping this question. I hate that I'm doing this to you, to us, but can't force myself to compromise anymore. Not on my future. You hate making me feel like this, don't want me to think this is about me. I say it's about me whether you want it to be or not. When you're at your most dejected, you tell me I deserve to be with someone who knows what they want, who's ready to commit to a lifetime with me and a child. You weep when you tell me you're sorry, but you don't think that person is you. You apologize for the way you are, ask me to forgive you, your fears, your personality generally. It hurts me that you seem so close to giving up. I don't want to give up and absolutely don't want your apologies. I want you to believe in us, our future, in building a family together. Why is that so hard? Many times the conversation ends because we simply run out of words.

Two months after our first conversation, we finally come to a decision. It's not really that you decide—it's more like you give up. Reluctantly, you realize that the least costly option is to stay together and try to have a child. You still claim that you're not ready. I still claim that you will be, when the time comes. I'm relieved that this is where we landed but sad because I wish we'd gotten here another way. I'm sad because I know I'm the reason you feel cornered, but at the same time I'm angry that I've had to put so much effort into negotiating this. I tell you I think I'm worthy of being loved by a person who wants to share a life and a child with me, and you agree with me. That makes me even sadder, because you agree, because I love you, because you're the bigger one of the two of us, but still we never really seem to be in sync nowadays.

This wasn't how I imagined starting a family would happen, but I try not to be sentimental. We're not sentimental, you and me—that's not our thing. I feel ashamed when I look at my list of options one last time. Pros and cons are listed with small plus and minus signs after each solution. The one with "stay together . . . have a baby" has the most pluses and least number of minuses. After one of the minus signs it says, "May not be able to cope." You were the one who wrote those words. Your neat handwriting is in contrast to my large scrawl. The words are tiny, but their meaning is enormous. It cuts me, but I convince myself you're wrong, you will have the energy, you will cope, and this is going to give our lives a whole new meaning. Our love will be easier later, when there are fewer opportunities to question every little thing. This is the last big change I'll ever force on you. I promise myself that this is the last time. I put the paper into a folder and hide it in a box with a bunch of old tax statements.

November 2014

I'm now a customer of a funeral home, and in the papers I brought home with me after the meeting, I see that they call me their client. I'm a client of a funeral home.

The sky was dark, and rain poured down as I made my way to the funeral home. I saw your parents' car in the parking lot as soon as we arrived, fifteen minutes early. Your mom was smoking a cigarette, her shoulders hunched, a coat wrapped tightly around her thin body. Her posture was tense. She seemed cold. Your dad was pacing impatiently between the car, a sign at the corner of the parking lot, and the door of the funeral home.

Your parents and I haven't talked much in the last few days. It hasn't been easy for us to share in our grieving processes. They call often, and your dad always tells me he loves Ivan and me, and that they'll always be there for us, that we will always be part of their family. I say that's what I want too, because I do, but right now I don't know how. Right now I don't know how to be part of anyone's family, not even my own. Your parents seem to want to meet more often than I do, and I'm not sure if it's to try to take care of us or if they're worried they'll be pushed out of your son's life. Probably it's because they think I need it. But I just don't have the energy. Any interaction with people generally exhausts me but especially those with the people who are also grieving for you. I can't listen. My brain shuts off. I don't know how to offer comfort or end sentences. I just want to run away, lock myself inside, when someone else starts to cry. I want to run away, lock myself inside, when I start to cry too. It's hard to know what to do with the impulse to shut out the rest of the world. Sometimes when your parents call, I let a friend answer the phone and tell them I'm busy with Ivan or asleep. Afterward, I feel ashamed. When we see each other, our meetings are short, and when I see them walk out the door, headed home again, I feel even more ashamed. But the fact remains. We are unable to comfort each other. We can't understand what's happened, and we are all struggling with our own demons. I think, Well, at least they have each other. When I shut them out, at least they can find comfort in each other's arms, each other's words, their long, shared history. But today we're meeting to talk about your funeral. It's unavoidable, and none of us has been looking forward to it.

Once inside the funeral home, we meet with the person who is going to be our funeral director. A short woman, whose name I forget as soon as she says it. I don't like the way she looks at me, how she puts her hand on my arm and offers her sympathies. It feels routine and not warm. She's done this so many times she doesn't mean it. We're just a part of her everyday life. Her thoughts are elsewhere. What to cook for dinner tonight or all the places she'd rather be right now. I despise her and her kind words. Decide to make the meeting as brief as possible, then leave here, and if at all possible never come back again.

The door opens and my friend enters. She's rushed here from work, has a dark dress on and high heels. She's out of breath, and I realize she must have jogged the short distance from the parking lot to the door of the funeral home. Probably she's missing some important meeting at work to be here. I feel guilty when I think about how she's taken time off for this, for us, for me and Ivan and this terrible situation. When I mime a "Thank you," she wrinkles her forehead and hisses, "Stop it." I love my friend and her brusqueness. She squeezes me quickly from behind, then sits down on the chair next to me. The meeting can start now. Only the funeral director is missing. I stare straight ahead and avoid meeting anyone's eyes. I will not break down today.

A box of tissues sits on the round table next to a stack of papers. The top one has your name written on it. Without expecting it or meaning to, something breaks inside me when I see it. No warning, just suddenly your simultaneous presence and absence in this room feels unbearable. My tears are sudden, a surprise even to myself, but I can't stop them. Your mom and dad are watching me. Your dad starts to weep too, and says my name over and over again. No one tries to hug me, and I'm grateful for that. My friend strokes my back and nods to our funeral director, who makes an apologetic entrance. I take deep breaths, trying to calm myself down so the meeting can begin. We need to get this over with.

I fail in my attempts to calm down, at least for the first fifteen minutes of the meeting. Every word the funeral director says brings a new flood of tears. "Your name is Carolina," she says, and I cry so intensely I can only nod in reply. "And you were Aksel's partner," she continues, and I keep crying and nodding—there is no end to it now. "And together you have little . . . Ivan," she says, glancing down at her papers to remind herself of his name, and I dissolve into a puddle across the round table. When I've nodded my way through the formalities and confirmed the deceased's address, my tears suddenly run out.

We start to go over the practicalities around the ceremony, and everything suddenly becomes easier. The bulleted list of questions to go through reminds me that this meeting will end. My worries that your parents and I would have different ideas about your funeral also proved to be unwarranted. You'd made it just as clear to them as you did to me that you didn't want a grave. What you wanted was for your ashes to be scattered to the wind, but we agree that the memorial grove at Skogskyrkogården is a reasonable compromise. We want something small and intimate, but when we start to list the names of colleagues, friends, and relatives who need to be invited, we quickly end up with a hundred people. Maybe even more. We decide to hold it at the Holy Cross Chapel at Skogskyrkogården, which has seating for two hundred. We choose an officiant to lead the ceremony, someone recommended by the funeral home. Before I know it, we're at the end of the meeting. Just as we're rising from our chairs, my phone rings. Unknown number.

My friend answers without even asking. She reads me so well now, knows that every intrusion from the outside world causes me anxiety. The flower deliveries still haven't slowed—at least several bouquets a day. And every single one means a call to be let in the front door. I hate them. Don't have vases for all the flowers. Can't stand the smell of the water when it gets old. My friend apologizes, gets up, and walks out of the meeting room. I hear her talking to the delivery person, redirecting them to the address we're at. I swear inwardly, thinking, Goddamn fucking flowers, but then immediately feel bad. I have no right to be so angry at the flowers. They're sent out of thoughtfulness and love, not to make my life more difficult. I have to remember that. I have to pull myself together.

As we're all hugging each other goodbye at the funeral home's reception desk, a truck pulls into the parking lot outside. My friend gives me a questioning look, I nod to her, and she runs out to talk with the driver. It passes through my mind that it's a very big truck for a flower delivery before she returns carrying a huge cardboard box in her arms. It's almost bigger than her. She totters in her heels and has to turn sideways to fit through the funeral home's front door. Just as surprised as me, she's realized it wasn't flowers arriving. Instead, it was ten kilos of cat food, for the cat who no longer lives with us but who moved in with a friend's family after you died. I obviously placed an order for cat food on the internet a few days before. I'd forgotten that. And now here we are. My friend standing in high-heeled shoes with ten kilos of dry cat food in her arms. Me and your parents at a loss for what to make of this situation. My friend's mouth starts to tremble as she looks at me over the top of the cardboard box. I can see that she's about to start laughing, struggling to push it away. I turn my eyes away from her, thinking it's not right if we start laughing now. Glance at her again. She really does look improbably tiny behind that cardboard box. Suddenly I can't hold back either. We burst into laughter, which keeps coming and coming, tears stream out of my eyes, and I don't know why I think it's so hysterical, but I do, and it's the first time I've laughed for over a week. In the end, I don't think it's funny anymore, but I keep laughing because it feels like I might never laugh again, so I might as well wring what I can from this. I laugh as I say goodbye to the funeral director, and I can just barely hold it back as I hug your parents goodbye and wave to them as they roll out of the funeral home's parking lot.

June 2013

My period is five days late, and I'm not yet brave enough to tell you. I still feel guilty for pushing you into this decision. I emphasized, maybe too many times, that it would surely take a long time for us to get pregnant. If we even are able to. For many couples our age it can take a year or more, or so I've read. I told you this to comfort you, since you still don't seem comfortable with the decision that we made "together." Our intimate life has been anything but pleasurable in recent months. After I pee on an ovulation stick and it shows I'm fertile, you have sex with me, guiltily and sometimes with eyes averted. I've stifled my impulse to thank you afterward. Instead, I've reiterated that it's going to take time. And you've muttered a no in reply, said it'll probably happen right away. Every month after ovulation, a giddy feeling has come over me. Did it happen now? Will a baby come from this? It's been three months since we started trying, I'm five days late, and I don't dare tell you. Nor do I dare tell you that this morning I'm going to take a pregnancy test. I think maybe I won't even be brave enough to tell you if it's positive but then realize that's a crazy line of thinking.

It's Monday morning, and we're both headed to work soon. You're sitting on the sofa with your computer on your lap, while I sneak into the bathroom, whistling on my way there to prove there's nothing special about this bathroom visit. My hand shakes as I try to pee on the stick's measuring range and nowhere else. I'm nervous about the result, whatever it will be. I hope I'm not pregnant, I think. And I hope I'm pregnant. On and on, one or the other. There is no ideal outcome in this situation.

I put the stick on the sink, just like the instructions say to do. Staring intently at the area that will soon show one red stripe, meaning I'm not pregnant, or two red stripes, meaning I am. The seconds creep by. I stand up, wash my hands. Manage to splash soap onto the stick as I do. My movements are jerky.

There comes the first stripe. Clear and indisputable. I keep staring at the area where the other stripe will appear. Holding my breath. Damn, there's nothing! Why is there nothing? Is there something wrong with me? What if I can't get pregnant! But wait. Isn't there something there? Am I imagining it? Is there another stripe? Weak and light pink? But still a . . . stripe?

Yes. There is another stripe. I pick up the little stick and study it for a while. The second line is becoming more and more clear. There are two stripes on the stick. I'm pregnant. Holy shit, I'm pregnant! How am I going to tell you? I'm alone in the bathroom in the apartment I bought a year ago, and you're sitting on the other side of the door working on the sofa. The cat is lying next to you, half asleep, and I'm pregnant. Someone is alive inside my body! A tiny product of you and me! It's incomprehensible.

My heart is pounding so hard it feels like it might escape my body. I have to tell you this right now, right away, it has to be now. But I'm afraid. I feel like I've betrayed you by getting pregnant. I fumble with the lock on the bathroom door, holding the positive pregnancy test, and go and sit down next to you on the sofa.

You don't look up when I sit down. I end up in an awkward position, a little too close but not touching you. I tap you on your shoulder, and you look up at me, wondering what I want. "We have to talk," I say. "About what?" you say. Looking into my eyes questioningly. Not noticing the test in my hand. I lift it up, wave it, take a deep breath, and reel off the essence of what I need to say. "I'm pregnant." My voice turns to a croak at the end of that statement, running out of air halfway. At this point my heart is pounding so hard it fills the room. I can feel the vein in my neck bulging out of suppressed tension. I can't help but smile too. I don't know if I'm smiling because I'm nervous or because I'm happy. In either case, you don't smile back. You're silent. Your fingers are frozen above the keys of your computer, your whole body rigid. Something is happening in your eyes, but I can't figure out what. You sit there silent and petrified, your eyes roving back and forth between me and the rest of the room. My smile has stiffened on my face. It feels like I'd have to grimace to restore it to neutrality again. Something that seems like an eternity passes by. I don't know what else to say.

I want you to respond. I want you to tell me what you're feeling. Your silence terrifies me, and I'm afraid of what's going to happen when it ends. I have a sudden urge to apologize but stop myself. You're the one who has to say something now. And finally, you do.

"Are you sure?" you say quietly, almost whispering. "I think so," I say, looking at the test again. There are now two clear stripes. "You said it would take time," you whisper. "I said that it *could* take time," I reply. You're silent. We sit next to each other on the sofa, and I don't dare touch you. Don't know if you're angry or sad or shocked or maybe even a little happy deep inside. As for me, I feel guilty. Guilt, mixed with wonder and a calm determination. This has to go well. It will go well. I'll make it go well.

Now you speak. You tell me you need some time to process this, then you stand up and start packing your bag. You put on your coat and shoes in the hall, stop at the door as if you're about to say something more. I stand opposite you, after following you out here, trying to catch your eyes. You say you have to go to work now; we'll talk later today. I take a step closer to you, so close that if you just stretched out your arms we could hold each other. But we don't, you don't stretch out your arms, and neither do I. Instead, I ask you for a kiss. Which you don't give me. You look at me for the first time since I told you we're expecting. "I have to process this," you say again. "Sorry." Then you leave. I stare at the closed door. Your steps move quickly down the stairs toward the street. I hear the front door slam shut after you. Soon you'll be on the subway, probably heading to one of your jobs. I wonder how you're feeling, what you're thinking, why you don't want to share it with me. At the same time, I feel I don't deserve to know.

I go back into the living room, where the cat has now left her spot on the sofa. I hear her meowing at the front door in the hall. She too is confused by your sudden retreat. A soft imprint is still visible in the sofa cushion where you were just sitting. On the coffee table the pregnancy test lies next to your earbuds. I don't remember putting it there. My memory of the last half hour has dissolved into a blur. I try to gather my thoughts and breathe deeply. Don't be sad now. Give it some time. Be the bigger person here. I'll treat you perfectly from now on. I'll be so perfect you'll have no chance to feel like this is anything but good news. We're expecting a child. We're making a family. We're going to be three. That has to turn into good news somehow. Even for you.

November 2014

My apathy has gained competition from a growing restlessness. I need something to do, a task to focus on, but even the simplest tasks exhaust me, push me back into apathy, and to my prostrate position on the couch. It's a problem. Today I'm out for a walk with Ivan. My goals are to go to the library and to buy stamps. They seem like completely reasonable challenges.

In one of the books I read on grief—which I'm now returning to the library—it says it's common for the grieving to do this. Manifest their irrational search for the missing person by creating tasks for the purpose of finishing them. The subconscious is searching for meaning, trying to find its way back to normality, and the conscious mind turns that into assignments, creates tasks.

Something else I've realized is common after reading these books is how I seem to see you everywhere. A tall figure in a hoodie walking down the sidewalk near the grocery store. The sun is in my eyes, and I can only make out his silhouette. My body always reacts instinctively: there you are. For a moment I think it's you. You're on your way to meet me and help me carry the groceries, just like you've done so many times before.

Or no.

Oh, right.

That isn't you.

It will never be you again.

I will carry my groceries home by myself from now on. The insight hurts so much my whole body goes numb. I keep moving forward mechanically. The grocery bags hanging from my wrists, as I push the stroller, imprinting marks in my skin though I don't feel it. I don't feel anything then. My brain recharges, headed again toward the practical. What do I need to do? Where do I need to go? What was I just now doing?

Then a few hours, or maybe just minutes, go by. I forget to stop myself from looking for you. And I'll see you again and the procedure will be repeated. There you are! No. That isn't you. That's someone else, that's someone who's still alive.

All of a sudden everyone seems to be the same height as you. Everybody is tall, wears dark blue hoodies, walks toward me exactly the way you used to.

There you are. And there. And there. No. That's not you either.

August 2013

It's summer now, so here I am sweating again. Is it me, or are the summers getting warmer every year? I don't remember summers like this in my childhood. I wonder if there's something wrong with my thyroid. Or maybe it's just because I'm pregnant.

A heat wave has hit Stockholm, and today I'm sweating in our car as we drive past Thorildsplan, then Kristineberg, Alvik, and Stora Mossen. I curse to myself that I didn't invest a few extra thousand kronor in a car with air-conditioning. In April, when we bought this used 2000 Volkswagen Polo, saving money by buying an older model sounded reasonable. April and May were cool. We weren't planning to use it for much besides shopping and going to the stable. A simple car, which, according to your dad, was also easy to repair if it broke down. But then summer came with its obligatory heat wave, and now our car is impossible to use except in the early morning and just after dusk. Nevertheless, it's the middle of the day now, the car is so packed I can't see out the rearview mirror, and we're on our way to the summerhouse we rented for two weeks starting today.

I entered the twelfth week yesterday. My pregnancy has so far been completely unremarkable. I've felt a wave of nausea a few times, but otherwise everything has been normal. My stomach hasn't started to swell, and no one besides my closest friends and family knows about the pregnancy. I don't think you've told anyone besides your parents, your brothers, and your best friend. You say you want to wait a little longer. Now it's vacation, most of the people we know are gone, and we are on our way to the house we rented on the island of Färingsö. As usual, I'm driving—anything else would be crazy, since you don't have a driver's license—and you're sitting next to me with the cat carrier and a howling cat in your lap. I drive as carefully as I can. Getting annoyed at the many red lights on the stretch between Fridhemsplan and Brommaplan, where we'll turn toward Ekerö. How can traffic lights always be red? How can there be so many? How does anyone make any headway on this road? It's probably thirty degrees Celsius in the car. The heat annoys me. So does the car, and the whiny cat. I just want to get there.

After a shaky introduction to the pregnancy in June—during which you retreated into yourself, asked for space to deal with what I assumed was your dismay, and I followed your example and retreated into myself to deal with my feelings of anger and loneliness—our day-to-day life slipped back into a normal rhythm. I did my thing, devoted my time to riding, meeting friends now and then, and working full time. You did your thing, and we rarely spoke about the pregnancy. When we did, it felt forced and we quickly abandoned the subject. I realized I enjoyed the pregnancy much more if I didn't share it too much with you. Convinced myself that at this early stage it was simpler like this, and of course it's difficult for you to feel anything until my body changes and it becomes more real for you. Better then to just take care of it myself.

I downloaded apps that told me about how the fetus was developing and what's happening in my body. I shared my thoughts with my close friends who'd also been pregnant. I talked to my family during my commute rather than when you were nearby, so as not to remind you. I asked my colleagues to take pictures of my stomach in profile, one every week. Saved the pictures in an album on my phone without sharing them with you. I avoided pushing my pregnancy in your face, ashamed of how it came to be and so quickly. I thought it would be easier later. Once the belly arrives. Once the baby arrives. At the very latest when the baby arrives, then everything will change.

June became July and now August. Our little blue car rolls past Drottningholm Castle, and soon we'll be on Färingsö. When we arrive at the summerhouse, we're going to unpack. I'll make the bed with our freshly washed sheets, take a shower, turn on the radio in the kitchen to listen to public radio. Tonight we'll grill. Maybe we'll take a walk to the dock and you'll swim. Tomorrow one of my best friends is coming after work, and a few days later my brother and sister-in-law arrive.

Then a good friend of yours. Later in the week, your parents and then my mom. I look forward to the next two weeks. Can't wait to read books and hang out with you all day long. This is the first time we've rented a summerhouse in Sweden, but if it's similar to how it works when we travel, when we live in exceptional circumstances, this will be a great thing for us, exactly what we need right now. We need to get away. Pause. Take care of each other.

As the car rolls into the driveway of our rental, the cat is silent. We've been talking freely for almost a half hour, and once you even spontaneously put your left hand on my right thigh. Warmth spread through the thin fabric of my pants. I felt so moved, almost to tears, by that touch. It's been a long time since you put your hand on me like that. I realize I've missed it. I realize I've missed you. This vacation could not be more needed.

November 2014

On the ninth day, Ivan sleeps in, and we stay in bed until nine o'clock. The chance to sleep in came so unexpectedly that for a moment I feel bad for my brother, who's probably been waiting hours for us to get up. It's not unusual for us to get up before six o'clock. Always accompanied by whoever slept over the night before. They don't seem to want to leave us alone for a moment other than when we're sleeping. I don't mind the company.

The sun has long since risen outside our bedroom window as we finally make our way into the living room, where my brother sits drinking coffee in front of the morning news. It's a familiar sight to find him here; he's already made himself at home. In a way, he's picked up where you left off. He's sitting in your spot on the sofa, leaning back in the same way with his laptop on his thighs. Just like you, he can work from home when he needs to—as a freelance translator he's not bound to any particular workplace—and like you, his workload varies between almost nothing and, at times, so overwhelming he has to work night and day to meet his deadline. It feels safe to have him here. We're able to spend hours together without needing to talk. He's better at reading me than anyone else, and our communication is mostly nonverbal. I appreciate his presence as much as I do his ability not to need to talk about everything all the time. He doesn't constantly ask me how I feel, how I'm doing, if it feels any better, if I've eaten something, if there's anything I need. He trusts me to tell him when I need him, and I do. I say when I need a shower or a break. Then I ask him to take care of Ivan. But for the most part, I just like having him here, close by, without needing to talk to him. And even if he doesn't ask me what I want for dinner, he does the shopping, cooks the food, serves it. When he's nearby, I can relax, and now and then I almost, almost feel content.

I say, "Good morning," tell him I slept in, and ask how long he's been up. He answers, "An hour or so," says he's working on a contract that needs to be translated from English to Swedish, and I pass by him and go into the bathroom. "There's coffee in the kitchen," I hear him shout as I close the bathroom door behind me and Ivan. As I change Ivan's diaper, it occurs to me that I haven't given him a bath since you died. Our evening routine has fallen apart, and I haven't even thought about picking it up again. Until today. I decide to remedy this right away. When I take off his pajamas, I sniff him, kiss his soft stomach until he laughs, and it hits me how good he smells, despite the days without a bath. How is it possible that a baby could smell so good?

When we're done, I pass by the entry hall and see that a letter's come through the mail slot. It's lying on the floor. An official-looking envelope with the Swedish Tax Authority's logo in the corner. I snatch it up, take a detour through the living room to put Ivan in my brother's arms, pour a cup of coffee, and then open the letter at the kitchen table.

It contains a single sheet of paper. The headline is only the words "Death Certificate." The public records office has sent it. Then: "Information About the Deceased." There it is. Your name, your long beautiful name, your social security number, and the word "deceased" next to it. The next heading reads "Children of the Deceased," and there I see Ivan's name and social security number. That's it.

I stare at the document for a long time in silence. I read it over and over again. My gaze wandering between the word "deceased" and the line "Children of the Deceased." I stare at all of your names. Then at all of Ivan's names. I feel a knot in my stomach. I don't know what to do with this paper. It tells me nothing I don't already know, and yet it hurts to hold it in my hands. I'd like to throw the letter in the trash, tie up the trash bag and take it to the garbage can in the courtyard, throw it inside, slam the lid and pretend the letter never arrived. The letter hurts me because I don't know what it wants from me, what it wants to tell me, what I'm supposed to use it for.

I stare at Ivan's names one last time. There's something that chafes at me about it. It feels like there's something missing in the middle, between his first and last name. There's a gap there, room for something else. When I realize what it is, I'm overcome by relief—this is how it has to be, of course it is. I can't believe I didn't think of it before. It's the only logical solution. Now that you've gone from living to deceased in the Tax Authority's registry, now that they've decided to push it into our faces with this letter, Ivan will inherit your first name as well. Your full name will sit nestled there among Ivan's middle names. Your name shouldn't just belong to a deceased person. Death doesn't deserve all of you.

Decisively, I open up my computer, go to the Swedish Tax Authority's website, where I download forms to change Ivan's name. Feel a moment of triumph when I realize the procedure is both simple and free: it's just to fill in the information, attach the registry I've just received in the mail confirming that you're dead and that I'm now Ivan's sole guardian, put the papers into an envelope, and send them away. I call out to my brother in the living room and tell him about my plans. "I'm giving Ivan his father's name as a middle name," I say. My brother answers the way I knew he would. No frills, no emotional expressions, no follow-up questions, just a simple: "Of course you should. That's really smart."

September 2013

You're with me at the prenatal clinic today. It's the first time you've come along, the first appointment I haven't gone to alone. You've had work, looked harassed when I asked if you'd like to join. So I stopped asking. I didn't want to force you to talk to my midwife. Maybe I also felt embarrassed. The thought has crossed my mind more than once: we must be the only couple she meets in which both parents aren't happy and expectant. I've reasoned that as long as we can keep that information to ourselves, it will be easier to bear. The rest of the world doesn't need to know. Not even our midwife. Better that you work, move forward at your own pace, and I'll go to these appointments alone.

But today is special, almost solemn. Today is the anatomy ultrasound. Today we'll find out if our baby is thriving, has ten fingers, ten toes, if it's growing like it should. We'll also find out the sex. I'm very excited about today's visit. In part, though I wouldn't admit it to you, because I hope something will happen inside you when you see the baby inside my belly on the screen. I'm hoping it will spark some joy. Some glimmer of hope for the future. That the little fetus will start to take over your heart, replace your fear with a belief in the future and some confidence in us. I know that's a lot to hope for, but I can't help it.

There are a lot of couples in the waiting room. Some of the pregnant women are so big it looks tough for them to even breathe, not to mention get in and out of their chairs. Some have no noticeable baby bumps; maybe it's their initial visit. Some couples have a child with them, a soon to be older sibling. Some couples hold hands. Others sit in silence flipping through magazines. Some, who I inwardly snort at in contempt, hold four hands over one pregnant belly. As if it needs to be protected at any cost.

I feel a wave of intense jealously for the couples talking to each other freely, their conversations unencumbered by the fact that the other people in the waiting room might overhear what they're saying. One couple interrupts each other, completes each other's sentences, and laughs in unison when the conversation turns to some hilarious anecdote. I wish we were that couple. I wish we were sitting in this waiting room talking to each other, laughing at each other, holding each other's hands.

But we're not. We're the couple in which the father-to-be flips through the newspaper while the mother-to-be envies the loving dynamics of other couples. I wonder if others can see it. Wonder if someone is watching us the way I'm watching them. If someone is feeling sorry for us, thinking, Poor people, they sure don't have much to say to each other. How did they end up together? Was it really such a good idea to have a child together? I push these forbidden thoughts away. They're of no use to me now. Besides, I've kept myself from thinking them for a long time. Do not envy other couples. Do not compare yourself. Remember: you can never know from the outside what it's like for other couples. I'm just projecting, and I have to stop it immediately.

The situation resolves itself. My envy, my small-mindedness, and my projections are interrupted by our midwife calling out my name. I bounce up. As we make our way through the waiting room, I take your hand. Holding it as demonstratively and as lovingly as I can as we pass by the couple talking and laughing. I glance at them, wanting their confirmation, wanting them to see us, but they don't look up. They're engrossed in their conversation. We mean nothing to them. I can't live with being nothing to them. Purely on impulse, more quickly than I can analyze what I'm doing, I tap the woman's foot with my own as we pass by. She lifts her eyes, still shining with laughter, and she looks at me warmly, says, "Oh, I'm sorry." I smile at her and say, "It's me who should apologize." For a moment, I exist, we both exist, we're two pregnant women smiling at each other because the future is so bright. A second later, the moment is over. We pass by them and walk toward the midwife's office. They continue talking, probably never giving us a thought. Your hand is cold and sweaty. Or maybe that's mine.

We enter the ultrasound room, and I let go of your hand. You make no move to stop me. I shut down and retreat into myself, want to get this over with, lie down on the bed, pull up my shirt, feel the ice-cold gel being spread across my stomach. The procedure can begin.

November 2014

I'm in the waiting room at the doctor's office just down the block from home. I left Ivan with the friend who's currently on call. I insisted on going here alone.

I've received clear instructions from my friend that I need to go to the doctor and describe what happened, so that I can go on extended sick leave. I don't understand why, since I'm already on parental leave, but I don't question her, just do as she says. It has something to do with saving my parental leave for later. In case I need it in an emergency. Just because I'm not working right now, doesn't mean I can't go on sick leave. I trust my friend. She said the doctor sounded nice on the phone. I hope she's right.

When the doctor sees me in the waiting room, he turns around without meeting my eyes, sighs out a "Follow me," and starts back down the hallway. I stand up, a little confused, and follow after him. Why didn't he say my name? How does he know who I am? He moves slowly, almost as if in pain. I have no trouble catching up. The corridor is quiet. I stare at his back as he slowly makes his way in front of me, limping slightly. There's a heaviness about him. He doesn't really lift his feet between steps. His office is at the end of the hall. He opens the door, walks in before me, leaves the door open, seems to assume I'll follow behind. And I do. But I already have a bad feeling about this.

Once we're inside, he sits down at his desk, stares at his screen, and starts tapping away at his keyboard. He starts to clear his throat. Doesn't look at me. Finally, he mumbles something.

"Well, what seems to be the problem?"

I don't know how to respond, so I remain silent. Staring straight at his face, now determined to wait him out, to sit quietly until he looks up and meets my eyes. It takes a while. He scratches his head and continues staring at his screen. There seems to be something that's not quite right there. And now, now finally it happens. The doctor lifts his eyes. For the first time he looks straight at me. Raising his eyebrows and asking his question again, this time more clearly. It's almost possible to hear the whole sentence.

"I said, what seems to be the problem?"

Before I even realize it's happening, I'm furious. Enraged. So intensely angry that I want to hit him, hurt him somehow. I take a deep breath, my heart pounding in my chest, my throat tightening in a way that makes me know my voice will break when I speak, robbing it of the authority I so desperately need right now. I can't help it.

"You mean you don't know why I'm here?"

Silence. The doctor turns his eyes back to the screen. Pushes a few keys absently. The computer doesn't seem to be of help to him. He glances back at me.

"Well...memory is fleeting."

Memory is fleeting. I want to kill him. I want to strangle him with my own hands, for forgetting why I'm here, for forcing me to tell him my story, the story I can barely stand to live, let alone tell over and over again. But I talk. I have to talk.

"Okay. I'm here because my partner died in his sleep a week ago, and because I have an eight-month-old baby to take care of, and because I have no idea how to do that right now. You don't remember someone calling and telling you all this, someone booking an appointment for me to meet you? Don't you write down what your patients book appointments for? Is this even possible?"

The doctor looks at me. His eyes lack emotion. He looks as dead as you did on Monday. Even deader. He's uglier, mean and ugly, with eyes that are dead even though he's apparently alive because he speaks, his obnoxious vocal cords forming words again.

"So . . . what do you want from me, then?"

Now I start to laugh. I can't take it anymore. This is too absurd. I say I'm here so he can put me on sick leave, and he asks for how long. I say, "You're the professional. I have no idea how this works. I don't know if I'm burned out or traumatized or in shock or how long it will be like this." He asks why I need sick leave when I'm on parental leave already, and even though I don't really understand that myself, I answer him as authoritatively as I can, trying to sound like I've done my homework. I say I can barely be a parent, can't take care of my home at all. That I'm basically a vegetable that needs help getting dressed in the morning. He stares at his screen again. Seems to be pondering.

"Grief isn't an illness. This would be an acute stress reaction. I can give you two weeks."

I stare at him. Give up. My anger has flowed away and been replaced by overwhelming fatigue. I don't care what he says. I don't care if I get on sick leave. I can't take in what he's saying. He slowly taps his fingers across the keyboard, filling in boxes to put me on sick leave for two weeks. Asks me for my social security number. I give it to him. Asks for my address. I give that too. Asks me the date my partner died. I tell him, though I'm convinced he should know that by now. He asks me what part of my daily life I don't feel I can cope with. I say, "Everything, nothing. I can't handle anything." He asks whether that includes vacuuming and washing the dishes. I confirm that it does. He asks whether that includes shopping for food and taking out the garbage. I confirm again. Slowly he types the information into what I assume is the Swedish Social Insurance Agency. Mumbles while doing it. I think he may be dyslexic and need to say the words out loud in order to write them. I've stopped looking at him now. I stare straight ahead at a point on the wall above his head. I've decided not to look this doctor in the eyes ever again for the rest of my life. Now his cell phone rings. He takes it out of the front pocket of his coat. Answers. Starts talking to someone about where and when they should meet for lunch. Says he has to go, he's with a patient. I can't believe my ears. I give up on humanity. I stand up, ask if that is all. He says, "Good luck. Let me know if you need anything else."

What was the outcome of this meeting? Grief is not an illness, it's called an acute stress reaction, and I have six days left of what is now a two-week sick leave. I don't know what to do with that information. On my short walk home, I call my friend, the one who booked the doctor's visit, and tell her what happened. She gets angry, starts to swear so loudly I have to hold the phone away from my ear. She says she's going to call and chew somebody out immediately, hunt down his boss, report him to the Patient Board, find a new doctor, one who isn't an idiot. She apologizes to me and tells me she's so sorry she put me in this situation. She promises she'll fix everything. I tell her it's fine. I don't care. I want to go home to Ivan, lie down on the sofa, maybe sleep a little. I don't care if I'm on parental leave or sick leave, as long as I never have to do this again.

December 2013

It's afternoon, and I'm lying on the sofa with a blanket over my legs and our cat beneath it. The outline of my body looks like a mountain chain, with peaks and valleys. First the breasts, then a valley. Then the round stomach, then another valley. Finally the cat, who's draped across my calves and sleeping, then a final valley before the last peak, my feet, which finish out the range of highs and lows beneath the blanket. Then your body begins. You're reclining near where my feet end, your computer on your stomach and a pair of earbuds in your ears. Sound leaks out of them, and I can make out what you're listening to. The way you move reveals you don't yet know that I'm awake, or that I'm lying here observing you. Your head bobs, your fingers drum, your feet wag with the music. You're relaxed and in a good mood, half dancing at your end of the sofa.

I'm also happy. It's Sunday, and I've just woken up after an hour's nap, and I feel like I could be pregnant for the rest of my life. It's not unpleasant. After summer turned to autumn and the ultrasound showed a healthy little boy growing inside me; after the leaves fell off the trees outside our bedroom window in Enskede and the nights got so long that they seemed to start just after lunch; after all that, everything's become . . . calm. My pregnancy is going well, and as the months pass by it feels like I'm in a frame of mind and moving at a pace that's more and more like yours. For the first time I don't feel the urge to fill my calendar with activities. For the first time in my life I can fall asleep, in the middle of the day, and not feel stressed by it. For the first time all I want to do is spend my weekends on the sofa, preferably binge-watching our favorite shows with you, with only short breaks to eat and go to the grocery store.

Also, you seem to enjoy our pace. We still don't talk very much about what's coming. I rarely ask you to listen to the information I'm devouring about what's happening to the baby in my belly. When he kicks so hard its visible from the outside, I pull up my shirt, point, ask you to look. You pat me sometimes but pull your hand away when he kicks, tell me you think it looks scary. You ask me if it hurts, and I say a little, but not so bad. You look away. I take out my camera, film my stomach as it bends and moves. Think that these movies will be fun to watch together, later. Maybe our child will want to see them too. "Look, honey, here you are in Mommy's tummy." I enjoy imagining that moment.

On our refrigerator door I put up a list of things that, according to a parenting magazine I bought, need to be completed before I give birth. Methodically, I've ticked off point after point on the list. Purchased baby clothes in sizes 50 and 56 because we don't know how big the baby will be when it comes out. Purchased a changing table, changing pad, and washcloths. Packed a suitcase to take to the hospital. Wrote down my birth plan. Bought a crib, a co-sleeping nest, and a car seat. Researched, test-drove, and finally bought a stroller. In fact, most items on the list have been checked off by now.

Either I've gotten used to doing most things related to the pregnancy and preparation for the baby on my own or maybe I simply enjoy being in total control. It doesn't bother me that things are like this. We're in a good place right now, and as long as I don't put any more demands on you, everything seems to be working well for us. You hold me at night again. I squeeze your hand as I fall asleep and think how lucky I am to have you by my side.

November 2014

I'm sitting at my kitchen table, staring at the white folder, where my friends have collected all the cards from the flowers we received over the past couple of weeks. It looks like it's about to explode, as if one more letter or card would do the trick. Most of the bouquets have by now ended up in the garbage, but the pile of cards and letters hasn't decreased. Even though I haven't opened the folder, it lies there bulging and demanding my attention. "Open me, read me," I feel like it's saying. I decide to take action right away, read all the cards at once and then never again.

The handwritten notes wash over me. They talk about thoughts, everyone's thoughts are with me now, and they talk about love. Everybody loved you, still loves me, and everyone is there if I need them. One colleague put a few pieces of candy in an envelope. One childhood friend writes that she understands that existence might feel pitch-black right now. One friend from the stables describes me as navigating "stormy seas." One friend's mother has knitted a pair of baby-blue socks for Ivan, which are included with the card. After a dozen or so messages, I stop reading. I just can't.

I find no comfort in their words. The cards don't work like they were meant to, or maybe I'm the one who doesn't work like I'm supposed to. But I don't feel anything when I read them. I don't cry. I don't mourn. I don't feel warm or grateful. They are just sheets of paper with words on them. They change absolutely nothing.

Everyone seems to think what's happened to me is unfair. It feels like every conversation, every text or meeting with friends, is filled with that word. "It's so unfair," they say. I don't know how to answer when they say that. It annoys me, but I try to hide it. Life has never been fair, I think. Surely no one believes that good and bad, sorrow and joy, are divvied up fairly in a person's life. Who believes that? Does everyone besides me? That's not how the world works. Not how life works. I suddenly remember when my dad died of cancer. I was eighteen years old, and none of my friends had parents who were sick or dead. It was the same old song back then. "It's so unfair. You didn't deserve this," they said, and they meant well. Then, like now, I had no idea how to cope with their sympathies. I kept my mouth shut rather than tell them what I thought. It sounds bitter and mean enough in my head.

No, I think. It's not fair, what happened to me, but do you know what else is unfair? What happened to you. You didn't deserve to die. You were the better half of us. You were the one who should have survived, and I, if someone had to, should have died. That's how I feel. If we're talking about fairness. Which is pointless. Where I'm at now, I'm not interested in fairness. It feels like an insult to you to claim I've been treated unfairly. I'm still here. I still have Ivan. I'm alive. I won; you lost. Don't feel sorry for me. It's not unfair to me. They've misunderstood it all. It's unfair to you. Nobody else.

Another comment I keep getting is that they've been so "affected" by my fate. It reminded them of the fragility of life. Some say, "Tonight I'm going to hug my husband and my children a little closer." I don't know why they tell me that. I don't understand what I'm supposed to do with that knowledge, except be reminded that I can't do the same thing myself. I can't hug you extra close tonight, I didn't hug you extra close on our final night together two weeks ago, and I bet that everyone who's hugging their families extra tight will wake up still together tomorrow morning. Because life is unfair.

I guess I'm starting to get bitter. I don't care.

February 2014

I've been off from work for a week, and still no baby has arrived. I'm extremely bored. Yesterday I walked around Årstaviken, a walk of more than four kilometers in hilly terrain through wet snow, wearing shoes that were way too thin. When I passed by Söder Hospital, I increased my pace, hoping that pure physical exertion might put me into labor, but nothing happened. My body seems content to remain heavily pregnant, and the baby seems to like it in there. Way too much.

I kept walking, eventually ending up at home, tried to feel once more: Is it happening? Is this how it starts? Will it happen later tonight? At eleven o'clock I headed to bed with a light ache in my groin and frequent Braxton Hicks contractions, so I felt hopeful that it might start in the night. Then I slept. And slept. And woke up to another morning of being heavily pregnant and not particularly close to giving birth. The contractions are only a memory. My disappointment is palpable. It feels like it's never going to happen. I'm over waiting for my baby now. It was cozy for eight and a half months, but not anymore. I'm ready for the next phase. I want the baby here. I want him living outside my body. I want a baby we can share, a baby who's yours and mine, who we love together for the rest of our lives. It's time for him to arrive now.

You're working as usual. I'm not sure where you head off to every morning, but we've agreed that from now on you'll always have the sound on your telephone turned on and you'll always pick up no matter how important your meeting is. It can happen at any moment now. We're six days past the due date. The hospital suitcase, which turned into two suitcases by the time I was finished packing, stand ready in the hall, and our fridge is full of nuts, candy, sodas, fruit, and smoothies that are getting closer and closer to their expiration dates. It could be that I overdid it a little when I went shopping for the goodies and nutritional supplements. It might be possible I won't need two full bags of groceries. But isn't it better to have too much than too little is how I thought about it when I went shopping like there was no tomorrow.

Inside me, besides the baby, there's a growing restlessness. I've seen every movie I wanted to see, met with every friend, talked my fill about being pregnant, and I even went to a three-hour-long play with no intermission last week. It's getting harder to sleep at night. The baby doesn't seem satisfied with any sleeping position besides me on my right side. If I try anything else, he lets me know. My hips hurt now when I move, it's hard to tie my shoes, and basically every physical activity causes noxious belching, including just going to the bathroom or into the kitchen. I feel done with it all.

Today, the sixth day after the due date, I'm going to take the subway from Sandsborg to Slussen, have coffee with my cousin, and then buy some books. I imagine I'll have tons of time to read after the baby is born. I imagine peaceful hours on the sofa with a sleeping baby on my chest or in the cradle next to me. I've purchased a new fruit bowl that I imagine will always be filled and just an arm's length away, while I recline and read and breastfeed for days on end.

Today I've put on makeup and pulled on a pair of tights and a short black jersey dress. When I look at myself in the mirror in the hall, I think I look hot. My skin has never been so soft and smooth as it has during my pregnancy. I think my new belly and breasts suit me. I imagine I'll miss them when this is over. Then I waddle off to the subway, whose schedule I've now memorized. Fifteen minutes later I meet my cousin.

As I hug her in the doorway to the café where we're meeting, I feel something in my underwear. Did I just pee myself a little bit? Was that the famous mucus plug sliding out? Or is my water breaking? I don't say anything to my cousin, want to be sure first, wait and see. Nothing else seems to happen in my underwear. Maybe I imagined it. I sit down, and we talk, laugh, drink coffee, eat lunch. I forget about that strange feeling. A little more than an hour later we finish up. My cousin has to go back to work. We pay the check and I'm standing up, just about to hug her goodbye, when it happens again. Something flows out of me. Not much, but it is flowing. I still don't say anything. I hug my cousin and go to the bathroom. Examine my underwear carefully, conclude my water didn't break—there's not enough there. I decide to wait and see again, slowly make my way toward the bookstore farther down the street, don't find any books I want to read, head home again. It's starting to get dark as I exit the subway, and it's soon time for dinner.

By dinnertime that strange feeling in my underwear has happened often enough for me to call the delivery ward at Söder Hospital and ask what they think it might be. The friendly woman who answers says soothingly that it's definitely nothing to worry about, but she thinks it's best if I go to the hospital so they can take a look at me. After all, I am six days overdue. But it's no hurry, she emphasizes. I can go in after dinner. So I eat dinner with you. We have meatballs, decide it's best that I go alone, because it's probably nothing, and it seems unnecessary to drag all our bags along with us if we're just heading home a half hour later. We decide you'll wait at home with our cat, ready to go if it's required.

By the time I reach the delivery ward it's seven thirty. It takes the midwife about three minutes to determine that amniotic fluid is leaking out of me and there's meconium in the water, which means the baby has defecated in the water. Which I soon learn means that I won't be heading home tonight and I'm going into labor whether my body is ready or not. The baby is clearly stressed inside and needs to get out. The information I receive gives me butterflies in my stomach. It's happening. I'm finally going to give birth.

After a quick and surprisingly pain-free examination, I'm told I'm dilated three centimeters, starting to have contractions, and that I should call my partner immediately. So I do. I call you, and you, in turn, call my brother, who's ready on our signal to move into our apartment and take care of our cat for as long as we're gone.

I've already made myself at home in my room in the delivery ward when you walk through the door. Your cheeks are red from the exertion of lugging my two suitcases, two grocery bags, your own bag, and the car seat for the car ride home through the hallways on your way here. I start to laugh when you come in; it looks like we're moving in permanently. Also the midwife, who brought you to the room and who is now looking at the monitor where our son's heartbeat is being recorded, comments on our packing, but without laughing. I see you've had to work hard to bring everything with you. There's sweat under your black knit cap. I also see you're relieved when you see me laughing. You're not fond of hospitals, and you haven't exactly been longing for this experience.

As for me, I'm more cheerful, determined to make this the day it all turns around for both you and me. Besides, I feel so elated that it's finally happening, that I'm finally technically in labor, and I still feel good. It almost doesn't even hurt. You come over to me where I half lie on the delivery bed, put down the suitcases and grocery bags, kiss me on the cheek, and ask me if I'm okay. I tell you that I am. Point apologetically, as if I were the one who put it there, at the chair you'll be confined to for the next hours. It doesn't look particularly comfortable. You won't be able to sleep in it. I tell you, "You can lie down next to me on my narrow bed if you want," but you shake your head, look at me to see if I'm joking, say you have no intention of sleeping and that the chair will be fine.

You sit down, take out your phone, and start typing on it. Tell me you have to send a few emails to your clients, let them know you won't be available for the next few days. I ask you to take a picture of me, a memory for us, a picture in those hours when I still look fairly fresh, those last hours with the belly. "Just a minute. Soon," you say, and keep typing on your phone. I wait. Excited. Hardly feeling the contractions—they feel like the ones I've been having for the last month—but the midwife says they're real, and I'm very proud of the fact that I'm not suffering.

When I tell the midwife, as she's on her way out of the room, that I can barely feel the contractions and that I thought it would be a lot more painful to give birth, she clucks and says, "Just you wait. It's coming." Then she tells me to relax, stay calm, and rest as much as I can. She suggests I think of the pain like waves crashing over me and then passing by, focus on the fact that every wave/ache is pushing us closer to our goal. I nod and pretend I haven't heard exactly the same thing a hundred times, seen it in every birth story I've read on the internet, and she leaves us with the instructions to push the red button next to the bed if we need her. We're now alone together in the room. You're done with your emails, but you've forgotten to take a picture of me. Your phone is back in your jacket pocket. The jacket you hung over the back of the chair. It feels vain and silly to nag you about the photo, so I drop it. Take a picture of myself in the mirror above the little sink in the corner of the room, then return to bed. We start watching a TV show on your computer.

A few hours later the pain arrives. With a vengeance. It's just after eleven in the evening when I give up thinking about waves and breathing exercises, stride out to the dimly lit hospital hall and yell "EPIDURAL!" so loudly it echoes between the walls. I've forgotten about the red button. My midwife meets me, puts her arm around me, leads me back into my room, and says I'm in luck because the doctor who puts needles in people's backs is on his way up from the emergency room to this department right now. Less than an hour later I get a shot in my back. It hurts, and I squeeze your hands hard when they stick it in, but I experience almost immediate relief and return to being elated for another hour or so. More than once I tell you, or maybe I'm telling myself, that the worst is over. "Now that I got that shot in my back, there's not much pain left." I'm not sure where I got that idea from, but I believe it.

Until I don't. I realize my research on childbirth has left much to be desired. I must not have read very closely on the difference between contractions and bearing down contractions. At one o'clock I whimper to the midwife, who never leaves our side now, that I feel like I need to poop, and I think the baby is coming out the wrong hole. Then everything happens pretty fast. The bearing down contractions start in earnest, and suddenly there are two midwives and a doctor and they dig around inside me and stare at the monitor and raise and lower the dosage of Pitocin and the epidural and I don't even know what I'm getting anymore. I disappear further into myself and what's happening to my body. They give me instructions not to push yet, the baby hasn't finished rotating, I have to wait a little, but I can't help it; my body bears down whether or not it's supposed to, and they tell me to try screaming instead of pushing, so I do. I'm screaming, but I don't recognize the sounds coming out of my throat, and with every contraction it feels like I stop breathing for longer and longer, and soon everything's just one long howl, like a wounded animal. I close my eyes, change positions between standing, crawling on all fours, lying on my back; I do whatever the midwives tell me to do, but I don't look at them, can't open my eyes, it hurts too much. I scream and snort, and it feels as if I'm being ripped in half.

I have no idea where you are in the room, what you're doing. Perhaps you're the one who brings water, puts a straw between my lips when the contractions ebb; maybe you're still sitting in the chair, a safe distance from the howling animal that until recently used to be your pregnant girlfriend. It doesn't matter. I can't see. I can't think. I can't follow instructions. I can only howl. Soon I'll split in two, soon I'll break apart, I think, and at that very moment as I try to muster the self-control to form

words, to cry out that we have to stop, that this is never going to work, you'll have to cut me open, at that very moment
I know the end is near. This is something I've read about. I've
read enough birth stories to know that just at the moment when
you feel like it's impossible to keep going, then it's almost over.
Just one more contraction.

At a quarter to five in the morning he gushes out of me,
and everything that hurts fades away, and I fall silent and suddenly I'm able to breathe again. The pain stops and for a few
seconds I hear my own breathing until the room is filled with
screams again; this time it's an infant's cry. I open my eyes when
I hear the screams. They sound so thin compared to mine,
which still echo between the walls of the delivery room. The
light in the room is blinding. I blink. It takes a moment for
my eyes to focus, but when they do, I see you, standing beside
me, next to my head. It must have been you giving me water between the contractions. You are the first thing I see, and
you whisper to me that I was amazing, that everything went
well, our son is healthy and beautiful, you say, and you pat my
cheek, and I realize it's wet with sweat. The screaming rises
from somewhere between my legs, and the midwives laugh and
say, "Aren't you an angry little one," and it takes a few seconds
and then suddenly he's on my chest. An angry baby with an offended wrinkle between his eyebrows and a burgundy hat on his
head pecking at my breasts. I try to hold him steady but realize I
don't know how I'm supposed to hold a sticky infant. It doesn't
come naturally. He's slippery, and his eyebrows are the angriest
I've ever seen in my life. I try to help him find my nipple while
you, with the help of the midwives, cut his umbilical cord, and
he screams and screams. I look at him without feeling anything
besides relief that the pain is over and an overwhelming fatigue.

One of the midwives says I have to push again, just once more, because the placenta has to come out, and I obey her, and it hurts only a little. She asks if I want to look at it, and I say no thank you. She tells me I did a great job, and now it's gonna sting a bit because she has to sew up my genitals. I don't care what she does to them as long as I don't have to give birth to another baby, and now you take a picture of me, finally you take a picture of me. I notice that you smile when you do and that I've almost never seen you smile when you take a picture of me. Then I think I'm probably ugly right now. Our son is screaming, still chomping at my breast. I think this is the angriest infant I've ever seen, but suddenly he falls silent, sucking on my nipple, finds the right position, and the line between his eyebrows smooths out a little bit. It feels strange when he sucks. It tickles and stings at the same time, and I look at you and you meet my eyes and you whisper that I did so well and now we smile at each other for the first time in quite a long time, and suddenly it's not just you and me anymore. It's us, all three of us. We're a family now.

November 2014

This morning I took a shower. Lately I don't do that every day; I've gotten used to greasy hair and the smell of sweat in my armpits. But today I have a visitor coming. The officiant is on her way.

It takes so much effort to meet new people. And it hasn't gotten any easier since my disastrous doctor's visit. Every meeting saps me of energy, leaves me empty, tired, in need of rest. The funeral director thought this officiant would be a good fit for both you and me. Though how the funeral director would know anything about who we are as people is beyond me. The officiant was described as unconventional, warm, passionate about culture, an amazing speaker, earthy, and incidentally the person who happened to train our funeral director, many years ago. At the time, I wasn't even sure what an officiant was, but I assumed it was a nonreligious version of a priest. A quick google confirmed that I was correct.

The date we received from the funeral home is several weeks from now, six weeks from the time of your death. When we booked it, it felt like an eternity until the day arrived. Now time suddenly seems to be moving so fast. Soon you'll be cremated. Soon I'll sit on a chair staring at an urn with a picture of you leaning against it. In the company of more than a hundred people. I feel sick. My stomach flips when I think about it. My thoughts are interrupted by the ringing of the doorbell.

Sitting at the kitchen table an hour later, I've come to realize that the purpose of the officiant's first visit was to get a sense of who I am, who you were, our history together, in my own words. She's listened and nodded. Taken notes and asked questions. My tears didn't seem to make her uncomfortable, not even when I had to stop and go to the bathroom to rinse my face with ice-cold water. She also hasn't shown much pity. It doesn't seem like this is the worst or saddest story she's ever heard. I appreciate that.

When she hobbles out of the apartment in her cast after two hours together, she leaves me with some homework. I'm supposed to figure out what songs should be played at your funeral, and I'm supposed to write a letter to you that she, or maybe me if I'm up for it, will read at the funeral. I'm also going to—and this I came up with myself—ask some of your friends and colleagues to write to me and describe you in their own words. Say something about their friendship with you. How they saw you, how they will remember you. As for her, she's going to send some poems to me that I can read and choose among before the ceremony.

It occurs to me that we, the officiant and I, have had an initial meeting in order to produce an event together. That's something I know how to do. I'm comfortable in the role of producer. Having homework to do this week, then another meeting booked in nine days with your parents, feels almost pleasant. Now we're rolling.

March 2014

Ivan is three weeks old, and he screams for hours every evening. It starts around seven thirty and goes on for what feels like an eternity, but it does actually end with him passing out in exhaustion at around ten or ten thirty. By that time, I'm exhausted too. I've cried in powerless despair at least once. Sometimes you're so panicked that you get up, put on your clothes, put our baby in his stroller, and take him out—still screaming at the top of his lungs—on a nighttime walk through snow and slush. So I can calm down. So I can get a break from the noise. Because I can't stand the emotions that the hours-long screaming evokes in me. This wasn't what I imagined having a newborn would be like. This wasn't the picture I had in my head. Not at all.

This has shown me that my ability to handle unforeseen events is somewhat lower than I expected, shown me I don't have the energy and self-confidence that I believed I would as a new parent. I thought I'd adjust quickly to my new role. That parenthood and its responsibilities would come naturally to me. That as long as I gave birth to a healthy child, the rest would fix itself. I've always been so good at making things happen. Such an efficient project manager. Capable of handling extreme stress. I'm so disappointed in myself. And that overwhelming love I thought would carry me through any difficult situations hasn't turned out quite as I thought.

Most of all, I feel stressed and weighed down by a responsibility I hardly can bear. Stressed because I can't comfort him, my own son, when he starts screaming. It doesn't matter how much I hush, rock, sing, breastfeed, change diapers, rock again. Nothing works. He writhes in my arms, and every night I lose a little more self-esteem—I feel more incompetent, worthless, unfit to be a parent. I want somebody to save me from this situation. When these outbursts have been going on for a week with no end in sight, I say, "There must be something wrong with him. He has to be in pain. Something's not right. Should we call the doctor?"

You remind me that we called the pediatrician earlier today. Repeat what they said about how normal it is for babies to cry at night. It's probably a little colic and some gas and who knows what else, but it's not dangerous. Not as long as he's eating and sleeping and in generally good condition. Still, it feels dangerous to me. I'm losing both control and confidence in the situation. Our pediatric nurse reminds me that it's a big shock to a baby to enter the world after ninth months inside the womb. She says I just have to give him a little time, and it'll all work out. "You're doing what you're supposed to do," she says, trying to comfort me, but it doesn't help. When his bout of evening crying starts, I break down again. Overcome by a totally unfamiliar flight impulse. You don't seem to be as shaken by our son's crying as I am, and you try to calm me while rocking and talking to him. "Remember what the pediatric nurse said. We're doing the right thing," you tell me on those evenings when I want to call someone, take him somewhere, maybe to the hospital, hand over the responsibility to someone else, someone who knows what they're doing. My skin crawls when he never stops. Actually my skin crawls before he even starts. My anxiety increases throughout the day, grows as afternoon turns to evening and the hour approaches seven thirty. Something feels terribly wrong, but I don't know how to fix it, don't know what I've gotten myself into, don't know how to get free of it. I feel ashamed of my thoughts, and my incompetence.

We've been home for just over two weeks, and so far you've been able to do most of your work from home. You've made some short trips to the store. When you leave, I feel nervous. Can I really take care of our baby on my own? What if he starts screaming and never stops? It's best if you work from home one more day, and maybe one more after that. I say, "Soon I'll be ready to be alone all day, but not quite yet." You stay home another day. And one more after that.

But as the third week nears its end, you tell me you have to start going to your clients' offices to work soon. You can't do everything you need to do from home. You say it will be just for short periods in the beginning, just a few hours here and there. "A few hours," I complain, "that's a really long time!" You say everything will be fine, and if something happens, you'll head home immediately. You ask me which I'd prefer. Should you go first thing in the morning or after lunch? Do I want to make plans with a friend or do I want to go to Uppsala and visit my stepmother for a few days? You're calm and focused on solutions; as for me, I feel unsure, afraid, trapped, and panicked.

Our roles have reversed, and I don't like it at all. I answer un-willingly that the mornings are better. That's when Ivan seems calmest. Force you again to promise you'll come home if he's inconsolable. If hours go by and he won't stop crying. "Will you come home then?" "Yes," you say. "I'll come home. I promise."

So we decide that on Monday you'll go back to work, and I'll start my parental leave on my own. Ivan is almost a month old. I'm ashamed to admit it to you, but secretly I long for Ivan to reach nine months, so I can go back to my job again, to an environment where I feel confident, where I have tasks I can handle, something I do well. I envy you that you're going back to work on Monday.

At night, when you're sleeping, after Ivan has woken me up to breastfeed or because he needs a new diaper, I rarely fall back asleep. Instead, I google postpartum depression and wonder if that's what I've got. I don't recognize how my mind works. I don't recognize how weak I've become. Maybe I'm depressed? That would be very unfair of me. I promised I'd do all the heavy lifting in the beginning. I promised I was up for this, could do this, said you just had to come along for the ride and I'd take care of the rest. I can't burden you with my feelings right now. So I continue to google late at night. Ticking off a list of symp-toms, thinking maybe I do have postpartum depression after all. And I'll have to keep it to myself. Take care of it on my own.

I decide to talk with our pediatric nurse during Ivan's checkup next week. We've only known each other for a few weeks, but I've called her many times, almost every day, asking about Ivan's crying fits or the rash on his stomach. I decide to tell her how I feel at our next appointment, let her decide if I'm depressed or just a very, very fragile first-time parent. Whatever this is, I have to solve it quickly. Preferably yesterday.

November 2014

This morning I need to go through your clothes to choose what you'll wear for your cremation, what will end up in the urn with your dust. I've had a hard time imagining what will happen with these clothes. Today the funeral home needs them, which leads me to believe your body will soon be cremated. Even if they didn't want to tell me exactly when that will happen. Even though they claimed that, unfortunately, it was impossible to say exactly when, but they'll send me a message after it happens. That's just how it works. Routines. Processes. Things I don't know, don't understand, am not familiar with and prefer not to be either. So I didn't ask. And now I'm going to open your boxes so I can follow their instructions and deliver what they want without knowing exactly why or to whom.

When I open the top box, your scent hits me so powerfully that I'm completely bewildered for a moment. The smell of you is still alive inside these boxes. It hasn't disappeared. You're not gone. Your shirts smell like you: a mixture of your cologne and your skin. I'm struck by how good you always smelled. And I realize I never told you that. How good you smelled to me. Like home. Now that scent only exists in these boxes and soon that too will be gone. I know because I tried to hold on to the smell of my father in the same way. Slept on one of his pillows, walked around in one of his shirts right after he died, hoping it would smell like him forever. Like safety and something else, something indefinable, that was always there in his scent. The feeling of being his daughter, probably. I couldn't hold on to him either. The scent got fainter every day, and after a few weeks his shirt didn't smell like anything, just air, not my dad, and no matter how hard I searched, no trace of his scent was left behind. But this box still smells like you. It still hasn't disappeared.

I pick up the shirt on top, a checkered flannel in dark blue and black, and press it to my face. Close my eyes. Open my eyes again. Put my nose to your shirt collar. Close my eyes again. Breathe in deeply. It feels like you're here. It feels like I'm holding you, like you're holding me, like you're close to me. I sit there with my nose at your collar for a while, until I hear Ivan whining in the living room where my friend is watching him. It pulls me out of my reverie. I have to finish my task. Get through this.

I choose the shirt you were wearing the first time we met. I choose the worn jeans you owned for as long as I've known you, the ones with holes in both knees, whose back pocket carries the shape of your wallet. I choose a pair of neutral underwear, a white undershirt, and a pair of black socks. And then your knit cap. The black knit cap that you refused to call a hipster beanie, that I gave you such a hard time about. According to you, you were no hipster. Absolutely not some nervous, trendy guy who worked in advertising. You just happened to like black knit caps that stopped just above your ears. Just happened to look really good in them. I agreed with you. You looked really great. In fact, I never saw anyone who wore one better. Still, I couldn't give it up. The hat was trendy. Hipsters all over this city were wearing them. Couldn't you just admit that? I wanted you to admit it. That you liked something that was trendy. But you refused. You'd always liked this kind of hat. Your boots and thick socks with slim jeans tucked into them were also just a coincidence. It annoyed you every time I teased you about it. But I couldn't stop poking at you. It turned into a discussion that went on for months. Once you even sent me an email in which you'd collected links and pictures about the definition of what a hipster was. In the email you underlined everything that didn't apply to you. I responded by sending pictures of you where you looked like people in the pictures you'd attached. It went on and on. A non-issue that neither of us wanted to back down on. Half jokingly but half in total seriousness. Now I'm sitting here holding it in my hands, and I realize we never agreed whether or not it was a hipster hat. It doesn't matter anymore. Now your black knit cap will burn with your body. It's the only thing that makes sense.

I stuff the clothes into a plastic bag, wipe away my tears with one of your shirts, sniff once last time before closing the box and going back to reality, to Ivan, to being alone and the walk to the funeral home with the plastic bag that carries your clothes.

May 2014

I've been a parent for just over three months, and tonight I'll be away from Ivan for the very first time. I'm excited. Worried. Eager. Reluctant. I both want and don't want this. Either way, at six thirty it's going to happen. The plan is to be away from home for three or four hours. Clink champagne glasses with my friends at a bachelorette party. Hopefully succeed in disconnecting from all these sleepless nights and restless evenings, all this guilt and isolation.

One of my best friends is the bachelorette, and her day of celebration started with a horse race. I had Ivan with me in his carrier, and I was constantly sweaty and always one step behind. While my friends competed on the racetrack, I sat and nursed nearby. Waved happily for the camera and tried to hide how much I wanted to be part of the adult world again. I also wanted to toast with plastic glasses. I also wanted to sit in the sulky. But I couldn't. I was nursing. I had to drive. I was a responsible parent. I pretended it didn't matter. But I envied the others, the ones with no baby strapped to their stomach. My skin was crawling with envy.

Recently, I've felt an increasing compulsion to escape from Ivan, if not to cut then at least to stretch our bonds. Just a little while. Just a little. Just a lot. Of course it's not something I talk about, not even with you. But it worries me. I worry that I'll never be the naturally warm parent I'd imagined myself as. I'm worried that maybe I'm just not fit to be somebody's parent at all. I'm worried I don't have what it takes, that I'm not up for the task. I worry that everything you worried about before my pregnancy doesn't in fact apply to you but to me.

I've felt panicked by being the only one who can comfort him when he cries, suffocated by the idea that he'll be connected to me from now on. I've whined about my dissatisfaction at home, expressed loud and clear my wish to get away, and you've tried to accommodate it. You've encouraged me to leave the house, go meet a friend, take a walk, or go to the stable. I've said I will, very soon I'll do it. But it's never come to be. There's always been some reason not to. Ivan has a cold. Or he's in the middle of a growth spurt. Or his stomach is upset. Or he's inconsolable unless he has one of my breasts in his mouth. It's as if I can't handle either approach to him. I long for some distance from him, but I can't stand to be away from him either. I feel trapped by him but worried as soon as he's more than a few meters away from me. I fear it will be like this from now on. Never calm away from him, never relaxed with him.

So far the whole equality between the parents thing hasn't

gone so well either. It makes me feel ashamed, like a bad fem-
inist. Before Ivan arrived, I was confident: my child would feel
equally safe with both his parents, oh yes. He'd drink breast milk
or formula from bottles, and both his parents would experience
tranquil moments of freedom both with and without him. We'd
divide the nights equally, sleeping well with the assurance that
the other one was on top of things. We'd be well rested at least
every other day. Then he arrived, and it didn't turn out like that.
In fact, we were soundly defeated.

Ivan doesn't drink milk from bottles. He spits it out and sputters, and his crying escalates as he gets hungrier and hungrier.
And I can't stand to let him cry. Not with me and not with you.
Quick as lightning, I grab him, take him from your arms, and
put my breast into his mouth. When you calmly point out that
it won't get any better if I don't give you the space to at least
try, it feels like a dagger inside. I know you're right, but I can't
help it. It's just not possible. On those rare occasions when I
force myself to leave the apartment, I text you every ten minutes. When you truthfully reply that he is in fact crying, I run
back as fast as my legs can carry me. Feeling like a failure and
promising myself never to speak about this out loud. This isn't
the way I thought it would be. I see my friends with babies the
same age moving freely outside their homes, among friends and
at work meetings, some even going out for a glass of wine. As
for me, I just breastfeed and struggle to force myself to go out
even with the recycling. It's utterly embarrassing. Most of all,
this is not how I planned it.

Not that you seem completely calm when he cries. You don't
get angry with me when I take him out of your arms, usually
with my bra already open and a shirt hanging off my shoulder,
ready to breastfeed. It's as if breastfeeding is the only thing we

know for sure. Everything else seems impossible to plan for, so I mostly stay home. And you've taken on every other practical task around both of us. You do all the shopping and cooking, cleaning and picking up, changing the sand in the litter box, playing with our restless cat, changing Ivan's diapers and carrying him around when he's happy. And you work. You've started working quite a bit again. Whereas I've never been away from home for longer than a half hour.

But tonight I'm going out. And now that moment has arrived. I've nursed and nursed until Ivan has made it clear he doesn't want to nurse anymore by, for example, vomiting on my shoulder. Which means the dress I'd been planning to wear has a slimy white stain of spit-up on it. I wipe it away with a wet washcloth and hope it doesn't leave a trace. Convince myself that spit-up hardly smells at all. Because no matter what, this is the dress I'm going to wear tonight. I don't have time to change, and besides, I don't have anything else to wear.

I've pumped myself empty, put four bottles, boiled and sterilized repeatedly, of breast milk in the fridge. We've been trying to get Ivan to take the bottle for several weeks in preparation for this evening. It hasn't gone so well. He spits and sputters at anything but the breast, but we haven't given up. Only once has he been able to get down the contents of a bottle. I'm not optimistic, but hope is the last thing a person surrenders, and this person wants to go to the bachelorette party without her son tonight. Just one night. Just a few hours.

I already have to resist the impulse to text you worriedly in the stairwell. Remind myself that we've gone through every practicality not just once but twice. You know where the milk is stored. You know what temperature it should be heated to. You know how to put a bottle into Ivan's mouth. You know how to change his diaper. There's nothing new I can tell you right now, and yet I feel a creeping uneasiness as I climb into the taxi waiting outside our front door. I check my phone worriedly on the ride into the city. Finally, I give in and text you to ask if everything's okay. I emphasize, for the eleventh time in the last hour, that it's fine, really totally fine, if you need me to come home from the party. Ask you to promise me that you'll let me know about even the most minor problem. You write back, "Everything will be okay. Just have a good time. We're doing great here." I put the phone back in my pocket. Decide to try to have fun tonight. Wondering if I even remember how to have fun. It feels like such a long time ago, like another life.

I arrive at the event space, run up the front steps, and enter out of breath. I hug the other guests, who've been partying since before lunch today. They all seem weirdly refreshed. They're radiant, laughing in their glittery dresses and shiny eye shadow. As for me, I have vomit on my shoulder and dark rings under my eyes. And there's probably something hunted about my expression, but it's hard to know exactly. Maybe that's just a feeling.

I grab a glass of champagne at the bar. Continue my round of hugs and hellos. My former boss asks how things are going for me these days. I say, "Good." "How old is your baby now, six months?" I say three months. He laughs loudly. "Oh dear, three months. You've got a ways to go. Those darn infants never let you sleep." I nod, laughing as well, trying to appear as if I have some distance from my situation. Taking too-big gulps of my champagne. It's already gone. I glance at the bar and wonder if there's enough left for another glass. If I'm discreet, nobody needs to know. I'm out so rarely. I sneak over for a refill.

The music is so loud I have a hard time hearing what my

friends are saying to me. I wish somebody would lower the volume. Aren't we supposed to be able to talk to each other? I do my best, play along, improvise my way through the conversation. Mostly it's about Ivan and my new situation as a parent. They tell me that Ivan is so cute in the pictures they've seen. That he seems like such a happy, sweet little baby. I agree but don't expound on the subject. I don't want to think about Ivan right now. I'm doing my very best to stop thinking about him. Instead, I ask the other guests about their day, what did they do after the horse racing? How was the bartending school? What treatments did they do at the spa? When a conversation runs out of steam, I move on. I've decided to talk to as many friends as possible before it's time to head home. I move a little too quickly between people, can't really land in any conversation. Don't really remember how we used to talk or what we talked about. My mind is still on Ivan and you. The music is too loud in the background. My smile isn't genuine.

Suddenly a friend is at my side. I can feel myself brightening up and relaxing. My best friend, my safe haven—this is where I want to be for a while. I hug her and say I've missed her. She hugs me back and says she wants to show me a text. It's from you and she just got it.

Hi. If you're near Carolina, can you ask her to call me? Nothing serious, just something with Ivan. xo Aksel

I give the phone back to my friend. Realize I left my phone in my jacket, which I hung at the entrance. How could I be so stupid? How long have you been trying to get ahold of me? What could have happened at home that would make you text my friend when you couldn't reach me? It was a mistake to come here. I'm a horrible parent for even trying. I feel so ashamed that I'm crying by the time I wave down a taxi outside the event space. I reel off my address, ask the taxi driver to drive as fast as possible. Tell him it's kind of an emergency.

As we roll over Skanstull Bridge on our way to Enskede, to home, to you and Ivan, I text you that I'll be there in five minutes. Write I'm sorry I left. As we turn onto our street, I get a response from you.

> Damn, I'm sorry, he fell asleep now. Things got a little rough when he wouldn't take the bottle, but we got through it. Everything is fine now. Can't you turn around and go back again? Sorry I worried you!

I pay the driver and enter our building. Nothing, absolutely nothing inside me wants to go back to the party. I regret I even went there at all. Not just that: I feel ashamed for going. Ashamed that I left you alone with Ivan, who apparently wasn't ready. I feel ashamed that I was so nervous around my friends, and that I stayed only forty-five minutes, and now I'm the parent who can't handle being away from her child. I feel more ashamed when I realize that I didn't even talk to the bachelorette herself, who should have been the first person I sought out in the crowd. With shame in my chest and a paradoxical feeling of relief in the rest of the body, I open the front door of our apartment as quietly as I can, sneak inside my home. Decide to avoid situations like that from now on. It's not good. Not for you, not for Ivan, and not for me. Might as well capitulate and stay home for a while.

I sneak into the living room and find you reclining on the sofa. You have the computer on your lap and a glass of Coke next to you on the sofa's armrest. I can hear a song playing quietly from the computer's speakers. Our son is sleeping in the baby nest beside you. He's sleeping silently on his back, with his chin up. He looks like he's smiling. You lift your eyes as I approach, tiptoeing over the living room rug. I see you trying to quickly discern if I'm angry or disappointed, trying to figure out if there's going to be an argument tonight. I'm neither. I just want to sit on your lap, bury my face in your neck, inhale your scent, watch our sleeping child, and never, ever leave either of you again. So that's what I do. You open your arms and welcome me back into the family again.

November 2014

I'm not sure how it happened, but over the past week I've been doing more and more things on my own. I took the trash out, opened the mail, loaded and unloaded the dishwasher several times. I've gone to the grocery store, and I cooked for Ivan. By "cooking" I mean I warmed up some cans of baby food, spaghetti and meat sauce, the only food he'll accept besides breast milk, but still. It's something. It's progress. My friends are no longer with me twenty-four hours a day. I'm usually alone for both the mornings and early afternoons, and then I'm relieved by my on-duty brother or mother or friend, who pops in around four or five. The feat of cooking dinner or getting through an evening on my own is not something I've accomplished yet, and I'm not looking forward to when the time comes that I do. I wish things could go on like this forever.

We're going to sell our car now. It doesn't occur to me until after I have this thought, made this decision, that I still think in terms of we, our, us. It's our car, and we're going to sell it. That's what we've decided, you and I. You're easier to convince when you're inside my head. You don't disagree nearly as often as you did when you were alive. In fact, you often agree with me, think I've come up with smart solutions and don't ask so many questions.

June 2014

My therapist has told me I need to train myself to handle Ivan screaming. She calls it sheltering; I have to work on sheltering both Ivan's and my emotions when he cries. I have to take a deep breath when it happens and remind myself that this isn't dangerous. I have to remember that crying is the only way an infant can communicate, and that I'm doing everything a parent can do to comfort him. It's not my fault when he cries. He's fine. The problem is not Ivan's, it's mine, and through training I'll get better and better.

I'm very grateful for my psychologist, whom I've visited every week since I finally dared to tell Ivan's pediatrician what a difficult time I was having. Once a week I receive confirmation that I'm doing the right thing. Once a week we talk about how I feel every time Ivan throws a fit and seems impossible to comfort. Once a week I'm able to tell someone about my impulse to run away, to hand over all the responsibility to someone else, some other adult, anyone else who would be capable of doing this. Once a week I cry because I feel so sad about our relationship, how things have turned out between us. How she manages it, I don't really know, but once a week I leave her office happier, stronger, and with my steps lighter. She gives me concrete tasks to practice and encouragement to believe in my own capabilities. "You have the strength inside you," she says. "You can do this," she says. And I believe her. I'm trying very hard to believe her.

But now it's summer break. The last task she gave me was this: under no circumstances should I go through with my plan to put you and Ivan on a train for two hours to the summerhouse we rented this year. I should absolutely not give in to my fear that Ivan will cry in the car when we're stuck in traffic by making impractical plans for your transportation. Instead, I'll get into our car, put my family in the back seat, and drive us to our rented house. Everyone will be together. I have to remember that Ivan is perfectly fine in the back seat, that he has *two* parents, that he's sitting with one of them, and that I'm not alone. That's what I'll think, and that's what I'll do. There's nothing more to it than that.

So that's why we're sitting here now, the three of us and the cat on your lap in the back, heading toward a summerhouse. This year our family is bigger than ever before, the car more crammed. We planned the time of our departure carefully: Ivan usually falls asleep just after ten in the morning and that's when we took off. I prayed to the weather gods for a cloudy day, and because this is Sweden in mid-June, they listened—the sky is gray and the temperature in the car is not unbearable. We already packed the car last night. Everything's been meticulously planned.

Before we've even left our neighborhood and its tiny streets, Ivan's eyelids start to grow heavy. You give me regular reports from your position next to him in the back seat. I catch your eyes in the rearview mirror, and you raise a finger to your lips to show we should be quiet now, that soon our child will be asleep. As we get up onto the highway, our car is completely silent. Ivan is sleeping, the cat doesn't make a sound, your head is bent over the screen of your phone, I have my hands on the wheel and my eyes on the road, and I steer our little family forward, toward our sixth summer together, our first with Ivan. I'm already imagining how proud my psychologist will be of me when we meet again in a month, when I tell her about my achievement. I can't wait to tell her all about it.

November 2014

Now your parents have also met our officiant. At our house — that's where we meet nowadays because I don't seem to be capable of functioning anywhere else. Also the officiant lives nearby. It seemed logical to have the meeting here.

I sat in the room next to them while they spoke to her, but I could hear every word.

Through anecdotes I hadn't ever heard before, I learned that you were a cautious child, much more inwardly focused than your extroverted and seven-years-older brother. I listened as your dad talked about how he couldn't entertain you in the same way as your big brother. He talked about how you cried when he sped down a hill with you on the back of his bike, about how you wanted to climb off and go back to your mom inside the house. I heard your father talk about the symbiosis that existed between you and your mom as you grew up. "He was a mama's boy. It was always the two of you," your dad said. Maybe he even turned toward your mom at the kitchen table. You stayed home with her until you were five years old. Your little bed was in their bedroom, at the foot of their bed. You and your mom liked to bake together, read Tove Jansson's stories about the Moomins, preferred to stay indoors. Your dad said you used to cry when they put you down on the grass as a small child. I heard how you sometimes feared your dad, his hot temper and loud voice, how you didn't resemble your big brother at all. You were the calm one, the thinker, the dreamer who didn't mind playing on his own. You were clever. "He was smarter than the rest of us," your dad said. I heard him stop often to cry and blow his nose into the roll of paper towels on the kitchen table.

Your mom sat in silence for most of the conversation. She's quieter than she used to be. Her grief doesn't gush out in the same way as your dad's, but I sense that it's eating her up inside. She looks tortured, and she seems to be thinner every time we meet. Excuses herself all the time to go out to the balcony and smoke. Stands quietly in the darkness, thinking. I suffer with her, wish I could find a way to comfort or at least reach her, but I don't know how. I have no comfort to give, have trouble initiating conversations on my own. With your dad it's easier. He does almost all the talking. Cries, talks, laughs a little sometimes, cries a little more. His gestures are still sweeping. He's the one who seems most like himself in his grieving. In the kitchen, with the officiant listening and taking notes, he unburdened himself and seemed for a moment to draw energy from all the stories of you and your childhood.

Those stories painted such a vivid picture that I could see you so clearly in front of me. A spectacled, scrawny little boy with big blue eyes and mousy brown hair that was cut at home. A thoughtful and subtle child who never wanted to go to bed, always wanted to sit up with the adults at a party. Who read lots of books and daydreamed all the time. A bit anxious. A child who preferred that things remain calm and still.

It's so strange that we never talked about your childhood, you and I, except in fragments. As I listened to your dad, I wondered how you managed to avoid that over our years together. It struck me that maybe I never asked you much about your past. Or was it you who didn't want to talk?

I remember the first week we met, the one we mostly spent in your bed in your spartan apartment in Hornstull. I remember how one day out of nowhere you claimed you had no childhood traumas, and I remember thinking you must be in denial. I remember you telling me about the glasses you hated, that you were so happy to get contacts at the end of middle school. I remember you mentioning in passing that you sold home-brewed liquor you hid in your room to your friends during middle school, and I remember your stories about binge-drinking and the ditches you tumbled into on your way home, and that time when you averted a fight. I don't remember much more. Did we not care about the past, or was that just me? What did you really know about my upbringing? About the divorce and my stepfamily and the move and the fights and the disease and the death? I can't recall a single conversation we had about my childhood. I wonder if it was because I thought it hadn't affected me as an adult. Now I feel like an idiot. I don't know what it says about us, about you and me, that we just skipped over that part where we got to know each other. Maybe it means we lived more in the now rather than in the past and the future. Maybe it says that neither of us was very interested in the subject. Maybe it doesn't say much at all.

I wish we'd talked more. I wish it hadn't been so quiet between us in those last couple of years. When I hear your parents talking about you, you appear so clearly inside me. It feels like I suddenly see you, all of you, who you were and who you became. Everything seems more logical now, now when it's too late. I wish I had another chance to love you. All of you. I wish I could redo our story, be another person with you. Somebody who asked more, listened more, understood more, had more patience. But it's impossible. Instead, I listen for the pieces of you that I missed.

When your parents and the officiant have finished talking, and she takes off, they stay behind for a little while. Cuddle Ivan, seeming noticeably relieved that the conversation is over. "Goddammit," your father says over and over. "Goddammit," I answer for lack of a better response. They ask me how I'm doing, if I can manage, am keeping it together, if they can help with anything. I say, "I can't think of anything. I'm making do somehow." Then they pat Ivan on the head one last time, put on their coats and shoes, and go home. I watch them from the bedroom window as they cross our courtyard on their way to the parking lot. Your dad's arm rests on your mother's hip, and he gestures to her with his free hand. I see her nod to him. I think it's so nice that they have each other. I try my best not to envy them, but I fail. It feels like all the people I have around me are only borrowed. It feels like in the end I don't have anyone anymore. Other than Ivan. It also feels like it's my own fault it ended up this way.

August 2014

Today my best friend is getting married. I call her Little Shrimp because she's younger than me and when I got to know her she was an intern at my previous job, but in the speech I've written for the wedding dinner, I plan to retire that nickname and accept her as an adult. She doesn't know that yet, where she sits with her back to me while a hairdresser arranges her hair. There will be flowers in it and twigs. I see her face in the mirror, and I know she's happy because I know how she looks when she's not, and today she's glowing. She's radiant and laughing and toasting with us. We are here to be at her side all day, up until the moment it's time for the ceremony and the reception. As for me, I'm in a pair of sweatpants, sitting on the double bed in the suite she's rented, watching her. I have a glass of champagne in my hand, two dresses in front of me on the bed that I have to choose between before this evening, and in my throat is a sob I'm trying my best to hold inside because I'm not entirely sure if my tears are joyful. I smile when the photographer documenting this day takes a few shots, but I doubt it looks genuine. I empty my glass too fast, stand up, and go to the toilet. Stare at myself in the mirror, see the bags under my eyes, tell myself to cut this out immediately. This can't go on.

Is that a jealous person staring back at me in the mirror? Is it envy I feel, the ugliest feeling of them all? Maybe I'm just an envious person, unable to enjoy other people's happiness? Somehow in the light of Little Shrimp's joy, my own life seems so dry, so empty, sad even. Since she met the man she's marrying we haven't talked as much as I would have liked. I'm not sure I've really been there for her like a good friend should be. I'm not sure she has either. Ever since you and I started to pull away from our social life and parties in the inner city, moved to the suburbs and had a baby—now six months old and currently at home with you in Enskede—I've increasingly followed her life from afar. Via text message and social media. I've watched her travel the world with her soul mate and fiancé. She's still working with concerts and going to the parties, but now with him at her side. When they toasted with their friends after their engagement, I participated by putting a heart under the picture on Instagram, pregnant and parked on the sofa with the phone in my hand. I've realized that she has found the love of her life. In the past, she and I used to travel together. In the past, we were each other's plus-one to every event. In the past, we talked about everything with each other. But that's starting to be a long time ago now.

I realize my sadness is a form of grief. This feels better than envy, so I let myself cry a little bit. But just a little. I can't ruin her day with my sentimental nostalgia. She found the love of her life, and I found mine. I have Ivan and you, and everything is as it should be. This is what growing up means. Keep it together, Carolina.

I wash my face with ice-cold water and text you to ask how you're doing. I'm worried because Ivan still won't drink formula from a bottle. We've never made it happen and have basically abandoned the project. So instead I nurse night and day. Today our plan is that you'll come to the hotel in an hour, and I'll give Ivan his lunch. Then my stepmom will come and take care of him during the ceremony. Take a walk in the neighborhood and then meet us again as the guests move on from the day's first location to the second. Then I'll breastfeed on a park bench. I don't care if strangers see my breast; I've long since gotten used to the feeling. Once Ivan is full, they'll head home. We've stocked up on every kind of baby food Ivan might possibly like. Bottles of breast milk and formula stand ready in the fridge. My stepmother's self-confidence as a babysitter is unshakeable. She refuses to consider any of my worries or emergency plans. I've still left them behind, though, in the form of lists, written in capital letters and posted on the fridge door. I've also made her promise she's prepared to take a taxi to the reception hall, where I can nurse him once more during the party. Everything is planned down to the tiniest detail for the first night we'll be away from Ivan, and it will surely go well. Still, I feel uneasy. Why did nobody warn me that being a parent felt like this? Will I ever feel free again?

It's almost lunchtime for Ivan, time to get ready and meet you in the hotel's foyer. As I step out the door, I shout into the room that I'm going to go nurse a little. I'll be back soon. I say it a bit too loudly, but nobody hears me. They're toasting and hugging and admiring the bride-to-be. I leave the room with my unanswered shout echoing inside. I feel stupid for interrupting them, trying to steal their attention for something so insignificant, answering a question nobody asked. My breast-feeding plans are the last thing on anyone's mind today. Once again I realize how far apart we've grown. Once again my eyes fill with tears. Stupid tears. I don't have time for any more tears today. I have to do my makeup and smile for the camera and talk to whoever is placed next to me at the dinner table and give a speech and go to a party. That's what I intend to do. No more crying.

November 2014

Today it's been a month. I've been waiting for this day. One month is a milestone. I still haven't really understood what happened, and maybe I'm even less sure now how to keep going. I realize it's not a sustainable strategy to just count the days and months. Soon I have to start filling my life with something meaningful, build something from the wreckage. But I'm not there yet. Ivan is nine months old, and I'm on sick leave from my parental leave.

The rolling schedule of family and friends is still working almost flawlessly. I have somebody with me every night, but I spend more and more time alone every day. My brother comes most often, along with the rest of my family: my stepmother, my little sister, and my mother. And several of my friends. The schedule hangs in my kitchen, a grid with morning duty, afternoon duty, and night duty, but I hardly glance at it anymore. It doesn't matter who comes as long as someone does. My family and friends work with a silent and firm resolve to keep me from going under. They clean, buy groceries, cook, keep an eye on my supplies, and fill my cabinets without asking me what I want. They know I have no idea what I want, at least not from the current selection. What I want I can never get back, and we try to talk as little as possible about that.

They give me food, pick up after me, sit with me on the sofa while I stare blankly into space in the evenings, sleep in the room next to me and Ivan, get up when I get up, and fix breakfast for me. Brew coffee. Play with Ivan and make sure I take a shower. I spend the day trying to come up with errands to do and walk around with Ivan in his stroller, trying to make it to the evening without anything terrible happening in between. This life is almost starting to feel like a routine, but I know it won't last forever and that I have to start moving forward more quickly.

I haven't felt much of a fighting spirit. The only thing that resembles any kind of ambition or plan for me has to do with Ivan. I have to give Ivan a good childhood. I *want* to give Ivan a good childhood. He needs happy memories, and I have to process my grief so that his childhood won't be filled with sadness. I know that's where I want to arrive but have no idea how to get there.

September 2014

Lately, while Ivan's asleep, you and I have been discussing our immediate future. These are not pleasant conversations. Neither of us likes doing this, but it has to be done: we're facing a change, and I don't think you've realized the extent of it. Soon you'll be on parental leave at half time and you haven't told your clients yet. You seem to think you'll be able to keep working full time while taking care of Ivan half the day. You tell me it just has to work, you have to make it work. And I'm worried.

I'll come home for dinner, we'll spend a few hours together, and then you'll work nights, you tell me. "Do you think that sounds sustainable?" I ask you. "Has to be done," you say. "I don't have a single project I can be away from. If I leave my clients for half a year, they'll replace me. I've been struggling to build this my whole adult life," you explain, hoping for my sympathy, that I'll understand why you intend to live a life of constant work and no rest. I ask if you intend to bring Ivan to your job, put him on a sofa and ask a receptionist to babysit him. The question makes you justifiably angry. You ask me if I really think so little of you. I don't respond. Instead, I say, "Can't you hear how crazy this sounds, working full time, taking care of a baby half time? I'm sorry, but I don't think it will work out." I say, "This wasn't what we agreed on." You mumble something. I ask you what you said. You say, "We didn't agree to anything earlier either." I just refused to listen to you back then. I fall silent.

You sigh, and your eyes focus somewhere in the air in front of you. You have no real argument for me because you can hear how crazy it sounds, but you're determined to do it anyway. You don't intend to give up any of your clients; they're too important. You're not going to compromise. You'll just have to sacrifice your own energy. You've made up your mind.

I spend another night with a gnawing anxiety in the pit of my stomach. A voice inside me calls out, "This wasn't supposed to be like this," and I ask myself what I got us into, forced us into. I wonder if it would be better if I didn't go back to work now. Ivan is after all only seven months old. Could I stay home through the autumn as well? What if I postponed going back until after the New Year? But I want to work! I've been longing to go back to a life where, at least for four hours a day, I'm the adult, the competent one, the one who works and laughs and lunches with colleagues. I don't want to compromise on that! And I want you and Ivan to have more time with each other without me. I want to see you grow into your role as a parent, and I'm sure it will happen if you spend more time with him on your own. Once you've comforted him, solved more of his problems, you'll grow. And when that happens, my feelings of being burdened by responsibility, almost buckling under the anxiety, will ease. I so much want that to happen. Besides, my employer is expecting me back in two weeks. It's too late to change course now.

I can't fall back asleep between nursing on this night either. I lay awake for hours, the thoughts running on a loop through my mind. On your side of the bed you seem to be sleeping well, or at least deeply, and yet you rarely wake up rested nowadays. I nag you constantly about your workload, pointing out that it's too heavy, that this situation isn't sustainable. You're increasingly quiet. Retreating into yourself. Telling me you have to work just a little longer when I head off to bed. Then the hours go by. I hear you tapping away on your computer in the kitchen outside our bedroom. When you finally come to bed, it's past midnight. I pretend I'm asleep. Ivan turns and grumbles when you rustle with your blanket next to me. We don't hold each other when we sleep. It's been a long time since we did that.

In addition, we've said yes to a rent-controlled apartment a few blocks from where we live now. It wasn't our plan, but an opportunity arose, and we couldn't say no. And now there's just a month left before we have to move, leave our beloved apartment for something newer, uglier, but much more practical. After thirteen fruitless years on the waiting list for a Stockholm rent-controlled apartment, I've suddenly been offered a large two-bedroom in our neighborhood, and in one of our many conversations about the future, I argued that we should take it. Because it's more practical. Because it's bigger. Because it has an elevator. Because it has a large balcony. Because we'll have more room. Because it's a rent-controlled apartment and those don't grow on trees in Stockholm. Because it just seems like the most sensible thing to do. At the moment, it feels like too much to handle, but in the long run it's a better choice. With a new, big elevator we can take the stroller all the way up to our apartment with a sleeping Ivan still inside. Ivan will have his own room. We'll have a giant, westward-facing balcony where we can have dinner in the evenings during spring and summer. You'll be able to have your own space to work from home.

161

I argued for it, and you agreed after a while. "We have to take the opportunity when it's offered, even if the timing is bad. We can hire a moving company. All we need to do is sell our current apartment, pack our lives into boxes in the coming weeks, and then unpack them in a month. Surely we can handle it." We agreed we could. We should be able to handle it. Just like so much else. "Who knows," I said, "in a few years we could be sitting in our big apartment, laughing about this chaotic period in our lives." "Maybe," you said, but you sounded defeated. Doubtful. I was too. I still am. I really need to start packing now.

November 2014

The day after tomorrow is your funeral. We've waited more than a month. I've felt increasingly restless and impatient. Can't we just be done with the funeral so we can move on to the next stage? I've joined several online groups for grieving young people where we can share thoughts and experiences with each other. I haven't contributed anything yet, but I've been closely reading what other people write. Especially about the time period right after a loss. One thing that keeps popping up is how many friends and people in one's network disappear after the funeral, return to their own lives, and a new type of loneliness and emptiness sets in. Another reoccurring theme is that the funeral is a milestone, the real goodbye; before that, nothing feels real. That, in combination with my desire to race through the first year and arrive at the fourth stage of grieving, makes me eager to get the funeral over with. Eager but simultaneously afraid.

It's been explained to me that we, your immediate family, will sit in the front row in the big chapel, near the urn. Everyone's eyes will be turned toward us. We've received close to 150 RSVPs for the ceremony. I haven't been around more than a few people at a time since you died. It feels hard enough to just sit there. Holding Ivan, trying to breathe. Exposing our grief to so many people at the same time makes me nervous. It makes me uncomfortable to think about how sorry they're going to feel for me, how I'll be the living embodiment of their worst nightmare. How they'll squeeze each other's hands more tightly on the benches, thinking how grateful they are that they haven't suffered my fate. I push away the thought of canceling the whole ceremony and try to find a more realistic approach. I focus on what Ivan will wear. Who will sit next to me and take care of Ivan in case he starts to scream or I lose control. How we'll get to the chapel. How we'll get home from there. What we'll eat for dinner that evening. Who will sleep over.

Lately thinking about practicalities has made me feel calmer. It has proven to work well as a distraction. I feel less sad when I'm being practical. The activities, which in the first couple of weeks were limited to going to the grocery store or returning library books, have increasingly been about arranging our future. Mine and Ivan's. I think about our apartment and how I want to move away from here. In the evenings, I spend my time searching the internet for rental apartments we can trade. I respond to ads. Put up my own ad. I wonder how small the apartment can be and still have enough room for Ivan when he starts walking, when he wants to do more things. Could we live in a tiny one-bedroom? Could we maybe even manage to live in a studio?

Recently I've also found it comforting to think more pragmatically about our relationship. Somehow it's easier to think of us as doomed even before you died. I think about how we might have broken up if you hadn't died. That I might have ended up as a single parent sooner or later. I think about how bad we were at making each other happy, how bad I was at making you happy, how you probably would have gotten fed up sooner or later and left me. You probably would have been happier with someone else. There's some comfort in admitting to myself that on some level I've been alone for a long time, even when you were alive, even in our relationship. For a moment or two these thoughts give me some peace. But they're soon replaced by other thoughts in which no peace can be found, no matter how hard I try.

Other times I think about you, about how unique you were. Then I have to admit to myself how terrible I was at seeing it, how I pushed away the things that made you special. Sometimes I think about how I'll never meet anyone else like you, and no one will ever be so good to me again. No one will ever love me so unconditionally again. Nobody will ever make me feel so calm again. No one will ever be like you.

I think about how I fell in love with you and immediately started complaining about the characteristics I fell in love with. I think about how I was always trying to change you. I wonder what kind of person falls for somebody and then immediately tries to change them. I think of all the times I pushed forward when you wanted to go slow. I don't deserve to be the one who survived.

I've written a letter to you. It started out as a sketch for the ceremony, but once I got going I couldn't stop. I didn't know I had so much to say to you, but the words rushed out of me and you felt so present in the room while I was writing. The letter ended up being four pages long. I tried to capture you, what you were like when we first met, tried to define what made you so lovable and unique. How uncompromising you were, how straightforward, your inability to dress things up or embellish them, how you never lied. Your loyalty. Your kindness. Your calm. Your dependability.

The letter became a tribute—I couldn't help it—and every characteristic I described cast an ever-darker shadow on me, my personality, the qualities you had that I don't, my inability to let you live in peace. I edited it, toned it down, read through it again. Put it aside and picked it up again. For two days I worked on the letter. Then suddenly it felt done. I sent it to my step-mother and two of our friends. Everybody called me crying, said I captured you so well. At the end of the third day I sent it to the officiant. Told her she could do what she wanted with it but that it should be supplemented with words from your friends and colleagues.

Now everything's been sent in, and the officiant has written her final script. I've seen and approved those pieces from our letters that she's going to read. One of our friends has designed a program for the ceremony. I approved that too. The songs have been chosen and sent to the chapel. Your little brother has written his own speech, which he'll give himself. How he can have the strength, I don't know. The officiant is ready to take over if it's required. She calms my every worry, says it will all go well, beautifully, and now there's nothing else to do but rest and wait. Let emptiness be emptiness, let loss be loss. That's a line from the poem that will begin the ceremony, and its command follows me through the final days leading up to our goodbye to the dust of your body on one morning in December of 2014. Let emptiness be emptiness. Let loss be loss. While waiting for the light.

October 2014

I'm standing on our new balcony, staring out over a concrete courtyard in shades of gray, wondering what Ivan will think of its tiny playground, two swings and a sandbox, when we introduce him to it soon. Maybe as soon as this afternoon. This is where Ivan will grow up; this will be his backyard. When he's older, will he remember it as much larger than it actually is? Will he climb the little jungle gym, swing on the swings, play in the sandbox? Will he learn to walk here, play hide-and-seek? Will he watch trains go by next to the courtyard, learn to ignore how often they pass and how loud they are? Will he make friends here, turn into a teenager who hangs out and sneaks a smoke in some other nearby courtyard? Will he have his first kiss here, or will that happen farther away, maybe in the city? The thought of Ivan growing up is dizzying. Feels like a distant future, difficult to imagine, but still I try. I don't have anything better to do. This is where we live now.

Today the apartment is empty, and it doesn't smell like home. There are still no light bulbs, and in the bathroom the faucet is dripping. The windows on one side of the apartment overlook a busy road where city buses pass by regularly. The other side overlooks the concrete courtyard. If you stand out on the balcony, you can watch the subway trains pass by every five or ten minutes, depending on what time of day it is. Right now it's just after two in the afternoon.

In less than an hour our things will arrive. You and my brother are currently finishing packing them into a moving truck at our old address. When you arrive, I'll be here ready to help, with Ivan on my stomach and my fingers ready to point. Directing the movers, making sure our furniture and sixty-some cardboard boxes end up in their proper place in the apartment. How did we end up with so many things? How did they fit into our one-bedroom apartment? How will they look in this apartment? I put the phone back in my pocket and go to the kitchen. Pushing away the thought that this place is ugly and almost absurdly soulless. Telling myself that at least it's practical. Convincing myself that we'll put our own personal touch on it. We'll make a home here, you and me and Ivan and the cat. This is the place where Ivan will learn to sleep through the night, I think hopefully. He'll have his own room, and you and I will find our way back to each other when that happens. In six months, when our parental leave is over and we're both back at work, the rent won't feel so high, since currently my income is reduced because I'm on parental leave. Soulless or not, this apartment is where we'll build a future together. The old one has been sold. The money is sitting in our accounts. We have a buffer if we ever need it. We can take trips in the summer. The future is pretty bright after all.

My phone vibrates in my pocket, and I know before I take it out that you are on your way. It's my brother, not you, texting me again. "Prop open the door," he writes. "We're on our way." He illustrates this information with a picture taken from the front seat of the truck. You're just now pulling out of our old street. There's a pang in the pit of my stomach. Now you've closed the door for the last time. Now it's happening for real. I take the elevator down five floors and do as he says. Staring out over the highway, waiting for the outline of a moving truck in the roundabout. Ivan starts to squirm in his carrier. He's just learned to crawl and hates to be still now. Every floor, piece of furniture, pant leg, and door threshold needs to be examined. The cat has to be chased. Chair legs must be chewed on. He's been in his carrier a long time now. Soon I'll have to let him out on the floor. But not quite yet. Because the silhouette of a gigantic moving truck just entered the roundabout.

The truck arrives, and one by one you jump out of the cab. First my brother, then the mover, and you last. You have your black knit cap on your head, and your cheeks are pale. I notice how tired you look as you head my way. I hug my brother, then you, kiss you on the cheek. Ask if everything went okay. You say yes. You rush over to the back of the truck. Focused. Pale.

December 2014

The chapel is packed with people. Not a single empty seat. I didn't even recognize everyone. But now it's over. My knees tremble as I stand up. One of your favorite songs is blaring out of the speakers. It made me sob even before the ceremony started, when they were just doing a sound check, and now I've cried for two hours straight, and I don't have anything left in me to cry. Now my focus is completely on keeping myself upright until we can get out of here.

I want to fast-forward through these final minutes and allow the guests to depart, wish I didn't have to take their hands, meet their eyes, accept their condolences. I'm standing now, receiving hugs. Hundreds of arms want to reach me, hold me and cry, thank me, tell me how beautiful it was. And I should let them know if there's anything I need. I say thank you, thank you for coming, thank you for your words, thank you for your thoughtfulness. It feels like this river of people, friends and acquaintances and relatives and colleagues, will never end. Until suddenly it does. Now it's just family in the chapel, and all that's left is to say goodbye to each other. And you, one last time, if we want to.

I haven't dared to look at your family through the ceremony. I glanced at your little brother when he stood up and read his speech. He was the only family member who spoke for himself, and I heard more guests in the chapel start to cry. He talked about what you were like as a big brother, and how he'll remember you. He talked about how you taught him to throw a Frisbee when he was little, told him to stop whining and just try again when things went badly. He said he wants to be a role model for Ivan, just like you were for him. From the reactions in the chapel, I could tell we all thought it was a beautiful speech. It must have been very difficult for your little brother to stand up there and give it. His voice trembled but didn't break, and the room was full of suppressed weeping. I blinked through my tears, let them fall on the back of Ivan's head. Thought about how soon Ivan will be ten months old. I hope that he, just like his uncle promised in his speech, will have many people around him to love him through his childhood now that you're not here anymore.

Your family stands around as perplexed as me. None of us really knows how to end a day like this one. That we would be left standing in the chapel after the guests had gone was never explained to us. What now? The music has stopped playing. Our steps echo against the stone floor as we move around the chapel. We give each other some confused hugs. Your big brother stands by the urn, puts a hand on the portrait of you that's leaning against it. His bobbing shoulders indicate that he might be weeping, but it's hard to know for sure. Maybe he's whispering something to you. Either way, I don't plan to approach him. It would be an intrusion. I feel defenseless without

Ivan in my arms. He's become my protection against reality, a shield between me and everyone else. His presence makes people cautious in their words and gestures toward me. Without him, people can say whatever they're thinking. They can say it like it is. And I don't like that.

The table next to the urn is covered by hundreds of roses. There are also white lilies and flowers whose names I don't know. And just as many cards. Plus the wreaths. The funeral director comes over to my side, and I scour my mind for something to talk about besides the obvious. Can't stand any more awkward praise about how lovely the ceremony was. I forestall her by asking if I need to memorize who bought wreaths for the funeral. I need to send thank-yous, I say. And did anyone donate money to the research fund included in the invitation? Should I check that too?

The funeral director tells me there's no need to think about that right now. She says I don't need to keep track of anything. She doesn't understand. She never has. She doesn't understand that I need this, need to be in control of something, need a task. I tell her that. She says she understands but gives me no further information. Instead, she says everything I need to know will be mailed to me. Then she puts a hand on my shoulder and says exactly what I don't want to hear. "It was a lovely ceremony," she says and meets my eyes, the ones that are too tired to cry any more tears today. "You did a good job." I nod and twist my face into something resembling humility and gratitude. I thank her. Without really knowing what she's referring to, what it is that I did so well, but I can't talk anymore right now.

In the room behind the chapel I find Ivan crawling around on the floor. He lights up when he sees me, starts to crawl in my direction, and I pick him up. My stepmother hugs me. She also says I did a good job. I'm tempted to disappear into her arms but end the hug. We have to leave here now. She asks how I want to get home. It's a fifteen-minute walk, but we can also call a taxi. I say I want the walk. Maybe we can buy food on the way home. My mom is coming with us too. And my brother. And my little sister. We'll all be having dinner together tonight, and I suddenly feel like celebrating. Drinking wine. Toasting the fact that this is finally over. Done. One more milestone, one more day between what happened and me. We all leave the chapel together. Say goodbye to your family, hug them one last time, say we'll talk soon. Then we head into the December darkness. I don't turn back as we walk away, don't look at the chapel with the enormous cross at its front. I keep my eyes forward and down, on the footpath that leads across the cemetery, then on to my square, to my grocery store. I start thinking about what I want to eat for dinner. Wondering if I have a bottle of wine chilling in the fridge at home.

In the grocery store a man is giving out samples of cheese-cake. He has an apron over his chest, a funny hat on his head, and he calls out to passersby that they have to try the new flavor. I avoid his eyes and shake my head at the offer. "No thanks," I say and move on. No cheesecake for me today. After I've passed by him I hear his voice, speaking now to my back. His tone has changed. "Next time try a smile! Always nice when people smile!" Then silence. So silent that my ears start to ring. His voice, his suggestion that I should smile more often, echoes in-side that silence.

I shake my head and feel my tears start to flow again. Soon they're falling onto Ivan's hat. I have to get out of here. I move purposely toward the exit. Pass by the candy and checkout lanes. As I pass through the automatic doors to step out into the square, I hear my stepmother chewing out the man with the cheesecake. "She just came from the funeral of her husband. Jesus Christ. Think before you speak, you fucking idiot," is the last thing I hear as the automatic doors close behind me, and I'm left standing alone with Ivan in his carrier on my stomach on the square in Sandsborg. It's started to rain. I wrap my jacket around Ivan, cup my hands over his head to protect it from rain and tears. I don't feel like celebrating anymore. I just want to go home.

October 2014

You wore yourself out during the move. You're exhausted. All you want to do is sleep. You don't have the energy for anything. When you play with Ivan, you often lie on the floor next to him. When he crawls away, you don't always follow. Then Ivan turns, crawls back to you. Nobody makes our son's face light up like you do. Even when you're tired. Several times I've found you lying alone on his blanket on the floor while Ivan explores the rest of the apartment. When you lift him up, it looks like you're struggling, as if he's suddenly too heavy. I worry about you and wonder if it's a virus or if it's a psychological response to the move. You didn't feel good after our last move either. Does it take a toll on you to uproot yourself once again, to leave another place you've made into a home? Do you suffer from it afterward? Or are you already burned out? You've been working so intensely lately. There're only five more days until you're on parental leave half time.

To compensate, relieve your burden, and keep myself and my mind occupied, I've unpacked almost all our boxes myself. In the evening after Ivan falls asleep, now in his very own room, I've worked in a frenzy. Clothes go into the closets. Books go onto the bookshelves. Kitchen utensils into kitchen cabinets, and various other things into one of the many closets we have in our new apartment. We have plenty of storage space here.

During those late nights, while I unpacked our boxes, you sat in the kitchen and worked, and a new kind of silence lay solidly between us. You've mumbled and hummed an answer when I've spoken. You've had a wrinkle between your eyebrows. Once when I went into the kitchen you were slumped over the table, had fallen onto your computer, and you seemed to be asleep. I put a cautious hand on your shoulder. Asked if you were okay. You jolted upright, said you were just taking a break. Nothing was wrong, you said. I didn't press you for more. Instead, I pushed away my own nagging concern, continued unpacking, settling in, drawing from my own energy reserves to make a home for all of us.

On Monday I go back to work again. From eight thirty in the morning until twelve thirty I'll be at the office and you'll be home with Ivan. When I get home, you'll leave for one of your jobs. Come home for dinner, which we'll eat together. Like a family. We'll put Ivan to bed. Then you'll go back to work. That's the plan. That's what we've said. I'll continue to be the one who takes care of Ivan at night. So far he's never slept alone in his new room. About an hour after he falls asleep he cries for me. Nurses himself to sleep again. Then sleeps restlessly, pushing his foot in under my stomach or my thighs. Also, I haven't slept a wink in our bedroom, but I convince myself that will happen in time. We've only been living here for a few weeks now. All the experienced parents I know have told me that one beautiful day in the future I'll miss having my baby sleep beside me.

Our plan is that I'll take the nights and you'll take the mornings. When Ivan wakes up, I'll bring him in to you. Go back to bed, rest for a few hours if it's early. I'll have to get up at seven thirty in order to make it to work. Then you and Ivan will be alone. I've drawn a map for you that shows you all the public playrooms we usually visit. Circled the addresses, noted the opening hours, indicated which ones Ivan thinks are the most fun. You haven't had time to look at the map yet. Tell me you'll look at it when the time comes. Which is in less than a week. Right now you just need to work. Right now you're just tired from the move. Right now you're too exhausted to make plans for the future. But you promise me, over and over again, you promise me it will all be fine in the end. I force myself to believe you, mostly because I have no other option.

December 2014

Soon it will be almost eight weeks since you died. We're approaching the last day of the second month. Ivan has twice as many teeth as he did when you disappeared. Every time Ivan does something new—for example, he started being able to pull himself up last week—I feel a strong impulse to tell you. Send a text or call, let you know what's happening with our son's development. More than once I've taken out my phone and found myself staring at the screen. Who should I share this with? Who cares? Who, besides you, would be interested in daily updates on our little child's development?

Usually I choose your parents, my stepmother, and my mother. Sometimes in a group text, sometimes as a personal message. They're never slow to answer. They're committed to

Ivan, proud of his progress, post pictures of him on their social media accounts. They feel strongly about him, maybe even more strongly than for their other grandchildren. They're as involved as they can be. They're not doing anything wrong, and still they bother me. They annoy me for the simple reason that they're not you. They're wonderful both as family and as support, but they're no replacement for a father. No replacement for a life partner. However, in the absence of a partner and father for Ivan, I keep them informed about Ivan's development. It feels better to do so than to let it be. This week they've applauded his teeth and seen videos of him standing up holding on to furniture in our home.

Inside, I keep on talking to you. I share all the details of our son's progress and development, tell you off for not being here. Again and again I beg you to forgive me for how things were between us in the end, how I didn't just allow but also contributed to that dull and silent existence. You deserved better. I didn't appreciate what I had, so I let it, us, slip through my fingers. I don't know how I can ever forgive myself for that.

In the void you left behind, I think of your sounds. I miss your sounds. The subdued echo of your never-ending showers in the bathroom. You brushing your teeth and gargling afterward. Your sneezes and your yawns. The music that leaked out of your earbuds while you worked. The voice you used when you spoke to Ivan. I even miss your suppressed sighs when I pressed you about the future or logistics. Your voice when you just woke up. Your voice over the telephone in the afternoon. The sound of your fingers on the keyboard late at night. Your muffled snores in the room next to me when I lay with Ivan at night. Your steps in the corridor that led from the kitchen to the living room when you got up to pee early in the morning. I miss all of your sounds.

Our home is quieter now. All our family and friends have increasingly gone back to their own lives. It turned out just like I read—something changed after the funeral. Around that time my friends stopped watching over me around the clock. My twenty-four-hour schedule was replaced by increasingly sporadic visits and frequent texts reminding me that I was always welcome to call or visit, urging me to say if there was anything I needed, anything at all, at any time. The people who'd taken time off from work to watch over us went back. My calendar was once again my own to fill. I still go through my days waiting for them to pass. We still have company most nights of the week, but I'm starting to feel like a burden.

In the mornings the emptiness comes. Waking up with my child without any plans or fixed schedule creates a new kind of stress. An increasing restlessness. I have started making plans again. Shopping lists that lead me to the shopping center near our home almost every day. Doesn't he need a new hat? Now that it's getting so cold, he probably needs wool underwear. And then there are Christmas presents I need to buy. The coffee's running out. I'm not up to doing laundry today; I'll just buy new socks. I go to the shopping center again and again. And without finding what I'm looking for, I head home again. Then I come up with new tasks for myself and it starts all over again.

Yesterday, as I exited through the revolving doors of the shopping center after one more lap without buying anything, I saw an ambulance with its doors open outside. Two EMTs were unloading a stretcher from the back. Somebody must have gotten sick at the mall, I thought and considered heading back inside. My stomach flipped, and then the almost comforting thought: Now someone else's life is changing other than mine. I'm not the only one this happens to.

When the EMTs straightened up I could see that one of them was the same man who came to our door on that morning almost two months ago. His swift gestures, his slightly disheveled hair, his kind eyes. He was the first one, besides me and Ivan, to see you dead. He was the one who tried his best to reach me, who did his best to penetrate my shock, who wanted to comfort me by saying that you looked like you died peacefully in your sleep. He was the one who explained to me that it was standard procedure for the police to come to the apartment, that I wasn't suspected of any crime, and he was the one who put an arm around my shoulders and led me through the front door, the door I promised I'd never go through again. He was the one who kept a tight grip on my wrist when he finally explained that he had to leave now, and the police were taking over.

I try to catch his eyes as he passes through the revolving doors of the Globen shopping center. I stifle the impulse to stop him, wrap my arms around him, say thank you and ask him if he has a moment. But he doesn't meet my eyes. He walks past me, just centimeters away, his eyes focused on the door he's about to pass through. He seems to be trying to calculate if the stretcher will fit through the revolving doors. He's doing his job. He has to take care of somebody else today. Maybe someone who's still alive, who broke their foot or hit their head. He'll do his job and I'll continue with mine, being Ivan's mother, head home, give him some lunch, and then put him down for his afternoon nap. Then we'll go back to the mall again later. There was something I needed to buy, right?

October 2014

It's a sunny autumn Saturday, and we're on the subway into the city to have brunch with a friend visiting from Gothenburg over the weekend. He was my friend first, but you two hit it off immediately. You've been friends since you met the first time almost five years ago. He's straightforward, warm, laughs often and easily, and is the opposite of a snob. You like that. We've spent many a drunken late night together over the years. At one time we used to meet often at concerts and festivals, bars and restaurants, took advantage of any chance to visit each other's cities. A few summers ago we spent a week with him at his parents' summerhouse on Tjörn, and the private jokes that originated during those late nights still live on, repeated nostalgically every time we meet. But those occasions have become increasingly rare. We haven't spent many evenings outside the walls of our apartment since Ivan arrived. In fact, this is the first time we've met him in over a year, and both you and I are in a better mood than usual as we ride the subway from Sandsborg to Medborgarplatsen.

You have your black hat on today. Ivan is wearing one that's almost identical. Your shirt has blue and black stripes, and Ivan's sweater is in the same colors. He beams in your arms whenever you're the one wearing the baby carrier. Seems to love being held so high up. I'm struck by how much you look alike and take a picture of you two on the subway platform. In the picture Ivan is laughing and a dimple appears on his left cheek. You smile, revealing an identical one. I think you're both beautiful and feel so proud to exit onto Medborgarplatsen and walk across Björns Trädgård at your side. I ask you if you have to hurry home to work after this, and you say no. An unexpected

178

break in your workload, and you feel like taking it easy. It makes me happy. I look forward to relaxing with you. We talk about watching one of our shows after Ivan goes to bed. Discuss whether or not to pick up one of the old ones we abandoned months ago or start a new one. Agree to start a new one. Decide to buy some steaks in Söderhallarna on our way home. Then make plans for tomorrow to drive out to your parents and fix the car's broken windshield wipers. I wonder how long it's been since we've done something together, and I realize I've missed it. I take your hand as we pass by Kvarnen. It's cool out. Ivan babbles on your stomach in his baby carrier. When our friend meets us, I wonder if it's obvious how happy we are at just this moment.

December 2014

The first Christmas is here. Both of my mothers, my sister, my brother, sister-in-law, and two good friends have gathered in Enskede with me. We've never celebrated Christmas Eve like this before. For as long as I can remember, Christmas has been an endless series of train rides and advanced logistics in order to squeeze in as many visits to as many family members as possible. But this year we're all at our place. I feel almost happy. In the kitchen, Mom is making food, cooking a ham and baking a kale pie. In the living room, my stepmother is playing with Ivan, who just learned to cruise around while holding on to hands or furniture. My brother's playlist of American Christmas songs is playing over the speakers. As for me, I'm sitting on the sofa with a cup of glogg, drinking it at a rate that can hardly be classified as sipping. The apartment has been decorated from floor to ceiling, and in the corner of the living room there's even a Christmas tree. The amount of Christmas presents stuffed below it is almost inconceivable. Soon we'll eat lunch together, then watch the classic Donald Duck Disney special followed by opening Christmas presents. This evening we'll be joined by my cousin and his son.

Holidays are the worst—that's what everyone who's lost someone says. I was already aware of that fact. After my dad died, I remember that first Christmas, just graduated from high school and faced with the prospect of celebrating Christmas with a broken family that had lost the person who united us. "You just have to get through the holidays," they say. "They'll get easier over the years, but they'll always be tough. Once, twice, maybe three times, then it gets easier."

I know from experience it's true. That person is missed more during the holidays. But this Christmas Eve, the only holiday we never celebrated together, your absence feels no more gaping than usual. Maybe even slightly less so. Our Christmas tradition was to celebrate separately until Boxing Day. At this time on Christmas Eve, you were with your parents and I was here, so it's not so different from other years. Except my family has gathered here, and I don't have to go to them. Except I have a child this year. Except you aren't at your parents' house. Except you won't be back on Boxing Day, and we won't go back to our normal lives or start scheming about our New Year's Eve plans together. Except this year you're dead. Except for that, everything is almost as it usually is.

I try to avoid thinking about how your parents must feel today. I texted them, and they answered. We've wished each other as merry a Christmas as can be had "under the circumstances," but we didn't call. I can imagine what it must be like in their home right now. It's probably quite dark. Your parents don't seem to like the lights too bright; it's almost always a little dim in their kitchen and living room. At Christmas they light candles in the chandelier above the dining table. Your little brother is probably there by now. They're probably celebrating like usual. Or "celebrate" is not the right word. What is there to celebrate today? Missing you, the hole where you should be, it must be unbearable on this day when you have always been theirs and not mine. This is probably one of the worst days for them since you died. As for me, I'm gulping down glogg at rocket speed and trying to keep myself occupied. Ivan helps me with that task.

After lunch, I start to get antsy. It's snowing. It gets dark very early. My friends have gone on to their next stop, and Mom's taken out her knitting. She's sitting on the sofa now with a glass of red wine in front of her. Her knitting needles knock rhythmically against each other in her hands. My brother is cleaning up in the kitchen. Probably he'll put on another pot of coffee soon. He's always brewing coffee. Ivan's whining is getting louder. He's tired and bored. And I feel restless. I wonder what to do with the rest of this day. Its remaining hours seem suddenly endless.

I get an idea. It starts with a "What if," which quickly becomes a "Why not" and then finally an "Of course." Why don't I walk to the cemetery right now and light a candle for you? Wouldn't it be nice, Ivan and I in the snow together on our first Christmas without you? Not exactly sad—more beautiful and meaningful. If I wear my black winter hat, it will turn white in the snow. And the snow will make a crunching sound under my feet. Ivan will sleep well in the fresh air. I tell my family I'm going for a quick walk so Ivan can sleep in his stroller for a while, then I put our outdoor clothes on in silence, call out a cheerful goodbye from the hall, and leave before anyone has time to get worried or propose joining me.

Our grocery store is still open, and I note that there will soon be a sale on Christmas hams. I pass by the refrigerators, looking for the shelf where the grave candles stand in a row. A smiling teenager in a Santa hat stands at the checkout. When I pay, she wishes me a merry Christmas, and I smile back at her, say, "You too," then exit back onto the empty square and head on toward my goal.

In order to reach Skogskyrkogården cemetery, we have to pass by another, smaller cemetery. Several families are wandering around there. They hold each other as they walk, bend over candles blinking beside the graves of a grandparent receiving their traditional Christmas visit. I note that everyone I pass by is in groups of three or four.

The stroller in front of me is quiet now. Ivan's fallen asleep. Maybe it wasn't such a good idea to come here after all. It's not as beautiful as I imagined before we left home. The snow isn't powdery; it's wet and heavy. The roads are crisscrossed with tracks, and my toes are freezing. Families have gathered here, lighting candles at the graves of their loved ones who had long lives. And here I am, by myself in front of the memorial grove, where the ashes of your thirty-four-year-old body were spread just a couple weeks ago. I'm freezing. There's no crunching sound beneath my feet. My hat is wet and not white with snow. I consider turning back, heading home, calculate the distance and realize I've come more than halfway. Might as well complete my mission.

The whole cemetery is blinking with candles. I'm not the only one who was inspired to light a candle near the memorial slope today, but suddenly I'm the only one still here. Where did everyone else go? I look at the time. It's ten minutes past three. The traditional Donald Duck Christmas special that practically the whole country watches just started on television.

Candles gleam along the path to the small hill that constitutes Skogskyrkogården's memorial slope. They border the walkway. Their flickering lights shine through the winter darkness, creating a solemn, almost sacred atmosphere, and I don't know if it's that or the temperature, but I start to shiver. I stop on the walkway and look around, suddenly at a loss. Should I go all the way up the path or stop here? Where does the path end and the memorial slope begin? Where should I put my candles? Where's a gap for my two?

In the grocery store, the grave candles were sold in packs of two, and I thought I might as well light both, one for you and one for Dad, but now I don't know where to put them. There are so many other lights here. Every spot seems taken. My candles surely won't find a place. I squat down next to the stroller, glance at Ivan, who's still asleep, then pick up my candles. Light them, pushing them side by side into the snow, continue to squat down at that spot for a moment. When I'm sure they'll keep on burning even in this wet weather, I stand up. Turn the stroller and walk away as fast as I can without running down the hill. Surrounded by these flickering candles in a suddenly deserted cemetery, I've never felt more alone. Tears burn behind my eyelids, and because I can't find a reason not to, I let them fall.

My weeping, calm at first, escalates quickly to an intensity that's more like sobbing, which I stifle as well as I can to keep from waking Ivan. This was a stupid idea. I don't want to walk around alone in a cemetery in the snow on Christmas Eve with a sleeping child in a stroller. I start to walk faster, almost running, panting, and my crying starts to cease. The stroller stubbornly refuses to go fast through the slushy snow, and I have to concentrate on the ground so as not to wake Ivan.

When I get to the second cemetery, I hear someone on the walkway calling my name. "Is that Carolina?" says a woman's voice that I recognize but can't quite place. I consider pretending not to hear—just keep going, pass by her with my eyes on my feet—but I realize that's impossible. We'll crash into each other if I don't look up. Reluctantly I raise my eyes. The voice turns out to be an acquaintance from my past, the former girlfriend of a friend. We haven't seen each other for several years. You wouldn't have known who she was if we were here together today. She belonged to a life I had before you. Today she's walking through the cemetery with her mother and an older woman, probably her grandmother. She calls out to me again, and then our eyes meet, and she realizes I'm crying. I try to smile and say hello, but my voice is thick and unruly.

She hesitates a few seconds, then steps forward, puts her arms around me, and hugs me tightly. "I heard about what happened. I'm so, so sorry," she whispers. "I'm sorry," I whisper. Then we stand there. Over her shoulder I see the women she's with hesitate, then start to walk on. They don't want to intrude. I sniff into her coat, and she continues to hold me. She says she's so, so sorry for what I've been through. "Life is fucked up." I keep crying. I can't make sense of my own thoughts let alone put them into words.

After a while we part. Wish each other a merry Christmas and say we'll be in touch. I apologize for the shape I'm in, and she tells me there's no need. Still, I feel ashamed once I move on. Think I've lost control of myself in social situations. Wonder if she's going to text her ex and let him know she ran into me sobbing in the cemetery on Christmas Eve. I wonder if he'll write back, "Fuck, that's awful." That would be typical of him. I wonder if this is the saddest and most pathetic thing either of them can imagine. I've become the kind of person other people pity. The type who walks around a cemetery on Christmas with a sleeping baby in a stroller, sobbing. It's almost too much of a cliché to be true. I curse myself again for this stupid idea, promise myself never to do anything like that again. Then I head home. Donald Duck's Christmas special is almost over now. My Christmas is almost over too. Soon I'll have made it through the first one.

October 2014

On the last day of your life, we drive home from your parents' house at sundown in silence. You stifle a sigh when I get stressed about the traffic on Nynäsvägen. I see you suppressing it in the rearview mirror. Ivan is starting to whine more and more loudly in his car seat beside you. I tell you to find something new to entertain him with, make him happy again, emphasizing, though it's unnecessary, that I can't do anything about the stand-still traffic. You say everything's fine. Stifle another sigh. Tell me to focus on driving rather than what's happening in the back seat.

On the last day of your life, we park the car and go to our nearest grocery store before we head home. At the refrigerated display case, I ask you if blood pudding and lingonberries would be okay for dinner tonight. You say sure, you've got no better suggestions. I put the blood pudding into our basket and pass by the chips aisle on my way to the checkout. I don't even have to turn around to know you've stopped at the bins of loose candy to grab some caramel chews and some gummies. When I put the blood pudding and milk on the conveyor belt, you put the bag of candies down neatly next to them. I pay, you carry Ivan in his carrier on your stomach, and we walk home in silence.

On the last day of your life, we eat blood pudding and lin-gonberry jam for dinner. As seven o'clock approaches, I start to get Ivan ready for bed. I breastfeed him on the sofa. You sit down at your computer at the kitchen table. I can hear you unwrapping your candy chews. You eat them in front of your computer. Your back is curved. I call out to you, say it would be nice if you played with the cat for a while when I put Ivan to bed. You say you already were planning to, that you'll do it before you go to bed.

On the last night, I say good night to you at eight o'clock on behalf of Ivan. You look up from your computer at the kitchen table and kiss him on the head, then I take him to his bedroom. I breastfeed him until he falls asleep and stay in the bedroom in the darkness for a while. I feel like I should take a shower, but I'm too tired. Instead, I listen to the silence outside. You're still in the kitchen. If I concentrate, I can hear your fingers tapping away on the computer keyboard. It annoys me that you're not playing with the cat like you promised. I feel guilty about what a boring day she had. Alone in our apartment while we were with your parents. I stand up carefully, sneak out into the apart-ment, out to you.

The last time I see you, I'm standing in front of the fridge in our new kitchen. I ask you if you're planning to work much longer, and you answer not long, not much longer. You just have a few things left to take care of. You don't look at me when I speak to you. You're engrossed in what you're doing. Besides, I haven't been particularly friendly to you this after-noon. To lighten the mood, I pick up our cat, who just entered the kitchen and started stroking herself against my legs. I put her into Ivan's carrier. She likes it there, allows herself to be rocked, puts her front paws over the top edge of the carrier and parries her head to my swinging movements. She looks funny. I try to get your attention, say, "Look, look." You lift your eyes and look at us standing there. You laugh a little when you see her, seem genuinely amused for a moment. Then you lower your eyes to your computer again. I ask you to take a picture of us, and you pick up your phone. You take a picture of us, then one more. You put down your phone again. Your eyes are again focused on your computer screen. You want to return to what you were doing before. Whatever needs to be finished before you can head to bed.

The last time I say good night to you I don't know it's the last time. If I'd known, I would have put more energy into my goodbye. If I'd known, I would have kissed you, told you how much I love you, how sorry I am for the way I've treated you the last few months. Instead, I carefully lift our cat out of Ivan's carrier and let her down onto the floor. I say, "I think I'll sleep with Ivan tonight." I don't need to explain why because we both know that he'll wake up soon and cry for me and the milk in my breasts. You don't protest. Your eyes are still on your computer. You let me go, and I do it, I go. For the very last time I leave you. I think we'll see each other early tomorrow morning. But we won't. We will never see each other again.

The last time I text you it's about Ivan. I write to you that I think he's having night terrors, and you don't answer my text. I think we're going to talk about it in the morning.

The last night, in a bedroom next to you, I fall asleep believing we have thousands of days ahead of us. We don't. This night is our last night. We don't spend it together.

2015–2016

January 2015

ON THE EIGHTH day of the new year a letter arrives in the mail. It says your ashes were scattered onto the memorial slope at Skogskyrkogården. I read the letter at the kitchen table. It's short, just one sentence, and doesn't look official, more like it was written by a senior citizen who's been experimenting with typography. There's no return address, no personal greeting or signature at the bottom. I read the letter once, then twice, sitting at my kitchen table. Trying to feel whatever I feel after reading this letter. Trying to understand what to do with this information. I lay the letter down. Take a lap around the kitchen. Load a dirty glass into the dishwasher. Put on a pot of coffee. Wipe down the counter. I'm waiting for some sense of finality, an endpoint, some relief or at least an added intensity to my grief. But there's nothing. I remember how you told me you didn't want to be buried at all. You wanted to be scattered in a forest or in the sea. Someplace no one would feel obligated to visit. No fuss. That's what you said. But you ended up in Skogskyrkogården in Enskede. It feels like we betrayed you.

I'm sitting in a waiting room, flipping through a psychology journal. I'm about to meet with the therapist I was assigned after I called a clinic specializing in grief, which offers free therapy for the grieving. I got an appointment quickly because they prioritize young people who have children at home. I had to wait only a month. I'm grateful for that fact. I don't have all the time in the world. I have a baby to raise. I need help so I can move on as fast as possible. In the absence of any better ideas on how to do that, I'm seeking the help of a professional.

Their waiting room looks like most psychologists' waiting rooms I've been in. There have been a few over the years. I called my first therapist ten years ago, the one who was supposed to help me figure out why I had such a hard time being alone. I didn't particularly like her, but I stayed with her for two and a half years. By the time I finished therapy, I'd learned how to identify what was happening inside me when I was alone and analyze why I was running away from it in the past. I'd talked myself hoarse about my relationship with my dead father, my teen years spent arguing with my stepmother, and my lack of a verbal relationship with my biological mother. I'd analyzed my first loves and learned the difference between self-confidence and self-esteem. I was tired of talking about myself, tired of the cost, and tired of my therapist. I felt done with therapy long before my therapist agreed with my conclusion. I left my last session believing I was done, prepared to meet the future pure, wise, and insightful. I was twenty-six years old.

I took a couple of years off. I waltzed between jobs and traveling, dance floors and hangovers, moved between sublets and love affairs. The only thing that never fell into place was love. The ones I wanted didn't want me. The ones who wanted me I pushed away. The gnawing feeling that something was probably wrong with me kept returning, despite all the effort I'd put into therapy. I ignored it with the same strategy as before: diversions, work, and escape from reality.

Then I met you, and we became a couple. I fell so hard for you, and at the same time I felt so confused that I contacted a new therapist in panic. This time I aimed higher. Figuring I had nothing to lose, I wrote an email to a psychologist whose books I'd read and been inspired by. I asked if he might have time to see me, and he did. During so-called short-term therapy, we explored my fear of losing the ones I love. I realized that as a result of the losses I experienced when I was young, I'd developed a paradoxical need for control in my relationships while also being terrified of intimacy in general, and therefore I found you and your distance both familiar and safe. My new therapist explained terms like "repetition compulsion" and "projection" and thought they explained my decade of failed romances. I loved going to that therapist, his clinic, the smell in his waiting room, talking to him and listening to him. I went to him for three months. When I read in the newspaper that he'd passed away a couple of years later, I felt truly sad.

Then Ivan arrived, and I ended up with the psychologist who's still helping me with my role as a parent. There our focus is on my connection with Ivan. She props me up when I'm afraid I'm unfit to raise a child, calms me down when I worry I won't succeed, and comforts me when I cry. And she reminds me over and over that Ivan is doing well, Ivan is fine, Ivan has a great mother who's doing everything right.

At my first appointment with this new psychologist, when she opened the door to the waiting room, showed me in, and pointed to a chair where I was supposed to sit, I felt a tiny bit amused by the situation. It occurred to me that she looked exactly like the cliché of a psychologist. I thought, she probably pronounces the *p* in psychologist, probably spends most of her time with other psychologists, might even be married to one. Her precise haircut, her thin, orange bangs made me smile. I couldn't help but wonder why so many psychologists I'd met have red hair and a pageboy cut. Did she become a psychologist because she has red hair or did she start dying her hair red when she became a psychologist? I wondered. She interrupted my thoughts by starting to speak. Her voice sounded just as I had expected it would. Melodic but not dramatic, deep but not authoritarian, quiet but clear as a bell, all at the same time. She briefly introduced herself and asked me to tell her why I was there. Now it was my turn. I prepared myself to start talking. I've done it so many times before. I've got this down.

It's just that I lost the thread before I even started because suddenly I didn't know where my story began. The situation didn't feel very pleasant anymore. Suddenly, it was about me and not about her.

I cleared my throat and started talking, at first coherently, but when she didn't ask me any questions, I lost my way, didn't know what order to tell everything in. I hopped around, breaking chronology, interrupted myself, my voice breaking. I tried to take a deep breath but couldn't. Everything fell apart, and before I knew it, I was telling her in a completely incoherent way that I'm an evil and weak person who basically caused the death of my son's father and who's now facing the impossible task of raising that son alone, and I have no idea how to do that. Then I sobbed for fifty minutes, and when I stepped out of her office again after an hour, I couldn't remember what I thought was so funny at first.

February 2015

I get by pretty well on my own during the days now, but I still hate the nights. Once everything gets quiet, and I've put Ivan to bed, I know I have exactly forty-five minutes before the first outburst happens. Since I quit breastfeeding around the new year, he's been drinking enormous amounts of formula out of bottles, and between the bottles I supplement with baby food. I've never had to heat up a bottle during the night, and everything is pretty much exactly as I'd hoped it would be. Except for these night terrors. They've grown worse in recent months as Ivan's motor function has evolved, and I'm increasingly frustrated by my inability to calm my hysterical child every night.

During the day we're almost like any other family. We visit playrooms and meet up with friends. Grab a coffee. Hang out. Move around a lot. Ivan is developing rapidly. He's started talking and walking and seems to love life just like any other one-year-old we meet. We laugh together. He gives me joy, and I try my best to avoid thinking about how what happened has possibly damaged him. But then morning turns to afternoon and then to evening, and we go home and my anxiety increases as dusk falls. My brain searches for some way to escape. Could I sleep over at a friend's place tonight? Could somebody come spend the night with us? Can we move away from here soon?

I've been dreaming of moving away from the apartment you died in since you first passed away. Every day I think about it. Every night I mull it over in my head. I don't want to live here anymore. I want to move, start over somewhere else. There's an atmosphere here that I can't handle. I still don't want to go into our old bedroom. I hate how long the subway ride is from Enskede to see my friends. Hate the elevator that stinks of urine, which we have to ride to the platform at our station. I hate the street outside our window and the never-ending buses that go by on it. Hate our backyard and its many shades of gray. When the evening turns to night, I think about how I have to move soon. I never wanted to live here. It felt like an uphill battle ever since we moved here, but at least we were doing it together. We were going to build a home together. Without you, I just don't have it in me. I have to get away from here.

April 2015

I'm packing for another move when the letter arrives from the Swedish National Board of Forensic Medicine. After an intense month of bank negotiations and running between apartment viewings, we finally found our new home. In just a couple of weeks the moving truck will arrive, and I have newfound energy to carry us closer to that goal: our new address, the place where we can start over. The days feel almost meaningful now; my task is so clear and the goal even clearer. The future feels almost exciting with the move within reach. I'm on my way between the living room, where Ivan is taking his morning nap on the sofa, and the bathroom, where I'm working on sorting toiletries, when I notice the letter on the hallway floor.

Almost exactly six months after you died, it has arrived. They warned me it could take time, up to half a year, and I wondered how that could be possible. How could the information about your cause of death take half a year to get to me when your body was burned and spread in the wind just a few weeks after your death? "It can't take that long," I complained. "We need to know. There's a child to consider! We need answers so we can move forward." The police officer responsible for your case was a very nice man and dependable. He seemed to understand how painful it was not to know. He explained in a kindly manner that he wasn't completely familiar with all the details of these kinds of investigations, but he knew they'd be working with genetic samples and analyzing microscopic findings. They might even send those samples to labs all over the world. "It's not because they're lazy. It just takes time," he promised me.

As time passed, I focused less on the actual reason why you died. It was more important to me in the beginning, back when

I spent whole nights wondering what exactly happened inside your body that made you die. But over time, those thoughts faded away. Now I spend most of my time thinking about Ivan. It doesn't matter what disease killed you. It doesn't change anything. You're still dead no matter what happened. But *if* you died from some genetic disorder, then I might spend the rest of my life in fear that Ivan will die in his sleep too. I can't stand the thought of such a life.

I stand bent over the hallway rug, staring at the envelope without daring to pick it up. Within seconds my body has been flooded with adrenaline, and I notice how my hand shakes as I lift the letter and start tearing open the seal. It strikes me that I probably shouldn't be alone when I read this letter, but my fingers work on. I can't wait. The information is here now, and I have to know as quickly as I can. I can call someone later.

The letter starts with some short background information. I scan it quickly because I already know it. It states that you were found dead by your cohabiting partner on October 27, that no external injuries were detected. The second heading reads "Observed Pathological Changes." In list form, it states that your heart was enlarged, that you had mild arteriosclerosis in your coronary arteries and inflammation in the posterior wall of one of the ventricles of your heart. This information doesn't tell me anything. I read through the points again. Realize that I have no idea what a ventricle looks like or what mild arteriosclerosis is. I recognize the last point on the list. It states "possible cardiomyopathy." I read the word again. Car-di-o-my-o-pa-thy. I know that cardiomyopathy means heart disease because I've been researching what causes sudden cardiac arrest in young people. I read on. Under the heading "Chemical Analysis" it states that no drugs or alcohol were found in your system and that the amount of glucose found in your eye fluid is considered normal. Even though I long ago abandoned the idea that you committed suicide, I feel relieved to have this information. There it is, in black and white. You didn't want to die. Your blood values were normal. You died from something else.

The next headline and the sentence that follows it, I read several times. First I read it slowly, without registering the meaning of the words, then I read it again, now with a question mark added after the last word. Can it really be true? I read the sentence a third time.

Genetic analysis after cardiac death showed no pathological genetic variants.

No pathological genetic variants. The four most beautiful words I've ever read, if they mean what I want them to mean. I don't dare to hope. Does this mean Ivan will live? Does "no pathological genetic variants" mean that Ivan has been spared? Do I dare to hope? The letter concludes with a summary stating that the cause of death cannot be confirmed, but the investigation's findings strongly suggest that death was caused by disease, "likely complications related to the patient's heart disease."

I stand in the hallway for a long time. I read the letter again and again. No pathological genetic variants. No pathological genetic variants. No pathological genetic variants. I take a quick picture of that paragraph with my phone and send it to a friend, ask her to check with a specialist she knows to see if this means what we hope it means. Then I send the same picture to another friend who works as a general practitioner. Ask her to interpret the information and get back to me as soon as she can. I wait by the phone and continue staring at the letter.

After a few minutes, my phone rings. My friend has talked with her specialist friend, who told her that "no pathological genetic variants" means what we want it to mean. There's nothing to indicate that what you died from was hereditary. There's nothing to indicate that your disease was genetically transferable. They simply didn't find any genetically pathological variants. I sob into the phone, and my friend tries to calm me. I can't stop. Just ask the same question over and over. Does this mean that they're *absolutely sure* your disease wasn't hereditary, I ask. She says she believes so. "But just to be sure, we'll call a cardiac specialist and make sure Ivan gets an exam. You don't have to do this alone," my friend tells me over the phone. "You can relax now. Ivan is going to live. The results are good. It's the best we could have hoped for. Do you understand that? Can you believe in that?"

I don't know if I can. I want to hear from another doctor, and then another. I want a whole choir of doctors telling me that Ivan isn't at risk of dying from the same illness as you. I'm going to need to hear it many more times. But my friend's words are a good beginning. During the day, the information slowly sinks in. The results that arrived in the mail today were the best we could have received. I have to allow myself to be relieved by it. I have to believe, and to hope a little too.

May 2015

It's the first night in our new apartment. In recent weeks, I've been—with the help of my friends, your parents, your siblings, and my brother—working hard on this move. Your brothers painted every room, put down wall-to-wall carpet in the bedroom, and cut a hole in the wall of a closet, which will now become Ivan's bedroom. They put a door with a window into that hole, so light from my room will stream into his. It's been a very intense few weeks for me and the people I love. But we've helped each other out as well as we could. Worked hard. And earlier today the moving truck took off according to schedule. We succeeded.

As the truck rolled out of Enskede after its last, unplanned trip—I had accidentally rented a truck that was too small—euphoria washed over me. Goodbye, stupid Enskede! Goodbye, stupid apartment! I'll never be back! If it had been a movie, I would have opened the window of the car, stuck my upper body out the window, and screamed with my hair flying in the wind. In reality, I stayed in my seat, my seat belt tightly fastened, and swore a little under my breath. I didn't look back, didn't even glance in the rearview mirror, welcomed every meter the truck rolled forward toward our new home. When the moving truck crossed over the bridge that connects Stockholm's southern suburbs with inner city Södermalm, I allowed myself a restrained squeak.

My friends helped me frame pictures of you, which decorate the newly painted walls of Ivan's room. We put up the black-and-white one of you smiling, which we had at the funeral, and a large one of you as a child, which I got from your mom. Then a few smaller pictures form a collage of you and Ivan together. In one of them you and Ivan are lying together on our sofa. Your index finger rests lightly on his cheek, and I know exactly what sound you're making when this picture was taken. Ivan is giggling with his mouth wide open, and there are only two teeth inside. In another you're sitting on a dock. I took the picture from a cliff above you last summer. I remember thinking you probably should have life jackets on down there. The sweetest picture of all is of Ivan. Just your hands are visible in the photograph. You're holding him up to a clear blue sky, the lower parts of your forearms are visible as you hoist him high in the air, his face turned downward toward you. Ivan is laughing. There's a string of saliva dripping down from his mouth, a transparent ray headed straight toward the camera. The contrast between the sky and Ivan, whose face is shaded by a white sun hat, is extreme. The picture almost looks fake. I hope Ivan will find joy in this collage someday. I've already decided we'll call it the Papa Board.

There's also a wooden toy box in Ivan's room, which your dad made. He put his whole heart into the project, and it took him over a month to complete. He said he could feel you close by when he was working on it in his workshop. As if you were standing at his side. Your voice was inside him through the whole process. During your conversation, you made it clear to your dad what you wanted him to do. "Get it together now," you told him. "You can't just collapse into despair over this. Don't give up. You have a life left to live. You have people who need you. Take care of Mom now. Help Carolina take care of Ivan. Be there for them." You told your dad all of this while he hammered and sanded and screwed the boards together, and now the box is finished, just in time for the move, and stands in Ivan's room.

When your dad told me about his conversation with you, I recognized myself. I do the same thing, but in other situations. I still discuss things with you before making a decision. Ask you if you think this seems like a good thing for me and Ivan. Sometimes I have to nag you, argue and reason with and persuade you, just like when you were alive. I'm still in the habit. In my mind, you doubted the move. In my mind, you thought the bank loan I was about to take out as a single parent was too big and might lead to economic insecurity. What if you lose your job? you said. I'm not going to do that, I answered. And if I do, I'll find a new one. We can't stay here. It's impossible, I told you. We argued about the move all through the night. We weighed the security of living near my social network and getting away from an apartment that gives me anxiety against the huge loans and the smaller living space. At dawn we agreed I could move. And I did. Now I'm here, on the balcony, which I'll show to Ivan for the first time tomorrow, along with all of the other rooms and toys and furniture and the pictures on the walls. I miss Ivan. I wish he could have shared this first night with me.

June 2015

Our motto the first summer after we lose you is "Always take the path of least resistance." Say what you want about children and screen time, but for me it's become a lifesaver. For Ivan's meal intake too. Ivan has started to like *Teletubbies* in recent months and now spends most of his meals engrossed in the world of Tinky-Winky, Dipsy, Laa-laa, and Po. He watches, puts a bite into his mouth, laughs, takes another bite, points to his colorful friends, mimics their sounds, takes another bite. Meals seem to go much better when he's engaged with the screen, and I've long since capitulated to the impossible task of forcing, enticing, or just plain keeping him at the dinner table.

At least the weather is good. It's summer, finally. The last one before Ivan starts preschool and I return to work after a year and a half away. The weeks still feel long—many days are as empty of plans as they are of company—but we've built a routine that works for us, and life is considerably easier than it was in Enskede. There every street, every store, every square, every library, and every playground reminded us of you. There every inch of our apartment was missing you. There the silence echoed menacingly in the late hours of the night. There the future, the rest of Ivan's childhood, seemed like an impossible task. Here we've started to have something that resembles a normal life, something I probably still need to get better at handling but that doesn't scare me to death every waking moment of the day. It was a very good idea to move.

During the days, we visit playrooms and parks. We've discovered which parks are better suited to younger children, which have water fountains to refill our bottles, and which have no trees to shade us when the days are too warm and our clothes stick to our bodies.

One might almost say we've found our rhythm. One day a week we visit your parents, who we now call Grandma and Grandpa. One day each week we have dinner with my brother and sister-in-law. One day we usually have dinner with friends who live close by and have kids around the same age as Ivan. Some days we hang out in parks with other parents who are on parental leave. I've started counting weeks, rather than months, until Ivan starts preschool. The thought that in just two months he'll spend his days there, and I'll spend mine at work, seems surreal. I both long for and fear it, as this change approaches.

I worry that I won't have the energy for my job or that I won't like it anymore or that I won't be able to relate to my colleagues after everything that's happened. That I'll always feel incomplete without Ivan at my side, and that missing him or worrying about him will get in the way of me doing a good job. Even more, I worry about Ivan. What if he doesn't like preschool? What if they aren't able to master the trick of getting him to eat or nap? It's probably not reasonable to expect them to let him watch *Teletubbies* during every meal or to understand that he sleeps only when his stroller is moving and that it's very important he get his hour nap each day. I don't want to have to get used to the feeling of leaving a crying child, my own crying child, in the arms of someone else. I worry about all the illnesses that flourish in the preschool environment, and I don't want to become one of those parents sharing their sick days with their kids on social media. But most of all, I worry that Ivan won't connect with his teachers.

Yet I also know it's time for a change. Our life would become depressing if it went on too long like this. I'd end up bored and frustrated, and it would affect how I parent. Soon I'll run out of ways to fill our waking hours with fun activities. This works only because it's temporary. I need a break, need access to a sphere that's just my own, if I'm going to continue delivering when Ivan and I are together. I need to learn to be away from him, and he needs to learn that the world won't end without me.

July 2015

I fall asleep and wake up to the sounds of horses grazing and snorting, trotting and galloping, neighing and whipping flies away with their tails. All of it accompanied by the buzzing of flies. Hundreds of flies, Öland's flies, outside our window and close to my ears in the bedroom. Summer is nearing its end. We're in a house on the east coast of Öland, which we rented with my stepmother and little sister, and basically I spend all of my time doing nothing besides being annoyed with them. I feel ashamed of that fact, and the days go by in a blur of mixed emotions, in which I sometimes snap at them, sometimes avoid them, and sometimes fuss over them to try to make up for my bad mood.

It's the fourth day of our trip, our last trip of the season, during the first summer after we lost you, and today we're headed to the beach. I'm sitting next to Ivan in the back seat of the car, alternating between giving him toys, which he constantly throws away, and texting with a friend. I'm not participating in the conversation in the car. When I'm asked a question, I respond curtly, and my stepmother's attempts to keep our mood festive keep falling flat. In my texting thread, I'm trying to describe to my friend what exactly it is that annoys me so much, but I can see immediately when I send these words away that I'm being unfair. When I describe how my stepmother almost compulsively questions everything I say, I sound like a sulky teenager. Not to mention how spoiled I sound when I complain about how infrequently they offer to help me with Ivan. After all, they *are* helping. Several times a day they give me a break so I can take a shower or lie on the sofa with a book. A couple evenings I've even been able to skip the ever more elaborate bedtime procedures. Still, I'm annoyed. Annoyed with the dynamic between my little sister and my stepmother. Even more annoyed by how often I have my hands full while they seem to be on vacation. I think it's unfair. They play cards and sunbathe, eat candy and joke around, have no routines they have to stick to. My life is in sharp contrast to theirs. I run around constantly, or crawl, busy with my twenty-four-hours-a-day job: Ivan. It drives me crazy.

Next to their vacation, my life seems even sadder than usual. Every morning when Ivan wakes me up at six, and I try to make him play quietly so the other two can sleep in, I feel annoyed. Every time they laugh, I'm reminded of how seldom I do. While they're lying in the sun working on crossword puzzles, I'm inside with Ivan. Throwing angry glances in their direction, answering "Nothing" when they ask me what's wrong. As I'm making his lunch, they're just finishing breakfast. When I get a fifteen-minute break, I run to take a shower. When they're ready for their first outing of the day, Ivan needs to be having lunch in the shade and can't go anywhere in a hot car. When they remind me not to forget about Ivan's sun hat on the short walk from the car to the store, I mutter, "Thanks, I know." Our lives just don't fit together easily, and everything they take for granted is everything I don't have. It makes me furious. I feel like a martyr when I'm near them.

I get that I'm projecting. I shouldn't be angry with people who are helping me, who invited me on a trip with them, who want to help me and be there for me. It's not okay to be angry and want more from the people trying to support me. Still, that's what I'm doing. I'm furious with my family, my friends, my entire network. I hate them because they've got everything I don't. I'm furious at the world and my lot in life. I'm incapable of being happy in this situation, and deep inside I hate myself for it, for becoming the kind of person I promised myself I'd never become.

Once we're at the beach, I realize we've missed Ivan's lunch, which is probably why he's so hard to please right now. He's whining in the sand, doesn't want to eat the banana I try to entice him with, and isn't interested in his beach toys. He bursts into tears constantly, throws his sun hat away, and won't stay in the shade. In frustration, I run off, quietly and still furious, in search of a restaurant that serves something Ivan might like. I struggle not to scream when the stroller's wheels get stuck in the sandy tracks as I push us forward on the path between the beach and the restaurants we passed by on the way here fifteen minutes ago. I swear silently and turn the stroller, pulling it behind me toward our goal. I wonder if that's what I'm doing with my life in general, moving backward. Right now it sure feels like it.

After a third of a hot dog and a few french fries, Ivan is tired and needs a nap. The time is approaching noon. The sun is bright, pierces the hood on the stroller, and no matter how carefully I steer, I can't keep Ivan in the shade. I need to find somewhere to walk that's both shady and flat. I text my family, still on the beach, that I'm taking Ivan for a walk. I tell them to eat lunch if they're hungry and that I'll let them know when he's fallen asleep. I haven't eaten since I woke up at seven this morning, but that's a problem for later. I'm used to putting Ivan's needs before my own, and my body's used to working on reserves. I've lost weight over the last year, and seeing my ravaged body in the mirror comforts me in some way. I look like shit. I look like I feel. But my body keeps on going; through wet and dry, it keeps marching on. Today is no exception.

The little path I found is getting narrower, and there are more tree roots in the ground. The stroller bumps along, and the front wheels hit the roots more and more often. I try to see how the path looks farther ahead—surely it gets flatter after this slope. I stomp on. Avoiding the roots, trying to find a pace that will put Ivan to sleep. The stroller ride gets even bumpier, the roots arrive more often, and the path becomes even trickier to navigate. For the second time today I start swearing under my breath. Why wasn't this information offered on the sign at the beginning of this path? Why can't the birds just shut up? Fucking hell.

I decide to turn around. I'll eat lunch some other time. We need to get back up to the road. Otherwise it'll be a nightmare to maneuver his stroller from the beach. Otherwise I won't be able to deal with the consequences. Using the last of my reserves, I manage to find a forest road where cars pass by only occasionally. With my jaw clenched, I hum the lullaby I use to put Ivan to bed at night. When he closes his eyes and falls asleep, it's been more than an hour since we started our walk. I count nineteen days and eighteen nights until he starts preschool and the next phase of our life begins. I think, Surely it can't be worse than this. Soon my eighteen months of parental leave will be over. Something new is on its way. Please let it be easier. Please let me become a better human being, a better parent, a better friend, and a better daughter then.

August 2015

I'm on the subway, on my way to the city to meet my sister-in-law after she gets off work. I'm in an unusually good mood. It's Wednesday, and tonight my brother and sister-in-law are coming over to our place for dinner, which means that this is the best night of the week. Hanging out with them doesn't offer much in the way of surprises, but our nights together are cozy, make me feel less lonely, and we have an established routine. First my brother and I decide over text what we'll eat for dinner. Sometimes we buy a bottle of wine; other times we drink water. We meet just after five o'clock, and Ivan positively glows whenever he catches sight of his uncle. We walk together to our apartment, and my brother plays with Ivan for a while before heading into the kitchen. While he cooks, I switch between talking to him, playing with Ivan, setting the table, serving wine, and tidying up in the kitchen. We have an early dinner, and Ivan is usually in an excellent mood. After dinner, my brother puts on a pot of coffee, asks me if I want a cup, and I say I do even though I don't. We move to the living room, and he sips his coffee. I don't really drink mine, but I put it to my lips now and then. After we drink our coffee, it's time for me to put Ivan to bed and for my brother and sister-in-law to head home. Our evenings end early, at barely half past seven. A total of less than three hours. But they happen regularly. And they are a secure tradition I have come to build my life around.

Today the sun is shining, and my sister-in-law and I have decided to walk through Gamla Stan on our way to Södermalm, buy some food and wine on the way, and then meet my brother at my place when he gets off work. My sister-in-law has become part of the family in recent years. During that period right after you died, she was at my brother's side, and thus also mine and Ivan's, almost twenty-four hours a day. But even before we lost you, we spent a considerable amount of time together. Hanging out with them is uncomplicated. We rarely talk about serious things. As we walk with Ivan in front of us in the stroller, I ask her about her day at work. She talks about the customers she met and the new products she's thinking about trying. She works in beauty care. I'm not particularly interested in the subject, but I listen hungrily to everything she says. Conversations with adults are rare occurrences in my life.

As we cross the bridge that connects Gamla Stan to Slussen, our conversation slips into ideas about the future. I ask if they're saving money for a trip. They usually are. Just like you and me, they love traveling far away together. They usually have some future date circled on their calendar. I ask what their next trip is, but my sister-in-law doesn't answer the question. Instead, she avoids meeting my eyes, sighs, and stops in the middle of the bridge. I stop too, and we stand facing each other on a footpath that overlooks Riddarfjärden with subway trains rolling by. She puts her hand on my upper arm, and I look into her eyes. She seems embarrassed or sad or regretful—I can't decide which. Her hand is cool against my arm, which is sticky from sweat after pushing the stroller under the August sun. I look at her and wonder what she's about to tell me. She meets my eyes, takes a deep breath, trying to say something she doesn't know how to say. Then she says it anyway.

"We're moving to Umeå. In three months. We've been offered an apartment—a large, rent-controlled apartment—and we've decided to take it. I've wanted to move home for a long time, and your brother wants to go. We've known for a few months now. He's felt bad about leaving you and Ivan in Stockholm so didn't want to tell you until you got on your feet again. I know this is hard for you. You two are so close. And you've been through so much. I'm so sorry."

Tears started streaming down my face as soon as she started talking. They're already dripping into my mouth and down my chin and onto my shirt. I'm standing with my hands on the stroller's handle, frozen in the same position I was in before she started her monologue. Silent in the face of this news. Though I sometimes managed to nod. I listened to what she said, and I could hear how logical it is. I should be understanding. Say it's okay, I get it, of course you should move, how exciting for you. I should say that, but I can't. My mouth cannot form the words. And the thoughts forming behind my mouth and my weeping eyes offer me no support. All I can think is: No. You can't move. You're not allowed to. You just can't. I can lose anything, anyone, but not my brother. Not him too. Now I have no one left. Now I'm completely alone.

My sister-in-law hugs me. We stand there on the pedestrian bridge, and people have to swerve to make their way past us. She holds me, says she understands how hard this is for me, tries to comfort me with the promise that they'll visit often and that it's only an hour plane ride away, and we can visit them as often as we like. She says it's all going to work out. It won't make such a big difference. I still can't answer. I don't say what I'm thinking because what I'm thinking is grim and has no place in this new reality.

I'm thinking about how now my brother will never be Ivan's rock. My brother won't meet Ivan regularly during these formative years. He'll never pick him up from preschool, and our weekly dinners will come to an end. We'll promise to meet often, but we won't. Because Umeå is seven hundred kilomenters from Stockholm. Life will get in the way. Plans and money and distance. Once again I'm losing something I took for granted. I feel stupid for taking it for granted. I should have known better. I'm an idiot. An idiot standing on the bridge between Gamla Stan and Slussen.

"Almost nobody knows about it yet," my sister-in-law tells me. "Your brother wanted you to know first. He's been so worried about you. He needed to see you get back on your feet. When we move, it will have been a year since Aksel died. You'll be back at work again, and Ivan will be in preschool, and everything will feel better than it does now. It's a long time until we move. Three months is a really long time. It's all going to work out," she promises me again.

Her promises land in the air between us, and we finally start moving forward. I manage a nod but still can't bring myself to look at her. I keep my eyes straight ahead, on the stroller and the back of Ivan's head. Curse my brother for his cowardice and his betrayal, curse my sister-in-law, curse the city of Umeå so far north, curse the whole damn world and all the people in it. Curse myself and my lonely, pathetic life. Increase the pace of my steps. My sister-in-law almost has to jog to keep up.

We make our way through the evening, and I cry a few more times, but not many and not for long. The atmosphere at dinner is oppressive, and our conversations flow sluggishly. I don't want to talk about what I'm thinking. Whatever we start to talk about I stop listening to after just a moment. I alternate between anger, sadness, resignation, and a vain desire to restore my pride. Anger that they let me down in order to devote themselves to their own lives and future. Sadness that I'll be alone again. Resignation because I might as well learn once and for all that nobody stays. Not in my life, anyway. A desire to restore my pride because I'm fed up with being a victim. Somebody who's always in need of help. A charity case.

———————

At Ivan's preschool, there are no adult-sized chairs, so I'm squeezed into a child-sized chair made of braided material. The chair is so low that I have to hunch over with my knees crammed in under the little table, while my coffee cup sits surrounded by the scattered crayons and notebooks from this morning's activities. I'm drinking coffee with another parent. It's my third and final day helping Ivan transition to preschool, and today something happened that I never thought possible: Ivan fell asleep at nap time. He did it in a crowded room whose floor is covered with mattresses, whose walls are lined with pillows, and with twelve other one-year-olds and just as many parents surrounding him. I'm so exhilarated I can't stop talking; it doesn't matter who's sitting opposite me. I have no idea which child's parent I'm unburdening myself to, but it doesn't matter. The important thing is that Ivan fell asleep. My child, who's never fallen asleep other than in a dark and silent room or rolling in the stroller surrounded by monotonous sounds, fell asleep in a room with other children and adults. It's inconceivable, unparalleled, magical! I've already sent the big news to all of Ivan's grandparents, his aunt, and even a few friends.

When we took a round introducing ourselves on the first day, I realized I was the only single parent in the group. The parents of the other twelve children were all alive and together. Maybe I imagined the mood changed after I introduced myself as Ivan's mom and quickly added that he didn't have a dad. Maybe the teacher wasn't hasty in moving on to the next parent in the circle. Maybe it was just in my head that some of the parents cocked their heads a little and nodded encouragingly, as if to prove they didn't think it was weird or sad that we lived alone. I was nervous, so it's hard to say for sure.

The father opposite me seems nice. He's drinking his coffee slowly, listening patiently as I keep repeating how I never thought this was possible. "Imagine that our kids are so big they're in preschool now! Just think, they can actually sleep in a group. They might become friends with each other. They'll have their own world where we can't follow them." I almost get tears in my eyes when thinking about it. The father nods. He agrees with me. Time has gone by so fast since they were born. "That's how it is with small children," he says, "things happening all the time." I have a sudden impulse to share our story, and before I consider that it might change the mood in our hour of triumph, I've already told it. "Ivan's father died just a year ago" comes out of my mouth, "and we've lived alone ever since. This will be the first time I'll be away from him," I say. "We've become very close," I explain. Still in a good mood.

The kind father doesn't know how to react to this information. He says, "Oh," and, "I'm sorry. That's very sad to hear." He doesn't ask me any questions about how or why, and I'm thankful to him for that. I don't feel like going into detail; I just wanted to say it. I wave away what I suspect is his discomfort with the answers to the questions he doesn't ask, and I say, "We're okay, me and Ivan. We've just been through a lot lately. This will be a welcome break, and furthermore, it's so important for Ivan to build relationships with new people, people he feels safe with, who he can seek comfort from." The father nods and says he understands. I stress that I'm looking forward to the future. I point out everything that's good about this situation. "It's such a great preschool," I say. "They're so good at what they do." The father agrees. "It seems like a fabulous preschool." The conversation is back on solid ground.

On the fourth day of preschool they've arranged boxes for the children's clothing in the hall, and above each one hangs a picture of a child taken on the first day. Above each picture they've written the child's name, and beneath, the name of the child's parents. The word "parents" appears on every sign, including Ivan's. Parents, plural. When I see that picture of Ivan, his cheeks wet with tears, his expression miserable, along with the words "Parents: Carolina," I freeze. Without even thinking, I break off my journey to the classroom, where today Ivan will be left alone by me for the first time, and take the stairs up to the office of the preschool's principal. I knock, ask if I'm disturbing her. I'm invited in a friendly way and assured that I'm not.

My intention is to as carefully and tactfully as I can ask them to change Ivan's nameplate so that the word "parents" isn't plural, but it doesn't really turn out like that.

Instead, I start to cry and list every single thing this week that hurt me. I tell her about the sign and how sad Ivan looks in the picture, how lonely my name looks after the word "parents," and how all the other children in Ivan's group have two parents while Ivan has only one. I tell her how every day after we're done I've wanted to call someone, talk about our day, and I've ended up staring at the phone in my hand, because the only person I really want to call is Ivan's other parent, the one who's no longer here. I tell her how I've listened to the other parents at the end of each day, heard them argue about whether their children should go home or go to a park and play. Then I tell her how I don't have anyone to discuss those things with, try to explain how that in combination with the sign, which just seemed to scream my loneliness into the hall of the preschool, is just too much for me. Then I apologize for crying. Emphasize how wonderful I think the school seems and how grateful I am that Ivan got a spot here. The preschool principal is a very kind woman. She promises to change Ivan's nameplate today. She apologizes, says the mistake is theirs and that I'm welcome to call her or book a meeting if I ever have any more thoughts or issues. She even thanks me for coming to her.

When I arrive at the preschool the following day, the sign has been changed, and now it says "Parent" followed by my name beneath a picture of Ivan. They've changed the picture too, and a happier Ivan without any trace of tears on his cheeks is staring into the camera. I try to figure out if it makes me happier, but I don't feel anything. Other than a drop of shame for my outburst in the principal's office yesterday.

September 2015

Our transition week is complete. The faux pas with the name-plate has long since been forgotten—at least that's what I pretend when I drop him off or pick him up at preschool with exuberant thank-yous to all his teachers for doing such a great job. I'll be going back to work again soon. My two-week break between being home with Ivan and going back is over in just a few days. Unfortunately, I don't feel particularly rested or recovered. That long-awaited sense of freedom has yet to arrive. Instead, I now live with an insatiable anxiety about being away from Ivan all day long. When he cries as I leave him in the arms of a teacher who's trying to comfort him, and I force myself to leave, every fiber of my being screams that it's wrong. I don't feel free at all. Sometimes I stop just a block from his school and cry too. Then I wish I could call you. Then I miss the co-parenting I think we would have done if things had turned out differently for us.

You should be here now. You would have talked sense into me whenever I considered never going back to my job, whenever I thought I was the world's worst parent for leaving my weeping and desperate baby in some stranger's arms. When my nerve failed me, you would have taken over. You would have dropped him off at preschool in the mornings, and when I called you just seconds after you left him, you would have lied just a little to make it easier for me. "It went well," you would have said, even when it didn't. But I would have seen through you, and you would have admitted he got upset again today, but then you would have convinced me that this wasn't harming our son. You would have told me for the thousandth time that there's no danger in being a little sad. You would've said, "He'll do great at his new preschool. It's just a phase. It will be over soon." I would not have totally believed you, but still your words would have relieved me of some of my agony.

Now I don't have anyone to call. So I cry a block from the preschool and then head home. Take out my phone to call them and see if Ivan's okay, but stop myself. I can't call all the time. I can't be that parent. They have more important things to deal with than a worried parent. I have to trust that they know what they're doing. They have experience with all kinds of children and parents. We're not the first to find it difficult to leave each other in the mornings. I have to tough it out. Maybe it's harder for me than for him. I find comfort in the words of other parents, parents with more experience than me, who say a transition period is very stressful even for the adults. That those days of transition are as much for the parent as for the child. It's natural for me to feel this way, I think. Unlike most parents, I have no experience whatsoever of being away from my child.

October 2015

The first anniversary of your death arrives on a Tuesday, just a regular Tuesday. I leave Ivan at the preschool and take the subway to work. I've decided not to say anything about the anniversary. I don't want any hugs, anyone's compassion, and I definitely don't want to start crying. I want to work, dig down into my tasks, let the hours go by, and pretend everything is the same as usual. Even though it's not. When I open the door to work and jog up the stairs toward my office—late as usual after a long and tearful goodbye at preschool—I hope nobody at work has noted the date on their calendar. I realize that clearly won't be happening as soon as I reach my computer.

On my desk sits a small dish with a cinnamon bun on it and a handwritten card. A beautiful bun—large, splendid, probably made with generous amounts of butter and purchased at a real bakery and not a grocery store. Before picking up the card, I glance around the office, but nobody looks up. I pick up the card as I sit down at my computer, hiding behind my screen. Written on the card in neat letters:

Dear Carolina! No need to talk about it, but I wanted to give you a bun and a hug on this day. K.

The card is from a colleague I don't know particularly well, someone who is obviously a thoughtful person and somehow remembered the anniversary of your death. I'm moved to tears by the gesture and struggle not to let them overflow. No crying at work. No making a scene, no making people uncomfortable, don't let them pity you. Not today. These commands to myself seem to work because no tears overflow, and instead I focus on opening the email program on my computer. I write an email to my colleague, who works in the room next to mine, and offer my warmest thanks with capital letters and exclamation marks. She responds quickly with a virtual hug back. Then we don't write anything more to each other. Nor does anyone else talk about it. The person at the neighboring desk doesn't even ask where I got the bun, which makes me suspect that everyone knows but says nothing.

At lunchtime another colleague offers to treat me to lunch. In a neutral tone, he says it's his turn. Because I like this colleague and don't have any other plans, I say yes.

Over pizza, he approaches the subject by first saying we don't need to talk about it, but he wants me to know he's there for me. He tells me that he lost a member of his family when he was a teenager and says he knows what it's like to carry grief in a family. He emphasizes that there's no right or wrong way to grieve, and he knows that everyone does it in their own way. I don't know how he manages it, but he makes me feel calm. There's no pressure to talk. Still, we do talk about it a little. Then we eat and discuss other things. I laugh several times.

I don't talk to your parents during the day, even though we're in contact often these days. They pick up Ivan from preschool one day a week and take him to my place so I can work later. On those days I pick up dinner on my way home from work and we all eat together, then they head home, and I put Ivan to bed. We've found a system that seems to work for all of us. They see Ivan regularly, and I can work a bit longer and meet them over a regular dinner at home. We text and call each other frequently. They've become the adults that Ivan sees the most, besides me and his preschool teachers. I think of them as part of our family. But on the anniversary we don't speak. On the anniversary we just text that we're thinking of each other, and then we let it be. Even in our grief we seem to be finding a way to make it work together. When it's at its worst, we give each other space, in a sort of unspoken agreement that works best.

That evening two of our friends come over, and we make meatballs and mashed potatoes. We used to tease and give you a hard time about it when you were still alive. You always used to order it when we went out to eat. You didn't like seafood and always made the safe choice. We used to say you were ordering from the kids' menu, but you never seemed to take it personally. And you always ended up ordering meatballs with mashed potatoes and lingonberry jam, almost on principle. You'd drink a low-alcohol beer if we were at home and a regular beer if we

219

were at a restaurant. In your absence, it's become a tradition for us to eat that meal every time we celebrate or remember you. On your birthday and on the anniversary of your death. Ivan loves it.

The evening is pleasant and not sad. Even when we toast in your honor and Ivan draws a face in his mashed potatoes, it feels nice. We laugh at Ivan when he shouts "*Cheers*" with a sippy cup in his hand. My friends take care of both the cooking and the dishes. I don't have to do anything at all. After my friends leave, I let out a sigh of relief, feel like I've gotten through this day admirably. We've completed the first. Many more are to come. But it will get easier.

Only after Ivan has fallen asleep do I cry. I look at pictures of you on my computer and try to call forth the memory of you as my partner, the person who was in my everyday life, the one I shared everything with. I try to imagine what our life would be like now, how you would be in the role of Ivan's father if you had lived. Then I think about the year that's gone by. I browse through the hundreds of pictures I have of you in my computer but rarely look at. I zoom in on your face and think about what a beautiful person you were. And how rarely I told you that. I cry for a bit, but I'm soon filled with contempt for myself because it wasn't easy to get it out. I feel ashamed that my tears are more about self-pity and not about unselfishly missing you. After a few minutes in front of the screen, I get up and shut down the computer. In the same movement, I stop crying. It's time to put away the last things in the kitchen, start my evening routine, head to bed, and finish the day. I'm looking forward to falling asleep tonight and waking up to a new day tomorrow. A next day.

December 2015

I'm walking across the meadows you grew up in, through the biting wind, hurrying so I don't miss my bus back to the city. I just handed my sleeping child over to your dad, who pointed out that this is the first time he's taken a walk alone with Ivan, without either your mother or me at his side. He looked proud when he told me that. Straightened his back and waved to me happily when we parted. He told me one last time not to worry, just to relax and have fun at my company Christmas party. "We'll take care of everything. Remember, we've raised four kids of our own. This is nothing."

I turn to watch them disappear over the meadow that leads to their house, and I hope he's right. I feel a twinge of guilt. Is it really okay for me to go to a party when Ivan threw up as recently as this morning all over the bathroom floor, and every diaper today has been more disgusting than the last? After the guilt comes the worry: What if your parents don't check his diaper before putting him to bed? What if he can't fall asleep without me by his side? Is it really a good idea that the first time he stays there overnight is while he's recovering from the stomach flu? But it doesn't matter now. It's too late to change my mind. Now just minutes remain until the bus picks me up and takes me to the city and my office, where my colleagues are waiting for me to start the annual Christmas party.

Once I sit down on the bus, I'm overcome by a sense of freedom. I feel like I've escaped. The feeling that no matter what happens to your parents in the countryside, I can't be there to change his diaper and wipe away his vomit. I need a break now.

I manage to pop into a clothing store and buy a glittery top on my way to work. The party's theme is "Glitz and glamour," and I've probably never felt less glamorous than right now. I don't own anything glitzy or glamorous. I'd decided to ignore the theme and go as I am, but then I saw my reflection in a display window, and what I saw was no fun. A tired face, pale cheeks, and unbelievably big bags beneath my eyes, a pilling knit cap, and an oversized coat that once belonged to you. In the store, I head straight for the first sparkly shirt I see, pay, and hurry out. Every minute is important now. Your parents could call me back to their house at any moment.

There's a buffet at the Christmas party. Two of my favorite colleagues are seated on either side of me. One seems to be as thirsty as I am; we toast frequently, sharing a bottle of wine between the two of us. The volume of the conversations in the room gets progressively louder. I'm laughing and enjoying myself. Soon I have to take the bus home. I told your parents I'd be at their house by eleven.

At half past nine I get a text from your mom. She tells me that Ivan is sleeping peacefully now and his stomach seems much better. I celebrate the news by opening another bottle of wine and toasting with my colleague. Now it's time for a music trivia quiz. The questions aren't very difficult, and my years in the music industry come in handy. My team wins a bottle of champagne. We open that too, toast again. The time is approaching half past ten, and I know I need to start heading home. But the party just got going. And I'm having so much fun. I don't want to go home. I drag out my exit. End up in a conversation with a colleague I rarely talk to. I ask her what her secret is, how she managed to stay married to the same man for twenty years. The conversation turns toward couples therapy, and we both agree that relationships are hard work. It feels like she understands me better than most. I want to be her friend. More colleagues join us. One of them announces that they've booked a karaoke room at a nearby bar. If we're going to be there by eleven, we need to start heading out. I think out loud: "I definitely can't join you." My colleagues try to convince me. One hour here or there, what difference does it make? Of course I have to go with them. I deserve it. I argue with myself. An extra hour surely won't hurt. If I take a taxi to your parents', I can be there by midnight. My boss tells me I have to go with them and that the company will pay for my taxi. I text your mom and ask if it's okay. She answers quickly: "Stay! Ivan's sound asleep." I go with them to the karaoke bar.

It's just after two in the morning when my taxi rolls into your parents' driveway. I've sung myself hoarse, and I surely stink of alcohol. It would be strange if I didn't. I sneak into the living room and see your mom lying reading beside a still sleeping Ivan on an inflatable double bed. I do my best to enunciate clearly as I speak to her. If she thinks I'm slurring, she doesn't show it. She's glad I had fun, she says, tells me good night and then heads down the stairs to their bedroom. I skip brushing my teeth and washing my face, slip out of my glittery clothes, and slip into bed next to Ivan. I'm still wound up. I smile in the dark at my memories from this evening. Note that I still have it in me. I can still have fun with friends on my own. I can still dance on chairs and tell jokes that make people laugh. I can spend a night with my friends without tripping over what I've been through, without dwelling, without needing anyone's pity or kid gloves. I'm still a person after all that's happened.

January 2016

Sometimes I wake up before Ivan in the morning. It happens more often than it should considering how badly he, and therefore I, sleeps at night. I should take every opportunity to sleep when it's offered, but still I wake up early every morning. And when I do, I never do what I should. I don't sneak out of bed and shower and get ready for the day that's about to start; instead, I lie where I am and stare at him. His features are beautiful when he's asleep. He looks so peaceful, in a way he seldom does in his waking state. His chin has a little dimple that's not visible when he's awake. He looks like you when he's asleep. His mouth forms a tiny smile. He seems satisfied with himself, like he knows something I don't. He lies on his back with his arms stretched over his head. His nightmares are mostly over; he no longer whimpers in his sleep. Sometimes I stare at him so intensely I'm surprised it doesn't wake him up. I look at him and wonder what his life will be like. I stare at him, and it awakens in me a love that's not all beautiful, a love that's filled with worry and powerlessness, which was the reason I had a hard time sleeping from the very beginning. I look at him and I long for him to wake up. Soon he'll turn two.

In Ivan's vocabulary you're a concept not a memory. For Ivan, you are Papa Aksel, who is dead. Ivan looks at the pictures of you that hang on our fridge and the walls of his room, but he doesn't understand who you are. Sometimes he asks if you're his uncle, especially when we look at the pictures when you're younger and have longer hair. Ivan knows that his father is dead, but he doesn't know much more than that. Not yet. He knows that his friends at preschool are picked up and dropped off by both mothers and fathers, but he still doesn't know why that's not the case for him.

When Ivan says that his papa is dead, there's no sadness or sense of loss; he states it as a fact. He just presents it as it is, and adults are the ones who react, who give his words meaning. In Ivan's world some children have a mom and a dad, some have two moms or two dads, and he has one mom. Me. Mama Carolina, who leaves him and picks him up from preschool every day. Mama Carolina, who takes care of him when he's sick with a cold or an earache or needs to go to the doctor. Mama Carolina, who sits up late with him when he's coughing. Mama Carolina, who wipes away his vomit and changes all his diapers. Mama Carolina, who rolls him to the park. Mama Carolina, who takes him on the train to meet his grandma and aunt in Uppsala and takes him on a plane to see his uncle in Umeå. Mama Carolina wakes up early in the morning and stares at him almost every day of the week. Mama Carolina worries and frantically tries to find a solution to how the next hour, day, or week will go by as painlessly and joyfully as possible. But he doesn't know that yet. What he knows, he takes for granted. I think that's good. I think he needs to be a child as long as possible.

When Ivan is awake, he's often anxious. He still hasn't got the hang of filtering sound input and reacts just as strongly to an airplane passing overhead as to a drill in a neighboring apartment. He's still sad when I drop him off at preschool in the morning and still sometimes has nightmares. It's become my full-time job, on top of my other full-time job, to provide him with a secure framework and stable routines. In doing so, I've become the kind of parent I promised myself I'd never be: the kind who constantly says no to parties that would be too stimulating or dinners that take place too close to bedtime, and I hardly ever use a babysitter because he doesn't seem to handle being separated from me very well.

The result is that we rarely meet people and spend most evenings on our own. I'm not happy that it's turned out like this, but I don't know who I can blame. My almost-two-year-old son is hardly at fault. That's why I have secretly started to blame the people around me more and more: my family, my friends, my social network, who have allowed my life to turn out like this. I'm furious with them for not regularly meeting us halfway. If they truly understood, they'd adapt more to us, come to our place more often. They wouldn't tell me to just bring Ivan along "and the rest will solve itself." They wouldn't casually offer that we're welcome to tag along; they'd understand we're in no position to tag along. If they understood, their dinners would start at four and end at seven o'clock. They'd keep me company in the evening, even if it meant a boring wait in the living room while I got Ivan to sleep, sometimes for hours. They wouldn't take jobs where they have to travel. They wouldn't move away. They would adapt to our needs and not content themselves with vague invitations and commands to holler if I ever want to tag along. If they understood, we wouldn't be as isolated as we are now.

In those forbidden thoughts no one is spared; everyone is strictly judged. I'm both ashamed and fascinated by how all my gratitude and humility evaporates in the darkness of the early hours of morning. I'm transformed into an angry and bitter person, jealous and envious, someone no one would ever want anything to do with if they knew. I don't share my thoughts with anyone, not even in the forums I've joined online for parents who've lost their partner. When other people discuss the same kind of bitterness, I don't participate in the comment threads. I don't want to admit to my self-pity in any way. It lives in a corner of my mind that no one has access to. It will remain there until I'm able through pure willpower to kill it and replace it with some other kind of thinking or feeling. I still hope it's just a matter of time. If I let time go by, let time do its thing, I'll grow out of these forbidden thoughts and return to being a normal person. Someone good-natured and grateful. I put a lot of weight on time going by. Getting through the days. Waiting myself out.

February 2016

It's Ivan's second birthday, and this year we're celebrating him at home, in our sixty square meters, surrounded by close family, which means a group of about twenty people, packed together in a not very large space. My own family is notably absent, my brother in Umeå, my sister busy with her own things, my step-mother traveling for work—to Ivan's great disappointment she's rarely around anymore. My mom will celebrate Ivan in a calmer setting later this week. It's fine, though, because the party is hardly shorthanded. People seem to be standing in line for an opportunity to play with Ivan, give him presents, or take pictures of him with their cameras. Most of the conversations are about him, his sweetness and intelligence, and how similar he's become to you. It's touching to receive so much support. That's how it is when you're popular, I think as I run back and forth between the coffee maker and the thermos. There are so many people here who love him, who want to celebrate him today. In your absence, he got twenty members of your family as compensation. That's not bad.

Even though we know each other well, I'm still not used to having them all together at the same time. So many people, so much noise, so many practical tasks. My ability to multitask is being put to the test, and even though I know it's unfair, I'm annoyed by this situation. The noise makes it difficult for me to hear Ivan, make sure he's okay, even though he's almost always in sight. It stresses me out. I'm unused to playing the role of both hostess and parent at the same time. I'm sweating profusely. My eyes dart between the floor in the living room and the conversations that keep being addressed in my direction. Keeping track of Ivan's state of mind and everything that encompasses, including diaper changes, mood, dirty hands, stumbling feet, acting as a wall between stimulation and overstimulation, is usually my only job, my full-time job when I'm free. Today I'm also a hostess. When I think no one's watching, I glance at the clock to see how much time remains of this two-hour party. One and a half hours.

Now your big brother tunes his voice in the living room. It's time to sing "Happy Birthday" to Ivan, who is looking around in confusion, searching for me among all the familiar faces that surround him in a ring. When his eyes meet mine, the rest happens in a silent mutual understanding. Three quick steps and he's with me, his arms stretched up, and I lift him so that his face is at the same height as the rest of his family, who are now singing at the top of their lungs. It's a little touch-and-go with the melody—hitting the right note has never been your or your family's strong suit—but they persevere anyway. I hold Ivan facing forward in my arms, and I look at each of your family members one by one as they sing.

There's your sister, who texts me regularly and always puts a heart beneath the countless pictures of Ivan I post on social media. Her eyes, which are glued to Ivan, shine with tears behind her glasses as she sings. I know she's thinking about how much he looks like you as a child. There's your big brother, who was the first person I called after I found you, who held me as we entered the bedroom to say goodbye to you for the last time. The one who cried and whispered "Little brother" to you then. The one who never mentions his sadness but who shows his love instead, who took time off from work to renovate our whole apartment before we moved in. There's your little brother, the one who looked up to you as a role model, who was the only one of us to give a speech at your funeral, who almost always shows up when I need a babysitter for Ivan, and the one who misses you so much he almost can't go to work some mornings. There's your dad—he sings the most loudly of all and never hits a right note. Your dad, who constantly tells me that he loves me and Ivan, and says that our mere existence gives his life meaning. Who brings Ivan to his workshop and teaches him about motors and saws and drills, who crawls around on the floor for hours with Ivan, who paints and sculpts clay figures with Ivan. Who talks with you in his head in an inner dialogue just like I do. Who never hides his sorrow or his joy. There's your mom, your still so beautiful mom, who will never get over losing you. Your mom, who is always available for Ivan, who sleeps on our sofa when he has the flu and I'm feeling terrified, who takes him for walks in his stroller so he can fall asleep, even on those days when her body is aching—there she stands, singing. And your sister-in-law, your brother-in-law, your nieces and nephews—they're all here. Encircling Ivan in a tight ring, encircling me, singing so that it reverberates between the walls, overwhelming the silence and the absence, doing what they can and can't do: they're singing. And they're here for us, for me and Ivan.

I look at them, and Ivan looks at them. When the last note sounds, he starts to applaud, shouts, "*More, more.*" They start to laugh. We all shout "Hurrah" four times in a row. I pretend to throw Ivan into the air at each hurrah. Just like always, I use Ivan as a shield between me and the rest of the world. He's my reason not to cry. He's the meaning of my existence. He's my savior and my ray of light. He's our common denominator, what connects us, what we stay together for, what keeps us going, what we can love now that we don't have you to love anymore.

March 2016

It's still winter, but the days are getting longer. It's no longer dark when I pick Ivan up from preschool. Sometimes the sun's even shining as we roll down the avenue to our apartment, where I immediately start making dinner, roughly the five hundredth since you died, which we then eat while watching a green dragon character on TV, who still seems to function as a kind of Pavlovian signal for Ivan to put his spoon in his mouth.

It could be the increasing light or maybe the never-ending winter, but for some reason I'm starting to feel restless. And above all, I'm tired of being alone. My thoughts—especially my forbidden, self-pitying, and bitter ones—often end up at the conclusion that a new relationship would be the answer to everything. My loneliness. Our isolation. Ivan's insecurities. My restlessness. It occurs to me more frequently that I might be getting close to ready to meet someone new. I note how lately my grief has turned more often to frustration, and in that there's a restless energy. If only I could meet a new person to share my life with, it would solve most of my problems. Ivan's too. The meaninglessness would disappear. The loneliness as well. Also, my feelings of isolation, and the alienation I feel from my family and friends. It could all be remedied, and Ivan would get a new father figure in his life before he fully realizes how much he's missing.

Unfortunately, I have no idea how to go about finding someone new. I don't know how people meet as adults, when they no longer spend their weekends at concerts and clubs. I have no idea how to flirt and have a sinking feeling that my market value has fallen sharply since becoming a full-time single parent. I also feel like my grief has made me ugly. Or maybe it's the bitterness. Or lack of sleep. Or aging in general. Plus, the logistics are not on my side. I almost never have babysitting help except when I need to work a few extra hours, and I still prioritize Ivan's stability above evenings on my own. Besides, any new person I meet has to want to share a life not just with me but with my two-year-old son as well. I have a very hard time imagining who this person might be and a nagging feeling that the odds just aren't on my side.

My friends don't want to hear any of that. They become enthusiastic whenever I hint at the subject of meeting someone new. They say people meet every day in all kinds of ways. It will happen to me too. But first I have to let people know that I'm available. While sharing a short after-work drink, one friend takes matters into her own hands. She downloads an app to my phone and shows me how to use it with patient world-weariness. The app is overflowing with the faces of men; according to my friend there are thousands to choose from. I feel like some kind of elderly Luddite sitting next to her, watching her tap away on my phone's screen.

When I got together with you, nobody we knew met people online. At least none of my friends did. At that time people met at parties and clubs, at concerts and after-parties, usually through common friends. If somebody caught our eye, we might send them a friend request on Facebook, but that was the extent of it. For the most part, the procedure was always the same, at least for me. I drank a little too much wine, found some object for my attraction in the crowd, stared down said object, and the rest usually took care of itself. I remember being good at it once upon a time. In the absence of any classical beauty or feminine charms, I worked with a kind of artificial self-esteem and cunning charisma that usually did the trick. But that was a long time ago. Almost ten years now. You were the last person I practiced my skills on, and then life and death came in between. We were drawn together, stayed together, and time passed. Ivan arrived. You disappeared. The conditions changed. My former self-esteem is nothing more than a memory I can only vaguely re-create when I try. Besides, I'm extremely doubtful that the picture of a face on a phone screen can provide any reasonable basis for the kind of relationship I'm looking for. Still, my friend perseveres. This is just as good a place to start as any. Probably better. This is how it works nowadays. Might as well get used to it.

So I try to get used to it. Inside the app I'm able to click through hundreds of men's faces. My friend teaches me how it works: Swipe left, and the face disappears instantly; it means "No thanks." Swipe right, and it's the beginning of an invitation; we're given the opportunity to start chatting with each other, discover more, but only if the man also swipes right on me. It seems complicated at first, but I pick it up quickly. I make my way through picture after picture of men skiing, climbing mountains, grilling huge pieces of meat. I'm terrified by what I see. One by one they're sent left, straight into nothingness, and replaced by another picture, another man. The app seems like a never-ending game, and I'm fascinated by how many single people are walking the streets.

I've carefully chosen four pictures that I think represent me and my life without revealing too much: one is of me looking happy at a party; one is me at my computer at work, professional but relaxed; one is me crossing a street while drinking a smoothie—I think I look cute in that one—and finally there's one of me carrying Ivan, whose face is turned away from the camera but whose presence is clear. I hesitated for a long time choosing that last picture. Didn't want the fact that I had a child on my hip to scare away potential men who might otherwise find me, or more specifically my pictures, interesting. I wondered how outsiders would interpret the fact that I'm the mother of a young child, barely older than a year in that picture, but it means what it means: I have a child. It's a central and non-negotiable part of who I am.

I amuse myself with the app for a while in the early spring. I pass the time with it after I put Ivan to bed. It drives away the bitterness and the forbidden thoughts, and I do my very best to stay hopeful and positive. Something better might just be waiting behind this picture. Someone I could see myself meeting in the future. I keep swiping forward through the men. My thumb cramps from all the times I swipe left. I say no to men who are fishing, men who are climbing mountains, men who are skiing, men in expensive shirts and silly hairstyles. I say no to men who seem to drink too much, men who work out too much, men who are too young or too old. I say no to men with ugly glasses, men whose beards are too long, men who write ridiculous introductory texts about themselves. Bad spellers are thrown away and the sporty, outdoorsy types as well. If they're looking for someone to share an adventure with, they're discarded. Too many children of their own: discarded. I make my way methodically through all the men. In the end, there are no more to choose from.

In just a few weeks, I went through every single man in a hundred-mile radius, and I haven't made contact with a single one of them. Disappointed, I text the news to my friend, who can't believe what she hears. She asks me to prove it with a screenshot and I obey. The application shows an empty map and asks me to try again in a few days. "That's impossible," she answers, followed by a lot of exclamation marks. "You didn't find one person cute or even interesting?" I answer, shamefully, "No." She criticizes me, justifiably, for being overly picky. She urges me, severely, to start saying yes to life generally and to the men in the app specifically. Nothing will happen if I say no to everyone, because then no one can say yes to me. She emphasizes that swiping right on a picture doesn't mean I have to spend the rest of my life with a person. I know she's right. A profile picture is hardly something you can build a future on. But maybe I'm just incapable of finding my soul mate and life partner through an app. Maybe it will just have to happen some other way. I need to figure out what that is. That night I delete the app from my phone and decide to put the project on hold for a while.

April 2016

My friends say I have to start living a little, and I know what they mean is that I need to live a little more *without Ivan*. I need to hire a babysitter more often, go out more often, join them in the evenings. "You'll be a better parent if you take care of yourself," they say, and use graphic descriptions to support their arguments. The most common metaphor is the one about oxygen masks on airplanes. The adult has to put theirs on first, before the child's; otherwise you both die. Apparently that's how parenting works as well. A happy parent is a better parent. When I do something for myself, I'm automatically doing it for Ivan. I know my friends mean well. Your parents and my therapist say the same thing. I should go out more. I know that, but it still feels wrong. They're right in general but wrong about my child. They don't know him like I do. They think we're like any other family.

Any time I receive an invitation to a social event where children aren't welcome, I start formulating my excuse. Ivan's a bit sick. We'll be away that whole weekend. My mom will be here for a visit. I'd really like to come, but I'm having trouble finding a babysitter right now. I'll try, and I'll let you know for sure soon. Thank you *so much* for the invitation, though.

The last excuse is no lie. Ivan has one grandmother who recently had double-hip surgery and now walks with crutches, and there's no way she could take care of a child as active as Ivan. His other grandmother, my stepmother, has a new job that requires her to travel most of the time, so that's not really an option either. In fact, it's almost impossible to find any time that works for her. And Grandma and Grandpa babysit all the time, at least once a week, so I can work longer days, and I don't want to saddle them with any more hours. But the main reason I say no so often is something I rarely share with my friends. And that is Ivan.

Ivan is even more prone to separation anxiety now than before. Our drop-offs at preschool are still—two semesters after he started—one of the most difficult, heartrending parts of our life. The days I've been able to leave him without him clinging to my legs and weeping desperately while a teacher takes him from me can be counted with the fingers of one hand. Every morning I head to work feeling like I let him down, and every evening I try to compensate for my betrayal by being extra present, extra safe, extra at everything I think he needs. In that equation, I don't have the heart to prioritize my own time or myself. Nor am I able to explain how it feels without it sounding like it's my problem, my sensitivity, my weakness as a parent. I've noticed the looks when I've tried. I've imagined how my friends must talk about me behind my back. "Can't she just relax a little?" I imagine they say. Over time it's just seemed easier to use white lies and excuses.

But today one of my closest friends is turning forty. We've known each other since we were teenagers, and she gave me a heads-up about her party months ago. Tonight Ivan's aunt will sleep over, and just in case, I've arranged to stay at a friend's place too. I agonized all week and considered canceling. I vacillated back and forth and could never make a decision. But when Ivan left me this morning with a wave and a smile in the yard of the preschool, and soon after I got a text message from my sister telling me she was looking forward to spending the night with Ivan, I took it as a sign. I should go to this party. I do my makeup in the bathroom while drinking a glass of wine and listening to music on my telephone's speakers. I can hear Ivan laughing with my little sister in the living room. I almost jog all the way to my friend's apartment and hope I'm not the first one to arrive at her party.

I'm not. My friend's apartment is packed with people, and the guests just keep streaming in. I haven't had a chance to look at everyone, but those I've seen seem absurdly rested. Full of life, clean, unburdened. There are no bags under anyone's eyes that

I can see. All the smokers and the people who are hanging out
with smokers are gathered in the kitchen. The host and hostess
take turns running to the door to welcome more guests. In the
living room people are dancing to music I don't recognize but
which I guess must be fairly new. I have a hard time figuring
out where to sit. I don't feel comfortable enough to dance, nor
do I dare to push myself into the kitchen with the smokers and
their friends.

I head toward the children's room, a little nook between the
hall and the hosts' bedroom that has been furnished for the
evening with a disco ball and a few chairs and an armchair. I
find an open seat there and sit down among a small group of
people. I know one person there, who soon invites me into the
conversation. We talk about introverted versus extroverted personality types. Everyone in the group claims to be introverted. I
don't believe them, think their claims seem like boasts, but don't
disagree. I too admit that I'm an introvert. We agree that the
fact that we've met in the most secluded room in the apartment
qualifies us all. The conversation moves on to gender, and we
talk about women's ability to make and hold on to their contacts. I recognize this kind of conversation; I've participated in
hundreds of similar ones, but it's been a long time now. Suddenly it all feels meaningless. Like we're just posing, pretending
to be smart for each other, doing nothing but agreeing. Nobody is talking about anything real or important. My thoughts
wander off, and I realize I want to sneak home. I don't want to
sleep in my friend's guest room tonight. I want to sleep next to
Ivan. But I have to make this count. I can't go home yet. It's
not even eleven o'clock. One of my friends looks into the room
and asks if I want a refill of my glass. I don't really, but I say yes
anyway. Soon she comes back with a whole bottle of wine, says

we might as well keep it here. We seem to be having a nice time here in the kids' room.

I stay here the rest of the night. Sitting in the same chair, in the same corner, and talking to a constant stream of random visitors about parenting and relationships, about recipes for drinks and music videos, about social media and psychology, about cat people versus dog people. The people I talk to seem to like to sit there for about a half hour or fifteen minutes, then they're replaced. As for me, I never quite manage to get up. The corner has become my permanent position. The wine bottle next to me has long since gone dry. I think I was probably the one who drank most of it. I wonder if I'd be wobbly if I stood up now. When I look at the time and see that it's past two, I try it. Stand up, think I should dance a little in the living room before I go home. Only then do I realize that the party is about to die. There are almost no people left in the living room. The music is still pumping, but no one is dancing. A man I don't recognize is sleeping on the sofa. In an armchair, a woman is sitting astride a man I recognize but probably wouldn't say hi to on the street. I move on, disappointed, looking for my friend whose guest room I was planning to sleep in tonight. I'm starting to get a headache. The smell of smoke in the kitchen doesn't help matters. Bottles and cans cover the counters. The sink is filled with wet cigarette butts. Four people are smoking at the kitchen table. One lets out a piercing and artificial laugh. I leave the kitchen. In the host's bedroom, another man has passed out and is now sleeping stretched out on the bed. I realize that my friend probably left the party, and I consider feeling hurt that she didn't take me with her, but I don't have the energy. I'm suddenly in a hurry. I have to sleep so I can wake up and go home to Ivan.

———————

Even though the dating app was a disappointment, and the party I went to ended up as a minor social catastrophe, I can't quite ignore the increasingly intrusive feeling that something is still missing in order to complete our family. Something, or more specifically, someone. It doesn't matter how many times I repeat to myself that families can and do look different, mine still feels halved. Damaged and hobbled. As if there is something fundamentally wrong about it. Surely life isn't meant to be this lonely. The problem is that I don't know what to do about it. In the meantime, I've started exchanging letters with a man.

He's a widower and a single parent. We have friends in common, and therefore his name has come up in conversation in the last couple of years from well-meaning acquaintances who have suggested we meet, since we share such a unique experience and situation in life. When people have told me I should contact someone they know who lost a partner, I've felt rejected by them. When they've hinted that it would do me good to make a friend who understands what I've been through, I've taken it as their way of gently letting me know that they can't handle me anymore. That I'm too bitter, self-pitying, and depressed to be around. In my heart, I've promised myself never to complain around them again. I've thanked them for their thoughtfulness but secretly felt that I'd rather live the rest of my life alone than make friends based on the shared experience of the worst thing that ever happened to me. It would mean giving up on a new life and staying stuck in the past. That's how I thought, continued to think, until the day not so long ago when I decided to write to the widower.

Right after Ivan had fallen asleep and the usual restlessness overtook me, I looked him up on Facebook. It didn't provide much information. It didn't say he was widowed; nor were there any pictures of his child. We had only a few friends in common, and his photos didn't offer much for a spy with too much time on her hands. I was reduced to doing what I usually do in this kind of situation: analyze what I see and speculate about the rest.

Through the captions on pictures he'd shared I was able to conclude that he could spell and express himself in writing. He also seemed to have traveled a lot in recent years. He'd also shared some songs, and after listening to one, I decided he's into something I like to call dad music. From the pictures in Paris and London, I concluded he has expensive taste in food and wine. He might be a snob. Judging from the number of comments and likes under his pictures and status updates, I interpreted him as being either very well liked or subject to massive flattery. He definitely didn't seem to be suffering from a lack of friends. And there were no clues that he had lost his partner suddenly a few years ago and was left alone with their newborn daughter.

All in all, his profile, for reasons I can't explain to myself, made me both curious and a little annoyed. How did he manage to maintain such a rich social life as a full-time single parent? Who cared for his child when he was off traveling to London and Paris? When did he have time to drink all those expensive wines and eat all that award-winning food? Why didn't he sit at home grieving more? And where was his daughter, the daughter he'd taken care of alone since she was born? The whole thing was almost disconcerting. It was something I obviously needed to dig into more deeply.

In between two of Ivan's nightly wake-ups I wrote to him.

The message ended up a little longer than I'd intended; it took two long paragraphs to introduce myself and explain how we were connected so he wouldn't think I was a crazy person. Then it seemed strange not to explain my situation and the reason I wrote to him, which I barely understood myself, so that paragraph became pretty long as well. And then the letter needed a little levity. So I added a short paragraph at the end. The letter was so long that it felt instantly embarrassing, but I had no idea what to edit away, and since Ivan was starting to stir and whimper again next to me, I just sent it as it was. I told myself that there was nothing to lose if he didn't answer, and besides, there might not be anything to win if he did either, so all in all it kind of evened out.

He answered by the next morning. He thanked me briefly for my letter and wondered tactfully why I had written it. A reasonable question since that wasn't clear in my letter, even less so in the bright light of the morning after. In an attempt to be more concrete, I responded to his letter on the subway on my way from preschool to work. Wrote it like it was: I'm not sure why I wrote him. Maybe because our shared friend recommended I do so. And from there our daily letter exchange began.

This pen pal of mine is often quite vague. We share anecdotes from our lives with our children and make them sound a bit more good-humored than they are in reality. At least I do. We've touched on our losses without digging deeper into them. Neither of us seems interested in going into detail, not about our private lives right now or in the past. But we keep in touch. Wishing each other a lovely weekend when it's Friday or sending suggestions for songs to listen to every now and then. Sometimes three or four days pass by without a letter; sometimes messages whizz back and forth all day long. Neither has suggested meeting. I get the impression that he's living with someone but don't dare to ask straight out. He hasn't mentioned this person, but from the varying frequency of his messages, I assume he's busy on weekends and in the evenings. Of course he must be. But I'm getting more and more curious. I'm considering suggesting lunch one day so I can see what he's like in real life, but I haven't dared to yet. Maybe soon. Maybe not at all.

June 2016

I'm sitting on a park bench and staring out over Årstaviken. The stroller stands in front of me with Ivan asleep inside. I know I'll have a hard time getting him to sleep tonight—he rarely sleeps in the daytime these days—but I didn't have the energy to keep him awake. I was so bored. Today we've already visited three parks, and it's not even one o'clock. I've tried getting in touch with my friends, especially the ones with children of their own, so I could meet somebody and kill an hour or two this Saturday afternoon talking to another adult and letting the kids play with each other for a while. I haven't succeeded. My friends are all busy. Some of them have country houses they go to on the weekends. Some of them have other plans. Some are at birthday parties or museums. A few haven't answered my text yet. This is a typical weekend in my and Ivan's life, a weekend with no plans during which I struggle to fill the hours with fun things for Ivan, make them go by as pleasantly as possible for him. As for me, I'm drowning in boredom.

I should be used to this by now. But I haven't yet managed to get used to the feeling of sticking out, being excluded, being alone. Especially if it's a holiday or long weekend. But even a regular weekend sometimes feels heavy. On Friday afternoon, when my colleagues end their shifts and let out a sigh of relief after a long week at work, it's as if I'm about to start another kind of shift instead. Now begin two long days with Ivan, who's two and still just as intense as the day he was born, though more mobile and with more specific demands. If I haven't planned well enough how we'll fill our hours, they feel numerous, long, and terribly lonely. I don't like feeling lonely. I like talking about it even less.

When I reach out to my friends to ask about their weekend plans, I always try to sound cheerful. Act like I don't care. Ask what they're up to and hope an invitation pops up. When their answers roll in and they tell me what parties they're going to, or that they're headed to the country with family, or that they're going to a kid's birthday party, I answer as lightly as I can. "Fun! Talk to you later! Let me know if you want to meet up!" I don't want to be a burden to my friends, someone they include out of pity; still, I wish they did so more often. I wish I wasn't so lonely. It's a tough combination to maintain. I solve it by stubbornly trudging forward, continually sending out these cheery text messages, continuing to spend the days the way Ivan likes them. I say yes to most invitations that pop up during the daytime, take the weekends hour by hour until they're over and we can go back to our weekday rhythm again. I've got a better grip on that.

By now, we've visited every museum in the city. We've also spent several Sundays at Ivan's grandma and grandpa's place. We know every park inside and out. Since evenings spent alone are long, I try my best to keep us outdoors and on the go as long as the daylight and weather permits. We eat lunch on park benches

and at fast-food restaurants. Change Ivan's diapers under trees
and on sidewalks. We roll around the city trying to find things
to do, at least one excursion every day. But today I feel tired of
all that. Today I'm having a hard time suppressing that feeling
of isolation. Today we have no plans, and none of my text messages have led to anything.

On a park bench in Tantolunden, where I sit staring out
over Årstaviken's sparkling water and at the commuter trains
rolling over the bridges, I allow myself to dream of another existence. I dream that you are still alive, that we're two parents
who spend our weekends with Ivan. I dream about planning
dinners with another person, cooking with another adult, eating together, and clearing away the dishes afterward together.
Maybe we drink a glass of wine. Maybe we watch a show together. I dream of sitting in front of the TV in the living room
and hearing Ivan laugh with someone else in his bedroom. I
dream of being able to say yes to a dinner or a party with friends
after Ivan has gone to bed. I dream of how every Saturday and
Sunday wouldn't feel so long. I dream of an existence in which
the thought of five weeks in a row of vacation makes me feel
not panic but longing. I realize I have tears in my eyes from
dreaming, and I reflexively pull my hat down lower over my
forehead. I decide to stop dreaming because it just makes me
sad. My dreams are so simple and yet at the same time so far
beyond reach.

I take out my phone and look at the time. Ivan has been
asleep for about a half hour. I have to wake him up soon. Where
should we go? Should we go back to one of the parks or go
home? What should we do at home?

I open Instagram and scroll through the images in my feed. I
see families in the countryside, friends at a demonstration, some

friends who appear to be shivering over beers at a sidewalk café. Suddenly I see a picture from a friend at a nearby café, just a few hundred meters away. The picture is half an hour old. It hurts—isn't she one of the friends I texted this morning to see if she wanted to meet? Didn't she answer that she couldn't? I search through my text messages to check. I've contacted so many people that I've mixed up their answers by now. They've blurred together into a single chorus of "No, not now, maybe later, that doesn't work for us, but let's talk tomorrow." I see her name. Read through our conversation from this morning. She writes that they haven't made plans for today, but we can stay in touch. I decide that's basically the same as an invitation. Even though it wasn't exactly formulated in that way, surely I'm welcome to pop over and join them for coffee. The pier they're sitting at is less than a hundred meters from here. Surely that won't be considered an intrusion.

I have neither the strength nor the energy for pride right now. I'm so devastatingly bored. With determined steps, I start to roll the stroller with my sleeping child inside toward the café on the pier, where my friend is. Wondering if I should tell her I saw her picture on Instagram or if I should just simply go into the café and pretend I was planning to have coffee there too. I decide it's better to contact her first. In an exaggeratedly merry tone, I write that I'm on my way, that I saw she was at the pier, that I'm walking by and thought I'd just stop in. I'm going as fast as I can now. She responds that they are about to go home, her child needs to rest, he sleeps best at home. "Come by. We'll say hi outside," she writes. I'm already outside when I receive her message. I stop the stroller and wait. Maybe I can join her on her walk home. Get a few minutes of conversation with another adult today. It's better than nothing. I wait and wait. The insistent feeling that my life is pathetic keeps knocking, but I don't open the door for it. The shameful feeling that I'm clingy and pushy comes next. I can't cope with that either. I don't have any alternatives. And now here I am. I see her coming, and I burst into the hugest smile I can manage when I wave at her as she nears the door. My smile has probably never been so fake. Maybe she looks a little embarrassed to see me. Perhaps I'm imagining it. It doesn't matter. This is better than nothing.

In the evening, after the day that seemed like it would never end but somehow finally did, I write to him, my pen pal and now—according to me—potential soul mate, to suggest a lunch. In exaggerated and humorous terms, I describe my boredom, say I'm dying for some adult conversation with a person who understands how it can be. I suggest a date two weeks from now so as not to seem too desperate. Tell him we could meet at a restaurant near his home if that's easier for him. I know that he works from home while his daughter is at preschool. Driven by a desperate desire for something, anything, new to happen, I don't care if he thinks I'm pushy. I just want a change. A lunch with a letter-writing stranger with dorky taste in music works as well as anything else.

He answers quickly. "Sounds great," he writes. "Let me just check about a babysitter so we can make an afternoon of it. Maybe get something to eat. Have a glass of wine too."

When I receive his reply, my stomach flips. What just happened? Did this just become a date? What does getting a bite to eat and a babysitter mean? Should I get a babysitter too? Why should we get babysitters? Does he think it will lead to something more? Do I want it to lead to more? What if he's terrible in real life? What if he has bad teeth and a weird voice? What if he never stops talking about himself? What if he expects me to kiss him good night? Or, even worse, what if I become interested but not him. Nervously, in the most casual tone I can manage, which makes me sound like a stuck-up teenager, I answer affirmatively to his suggestion, and we decide we'll book a date after we've checked with our babysitters. After that, I scour the internet for photos and videos of him, and for the first time in seven years I try to imagine what it would feel like to kiss someone who's not you. I can't help it. It just happens.

Ivan is going through a daddy phase. He asks about you often, looks at pictures of you, roots around in the Papa Box, and calls out "Papa" when he takes old cards out of your wallet or finds your picture in an old passport. He says over and over again that you're dead, and it doesn't seem to bother him. He's content with that fact, but then a minute later he asks me when you're going to stop being dead. He's started asking about his grandfather as well, my dad. He's dead too. He seems to be trying to put it all together. His father is dead, and his grandfather, but not his mom and not his grandma. And not his other grandmas or grandpa either.

I can see that he's struggling to make sense of the whole thing, but it doesn't quite fit together for him yet. He's too small. Death is too abstract. His thinking is still so concrete. It didn't get any better when at first I appeased him by talking about heaven. I thought it might be comforting for him but soon realized that the follow-up questions were impossible to answer. When he points to the clouds and asks if you're in them, I don't really know what to say. I say, "Nobody knows for sure. People believe different things, but no one knows for

247

sure." When he says he wants to climb into heaven and I say that won't work, he says he's going to get a ladder. When he asks if you're sitting on the moon and disappointedly cries, "But I can't *see,*" I realize I'm in over my head. We can't keep talking about heaven in this way. As cautiously as I can, I try to take back the heaven thing. "That's just something you say," I dodge. "Heaven is something some people believe in, but others don't. Nobody knows what happens when you die. I don't know either," I fumble along. "Isn't that strange?"

Ivan looks at me with distrust. He is waiting for me to continue, but I'm silent, searching for some way to explain this that's easier to understand. But I fail, give up, try to distract him with conversations about people who are still alive. Talking about all of his grandmas and his aunts and uncles and grandpa. They're easy to talk about. My attempts at diversion work most of the time. But the questions about you are becoming more frequent. I have to get a handle on this soon. Become a little more consistent in my answers about where you are and what death means. Read books about how to talk to children about death. It's time.

One day this week, when I was picking up Ivan from preschool, something unusual happened when he saw me in the doorway. He's always so happy when I arrive, comes running toward me with a delighted squeal, but this time his face held the unmistakable look of disappointment. Then he exclaimed: "Not you, Mama. I want Papa to pick me up today!" Then he sat down on the floor and started to cry. One of the teachers cocked her head in the exact way I've asked them not to do when Ivan talks about death. The teacher's eyes betrayed a feeling of pity I want to spare Ivan from, but I realized I would never be able to protect him completely. From the feeling that someone feels sorry for him. From the feeling that he's weird or different. From the idea that because his family is halved he lives a sad life. That a person has to cock their head to the side at the mere mention of his fate. I stared at the teacher imploringly, trying wordlessly to make her stop.

It seemed to work. The teacher quickly recovered, her expression changed, and she straightened her neck. She headed over to my crying child while one of Ivan's classmates stood next to him, reaching out to pat his arm as they have learned to do to comfort a sad friend.

As for me, I answered without even thinking. Without stepping into the room and without changing my tone, I spoke as calmly as I could. "I know you want Papa to come pick you up, sweetie. I miss Papa too. It's really sad that Papa is dead—really, really sad. But you know what? You have me, and I love you more than anything else in the world. We're our own family, you and me, and you have a lot of other people who love you too. Your grandmas love you, and grandpa, and your aunts and uncles and all of your friends too."

Somewhere in the middle of my speech about who loved him besides just me, Ivan tore himself out of his teacher's arms and threw himself into mine. He landed across my knees and I lost my balance, went from a crouch to half lying on the floor. I continued to talk to him while stroking his hair and saying the names of everyone I could think of who also loved him. A few of the children in his group stood next to us, listening carefully to the names I counted off, and I felt Ivan relax, then start to look around at the little group of children that surrounded us. Just as I started to run out of names, Ivan got tired of my stream of words and informed me that flowers can die too. Actually. One of Ivan's friends filled in. She knew a dog that died once.

The teacher joined the group, and we all talked for a while about who can die. Flies and grandmothers and trees and a little sister who died in the stomach.

The conversation was tender. I was touched by the other children's stories about death. Surprised that a group of two- and three-year-olds had so many profound thoughts. The logic was shaky, but the thinking was there. The desire to understand, categorize the living and the dead. Suddenly we found ourselves having a conversation that was no longer about your death but about death itself. Ivan was part of the group of children who were now wondering if a bike could die, or a tractor. When we agreed bicycles could break but not die because they're not alive, Ivan was happy again. Ready to eat his banana, put on his coat, and head home with me, his mother, who loved him more than anyone else in the world, along with a group of other living human beings. On my way home, I wondered if I'd made a mistake in preventing him from grieving for you by talking about all the people who are still alive. Maybe I did exactly what you're not supposed to do. Maybe I should have talked more about you.

It's been a few days since the incident at preschool. Since then I've gone to the library and borrowed a couple of books about how to talk about death with little children. I also borrowed a children's book about a guinea pig that is very old and will soon die. I listened to a radio program on this subject on the subway during my commute. I've also talked to Ivan's teachers and booked a meeting with them to discuss how we should approach discussions about death. I can't think of what else to do. We'll take it as it comes.

I wonder if he remembers you at all. I wonder what he thinks when he looks at pictures of you. His interest in you seems to be based on a new type of comparison: most of the people he knows have a father, but not him. Only now is he realizing he lacks something his peers at preschool seem to take for granted. The more I think about it, the more confident I feel that his tears weren't about remembering and missing you but about not wanting to be different. It makes me sad to think that way. I will never be able to protect him from the feeling of being different. I will never be able to help him remember you on his own. Most of the books I read claim that a child's first memories occur approximately at the age he is now. He's been without you for more than a year and a half. He was a baby, still nursing, when you died.

I wish he'd had the chance to get to know you. That he could have grown up with memories of you, the real you, memories of how you were and sounded and laughed and smelled. I wish he'd had a personal relationship with you, one that lasted longer than eight months. I wish he didn't have to start asking questions about you that we, the people around him, will probably answer in our own and sometimes completely contradictory ways for the rest of his childhood. But that's just the way it is. It is what it is and it was what it was, and all I can do is prepare myself the best I can, read and try to understand and promise myself that I'll save my memories of you and always try to answer your son as honestly and in as much detail as I can when he asks.

My friends maintain their hesitance about how events are developing with my new pen pal. Our planned lunch has gradually turned into a dinner at a restaurant, and then into a cheese and wine night at his home. They think it sounds like I'm headed straight to the after-party. "Shouldn't you at least meet in a public place the first time?" they ask and raise a finger in warning. Point out that he could be a psycho, and the rule of thumb is a first meeting that's short and in public. As for me, I respectfully disagree with their caution. I haven't done anything that's even close to exciting in recent years. And they don't know anything. They haven't been part of our correspondence in the last few weeks. They can hardly understand how much we already know about each other. If he'd rather meet at his place, I'm not going to argue. We're just going to nibble on some cheese, drink a little wine. Talk a bit. Maybe I'll make a new friend who understands me. I'm not going to let the opportunity pass by insisting we meet at some restaurant or bar and only for a certain number of hours. I've arranged for a babysitter whose hours are flexible, and his daughter will be with her grandmother when we meet. I'm very excited about our meeting.

When I go to buy new clothes that day, I convince myself it's just because all of my clothes are so old and worn out, and not because I'll be wearing them when we meet. When I try on countless combinations in front of the hall mirror after Ivan has fallen asleep, it has nothing to do with the meeting—I'm just having fun trying on new things. When I shave my legs for the first time in almost two years, it's because summer will be here soon. Might as well do it now instead of in a couple of weeks. No other reason. Absolutely not.

———————

It's Saturday morning, and Ivan wants to go out. He wants to go to the park, says he wants to meet his friends. Which friends he's referring to is unclear to me; to be completely honest, he doesn't have very many yet. He's a child who still prefers adults to kids his age. But he's restless by nature. He never wants to be inside, in our apartment in Södermalm. He wants to go out. He stands at the door repeating the same phrase but with an impressive creativity when it comes to variations of word order. "Come on, Mama! Come, let's go! Mama, come! Come, Mama! Mama, let's go!" He puts on his pink shoes in the hall. Tugs at the door handle. His mouth running nonstop.

I'm on the sofa with yesterday's makeup under my eyes, greasy hair, still wearing the T-shirt I slept in. My chin is red and chapped, and specks of mascara come off on my fingers when I rub my eyes. I should at least put some makeup on before we go out. Definitely I should brush my teeth. I try to negotiate with Ivan for more time, tell him I have to drink my coffee before we can go, promise to take him to his favorite park if he settles down. It works somewhat. Still, Ivan refuses to leave the hall. I move slowly through the apartment, trying to make a plan for our day while simultaneously texting with my friends. It's a regular Saturday in June, nothing special, but I'm trembling inside in a way that I haven't for a very long time. My head aches from the wine I drank yesterday. My phone is vibrating constantly. For once, my life is at the center of discussion. The bat signal has gone out, and unlike the last time that happened to me, the news I now have to share with my friends is fun. They're excited, curious, want to know more, use exclamation marks and emoji symbols with balloons and streamers. I don't have time to answer. Ivan has managed to unlock the front door and is headed into the stairwell. I force myself up from my reclining position, run after him, carry him back inside.

What's new—so huge that my friends are texting me in all capital letters—is actually pretty commonplace. If it weren't for the context. If it weren't for the fact that over the last few years my life didn't offer anything at all on that front. But now it's happened. I slept with somebody. For the first time since you died, and if I'm being completely honest, for the first time since Ivan was born. And well, maybe it was a while before that too. We might be getting close to three years now. I haven't exactly been keeping count. My body hasn't complained about that specific break.

I don't know if it's strange that I haven't missed it since you disappeared. The thought of sex and relationships exhausted me, and I haven't had much desire. I didn't really know what it was I was supposed to be desiring. Sure, I've missed having an adult in my life. I've missed having somebody to share my thoughts about Ivan with. A person to talk to in the evenings after Ivan falls asleep. A person who can help me with the things I'm terrible at. But sex? Not really. Maybe it's as simple as I just didn't have room. Maybe Ivan fulfilled some of my need for closeness. Maybe I'm just a less physical person than most. Maybe I've pushed away any hint of desire because it seemed so hopeless. Probably it's a combination of all of the above.

Nevertheless, I did wonder how I would feel the day it finally happened. If it were to ever happen again. I was repelled by the faces I swiped away on the dating app. And in my vicinity, I've noted that everyone seems to belong to someone else. There's been no selection, and my desire has been anemic, or almost nonexistent. It seemed like meeting someone was a long way off. Or sleeping with someone. Ever again. But then it turned out just like everyone said it would. He appeared when I was least expecting it.

It was half past three o'clock in the morning, already light out on our avenue, when I stepped out of the taxi. Dazed, drunk, with a rash on my chin from another man's stubble, I ran all five flights up to our apartment, sent the babysitter home with a whispered apology for being so late, took myself to the bathroom, drank the mandatory glasses of water, and brushed my teeth. Snuck in to Ivan, who was sleeping in my bed, listened to his breathing for a while, snuck out again. Stood on the balcony, looking out over the alley.

It had been a long time since I was up this late for this reason. Everything in the world outside my house suddenly seemed painted in such intense colors. So alive. For a moment I felt like myself again. Not Ivan's mother, not a grieving widow, not a wounded person with a heavy past. Just a normal, tipsy, soon to be middle-aged woman who somewhat unexpectedly got laid. Memories bubbled up of a time when I used to find myself in the back of taxis intoxicated and full of adrenaline. It would soon be four o'clock, and the sun was peeking up at the end of the alley.

Back in the bedroom, I snuck in beside Ivan. Hoping my movements wouldn't wake him. Or my breath. We must have had two bottles of wine over the evening. Maybe even more. I didn't count. Ivan seemed happily unaware of my sins. He flopped around a few times and finally landed with his feet under my thighs. I put my blanket over both of us, closed my eyes but didn't sleep. Something inside me needed to relive the evening in my memory one last time. And then just once more. And then again.

His mouth when he smiled. His slightly crooked front teeth. How his laugh came suddenly and without warning. The way he looked at me when I talked. How I stretched out on his sofa, luxuriating in that look. His arguments about how he doesn't believe in talent, but how he's convinced everything comes down to practice. How he burst out and said that I was beautiful long before he kissed me the first time, when there were still several meters between us in the room. How he touched the scar on my ankle and said it was the most badass scar he'd ever seen. How I started joking with him, at first carefully, then more roughly. How quickly he responded to my jokes and turned them back on me. How we started to bicker. How quickly he switched from joking to seriousness. How out of nowhere he stopped joking and started asking me questions that were difficult to answer. How he didn't look away when I fumbled for words. How between our first kiss and our second he told me to text my babysitter and say I would be late. The stubble of his beard on my chin and my cheeks. His scent. His cologne, which I recognized but couldn't place, until later when I peeked into his bathroom cabinet and saw it was a perfume that I owned too. It smelled different on him. Better. His text to me while I was in the taxi on my way home. "Let's do this again," he wrote. My reply to his text. "Gladly," I wrote.

Time after time, I relived in my mind everything that happened, as if I were studying one last time before a test. Who knows what I'll remember tomorrow. Or what will be lost to the late hours of the night if I don't repeat it one last time. It must have been during the third replay that I finally fell asleep.

Not until today, back in my normal life and with Ivan and on my way out the door, do I think of you. A wave of guilt washes over me. I count how long it's been since you passed away and realize it's almost two years now. If you count generously. Actually, it's less. It's a year and eight months, but I choose to think of it as two years. It feels better than one and a half. Two sounds like less of a betrayal than one.

As I roll Ivan down our avenue on this sunny June day, I wonder what you would think if you were watching me now. I conjure up an image of you, tell you what happened. I want to discuss this with you, and I want your permission. I go straight to the point; no long introduction is necessary for this kind of dialogue. "I slept with someone last night," I say to you. "Are you angry with me now? Was I allowed to do that? Is it awful that I liked it?" In my head, you respond quickly. Surprisingly fast, you give me your blessing, which makes me think I've lost the knack, can call you up no longer as you were but as I want you to be. Either way, you approve of my actions. You tell me it's okay, it doesn't matter, go ahead. "As long as you take care of Ivan, you can do whatever you want."

In my imagination, I thank you for giving me your blessing and decide to stop talking to you in my head for now. I always feel a little insane when I do it. Besides: it was just one night. Maybe there won't be any more. It doesn't mean anything. I thank you for understanding, then focus on what's outside of me, in front of me, Ivan, the world, the sky and sun and city, and suddenly it all seems so inviting, as if I am a part of it rather than standing on the sidelines.

Then I take out my phone, and before I know it, I'm drafting a text message to him. I have his phone number now. And the code to his building. And probably traces of his bodily fluids inside me. I think about the things he said to me, did to me, less than twenty-four hours ago. As I turn into the playground, and Ivan's legs start to kick in excitement, I do it. "Thanks for last night," my fingers write. "I had a great time and I'd love to see you again if possible," those fingers continue. Then they press SEND. The message has been sent. Something flutters in my stomach. I can't stop smiling. Laughter almost spills out of my mouth, and I have to control my facial expression to keep from looking like a crazy person who just wanders around laughing to themselves as I continue to push the stroller forward, toward the swings in the park.

I put the phone back in my pocket, my heart still pounding. I run after Ivan. He's already at the swings, and I lift him up, sing his favorite song to him, trying to drown out my thoughts with that song. Ivan cries out in delight as I swing him high, up toward the sky. I laugh when he laughs, and another day in the park begins. Another day just like all the others, but not really. Because I slept with somebody. And you gave me your blessing afterward. I got your permission. And I sent a message to him and asked him if he wants to meet again. Otherwise everything is the same as usual.

———

It's been forty-two hours since I last heard from him, and I think about him all the time. Midsummer came and went, and he didn't answer my text. I feel like an idiot. An idiot who in my eagerness forgot to consider that he probably already has a girlfriend. An idiot who, without hesitation, let herself be kissed, seduced, and carried to a bed with wrinkled sheets that were most likely wrinkled by another woman, a woman who isn't me. I blame myself for being naive and try my best to smooth over what happened, make it into something less than how it felt. It didn't mean anything. It doesn't matter if it doesn't lead to anything. It just was what it was. A first step for me as I move on to a brighter future, even if that future isn't going to be with him. It's not a disaster if he doesn't answer. We were just having fun.

These commands to myself do no good. They feel like something a wise, but not particularly convincing, friend would say, which I'd nod at but not be able to internalize. I'm doing a bad job of overcoming and pushing away my desire for him, just him, which has arisen after our first meeting, and I'm filled with dissatisfaction that he hasn't answered my text.

I've kept myself occupied as best I can. For example, I've scoured the internet for any scrap of information about him. I've saved all the pictures I've found of him, both on my computer and on my phone. I've memorized his door code and phone number, even though I've been at his place only once and our contact via phone so far consists of only two texts when we were drunk and one text from me the day after. I've stared at his address on Google Maps, even changed it to street view so I could walk his street virtually, just as I did for real before our first and so far only meeting. I go to his Facebook page at least once an hour when I'm at work. I've considered adding him as a friend but haven't yet. I've stared at his profile image, trying to figure out why he won't answer my text. I've spent a great deal of time and energy going through his friend list, trying to interpret if the women who are generous with likes on his posts are current girlfriends, ex-girlfriends, or just friends. I spend time thinking up ways of slipping his name into the conversation if I were to talk to our mutual friend. I've torn my hair out thinking that if he doesn't answer me within twenty-four hours, then I'll fall apart. I even wrote a poem about him. No one can accuse me of sitting around twiddling my thumbs.

After more than two days, he finally answers. He writes, "Thanks for a good time," and, "Of course we should meet again." He says he has "a lot on his plate" right now but that we can try to meet in a few weeks. He ends with "xo."

His message is short. I memorize it at my first reading but still read it another ten times just to be safe. I answer with a simple thumbs-up—no more and no less. I think it seems like an appropriately enthusiastic response. I don't want to scare him away by seeming too eager. Only after I reply do I realize I did so in less than a minute, after it took almost three whole days to get a message from him. I fret over that. I'm in agony that my eager thumbs-up might make him less interested in meeting me again. I have devolved to the emotional maturity of a thirteen-year-old.

I'm not so dumb that I don't realize I'm projecting, that he's become, without him realizing it, something bigger than just who he is. He symbolizes what I dreamed about without me admitting it to myself. Something I longed for without identifying it as longing. I know that, but it doesn't change anything. I desire him every single minute, and I can hardly concentrate on anything but desiring him. Despite my almost thirty-eight years of experience, I can't reason with myself, can't focus on more important things. Like, for example, my job. Or my friends. Or my almost two-and-a-half-year-old son. And if he doesn't contact me soon again, I'm afraid I might go crazy.

During the first week it was easier in a way. Then I was alone with my infatuation and naive fixation on a man I didn't know. Then it was alive only in my imagination, and I didn't feel guilty about that. But after he contacted me again, suggested we meet that very evening, everything moved fast. My fantasy became reality, and from that reality the conflict arose. I can't keep my eyes closed in the face of reality: I'm the one who's making it happen, and therefore I'm the one who's responsible. I'm the one who texts immediately as soon as he contacts me. I'm the one who arranges for a babysitter, pretending to work late when he wants to meet me. I'm the one who spends all night talking on the phone after Ivan goes to bed. I'm the one doing it, and I have a stinging suspicion that I'm doing something wrong. Nevertheless, I do it again. And again.

My crush on him is so all-consuming that I don't know what to do with myself, and I have no one to share it with. I can barely cope with my own thoughts about it. I've stayed silent on the matter, but inwardly I've fixated on it and fantasized. All the while my brain has worked feverishly to direct this romance, which is what I assume it is, so that it's acceptable from an outside perspective.

It hasn't been even two years since you died. It's been a year and eight months, and I don't know how it can be assumed I should wait any longer, dammit. It's gone from being a non-issue to one of the biggest dilemmas in my life. Am I allowed to move on now? Can I move on now? Does that make me a cold, almost evil person, that I'm in love—yes, love—this soon after losing you?

On top of my internal obsession, external events are proceeding as if on their own. It's as if I have no control over things. For example, I can't stop myself from answering immediately whenever he contacts me. And he contacts me often. Several times a day. Sometimes it feels like our dialogue never ends except for pauses to deal with our various commitments to work and children. Then we pick up the thread again. We share a seemingly meaningless yet carefully curated stream of images from our daily lives: from the elevator and street and subway and work and the food we eat and the dishes we wash and our faces with open, foamy mouths when we brush our teeth. I'm still self-conscious about how I look in pictures; sometimes I edit them before I hit SEND. I read through our text threads, trying to see them from his perspective, get some sense of how I appear. I don't want to seem braggy. Or unintelligent. Or too neurotic. Clingy, even. I want him to think I'm smart and cool and funny. Because that's what I think he is. And brave and mature and intelligent and handsome. He's all those things, and I want him to think I'm all those things too.

I wait impatiently for his reply from the second I send my message until the second his reply arrives. If that takes more than a few minutes, I panic. The minutes crawl forward. They feel meaningless and empty until his answer vibrates my phone, and I start to function again, throb again. Then everything starts over. The days creep and rush at the same time. I do one thing after another that takes me closer to him and further from you, and I can't help myself. I had no idea I had so little self-control. I also had no idea I had so much free time. Or energy.

Suddenly days pass, and I don't even think about you. Suddenly afternoons with Ivan after preschool don't feel as heavy as they used to. When we play in the park and go by the grocery store and then roll home to start another evening in front of some kids' show eating our meatballs, I don't feel like the tragic figure I used to. On the contrary. I feel like an exciting person, someone with a secret life besides just my single parenthood. I have a man who wants me, who's waiting for the signal from me to call me as soon as Ivan's fallen asleep, a man who finds me attractive and fun to talk to. Suddenly I'm not just a mother and a grieving widow. Suddenly I mean something to someone other than Ivan.

In the evenings after Ivan has fallen asleep, we call each other. Our calls go on for hours into the night. His voice makes me feel calm and exhilarated at the same time. We already talk about everything, even though we've known each other for only a few weeks. When we finish a conversation, we ask the other one to hang up first. Wait in the silence, and neither hangs up. Start laughing and try again. Force ourselves to finish up, and then we send a few more text messages until we finally fall silent for a few hours of sleep.

I don't dare tell my friends how much we talk. Three weeks ago we didn't know each other, and to everyone else in the world, those three weeks were normal. For me, everything has changed, ripped out by the roots and turned upside down. Suddenly my function, the reason for my existence, is more than just being Ivan's mother. I want to savor that feeling, keep it to myself, don't want to expose it to the world, or not yet. Besides, I feel like some kind of naive teenager when I try to soberly express to myself the nature of our intense connection. I feel like I might blush just talking about him. It will be obvious how in love I am, and I don't want to admit that to anyone because it feels inappropriate.

When my friends ask if I've had any more contact with him, I confirm that we're in touch. Exactly how much that might be, I keep to myself. When the more perceptive wonder what's really up, how I'm feeling, and where this is headed, I say, "We'll just have to wait and see." Tell them, "Someone has appeared out of nowhere who seems to understand me, who also has a history of grief and loss, who seems to see things as I do. Someone who makes me feel less lonely and makes me laugh." I say, "He might be my soul mate or might end up a good friend, maybe the kind of friend I keep for life." Then I change the subject because I don't want to admit how much it means to me already.

Your parents don't know anything. I'm not brave enough to tell them I've met someone who isn't you. Someone who's not just not you but not like you at all. A fearless person, a person who moves fast, a phone person, someone who wants to try everything, talk about everything, and doesn't seem to be afraid of anything at all. Someone who oozes words all over me that no one has said to me before. Someone who knows just like me that life can change in an instant, who knows there's no reason to wait when something feels right. I don't dare say that it feels right. That it gives me hope. Not to your parents, especially not to your parents. Not without anguish, I recall how recently I told them I thought I'd never meet another man and that I had reconciled myself to that thought. Now I feel like those words are a promise I'm breaking, a double betrayal. I'm betraying not only you but also your parents.

The fact that I fell for someone who's not at all like you feels like conclusive proof of my inability to love you just as you were. I wonder if I can keep this a secret forever. No matter what happens, that's a question for later. For now, this is our secret. What I do in the evenings after Ivan has fallen asleep is still my business. In one way, I hope it will soon end, prove to be a short-lived love that fizzles before I have to expose it to the world. It would be so much simpler in so many ways. But on another level, that feels like the worst thing I could imagine. I am very confused. I am very infatuated.

July 2016

He's the same age as me. He's much more experienced than me. He's been a single parent longer than me. His child is older than mine. He's had longer relationships than me. He's straightforward and doesn't mince words. He's not afraid of big gestures, or emotional statements about love and grief and dreams of a shared future together. When he talks, he talks quickly, spitting his words and thoughts out at a furious pace. When he writes, his language is poetic and filled with antiquated expressions that make him sound like someone a generation older than he is. He takes himself seriously, and he seems to think I should do so a little more often too. He says I protect myself with sarcasm and irony. He calls me a "cool cat" and I laugh when he does it. Nobody has ever called me a cool cat before. He also thinks I'm the sexiest thing he's ever seen, and he's not ashamed to tell me that. When he says those things, I try to play them down in embarrassment, make a joke of it, but he answers without irony. He stares at me until I stop joking and says he means it. He's more intense than I am. Way more intense. Everything about him. He suffers from unfathomable anxiety sometimes. Gets angry sometimes, irritated with people and events in the world around us, sputters and rages about all these idiots. He says he hates the entire advertising and showbiz industries. When he's angry, he's incensed. I'm fascinated by his anger and secretly inspired by his temper. It seems refreshing to get so angry sometimes. But usually he's happy. Though he doesn't say "happy"; he says "joyous." He's basically an all-or-nothing type of person, and I suspect—no, I hope—I'm right now becoming his all. He says his joy is because he met me. He says he's been dreaming of me, waiting to meet someone like me, claims I'm everything he dreamed about in a woman. That's another way in which he's different from you. He calls me a woman, not a girl. He doesn't like me; he loves me. I absorb his words like a sponge. It feels like I've been waiting my whole life to be loved in just this way, like he's the one I've been waiting for. He's the kind of man all my angsty teenage poetry was written about. He's the kind of man who suits me best. Someone intense, who challenges me, who wants to live in the here and now, not wait for another day. Somebody who lives at the same pace I do. I can hardly believe it. I finally met him in the end.

From the outside, there have been no major changes in Ivan's and my life. The change is internal. Inside, I'm imagining the future he and I will build together. In the future, he fills the empty seat at our dinner table, becomes a new father figure for Ivan, a living one. In this fantasy, he fills the void you left behind. He's the answer to all the questions I've had since we lost you. He's the answer to how I will live on. He's the meaning to all of this, to what kind of childhood and future Ivan will have, to what my context is, my sphere, my arena. He's my savior, my knight, and he fills my evenings and me with warmth, with thoughts and conversations that never seem to end. In my fantasies, he's the solution to everything that went wrong, gives meaning to everything that has happened, is the basis for a beautiful story about how life turns out, a happy ending. I'm letting my fantasies run wild, but I can't stop myself because I suspect they spring from a desire I haven't allowed myself to feel for a very long time. I think it might do me some good to acquaint myself with my longing now that it's suddenly so obvious.

It seems to be much easier for him. He seems more secure in his role as a parent, in his career, in his role as a person in general. I want to be like that too. I want to learn from him, and I want to lean against him, and then I want to live with him for the rest of my life if I can, thank you very much. Yesterday when we were talking on the phone he told me for the first time he loved me. He just said it, as if it weren't embarrassing or sensitive, something to be ashamed of or joke about. A simple statement rather than a fragile confession. I was extremely impressed. And embarrassed. Struck by an impulse to put my hand over the phone to make sure nobody could hear us. But I was alone in the living room, like always. Ivan was asleep in our bedroom, and I, his mother and your widow, was on the sofa with the phone pressed against my ear, my heart pounding for another man, who I'm dreaming about creating a future with, and he'd just told me he loved me. I didn't dare say anything back, but I smiled and then couldn't stop smiling for the rest of the night.

———————

Ivan is eating a Popsicle in his stroller. He's in a wonderful mood. Wants to jump around on every patch of grass, play in every park we pass by. I let him. Drawing out our walk, which I know by now takes exactly eighteen minutes if we go fast and twenty-two if we go slowly. I'm nervous and worried about the sweat stains on my shirt, both on my back and near my armpits, from this July heat. It's hot, and I'm extremely nervous—the two combine to destroy any chance I have of looking fresh. I try to stay in the shade, stop the stroller, much to Ivan's delight, sit down on the grass while Ivan investigates a stick in this random park. He's pretending it's a chain saw. He buzzes and waves it in the air at some bushes. I'm waiting for my sweat stains to dry. We're just a few hundred meters from his apartment building now. We're not really in a hurry. But dawdling isn't making me any less nervous.

We are on our way to him. We'll eat dinner together, the four of us, the kids will meet for the first time, and if all goes well, we'll sleep over. He bought an inflatable bed so Ivan can sleep on the floor next to his bed. There are Popsicles in the freezer, and kid-friendly sausage stroganoff is cooking on the stove. On the bedroom floor there's a dollhouse ready to be explored by Ivan's curious fingers. I've received several pictures via text and numerous assurances that everything will go well.

It's now been five weeks since we first met. Over those weeks, we've spent hours on the phone every night, told each other secrets we never shared with anyone, met for lunch during workdays to grab a few more moments together, and hired babysitters to have the chance to spend some time sleeping in each other's arms. We've become physically and psychologically addicted to each other, and we're convinced that we are each other's great love. Words that once felt unfamiliar to hear and uncomfortable to say now flood my everyday life. Nobody knows except the two of us that we've said "I love you." Nobody knows that we're already thinking about the family we want to build, about the future children we will have together and the apartment we plan to buy when we move in together. His name is followed by "darling" in my contact list, and when I call him, a picture of my lips forming a kiss appears on his phone screen. We call each other all the time. One hour without contact and I can feel it on my skin, it becomes hard for me to concentrate, I fumble for my phone and try to find the right words. Where is he? What if I lose him? But he never disappears. He is constantly present. Neither one of us seems to need much sleep anymore.

But then there are the logistics of being single parents. The never-ending babysitter jigsaw puzzle has made it hard for us to meet as often as we'd like. Just one or two days a week have felt like way too little. Four or five days apart feel unbearably long. We've become dependent on each other, constantly wanting more, never satisfied by the crumbs we can scrape together. We've become cut off from our reality in a way that's starting to be a problem. I hide our relationship from those around us as if it was something ugly, and I haven't seen your parents for almost a whole month. The nightly phone calls have led to sleep deprivation. The constant text messages have made it hard to concentrate. Our physical and mental presence in social situations and at our jobs has started to suffer.

Not to mention the absence from our children when we hire a babysitter in order to meet. The guilt arrives like a letter in the mail every time I choose to leave Ivan to spend a few hours next to his body. When I'm with him, I miss Ivan intensely and feel ashamed for sacrificing time with him in order to satisfy myself. I've started to feel like a bad mom. I don't want to be without Ivan. And he says he's ready to let the kids meet, says he's sure it will all be fine. During our previous night together we weighed the pros and cons. Ended up agreeing that if our feelings for each other are this strong, then we might as well let the children start spending time together. So here we are today. And here I am, sitting beneath a tree, sweating.

I'm nervous to meet his daughter with Ivan. Worried that she won't like me or, worse, won't like Ivan. Or that he won't like her. That he'll decide he wants to go home and will do everything in his two-and-a-half-year-old power to show his dissatisfaction. Worried that it will all feel weird or bad and that, in turn, will prove that I'm moving too fast and that I've lost my foothold on reality in this state of infatuation. Worried that I'm putting myself, not Ivan, first. No matter how much I try to convince myself it's just one dinner, one sleepover, and doesn't need to be any more than that, I know that's not true. This is a milestone. I'm introducing Ivan to my new love. Ivan, who's lived alone with me since he was eight months old. I, who've lived with an empty chair at the dining table since I lost you. Today I'm taking a step to change that picture. I don't know if what I'm doing is good for Ivan or traumatic. Either way, it's not a small thing.

And now it's going to happen. My sweat stains aren't going to dry, and Ivan has grown tired of his stick, or chain saw—it's unclear what it's supposed to be now. He's talking about ice cream. "You already had an ice cream. Let's go now," I say. A little too brusquely. A little too stressed. I put him into his stroller. Start walking up the last hill, the one that leads to his building. The sun is broiling hot. Ivan is whining. No turning back. Let's do this.

August 2016

And then suddenly it's like having a family again, one with two parents and two children. It should feel strange, but it doesn't. The days flow together into a blurry honeymoon in which everything we do, every excursion and dinner and evening on the balcony, slides forward smoothly. This time I have an older child: Unlike when you died, our son is now a person who can speak and has a will of his own. Someone who can sing most of the melodies he hears and switches back and forth between apps and games on his iPad with impressive accuracy. Someone who gets mad when things don't go his way and hates being naked, even when he takes a bath. Someone who hates going to bed and prefers staying up with the adults until he passes out on the sofa. A person who talks about his papa in heaven, and my current love as his papa here on earth. I thought it would be complicated, at least somewhat, but everything happened so simply. Unbelievably so.

My worry that the children wouldn't like each other turned out to be unjustified. And I had the experience for the first time of watching Ivan fall in love with another child. An older child, who shows him how to build with Legos and takes him by the hand when they cross streets. One who challenges him and makes him risk more, laugh more, want more. With the self-confidence and adventurous spirit of a five-year-old, she shows him the world in a way I've never managed to do. Sometimes they quarrel, but they make up afterward. When Ivan wakes up in the morning, it's no longer my bed he crawls into. For the first time in my life, I understand what other parents mean when they proclaim siblings are the best. "They take care of each other," they've told me. I believe them now. The stimulation and joy that Ivan finds in his new twenty-four-hour companion is unmistakable. My initial concern about exposing Ivan to something traumatic based on my own selfish desire for love has been abandoned over the summer month we just spent together.

I didn't spend this vacation on my own with my son. This summer we spent it together, all four of us. We went to beaches and made excursions to furniture stores to buy new children's beds—now we have sets in both of our apartments. We've stayed at castle-like hotels and hung out with each other's parents. We've showered each other's children with presents in our zeal to win their love and affection, and we've succeeded. We've played in countless parks. We've talked about booking a trip abroad together but haven't quite gotten around to it.

Suddenly we find ourselves in the midst of that utopia we observed from a distance in other families, the one where children have two parents and take them for granted. We love that almost as intensely as we love each other. He says he wants to have children with me, and I laugh at him. He says it again, and I laugh again. Then he says he's serious, and I answer that of course we'll have kids together. Someday. When we've built a family with the children we already have. He's satisfied with that answer but asks again the next day. I'm charmed to be living with someone who wants to build a future with me, who insists on it.

The ecstasy of suddenly being two parents is triggered by such simple things that no one who hasn't lived our lives could understand. Realizing I forgot to buy something at the store and being able to run back and grab it without having to drag my unwilling child along. Sharing all the chores of cooking, laundry, and dishes between us. Letting each other sleep in. Being able to stop a tantrum by letting the other person step in and take over. Being able to lock the door to the bathroom for some time alone on the toilet or in the shower. Four arms lifting and carrying, comforting and playing, hugging and tickling. Four legs that carry and walk, run and crawl, chase and are chased. This was what I wanted. This was how it was supposed to be.

When the children fall asleep in the evenings, we continue talking, drinking wine, sleeping together, and then talking some more. It's not uncommon for us to realize it's past three and we have to get some sleep. Soon the kids will wake up. We should catch a few hours of sleep as well. And then we go to bed, pumped full of endorphins, and continue whispering in the dark for a while. Until we finally fall silent. He falls asleep first. He sleeps on his back, and a small puffing sound comes out of his mouth when he's in that state between waking and sleep. I listen to it and think it's the most beautiful puff I've ever heard. My hand lies firmly between his two, centered in a tower of hands on his naked chest. I look at him one last time, then I close my eyes. Soon a new day will begin in the family we've become, the family we thought would never happen to us.

Summer vacation is grinding toward its end. Stockholm is starting to fill up with people again. The subways are no longer empty, there are cars in every parking spot on my street, and the parks are crowded with children playing again. My phone beeps more and more often with messages from friends returning from their vacations. They say they want to meet soon, and I avoid making any concrete plans. There's still a week remaining until the preschools open and I return to my job. I want to spend it with my family and not make any plans. I want an empty calendar except for the activities we do together.

My friends seem to think I've joined a cult. One said exactly that when I told her we're thinking about getting engaged and moving in together. In the last month, I haven't had time to meet the people I usually do. Via text messages, I kept them updated on my life. Made excuses for my sudden absence, saying it's just a lot right now, the weeks rushed by, but I promise we'll try to meet soon. They tell me they're happy for my sake, but they've increasingly started to point out how strange it is that they haven't met him yet, my new love. They say it feels weird. And they'd very much like to meet him. And they point out, a bit too frequently to ignore it, that this has all gone very fast. When they do, something happens inside me, something that reminds me of guilt, and it makes me quickly turn off my phone's display and abandon our text thread without answering. I tell myself I'll get back to it soon.

Your parents also point out that this all happened very fast. They're having a hard time keeping up, they tell me at the dinner table at my place after an afternoon spent with me and Ivan. They ask me to lay my cards on the table, probably because Ivan declared earlier today that he has a sister now. The shift in mood after that was unmistakable. I, who'd suggested earlier that we met now and then and weren't in the process of making a new family, felt caught in the act. My attempt to laugh it away echoes against the walls. At the dinner table, the questions arrive. "Who is this person?" they wonder. "Are you together? Is it serious?" they ask. "It feels like it's speeding ahead," they comment. "We just wonder: where is Aksel in all this?" they burst out in the end. This is followed by an uncomfortable silence. Your dad clears his throat. "We only want the best for you," he emphasizes. "You have to believe that. But surely you can understand why this is difficult for us. It makes it so palpable that he's . . . gone." With the word "gone" his voice cracks. That last syllable comes out like a whisper. He takes off his glasses, now wet with tears. Says nothing more. Your mom is also silent. I know it's my turn to say something, but I don't know what.

My cheeks are hot, and I curse myself for being so unprepared for this conversation. The seconds tick by. I don't dare look at your parents, so for the rest of dinner I stare down at my plate instead: fork and knife and lumps of food and a half-eaten bit of cucumber that offers no answers. I can tell my silence is just making things worse, but I don't know what to say, keep searching frantically for the right words. Your dad sighs and sniffs loudly. Ivan is playing in the living room. It's only a matter of time before he gets bored and comes back in here. Their question hits a sore spot inside me, one I haven't managed to define yet, and I'm even less prepared to answer any questions about it.

Because, where *are* you in all of this? You're in pictures on the refrigerator. In Ivan's vocabulary you're Papa, who is dead. In his room, we have framed photographs of you as a child and as an adult. We sometimes watch videos of you on the computer. We talk about how you two have similar ears and hands and feet. We talk about heaven and about how you loved him. About how you were there when he was born and always made him laugh when he was a baby. But you're not here. You're just not here.

You're not in my everyday life, except when I talk about you and re-create memories of you. You're not here to talk to in the evenings. You're not here to share Ivan's childhood with me. You're not here to make decisions about Ivan and the future. You're not here to comfort me. It's not your fault, but you're not here. You're dead, and I'm alone. You're dead, and I've fallen in love with someone. You're dead, and I want the chance to live with somebody again. You're dead, and I don't know if I deserve another chance, but I want one. You're dead, and I don't know if I'm sweeping every trace of you under the rug by meeting someone new, someone who's not you. I don't know if what I'm doing is allowed or if it somehow devalues my love for you. That could be the case. Maybe that's how your parents see it. But the fact remains. You're still dead. And I don't dare point that out to them. It feels like I'd only hurt them by telling them what they already know, the grief they've lived with every day since you died.

In the end, I start to talk. Tentatively, I try to answer their burning questions in a way that doesn't emphasize your absence more than is absolutely necessary. I say I understand that it's sudden for them, the way our lives have changed lately. I confirm that it's happened suddenly for us as well. I emphasize that you are still present for us, in the same way as before. That you will always be Ivan's Papa and they will always be Grandma and Grandpa. I say nobody can take that away from them. Your dad nods and says he supposes he's just surprised. That just a couple of months ago I told them I thought I'd never meet anyone again. It becomes clear to me your parents found some comfort in that, and when your dad points that out, I feel what I don't want to feel, what I try not to think, again. I've betrayed them. I've betrayed you. I've broken my promise.

275

After a while the conversation fades out. I run out of words, and Ivan comes in and interrupts our awkward silence. He demands that Grandma read him a story, and she gets up, excuses herself from the kitchen table, and follows him out into the living room. I stand up and start to clear the dishes. Ask your dad if he wants a cup of coffee. He says it's too late for him, and besides, they're heading home soon. We cautiously return to the kinds of conversations we're used to, to the type of meeting we're used to. But our hugs when we say goodbye in my hall are stiffer than usual.

"We just want the best for you and Ivan. You have to understand that," your dad tells me again.

"I know. I understand," I say again.

We smile at each other and wave in the stairwell. Say see you soon, let's be in touch as soon as we've looked at our calendars. But the silence they leave behind them in the hall is heavy. I try to shake it off by playing with Ivan, but I don't succeed. Your parents' concerns have touched on something I don't want to deal with. The same goes for my friends' text messages. They remind me of my guilt, make me feel coldhearted and naive to think it could be this easy. In particular, their worries threaten my trajectory. They pull me down to earth, illuminating questions I can't even answer for myself, and it puts me into the difficult position where my options seem few and none are completely satisfactory.

How can I hold on to you when you're not here? How can I hold on to you while moving on from us? Do I have to renounce the new love when I never even chose to lose the old one? How can I move on without the approval of the people in our life who matter the most to me? The equation seems unsolvable. The only remaining option is to keep the outside world far away from my relationship, and my relationship far away from the outside world.

———————

It's not like I make a conscious decision to do so. It's more that keeping the world and my relationship far away from each other feels like the most neutral thing to do right now. Just a little longer, I tell myself. Just until I've landed and figured out what's bothering me. Just until the people around me — my family and my friends — get used to the idea of what's going on. Then I'll confront everything and everyone. Then I'll explain to them they have no need to worry. Then I'll prove to them that even though we moved fast, this was all for the best: of all the futures that were offered to me and Ivan, this was the very best option, and I chose to indulge, for both of us. They'll understand eventually. They just need some time. I just need some time. Then I'll go back to a life that can accommodate everyone: your family, my friends, my old family and my new family.

Toward the end of summer vacation, we drink wine and eat lobsters in the kitchen while the kids watch movies in the room next to us. We toast the summer that's just passed and praise ourselves for making our first summer together such a wonderful one. When I stand up to clear the dishes away, he asks me if I want to marry him. At first I laugh, thinking it must be a joke. When he answers, somewhat defensively, that he's being serious, I stop laughing. "You're crazy," I say at first. Then I say I'd like to marry him. The contrast between my life before and my life with him today has become starker with each passing week, and I can't imagine a more sensible choice than living with him the rest of my life. With him, two plus two have become four, and it's four that I want to be. Why not get married when we've found our home in each other? Why not be spontaneous for a change?

Elated by our sudden decision, we look at rings online while eating chips on the sofa. Neither of us has been engaged before. Before this moment, it never came up, since somehow I managed to live more or less like a teenager until I was close to thirty, and then with you it never seemed like an option. It was hard enough to make you want to be with me at all. Not to mention getting you to move in with me, and have a child with me. Talking about marriage would definitely have been going too fast for your taste. And it was never that important to me. I never dreamed about being a bride like many of my friends. Though I have nothing against the thought. And being loved by a person who wants to share the rest of his life with me is undeniably flattering. Also, being engaged will be an experience unique to us both. It will give us something that neither has had before.

I say I want a simple ring. Thinking, but not putting into words, that I don't want my friends or your parents to know what we're up to. Not quite yet. Also, from an outside perspective, there's something a little embarrassing about getting engaged so soon after meeting someone. Getting engaged after two months sounds like something teenagers would do. Adults, especially ones with children, are cautious about new relationships. They wait, see how it feels, and proceed carefully. He doesn't seem to see it that way. He seems happy about our decision. He says I can decide what the rings will look like. I suggest we do it in a few weeks; by then we'll be past our two-month anniversary. If one counts generously. If one considers us a couple from the first time we met. Two months feels better than a month and three weeks, which is where we are today. He thinks

I'm silly to look at it like that but doesn't stop me. A few weeks from now will be fine.

The next day we meet at a jewelry store in a mall near me. I feel self-conscious that someone I know might pass by and see us in here. It would be obvious what we're up to. I try not to care, but I think about my friends who thought I joined a cult. This will confirm their image of me. I think about the conversation with your parents, who pointed out that it's all moving a little too fast for them right now. If they only knew. I try to rush through the process at the jewelry store, but the staff take their sweet time. Flipping through binders, making sure to spell our names correctly, trying various sizes on our fingers, fetching other models. In the end we agree on a plain ring in white gold, find the right sizes, put our names and the date of our intended engagement onto an order form. When it's time to pay, we ask to split the payment in two. I start to put my card into the card reader. He takes out his phone and takes a picture of me doing it. Asks me to look into the camera, says he has to preserve this moment for posterity. He smiles widely behind his phone. I follow his example. I smile into the camera and toward the man behind it. Between clicks, I glance out at the people passing through the mall, behind his back.

———— ——

Our first real fight takes place on the last day of summer vacation. The dispute is about Ivan. Or about me as a parent. Or about raising children in general. I'm not totally sure. It starts with him pointing out that he thinks I'm spoiling Ivan with so much attention. He thinks I treat Ivan like he's a baby, which makes for an unfair distribution of attention between the children. He says Ivan is at the center all the time. He points out

279

that Ivan is allowed to sleep in my bed whenever he wants, that he still drinks from a bottle in the morning and evening though he's big enough to stop, and that he still uses diapers. It's time to potty train him, he says and continues: Ivan throws a fit like a baby as soon as something doesn't go his way, and he receives comfort and distraction whenever he's the least bit stressed, overstimulated, or tired. I have chosen to respond to his every need instantly twenty-four hours a day, stop whatever I'm doing to pick him up, comfort him, and I seldom set up any clear boundaries. He points out that I can't even shower when I want because of Ivan's sensitivity to sound. Says I can't live like this forever, and I'm probably not doing him any favors in the long run. I explain this is my way of making the days go by as smoothly as possible. Happy child equals happy parent. My argument falls flat. His point is that Ivan would feel better if he had more boundaries and less coddling from me. He says he's bringing this up just as much for Ivan's sake as for mine. Stresses he can see how tired I am.

I feel annoyed by his concern and violated by his analysis. His guidance over the last few weeks has started to permeate our everyday lives and makes me feel incapable as a parent. Since he's the one who's already had a child Ivan's age, it's difficult for me to claim as much authority on the subject. I am and remain the less experienced of the two of us, no matter how much I argue that all children are unique and that I am working with Ivan in a way I think will benefit him in the long run. After all, we don't have the same child. They don't have the same temperament, aren't cut from the same cloth. I find it unfair of him to use his daughter as a model.

The discussion turns into a fight after I rebuff him and ask him to stop interfering. I point out that he's known Ivan for barely a month, and he gets upset with me because I'm not a big enough person to realize he means well. He raises his voice, and I ask him to lower it so as not to upset the kids, but he continues. Says I'm terrible at handling criticism, and there it comes: that he's the one who's already raised a child. He finishes off with saying that believe it or not, he loves Ivan, and I have to stop living in symbiosis with him and excluding the other half of my family the way I do now. The bottom line is clear: if I want to keep this family together, I need to stop walling myself off with Ivan and let others inside. I respond to what he says and how he says it with silence and suppressed anger. I don't want to argue in front of the kids, but I think he's being uncompromising and unfair.

I try to end the discussion by whispering, so as not to increase the intensity of his irritation, that I promise to think about what he's said. Unused to arguing, being questioned and reprimanded for my parenting, I can't find any other way to end this other than agreeing with him and telling him Ivan needs more boundaries, and that I'll work on myself. I do my best to appear accommodating, but I think my suppressed anger shines through. Besides, I'm almost trembling with shame. I feel like I've been caught in the act.

Because, yes, Ivan is still a baby to me in some ways. A baby who, without even knowing it, has suffered a loss that I'm constantly trying to compensate for. My child didn't choose to lose a parent at eight months old, and to hell with whoever tells me to stop compensating by keeping him in a good mood, keeping him feeling safe and secure. My own needs will have to wait until later in life—I've already reconciled myself to that. Don't come in here and demand I change more than I already have. Just meeting a man at this point in my life is a big change, revolutionary even. And here he has the nerve to tell me how to raise my son, to claim there's some better way than mine. If I would start setting boundaries. Be a little tougher on Ivan. Let him cry and whine for a while before picking him up. Let him learn how to play by himself. Not always make myself available, ready to divert, comfort, hug, or entertain. If I would just teach him to sleep in his own bed at night. Stop responding to his every peep immediately. Quit spoiling and coddling and comforting and opening my arms all the time. To hell with him for wanting to interfere. To hell with him for not just letting what's working right now keep working. To hell with him for making me apologize for one of the few things in my life I'm actually proud of.

The fight ends with not just my compromise, to think about what he said, but also he promises to back off and keep his advice for when I ask for it, then he pulls me into his lap. He kisses me all over my face and puts his hand on my breast, where my heart is still pounding hard and fast. "I love you so much," he whispers. "You are my family, the two of you. I want to live the rest of my life with you. Do you understand that?" I let him kiss me, relieved that the fight is over. Hoping there won't be a next time.

———

I lie in the dark, trying to get Ivan to stop singing. It's later than it should be, we've been in the bedroom over an hour, and he really should be tired by now. Soon it will be time for the next child to go to bed, and that fact stresses me out. I hush Ivan and tell him he has to be quiet, but he starts singing his song a third time. I threaten that if he doesn't try to sleep right now I'll leave the room. Ivan gets sad and starts to cry. Says I'm talking too loud and calls me "mean Mama." I apologize to him. Apologize for being angry and for making threats. "I won't leave you. I would never do that." I stroke his hair and whisper that we really, really have to sleep now. It's late. Tomorrow we have to get up early and go to preschool. The information about preschool doesn't comfort Ivan in the least, and he starts to cry even louder and says he doesn't want to go to preschool. Not tomorrow, not ever, no more preschool. I give up and change tactics. Tell him a quiet story, continue to monotonously stroke his hair, and it works: he quiets down and listens. My phone vibrates in my pocket, and I don't need to pick it up to know what it is. He's texting me to ask how it's going. He can hear how it's going, but he's getting impatient. He wants to put his daughter to bed soon. It's getting late for her too. She also has to get up early and go to preschool. It's a weekday, and we haven't really got our bedtime routines down yet. Putting them to bed at the same time has turned out to be an impossible project. She needs less sleep, but he's harder to get down. One at a time seems to be the only way to get both of them to sleep. With early wake-up times, a shared bedroom, and two kids who'd rather stay up half the night, the arrangements take a lot of time. So I wait. And pat. And feel more text messages from the room next door vibrating in my pocket.

When Ivan's breathing finally deepens, I stop whispering my story. Stroke his hair once more and make sure he's sleeping. Then I sneak back out to the living room as quickly as I can, find them at the kitchen table. She's eating a bedtime snack, drawing, apparently pleased with the situation. She points proudly to the figures she's drawn, tells me they're a family: stick figures with giant heads, which I assume are her, me, him, and Ivan. Everyone is of different heights and with different colors eyes and hair. Everyone is holding hands. My stick figure has long eyelashes, and Ivan's mouth is shaped like an O. I praise her, tell her it's a beautiful drawing and regret it immediately. Never pass judgment on a child's achievements. Instead ask them about what they've created, discuss the contents. Avoid words like "good" and "nice" and "beautiful." I know all that, but I forget it over and over again.

He's standing at the counter chomping on a carrot. He looks annoyed, and he asks me if I got his text messages, since I didn't answer. I say I got them but I couldn't take out my phone at the time. I'm annoyed with him too. Because he puts pressure on me during bedtimes, as if I had the power to make a two-year-old fall asleep according to a set time frame, as if this all depended on me. I hiss between clenched teeth that there's not much else I can do other than keep going when things don't go quickly. He points out that it never goes fast nowadays. He says Ivan is unusually anxious, and I ignore his comment and glance at the clock. Almost half past nine. I stifle a yawn. He sees me do so and tells his daughter it's time to brush her teeth and go to bed. She protests for a bit but soon gives up. They disappear into the bedroom, and I end up on the sofa. I can unload the dishwasher in the morning. I'm too tired now.

It's hard to put my finger on exactly why, but I often feel stressed. Maybe it's returning to normal life after a long vacation. Maybe it's because Ivan still doesn't really like preschool, and I feel guilty leaving him there every day. Maybe it's the transition to our new life, now a family of four instead of two, and the daily grind of that. Schedules to keep to, sleep to catch, food to make, and kids to pick up and drop off, look after and appreciate, divvy up attention for in as straightforward a way as possible and at the same time have enough for both. Maybe it's just being a parent to twice as many children as I'm used to. Maybe it's just that there aren't as many hours in the day as there apparently were in the summer. Perhaps it's the discrepancy between what's happening in my relationship and how I talk about it outwardly. Something is needling me.

I'm often stressed even before my workday begins. I rush into the office and throw myself down in front of the computer without chatting with my colleagues so I can make the most out of my hours. I usually eat lunch at my computer or while I'm on the phone with him planning our evening. Who will go to the store, what should we eat, where should we sleep, my place or his? When I leave work, I almost jog with my breath caught in my throat to the preschool. Once at the preschool, Ivan is invariably tired and whiny, and accuses me of being late, says he wants to go home. It worries me when Ivan doesn't seem happy. My brain searches feverishly for solutions, troubleshooting the day to find reasons for his dissatisfaction. Without discussing it at home, because I suspect we won't agree on the solution, I try to offer Ivan time alone with me for the first hour after pickup and the last hour before bedtime. It's hard to make this life we're building together work. Especially after our fight, when I basically promised to stop spoiling Ivan. Since then, we haven't talked any more about the subject, but I know he's still annoyed with me on some level. He still thinks I spoil Ivan and let him take up too much space in our shared lives. He thinks I distribute my attention between the children unfairly, and that it's silly of me to make simple foods like hot dogs and meatballs instead of cooking nutritious food from scratch and teaching the children to eat what they're served. There's an increasing feeling that not everyone's needs are being met, and with that comes the guilt.

★   ★   ★

The list of people I feel guilty about is quite long these days. I feel guilty because I don't see your parents as often as I used to, because I don't share what's happening in my life with them, even though I know they're wondering. I feel guilty because I don't hang out with my friends anymore, because I don't respond to their invitations and never show up. I feel guilty because I don't go out to lunch with my colleagues, since I leave earlier than they do so I can have time to pick up Ivan in the afternoon. At home, I feel guilty because his daughter suffers when I try to meet Ivan's needs and because Ivan suffers when I devote myself exclusively to her. I feel guilty because there always seems to be someone who wants more from me than I have time or energy to give. No matter what or whom I think about, it eventually leads to guilt. It's not rare for me to use Ivan as an excuse to go into the bedroom and close the door behind us so I can give myself an artificial break. Then I feel guilty because bedtime is taking too much time.

From my place on the sofa in the living room I hear him in the room next door whispering to his daughter that he loves her. He says she's the best thing he knows and tells her she makes him proud every day. I hear her giggle when he teases her, and I hear her ask him to rub her back. Then silence. It hasn't even been ten minutes since they entered the bedroom. Their bedtime routine is shorter than mine and Ivan's and definitely more harmonious. He rubs her back and watches a show on his phone at the same time. As for me, I grind my teeth after that hour-long session with Ivan, and I have no wish to do anything at all.

September 2016

One Thursday in September we meet at a restaurant in Gamla Stan and exchange rings. He posts an image of our interlaced hands on Instagram, and congratulations stream in from his friends and acquaintances. Afraid my friends might find out from someone else, I text them and share the news with them as well. I'm engaged now. Some of them respond immediately; others are conspicuous in their silence. I pretend it doesn't bother me, but it does. I compensate by toasting with my love, letting our glasses be refilled by the waiters, who also congratulate us on our engagement by uncorking a bottle of champagne. I kiss my fiancé over the table. We look at our rings over and over again. I swore my love to him in a letter I wrote at work before we met up. The letter describes our first meeting, how I memorized his door code immediately, and how he brought color back into my life again. Everything I wrote is true. He reads it and cries. Says he's happy for the first time in years.

Then we drink even more wine and eat dinner. I'm drunk by the time the main course arrives, and by eight thirty we take a taxi home because I'm feeling dizzy. The whole thing is extremely embarrassing. It's not like me to get so drunk. I feel nauseated as I take off my shoes in the hall. The champagne, standing next to an enormous bouquet he prepared and placed in the living room, we leave untouched. I fall asleep in his bed by nine thirty and wake up the next morning with an enormous hangover.

My first day as engaged stumbles by in a haze—I end up lying down on a sofa at work and have to go home early, pick up Ivan from preschool, and climb onto the sofa the moment we get home. I'm still feeling nauseated today. I wonder if it's something I ate.

On Saturday, I have a headache. We fought again. We've gone from a summer without even a hint of disagreement to drowning in them now. I'm annoyed by his intensity, his constant need for confirmation, how often he contacts me while I'm at work or with friends. I get irritated by how much space he takes up, by his eccentric mood swings. He, for his part, is annoyed by my temperament, how bad I am at treating him lovingly when he's feeling down, how I withdraw into myself when we quarrel, by my coldness in the face of every conflict. He says I'm prickly almost all the time, that I close up like a clam any time I'm criticized. He says that my mental absence is obvious even to the children and that I have to learn to communicate what I feel. He explains that I am easily offended and have an almost unhealthy need to be in control. In a whisper, in case the children are awake, I point out that his temperament isn't exactly the easiest to live with either. Dealing with his mood swings is like walking through a minefield, I say. I complain that he takes up so much room, makes such a mess, and leaves dirty dishes and glasses all over the apartment. I tell him it feels like I'm taking care of three kids, not two. I roll my eyes when he has to take a bath to relax, and I whisper through clenched teeth that I'd like to relax once in a while too. He counters that it's my responsibility to do so and points out that he cooks most of the food and goes to the store more often than I do. Then we go back and forth forever about who's grouchier, who was in a bad mood first, who's actually justified in their anger. We quote each other and accuse each other, and in the end we don't remember why we started fighting in the first place. Then we lay down our arms for a while. Return to everyday life, to the children and logistics. But our conversations at the dinner table become more fraught as the days pass.

I sneak into the bathroom more often than I need to and take longer showers than I've ever taken. Stand with the water directed at my chest and my gaze stuck on the tile in front of me. Startle and call out "Out soon" if someone knocks on the door, then curse inside. I catch myself wishing that he could just slow down, and I can't help but feel sad when I remember that's how you once felt about me. You and your showers. When it is far too late and of no use at all, I suddenly understand you. Our discussions often take place after the kids are in bed; there always seems to be something we need to sort out. I've been feeling worse in the last week, and now my period is late. I know I need to take a pregnancy test, but I procrastinate. Think there's no way I could be pregnant—we've been so careful. But the days go by and no period arrives and I continue to sulk, and in the end I buy a test.

He waits outside the door when I go into the bathroom. Wishes me good luck, and I promise, even though it's obvious and my only choice, that I'll come back out immediately. I'm so nervous that my hand holding the stick trembles. It's just over three years since I did this the last time. Back then I was expecting Ivan. Back then we lived in Enskede and the bathroom was almost as tiny as this one. You were sitting on the sofa working; I whistled on the way into the bathroom so as not to awake your suspicions. I was hoping for a positive result even though I was afraid to tell you when I got it. This time, I don't want the result to be positive. A positive result would be a negative answer today. This time I didn't whistle on my way in. I do what I'm supposed to, pee on the stick, and I hold my breath and count to ten, then thirty, then fifty. The stick shows one line, not two. I count to ten again. As slowly as I can. No second line appears. I'm not pregnant. I let out a "Yeeeeeeeees" in one long exhale, stand up, wash my still-shaking hands slowly while adrenaline pumps through me. Feel the nausea I've suffered for the last week flow away, and suddenly it's easier to breathe. I take a few more deep breaths at the door, smooth out my face, step out. He's waiting for me in the living room. His eyebrows are raised. He looks at me, questioningly. "Well?"

I can't help but smile. My face breaks into it when I look at him. I'm so relieved. His eyebrows are still raised, but he answers my smile with one of his own, seems happy, probably because I am. We smile at each other in tender understanding for a moment before I inform him of the result. I point to the stick, which still shows only one line. He looks first at it, then at me, and finally at the stick again. Somewhere along the way, his smile fades away. He looks away from the stick and his glance lands on the floor at our feet. Silence. I ask him what's wrong. "Isn't it a good thing that I'm not pregnant?" He doesn't answer, just gets up and walks past me to the balcony, sits down on a chair and stares straight ahead. I follow clumsily behind him. Stand at the doorway. He still won't look at me. I wait. He doesn't say anything. I try again. I ask him what's wrong. He says he doesn't feel like talking to me right now. He wants to be alone for a while and absorb this. Only now do I realize he thought my smile meant I was pregnant. That he was happy because he thought we were going to have a child together, him and me, that we were creating a family in the way he defines it. Now he's sad, or angry, or disappointed, and he doesn't want to talk to me about it. I linger at the balcony door, waiting for him to speak, but he stays quiet. A powerful feeling of déjà vu washes over me, and the scene in Enskede replays in my head. That time I was pregnant and you didn't want to talk to me. You wouldn't meet my eyes when I told you, and you fell silent and disappeared. Over three years later, here I am again. The situation is mirrored, but with a different premise. I've done the wrong thing again.

I try to save the situation. I apologize. "I didn't mean it that way. I just meant I was glad we weren't pregnant right now." I emphasize the words "right now" to make him understand. "We just met. We're already working on building a family. We just got engaged, we already have kids, two kids. That's quite a lot to handle already." I grope through the silence between us, seeking his forgiveness without knowing exactly what I need to be forgiven for. That I'm not pregnant or that I smiled when I announced the result? That I feel relieved and not sorry about the outcome? I fumble on. "Listen. Honey. We're working on building a family with those of us who are already here. Surely that's what's happening, even if I'm not pregnant right now."

He still won't look at me. He still won't answer my questions. All he'll say is that he wants to be alone. His silence is uncharacteristic, and therefore it scares me. I fumble to find the right words to compensate for my smile, my stupid, hurtful, insensitive smile, but it seems to be too late. My smile, my relief at not being pregnant, has hurt him deeply, and there's nothing I can say to take it back. With a heavy and anxious heart, I go back inside again. Go find the kids, who are in their playroom and proudly announce they're packing their backpacks for an adventure. I try to participate in their game. I can't concentrate. If only I could have kept myself from smiling.

The evening goes by in silence. I don't know what to say to comfort him, and it doesn't matter because he still doesn't want to talk to me. But after the children go to bed, we do so anyway. We talk—initially in whispers, but the conversation soon turns into a debate, and suddenly we're fighting again. He says my

smile proves I'm not ready for the kind of relationship he's looking for. He says he doesn't believe we have the same dreams, the
same image of the future, and he doubts my love. He says he's
been clear with me that he wants more kids, that it's important
to him, since the first time we met, and my relief over not being
pregnant was unmistakable. He says he feels tricked. He accuses
me of not wanting to have children with him and therefore lying throughout our relationship. He's not sure how he'll be able
to trust me after this.

I try to convince him that I want more children too. I really
want him to believe me. Just not right now, not when we just met,
not when we're still learning how to be parents to each other's
children, not when all this is so new. I say I'm not as relieved as he
thinks I am, say that if I'd been pregnant of course I would have
wanted to keep the baby. I struggle to convince him but fail over
and over again. After a while, I stop trying. He doesn't believe me
anyway. I don't know if I believe myself, but I desperately want
him to believe me. I don't want him to be angry with me. I don't
want him to leave me. More than anything, I don't want him to
leave me because I wasn't pregnant tonight.

The last thing he says, with his back to me, before we fall asleep
is that he doesn't know what he feels about us anymore. Then
silence. I don't dare try to put my hand on him, so I turn away
from him too. I wait for his breathing to deepen, think that
if we both just sleep something might change in those hours
and we'll wake up feeling warmer toward each other again. Isn't
that how it always works? The problem is, I never hear him fall
asleep. No deep breathing except for the children's. The bedroom is quieter than it's been for several months. I don't sleep a
wink that night.

I still haven't got my period. I still feel nauseated. I'm still shaken after what happened last Saturday. I don't want to end up alone again. I don't want to go back to a life of just me and Ivan. I want a family, and I want to keep his love. I definitely don't want to be the kind of person who gets engaged for a week then breaks up. I want him to believe in me again, in us, and I'm determined to do whatever I can to make that happen.

I'm sitting on a toilet again, peeing on a stick. We're at his place, and the kids are playing with Legos outside the bathroom door. This time I bought a more expensive test, with a digital display. For the second time this week I put the test on the edge of the sink. Stand up, wash my hands, wait. The test's display will soon blink either PREGNANT or NOT PREGNANT. Right now an hourglass is flashing on the tiny screen. It stops. Goes dark for two, three, four, five seconds. I've stopped breathing.

We made up the morning after the negative test result. I buried the stick at the bottom of the bathroom trash, and we never talked about it again. But a chill has settled over the atmosphere at home, and we haven't laughed together for several days. He seems lost in his own thoughts more and more often. Doesn't talk to me like he used to. Says he's tired and wants to go to sleep immediately after the children go to bed. As for me, I seesaw between my fear of abandonment and the feeling that I'm being treated unfairly. I start to doubt I did anything wrong. Why would I owe him any more apologies? In the midst of all this, I feel nauseated again, and my period still hasn't arrived. I've had better weeks.

I hold my breath and stare at the flashing screen. The hourglass has stopped blinking. The display is black for another second. Then it comes: PREGNANT 1–2 WEEKS. I stare at the screen. Still can't breathe. Pick up the test with a hand that's trembling again. Look closely at the screen. Searching in vain for a corner of the screen that would make this message ambiguous, open to interpretation, but I find nothing. Realize that I'm still holding my breath and force myself to start breathing again. I am not ready to leave the bathroom, I have to wait a little longer, so I turn on the faucet for a bit. I look at myself in the mirror. My face is expressionless, reveals nothing of what's going on inside. I'm pregnant. I'm pregnant after all. Somebody is alive inside me now. Even if I throw the test in the trash and never show it to him, I'm still pregnant. We've known each other for two months, and now I'm pregnant. I widen my eyes and stare at myself in the mirror. Trying to form a smile. The muscles around my mouth pull up the edges of my lips, but my eyes don't change. They're still expressionless. I wrinkle them up and keep smiling toward the mirror. It looks like a grimace. This wasn't what my life was supposed to be. Not now. Not yet. It doesn't feel real. It doesn't feel right. Nevertheless, this is how it is. I'm pregnant.

It takes a while. I'm incapable of going out just yet. I know that from the second I tell him the result my life will change irreversibly. In here things are still like usual. In here it hasn't begun yet. In here I can still pretend it hasn't happened. Just a little longer. But now there's a knock on the door. He knocks gently. A soft voice asks if everything's okay, wonders how it's going. I'm sitting on the toilet again. The test is damp with the sweat from my hand. I don't get up to open the door. Instead, I whisper that I'm pregnant. He doesn't hear me. I whisper again, this time a bit louder. Silence for a moment. He opens the door.

There he stands, trying to read my expressionless face for a

second time this week. "I knew it," I say. "I fucking knew it."
I look at him, see the shock on his face quickly changing into
something else. This time he's the one who smiles. He can't
help it. He smiles, and it's directed right at me.

Now he hugs me. Hard. He stands above me, and my chin
lands at his armpit. It smells a little like sweat, his sweat, his body
odor that I've never, not once, thought smelled bad. Even his
sweat smells like home. Why can't I just feel at home now? I
breathe in, bend my neck back and up to land in his hug. Put
my free arm, the one that's not holding the test, around his back.
My neck is strained in this position. He whispers in my ear. "My
beautiful Carolina." Kiss. "Everything will be all right." Another
kiss. I hide in his embrace, in his arms and his scent, and try to
land. I nod against his shoulder but can't manage to get anything
out. I'm unable to answer, unable to stand up. I just want to sit
here on the toilet and let him hug and kiss me forever.

Then the children come running. They've noticed that
something outside of the ordinary is taking place in the bathroom. They want to be included. They push themselves into
the room where he's hugging me, and I'm still sitting on the
toilet lid, bent over in a weird position, hiding in his arms. His
daughter climbs up to get inside the hug, pushes in between our
legs and reaches up to my lap. She pretends she's a cat and spins
and purrs in my arms. I'm hit by a sudden impulse to protect
my stomach from her sharp knees. Ivan is getting nervous. He's
stomping worriedly behind her. He can't find any gap to get
up into my lap, and he's whining more and more loudly from
his position at my feet. It feels crowded with so many bodies
in the bathroom. Instinctively, I throw the test away from me,
and it lands in the sink. I use my free arm to lift Ivan onto my
lap as well. I'm sweating. It's too crowded in here. We don't

have enough room. We're only four, and we can barely fit. The thought is dizzying.

"Okay, everybody," I say, "it's too crowded. Why don't we go out on the sofa instead?" My autopilot has kicked on, and once again I've become a mother who just wants everyone to have enough room, to not feel worried or disappointed. And above all I don't want anyone to get angry and leave me.

"We need to talk more about this," I whisper a moment later on my way to the bedroom to start Ivan's bedtime routine. "Of course we will," he replies from the sofa in a tone of voice that is supposed to instill trust but just annoys me so much I have to bite hard on the inside of my cheek to keep from screaming. "We have plenty of time," he continues meaningfully. "Nine months is an eternity at the rate we move. It'll all be fine," he promises again.

I force myself to nod. I so much want him to be right. I'd like to place my trust in his words, but I don't feel convinced. Instead, I follow Ivan into the bedroom. We lie close to each other in the bed, and another bedtime, maybe our thousandth, begins.

Only when Ivan has fallen asleep do the tears come. It starts as an ache in the pit of my stomach as I stare at his face in the light of the bedside lamp. He's breathing deeply, has hours to go before the nightmares begin. It rises up and presses against my lungs as I look at his peaceful face and see a stain on one cheek. I forgot to wash him tonight. It sticks in my throat when I see his little hands hugging his stuffed animal, the gray monkey he found when he started preschool and that soon became ours because he wouldn't be separated from it. It spills over when I rub

his back and reach the bulge of his diaper, realize I should start
potty training him pretty soon because he won't be the baby in
the family much longer. I breathe with my mouth so as not to
make any sound and wake him, and I think, What have I done
to you, little darling? How could I ever love anyone the way I
love you? How are you going to find your place in all of this?

I try to stop crying, calm myself, breathing as quietly as I
can. I can't wake Ivan now. Also, I can't leave this room with a
blotchy face and go out to the man who loves me, who's waiting in the next room, who's happy right now. I can't disturb
either Ivan in his sleep or my man in his joy. I stay in the bedroom for a while. Trying to collect myself to continue with the
evening routine we've only just now got going. First Ivan goes
to bed. Then we play with Ivan's new sister for a bit. Then she
also falls asleep. Then the adults have some time to talk. That's
what we'll do tonight too.

The difference is that tonight I'm not looking forward to the
conversation. I'm not ready to put what's happening inside me
into words. I don't know yet why this hurts so much. I don't
want to hurt or provoke him by saying I'm suffering before I
know why. I want to lock myself in this bedroom next to Ivan
and hide from the rest of the world from now on. But it's impossible. So I have to pull myself together. This is not okay. I've
been given love again, given a second chance. I'm probably just
scared. Shocked, of course. I can't let my fear or guilt get in the
way of what we're building. I just have to accept that it ended up
this way. Not everything goes according to schedule. That's not
how life works—I've already learned that the hard way. I have
to apply those lessons now, to this, with courage and flexibility.
Lying around crying will get me nowhere. I climb out of the
bed carefully and carry Ivan over to his own bed. I look at him

one last time, make sure that he's asleep. Then I leave. One last deep breath before I step out of the bedroom and meet the other half of my new family. We're four now. Soon we'll be five.

———————

The subway is packed with people at rush hour. I stand in the crowd, doing my best not to touch any of my fellow commuters. The smell of sweat disgusts me, and I wish I had time to walk from work to the preschool, where Ivan is waiting to be picked up. But I don't. I can't fit in my work hours and a walk from the neighborhood where I work to the neighborhood where I live. So I'm standing on a train, swearing to myself silently. I'm cursing the city I live in and all the people who live in it. The smell of their bodies and their breath and the whole concept of public transportation. I'm thinking it should be forbidden to eat garlic for lunch, there should be laws about proper oral hygiene, polyester should be banned forever, and every single dialect sounds equally ugly. A familiar nausea wells up, and I count the stations that remain until I'm there. Will I make it? Do I need to jump off and breathe? Will I vomit on the subway? I decide to chance it. Surely I can make it one more station. If I breathe carefully, turn my face away from the man who smells like garlic and has an ugly name tag on his chest.

There was never much of a discussion, but we agreed to keep the baby. At the beginning of our conversation, I brought up, as affectionately as I could, my fears and doubts. I gently touched on how I didn't feel ready, on my guilt about Ivan. Maybe I was too gentle. Maybe I didn't really discuss anything. Anyhow, each and every one of our conversations landed at the same conclusion. We love each other and want to live together. No, the timing isn't perfect, but not everything in life can be scheduled.

Who knows if we'll have another chance? I'm old, at least by the standards of female fertility, and we can't assume we have all the time in the world. Having more children is important to him, so important that he's not sure he wants to live with me if I don't, and I think—no, I hope—that I can come to a place where I too see this as...a good thing. I have to. This new child will bind our family together in a unique way. The children will share a younger sibling. It will tie them closer to each other than anything else we could give them. And I'll have more than seven months to get used to the idea. I hope it goes faster than that. Maybe once I stop feeling sick.

I feel intensively nauseated this time. I no longer like adult food. My diet consists of sandwiches, hot dogs, macaroni, and biscuits. On those days when fish soup or rich stews are served at the dinner table, I decline. Wait until Ivan's fallen asleep and then eat a few sandwiches in front of the TV. Watch something stupid before going to bed early. I'm rarely in a good mood. I'm constantly tired, I never have the energy to clean, and it takes me hours of rest to be ready for the grocery store. Plus, we basically argue every day. I don't think I'm a joy to live with.

My relationship with Ivan is suffering too. My guilt has not subsided. All I have to do is look at him and tears well up in my eyes. I can't play with him like I used to. I lose my patience faster when he's whiny and stubborn. I get angry and snap at him when bedtime is taking too long, and the second he falls asleep, I want to wake him up again and beg for his forgiveness. While he sleeps, I stare at him in the darkness and silently mouth my apologies. The next morning it starts all over again.

I try to convince myself that something wonderful is happening to Ivan right now. He's going to get a bigger family. He'll have more people to love and who love him. This will work out just fine for him. If only I could just accept this and stop feeling so trapped. If only I could just step onto the train that's already rolling and take that last foot off the platform. If only I could shake off this apathy and coldness that has so suddenly and uncharacteristically overcome me. Then everything would be fine. This all depends on me, and it's my own fault if it doesn't go well.

It's still too early to tell the children. But last week I told my friends and family. They received a text message from me that was equal parts defensive and desperate for their approval. The response was varied, stretching from no reaction to worried and skeptical to effusive congratulations. A few of my friends told me straight out that they thought this was a hasty decision. Pointed out that we've known each other for only a few months and there's plenty of time to build a family in the future. One asked me straight out: "What's the hurry?" I refrained from repeating what I'd already said, that this was unplanned, that it just turned out this way. Sometimes life doesn't happen like we plan, and now we're making the best of the situation. But instead, I didn't answer at all. I've distanced myself from those friends who have been open about their reservations. I have a hard time refuting their worries, which remind me far too much of my own, and so I've avoided answering them because I'm out of respectful responses. And to those who reacted with silence, I just let it be. Their silence is answer enough. I don't have the energy to meet them. On the other hand, I've turned more and more to those who were quick to congratulate me and confirmed their support for me no matter what decisions I make, via phone calls and texts, because we don't have much time to meet. We haven't met for a long time. A life with two intense children and an equally intense man, plus two apartments, a full-time job, constant nausea, and a fatigue that makes it hard for me to get up off the sofa, doesn't offer me many chances to meet anyone face-to-face. My understanding friends understand that as well.

———————

I don't make it easy for him to look forward to a future with me. Still, nobody can accuse him of not trying. He does the shopping and the cooking. Supplies me with prenatal vitamins and reads about the stages of pregnancy on the internet. Buys nonalcoholic wines and takes the kids to the park so I can rest on the sofa. Rents movies in the evenings and doesn't mind when I fall asleep in front of them. He does absolutely nothing wrong, and still I'm furious. Maybe for that very reason. Secretly I blame him for putting me in this position. If he weren't so impetuous, then he would agree this has gone too fast for both of us. If he weren't so hung up on having more kids, then he'd understand. If he were just a little more interested in listening to me, to what I'm hinting at even if I never say it out loud, then I wouldn't feel so alone right now. But he's not. And he doesn't. He doesn't want to hear that. He marches on: shopping, cooking, filling and emptying the dishwasher, buying me vitamins, playing with the kids, sending me encouraging text messages, and looking forward to the new addition to our family. I have no say in any of this. Decided is decided, and now it is what it is. Might as well try to get used to it.

The problem is that I can't. I'm afraid, angry, worried, and despairing by turns. And I have nowhere to work through it. So I stay silent. And I flee. I flee into myself, becoming ever more remote. The situation reminds me of one I've been in before. Three years ago, to be exact. But now the roles are reversed.

Against my will and for the first time in my life, I've become the brake pad, the mood destroyer, the one who doesn't dare and doesn't even know if they want to. When I'm not feeling deeply sorry for myself, or him, I think of you and how you must have felt at the end of our years together. Then I start feeling deeply sorry for you instead.

Even though I constantly complain about being tired, I sleep badly at night. When he asks me if it's because of the nausea, I say yes. In fact, I lie there thinking about Ivan. When he has his nightmares and whimpers in his sleep, I'm overcome by feelings of guilt and want to lift him over to the big bed we sleep in, but I don't. He has to get used to sleeping in his own bed now. A baby is on its way. Instead of bringing him to my bed, I lie on the floor next to him. Take my pillow and blanket and make myself a bed next to his, lie on my side and stretch my arm up and over the edge of his bed. Then I rub his back and hush him when he cries, waiting patiently for him to fall silent again and go back to sleep. Then I listen to his breathing, trying to decipher if he's dreaming or sleeping peacefully. He has nightmares often nowadays. I blame myself for that too. I go through every mistake I made on that particular day, counting everything I could have done in a better way. I should have moved more slowly into this new family. I should have had more patience. I should have put the brakes on when there were still brakes. I should have used contraception. I should have given Ivan more time to adapt to the change. I should have done more. I definitely should be doing more now.

If only this nausea would pass, then I could be a better parent again. Then I'd be a better partner as well. If I could just choke down a little food at dinner, then I'd have the strength to make it through an evening upright again. This will all be better in a few weeks. That's what I tell myself and him, the man who's doing the cooking, buying all the groceries, who also works full time and sometimes even drops off and picks up Ivan in order to lighten my load. If only this would pass soon. If only I could find my way back to myself, to us, to what we were, soon. After all, we have a plan. After all, we agreed.

October 2016

One morning when we woke up, summer was gone and autumn was a fact. Another morning, we said to each other it might be good for both us and our children if we slept apart sometimes. Ivan is so anxious during the night, he wakes up the whole family with his nightmares. We both have so much to do at work right now. Our kids might benefit from being apart now and then too. It would give them the opportunity to start missing each other. Let go of some of their jealousy, their competition for our time and attention. We talk about what's best for the children, but really we mean ourselves. There are so many things we don't say directly these days.

This week we sleep apart almost every night. His job is very demanding right now, he has to work late to keep up, and as for me, I collapse in my bed as soon as Ivan has gone to sleep, and I'm not great company either. We agree it's easier for us to do our own thing now when I'm so tired.

I don't admit it, but it's a relief. When Ivan and I are alone, I have a little more energy and temporarily feel like I have control over my life. We eat our hot dogs for dinner and nobody points out how little nutrition there is in it. Then we play for a while.

I can focus on Ivan, laugh with him. Bedtime is calmer when nobody is waiting in line behind us. When Ivan goes to bed, he can choose where he wants to sleep. Usually he sleeps in my bed. Often I don't even get up again. I lie there in the light of my phone screen. And I text the man who will soon be the father of my second child, tell him, "I'm falling asleep now. Let's talk tomorrow instead," and he texts back a short, "Good night." I suspect he's hurt—because I don't suggest we call each other and say good night instead, because I don't say I miss him, because we don't talk to each other like we used to, because I've disappeared into myself—but I don't confront him. I can't handle another conversation that goes late into the night. Instead, I lie in bed, rub Ivan's back until he stirs in his sleep and rolls away from me, pushes himself into a corner of the bed, sighs loudly, and then sleeps on. And another day goes by.

———————

Yesterday we were at the prenatal clinic. We'd asked for an early ultrasound because I haven't been feeling very good this time, not physically or mentally. The results of the ultrasound were positive. We were told that the fetus is alive and doing well. My values are fine. The nausea has almost passed. Soon I'll start having more energy again. It's only a matter of days now, at the most a few weeks, until the paralyzing fatigue goes away. Everything's going according to plan, and there's nothing to worry about, our midwife promised us, and I nodded and smiled, held his hand, and did my best to seem relieved and grateful.

We held hands as we walked from the restaurant where we'd had lunch to the subway station where we would go our separate ways to pick up our children at their respective preschools at either end of the neighborhood. Stated, as cheerfully as we

304

could, that everything was just as it should be, no clouds in our skies now.

Except this thing where I'm still not happy. And that I still feel exhausted by spending time together, by all my inadequacies, by the intensity of this life and my relationship with him, which seems to be increasingly distant and rife with misunderstandings. Except that I'm still eaten up with guilt about Ivan, who's happily unaware that his position as the baby of the family will soon be ripped away from him. Except for the fact that I still haven't quite landed in my role as a stepmom. Except that our entire family project feels overwhelming. Except my guilt when it comes to your parents, my parents, my colleagues, and my friends. Except that there's been an endless series of arguments and discussions both big and small in our new everyday life. Except that, there really are no clouds in our skies. It would be a shame to complain.

But I do complain, and I'm not the only one nowadays. He feels like he bears a heavier load than me and explains how it exhausts him. Nothing makes me happy, he says, and I never show the least bit of gratitude or love. He thinks I'm depressed, and he's probably right. But most of all I'm tired. Our life together is twenty-four seven, offers no breaks to catch my breath. I'm never allowed to be alone. There's always somebody wanting something from me. The thought of what's growing inside me paralyzes me with terror instead of filling me with anticipation. It hurts him that I still feel that way. It hurts me that he doesn't understand. I'm torn between anger and guilt—anger because I feel painted into a corner and guilt because I went along with it and can't seem to find a way to make peace with the situation. I despise him and feel sorry for him at the same time. I despise myself and feel sorry for myself at the same time.

My self-contempt expands along with my stomach, and it now stretches across several eras of my life. I despise the person I was with you. I despise the person I am with him. I feel sorry for how you must have felt back then, and I feel sorry for myself because I feel the same way now.

In order to compensate, to make him happy, I fill the time between these serious conversations with something a little more positive: I started working on a list of possible names. I put it up on my fridge and ask him to look at it and add his own suggestions. That seems to work. It makes him happy to read the list. He likes the names I've suggested, hugs me, tries out those names with the names of our other children. The list has only girls' names on it, because I'm certain it's a girl in there. I never felt this sick when Ivan was inside me. And I was never this tired. Nor did I feel this depressed. It must be a girl. I add more names to the list. We talk about Eli and Alice and Lo.

As the weeks pass, I think I just can't do this. A thought pops up compulsively more and more often. I'll be at work, in the middle of a meeting: I have to get an abortion. I'll say no to a glass of wine with my colleagues: I have to get an abortion. I'll look at my calendar, at any point past six months from now: I have to get an abortion. I'll snap at Ivan because he hits me and calls me stupid: I have to get an abortion. I'll be talking on the phone with my mom, who's started knitting a little sweater for her new grandchild: I have to get an abortion. I'll be texting with your parents to apologize for the fact that we're never in touch anymore: I have to get an abortion. I'll put Ivan to bed, and as he cries and fusses: I have to get an abortion. Before I fall asleep and as soon as I wake up, there it is. I can't handle this family project, I think. It's an idiotic idea, I think. I have to get an abortion. I really have to get an abortion, I think. The only problem is that I'm the only one who thinks so. And I don't dare tell anyone else.

I even lie to my therapist. Nobody knows that every time we quarrel I'm overcome by panic, real panic that pounds in my chest and makes it hard for me to breathe. Panic that makes me google "abortions" late at night. Nobody knows I've programmed the phone numbers to clinics in my phone. The thought is forbidden, and I can't, I just can't, go through with it. It would mean losing everything we've built over the last few months. It hasn't been articulated, but I just know that I'll lose them if I deviate from our plan, the one we both agreed on, the one I've promised to go through with. He'll never forgive me for an abortion. He'll leave me. If I back out now, I'll tear apart our family, and take Ivan's new sister from him, his possibility for a future with a family that's bigger than just me and him. His daughter will lose my presence in her life. She'll lose another mom, and Ivan will lose another dad. An abortion isn't an option. An abortion is unthinkable. Yet I can't stop thinking about it.

Every time we end up in a fight, in some serious conversation, trying to figure out what's gone wrong between us on the day in question, I think about it. Every time he blows up and gets angry or sad about something I've done or said or not said or not done. When he accuses me of being depressed, negative, impossible to live with, impossible to satisfy, I think about it. Everything is my fault. "You make your bed, you lie in it," as everyone knows, and I've made a bed, but I've found no rest. The time for regrets, for going back to the way things were before I was pregnant, has passed. Everyone knows now. Everyone except our children. They'll find out soon too, and I agonize about that day. Push it into the future with arguments that it's still too early, there's still a high risk of miscarriage.

Early or not, my pants are getting tight, and I hate it. My breasts hurt, and I have to be careful with them. My body seems to throw itself into pregnancy faster this time than the first. I swell, and I ache. No one can touch me. I would prefer to be alone. I rage about dishes that aren't cleared and toys that are left out. I push my anxiety out in every possible direction. Ivan gets nervous. His daughter gets nervous. I try to compensate and ask them to come to me on the sofa. I tickle them for a few minutes and they laugh. They climb all over me. I protect my stomach, shout "Ouch" when they get close to my breasts. I growl and sigh and compensate and spoil. I'm anything but a harmonious parent. It's only a matter of time before this bursts.

And then one day it does. But not for me, for him. One day he calls me at work—we were arguing this morning and went our separate ways in tense silence—and he's crying. He says it's obvious that I don't want the child, that I don't love him, that I'm not ready for the life we're building together. He weeps, and he screams that nothing matters to him anymore, that I might as well get an abortion. I'm silent during his call. Can't find the words to calm him, can't force myself to disagree. Not this time.

While we're talking, I walk around the block where I work. It's raining, and I protect the phone under my hood. I go round and round in silence. I listen as he weeps, stay silent when he quiets. I miss a meeting at work. Then I miss another one. I listen to his outrage, which seems to never end. He's so sad. So disappointed. It's clear to me that I can't deliver. I can't make him happy while also surviving myself. I can't do any worse to him than I already have.

Finally, I interrupt him. I have to raise my voice to do so. I start by saying that he's right, and then I tell him I think we moved too fast. I say I'm sorry that he feels the way he does about us and for the fact that I've been one big disappointment from beginning to end. I say I'm sorry that I couldn't be the person he wanted me to be, and that even though it doesn't change anything, I say I really tried. He tells me to stop being such a martyr. I apologize for that as well. Then I say I'll call a few clinics this afternoon and let him know if I can get an appointment this week. We don't have to decide this minute, I say. But maybe we need to look at our options again.

He's quiet. I can hear him blowing his nose. He says that's not what he wants. "Please, say you love me," he whispers. I'm silent. Just a little too long. Then I say it. For the first time in several months, I'm honest with him. "I love you. I love you so much every inch of me aches with it, but I can't do this. I'm sorry. It's impossible. It's just impossible for me."

That afternoon I call one of the abortion clinics I've had saved in my phone for weeks. I start to cry before I can even get my name out, and they give me an appointment. The woman on the phone doesn't seem to judge me for my ambivalence, and for the first time in a month, I talk openly about how I feel. By the time I hang up my face is swollen from weeping and my legs are too weak to hold me. I want to keep talking to the woman on the phone—she's the only person in the world I want to talk to about this—but I realize I don't even know her name.

———

One Tuesday morning we say goodbye and then we don't see each other again. I don't know that this is the morning it will happen, but I'm sure it's about to. This weekend's conversations were headed in that direction. When I said those words on the phone Friday, I realized I meant them and I could never take them back. Whatever the risks, no matter the cost, I knew. I'm not ready. I can't make myself ready. It's impossible.

We talked nonstop through the weekend with just a few breaks to deal with the kids, make food, and sleep. Sometimes we found our way to each other only to be torn apart again. He alternated between being furious and absent, lost in thought with sadness in his eyes. He alternated between saying that he would stay even if I chose to end the pregnancy and implying he would leave me if I went through with it. "If you don't want to build a family with me, have more children with me, then we don't want the same thing from our future," he said, and it was hard to argue when he put it like that.

Yesterday evening he stopped talking completely. He sat on the sofa with his headphones on and a glass of wine in his hand. Stared either straight ahead or down at his phone, never looked in my direction once as I moved about the apartment. His phone beeped regularly with text messages. I didn't ask whom they were from. Instead, I kept myself busy. I cleaned the counters. Hung up laundry. Picked up toys from the floor. Sorted the recycling into bins under the sink. By ten o'clock I was out of chores to do, and I didn't dare sit down next to him on the sofa. So I went to bed, but I couldn't fall asleep. I wondered when he was going to come in. If he'd want to talk when he did. I could hear him moving in the living room. I heard him pouring another glass of wine. I heard his phone still beeping regularly. In the end I heard him brush his teeth. But he never came into the bedroom. The clock passed midnight, and I must have fallen asleep because I woke up from a dream and instinctively stretched out a hand toward his side of the bed. He wasn't there. I snuck out. Found him on the sofa. He was asleep in a strange position, his headphones still over his ears. An empty wineglass stood on the coffee table, a tangled blanket over his legs. He still had his clothes on.

He woke up the moment I sat down by his feet on the sofa. He looked around in confusion for a few seconds before he saw me. He stared at me in silence. I stared back. We sat there for a while, just looking at each other and not saying a word. Finally he spoke. "I'm sorry, but I can't do this. I can't take it anymore." I nodded.

I gazed at him, and my vision filled with tears. For a second or two I struggled against the impulse to throw myself onto him, comfort him, apologize, and beg him to just forget everything that had happened the last few days. But I didn't. Instead, I just sat on the sofa and looked at him, the man I loved, but whose child I couldn't give birth to, and whom I was losing at this very moment. I looked at him and realized we'd reached the end. It was over. I looked away first. Stood up and went back to the bedroom. Gently, I opened the door. Just as gently, I closed it behind me again. I slipped into my bed, quiet so as not to wake Ivan, put my head on my pillow, and closed my eyes.

When morning arrived and first one, then two children woke up wanting breakfast, we acted like everything was normal. In unspoken agreement, we did exactly what we always do. We made breakfast and brushed our teeth, put on coats and searched for missing mittens. When we separated at the front door, he made no effort to kiss me. He bent down to Ivan, patted him on the cheek, and said, "Goodbye. Have a good day at preschool. See you soon." Ivan smiled at him, and he smiled back. I followed his example and repeated the same procedure with his daughter. She turned her face away when I was about to pat her cheek. My hand hung there in the air for a second before I changed position and started to wave instead. I stood up and looked at him one last time, but he didn't meet my eyes. We said, "Goodbye," "Talk to you later," and then went in our separate directions. I saw his back disappear out of the gate and waited a few seconds more before I followed. Outwardly, the morning had gone by just like any other morning. It's just that it was the last one.

At lunch, he calls me and says what I was waiting for him to say all weekend. He confirms my hunch that he can't stay with me if I go through with the abortion. He says he wants to be there for me during the procedure, but he doesn't think he can live with me anymore. He says he loves me just as much today as he has since he met me, maybe even more, but he no longer believes in a future together. He asks me one last time if this is really what I want. I answer, "No. This isn't what I want, but it's what I have to do. I'm not ready to be a mother again. I can't. It's impossible. It's too fast. I can't handle so much change in such a short period of time." I say it feels like I'll fall apart if I continue. Then he says it again. "In that case, we have no future together." Then says he has to go back to work. I can't stand to hang up even though we've already said goodbye, but I hear the phone click, then it starts to beep, and he's not there anymore, he's gone, but as long as I'm still holding the phone to my ear I can pretend he isn't. I sit there for a long time. Finally even the monotonous beeping stops and the telephone screen goes black. The call is over. Our relationship too.

At first I was sad. Then I got angry. Then I felt empty. Then I got sad again. Right now I'm angry, but I expect that'll change soon too. It's been like this all day.

Over the four hours that passed between our conversation and picking up Ivan from preschool, I managed to circle through a range of emotions. First: a bizarre feeling of unreality. Did this really happen? Am I alone again? I texted all the friends I could think of, explained what had happened briefly. The responses didn't take long. I reveled for a short period in the upset reactions of a few of my friends. They swore and used all caps. Some even called, and a few of those calls I even answered. That turned out to be a mistake, because the more I talked about it, the more the sense of unreality gave way to the comprehension that this had happened to me, not someone else. In a sudden impulse to protect him, I heard myself smooth things over, describe my own bad behavior lately. I explained how I more or less tricked him into believing I wanted the baby and was ready. I fumbled for words. Was interrupted, lost my train of thought, and tried again. My friends maintained what had happened was not okay. "You don't leave someone because they want to have an abortion four months into a relationship. You just don't do that." I gave up on my attempts to defend him and allowed myself to be a victim again, just for a little while.

In stepped grief. Like a punch to the gut, it spread through my body like a wave of nausea, and I sat there and cried again. Wiped off the telephone with the sleeve of my sweater, let the snot run down over my lips, tried through my sobs to find the words to describe how things have been lately, what caused my decision, what he said, what I said, how he reacted, how I reacted to what he said. Suddenly everything felt so unspeakably tragic.

And suddenly I was exhausted. I told my friend on the

phone that I couldn't talk anymore. She let me hang up with the promise that I call again soon. After the phone call ended, I calmed down a little. I opened our text chain and scrolled upward. Read through all of our recent text messages over the last few weeks, tried to read them neutrally and without judging either one of us. I failed royally. As I read, I became first irritated, then angry, and finally enraged. How dare he break up with me while claiming to love me more than he's ever loved anyone before? We've known each other for four months. A third of a year. Who the hell does he think he is with his ultimatums and emotional blackmail? What happened to me being his everything? The one he'd dreamed of meeting, who brought happiness to him again—what happened to that?

As soon as the rage washed over me, it was gone again. In its wake came the panic and an almost irresistible impulse to make everything right again. Should I call him now, say I've changed my mind, say we should follow through with it? Would he believe me, would he take me back if I just kept to the plan?

Then came self-loathing. What kind of person am I to think in terms of a love affair going according to a plan? Why would I beg a man who gives this kind of ultimatum to take me back? What kind of person am I to have given you a similar ultimatum once? What's wrong with me?

Two hours later, we're sitting on the floor of Ivan's playroom, loading small cars onto a tow truck. My interior is still chaos, but through constant practice in recent years I've developed the ability to keep the worst of my emotional turmoil beneath the surface when I'm with Ivan. I automatically save the worst for after he's fallen asleep. This evening is no different. I don't cry. I don't even sigh. Instead, we do what we always do. I make sure

I'm present for him, laugh when he makes jokes, look him in the eyes when he talks, and I make him his favorite food for dinner. He gets ice cream for dessert. We eat it on the floor and play with cars. My voice breaks only once and that's when Ivan asks me why the rest of our family isn't here. They're at their home, and we'll meet another day, I answer as calmly as I can, but my voice cracks on the last word, and I run into the bathroom, saying I have to pee. In the bathroom, I sob as quietly as I can. Stare at myself in the mirror and count to ten. Go out again. We go on. Like we always do, like we always have. We never stop, me and Ivan. That's not our thing.

In a week, I have an appointment at Karolinska University Hospital for a surgical abortion. The procedure will last twenty minutes, and I still haven't decided if I want him to be there with me. I think the next few days will tell. A part of me never wants to see him again. Another part of me wants him with me right now, wants his comfort and all of his love. I ignore that side, at least for now, to the best of my ability. That side has nothing to win by longing for a person who's decided not to be here. I tell myself he can't possibly love me if he'd leave me for this. I just have to make it work somehow. I've suffered worse losses than this, haven't I? I know how to keep on living. I look at the clock and see it's Ivan's bedtime.

We pick up the cars from the floor and start our bedtime routine. I put Ivan in his pajamas. We warm up his bottle together in the microwave, count to thirty together. We take turns shaking it, and we end up on the sofa. Ivan drinks it all down. We head toward the bathroom, and I brush his teeth with the green toothbrush while trying not to look at the yellow toothbrush standing next to Ivan's. I chat with Ivan about plaque monsters and dentists while I brush. Look deep in his mouth, inspect his teeth. He opens wide. He is terrified of the plaque monsters. I say the plaque monsters aren't real monsters, but they do like eating away at teeth. It's the same way we always talk. We go into the bedroom, pull down the blinds, and lie down together in my bed. Just as we always do.

At the other end of the room stands another bed, still unmade. In the dim light of the bedside lamp, it gapes open, empty, and looks like it's crying out for something. I don't want to look at the bed, but still my gaze is drawn there. Sticking out of the jumble of pillows and the crumpled blanket I see the silhouette of two stuffed animals, a sheep and a cow. They've been living here for two months now. They've spent every night in her arms since the first night she slept here. Tonight they're alone. When she woke up this morning, she thought she'd fall asleep here tonight again. Ivan thought so too. As if he is reading my thoughts, Ivan breaks the silence by asking where she is. Maybe he followed my gaze across the dimly lit bedroom. Maybe it's only now that it hits him there's something different about this evening. I tell him she's sleeping at her home tonight. "Why?" he asks. I say, "We'll meet her another day. Soon," I promise. "Sleep now." I kiss him on the forehead. He turns away. I stroke his hair. He tells me to stop. I lie silently next to him and stare up into the darkness. Trying not to look over at the shadows in that empty bed. How will she be able to fall asleep without her stuffed animals tonight? What will he tell her when she asks about us? What should I say to Ivan when we don't meet them tomorrow or the day after that? What have we done? What have I done? How could we do this to our children?

A day goes by. Then another one. Now it's been three. I manage to keep Ivan busy and more or less entertained. In a not completely unpleasant way, our life returns to the familiar. There's a kind of temporary calm. I have nobody to answer to except Ivan. No one to live up to besides Ivan. No one pointing out my shortcomings as a stepmom or life partner. No one accusing me of being impossible to live with or reminding me that I'm not enough. From an existence in which the number of roles I had to fill seemed overwhelming, I now have only one. And I know that one well. I'm Ivan's mom, no more and no less. It's all about getting through the days. Making them as pleasant for him as possible. It's about not dwelling on the big questions, everything that never was, everything that will never be. It's about taking the minutes and hours one at a time. Letting time pass, doing what's simplest in the moment.

My family and friends seem relieved and determined to help me through this crisis as well. Suddenly everyone is around again. On my phone and in our apartment. The ones who told me we were moving too fast seem relieved. Those who kept their thoughts to themselves do so no longer. Even those who, up until three days ago, were supportive of me in all my hasty life changes admit they were worried. The overall view seems to be that I've finally come to my senses and now I'm making the best of a difficult situation. I reinforce that impression in the conversation. In moments of doubt I call whatever friend is available, sometimes several in a row, and ask them to repeat it for me. I lean on them and repeat their words like a mantra: I'm doing the right thing. It wasn't meant to be, not this time, not for me. It never would have worked. It went too fast and I couldn't keep up. I don't have the energy. I wasn't ready. It's nobody's fault it turned out like it did. He's angry with me now,

317

but he'll forgive me one day. I'm angry with him now, but I'll forgive him one day. Everything will work out in the end. I just have to get through this.

In four days I'm going to Karolinska University Hospital to have the abortion, with or without him by my side. After the procedure, it will take me one or two weeks to physically recover. In a month, it will be as if it never happened. In four months, as much time will have passed as we spent together. In the long run, this is best for Ivan. He'll have me back as an attentive parent. He won't get a little sibling, probably not an older sibling either, but he will have a parent who hasn't mentally collapsed. I tell myself that's the most important thing. Ivan keeps me, and I keep Ivan. That's the only thing that matters in the long run. That's the only commitment I would never betray or fail. We have to stick together. I have to keep us together. It's on me. It's been on me the whole time.

For the first few days Ivan's questions come constantly: Where are they today? Why aren't they with us? Can we go to their house now? What about tomorrow? Why not? When will we see them again? Then the questions start to thin out. Today is the first day he hasn't mentioned them at all. Maybe Ivan understands more than is reasonable to expect of him. Maybe he can tell that talking about them makes me uncomfortable. Maybe he's noticed how I struggle to sound natural when I answer. Or maybe he doesn't think of it much at all. Whatever the reason, he seems to be happy with the flood of visitors and activities we used to spend our days and weeks with. One day my mom visits and sleeps over. They read fairy tales on our sofa, set up a train set over our whole living room floor, and Ivan helps her bake

cookies that look like chess pieces. He's never heard of chess before, let alone a chessboard, but he wrestles to both say it and
transform the brown and white dough. Another day, your parents pick him up from preschool and take him to their house,
where he's allowed to play, under Grandpa's strict supervision, in
the big workshop in the basement. When Ivan comes home that
evening, he talks nonstop about all the tools in Grandpa's workshop right up to the moment he falls asleep. On a third evening,
your little brother comes by. We eat an early dinner, and your
brother roughhouses with Ivan in bed, pretends to be an airplane
and carries him screaming with joy through all the rooms.

And so it goes. I try to take the days one by one. Tending to
what needs tending to: the dishes, the washing, the cleaning—
all are simple. Taking care of Ivan is also simple. As is doing
my job. Especially now, when I don't sneak away constantly for
hours-long private phone conversations. I get a lot done, maintain my composure, and Ivan's life looks basically the same as it
did before. The days fly by. I keep us occupied. Let time pass.
Waiting for now to become then.

When Ivan falls asleep, I pace around the apartment for a few
hours. The silence is palpable and my grief piercing. In the
evenings, only after Ivan's fallen asleep, I allow myself to mourn
a little bit. In the evenings, I miss his company, our conversations, the life I had with him. I miss being loved by him. I miss
his physical presence, his scent, his laughter, his teeth. I miss his
daughter and the messes she left on my living room floor. I miss
that first period, when we were newly in love, before the question of having more children cast a shadow over our lives. I miss
our phone calls and text messages.

In the evenings, I write to him. For hours. I start hundreds of text messages and don't send a single one. In some messages, I ask him how he's feeling, what he's thinking, if this is really how it's got to be for us from now on. In others, I chew him out, accuse him of being cold for leaving me just because I can't go through with the pregnancy. In others, I blame him for leaving not only me but also Ivan so suddenly. In others, I want to destroy him, mock him, hurt him by calling him callous, manipulative, and manically fixated on bringing more children into the world. Then I write other types of text messages. In them, I beg him to come back to me, to us; I plead for his love and for him to forgive me for wounding him so deeply. The tone of these messages changes as quickly as my emotions. One thing they all share: every single one stays on my phone. Not one is sent. Something stops me. Maybe it's that I'm pregnant and don't dare to confront him until I'm not anymore. Or maybe I'm just not able to handle another conversation in which he tells me how angry and disappointed he is with me. Maybe I just don't have the energy to be left again. Or perhaps it's my guilt standing in the way. Maybe it's that I don't know what being in contact again right now would entail. My messages end up unsent in a document on my telephone. They never reach their intended recipient. The document grows longer and longer as the days go by.

Around eleven, I permit myself to go lie down next to Ivan in bed. Commend myself for getting us through yet another day without any major traumas. Try to tell myself I'm a strong person, a good parent, someone who does the right thing. Say to myself in as mature a voice as I can muster: This is how it has to be. Even though it hurts.

———

One morning I wake up and it's been two years since you died. In the midst of those parenthetical days between what was and what comes later, suddenly the anniversary arrives. My phone reminds me of it before I even get out of bed. I wake up to several text messages from people telling me their thoughts are with me on this day. They send hearts and say they're here for me if I need them. Your mom writes to ask me if there's anything she can do. If I'd like her to come sleep over with me and Ivan, today or after the surgery, don't hesitate to ask. One friend asks me if I'd like to meet up after Ivan's out of preschool and go to the cemetery to light two candles together. She suggests a time and place, writes that all I have to do is show up, and we'll do the rest together.

My first impulse is to leave her question hanging, wait until it's too late to follow through on her suggestion, then thank her for her thoughtfulness. The thought of going there together feels overwhelming. It's bad weather and I'm tired. I have enough on my plate just making the days as humbly enjoyable as possible for Ivan, and I suspect that a trip to the cemetery might interrupt that flow. Not to mention if it's during that delicate time between preschool and dinner. Ivan will most likely have low blood sugar and be both whiny and tired. Besides, it feels inappropriate to go to the cemetery when I'm carrying another man's child inside my body. I feel like a complete failure as a grieving widow. It feels like the most respectful thing would be not to soil your day with my presence this year.

But after I drop off Ivan at preschool and arrive at work, the thought still gnaws at me. This is the two-year anniversary. I should do something special. Maybe it would be nice to go to the cemetery with my friend and Ivan and light a candle for you after all. It's not like you're sitting there judging me. After an hour of mulling it over, I answer her text, write I'd like to join her there today. I thank her for being there for me, always, supporting me in the way she does. She answers with a simple "Oh, stop it" and repeats the time and place we'll meet.

After I pick up Ivan, we meet at a subway station near his preschool. Your little brother comes with us. We meet by the tracks in the middle of rush hour, and Ivan, who was skeptical at first, lights up like the sun when he sees his uncle. Together we jump on the subway and head toward the cemetery. My friend explains to Ivan that we're going to light a candle for you. She talks about heaven, and I can see that Ivan is confused. It's been a few months since we last mentioned heaven at home. My friend's words stress me out, and I think I should probably talk to my friends pretty soon about how I want them to approach discussions of death with Ivan. I realize I should have done so already. The problem is that I don't really know what I want. And besides, I haven't been hanging out with my friends for quite a while. I'm not even sure I want Ivan to think about his father today. I'm afraid he'll connect the word "Papa" with someone who disappears.

I want the conversation about heaven to end for now, and it does, at Ivan's initiative. He tires of listening and starts talking about something concrete, something he understands. He asks what subways do, asks where the driver sits, mimics the voice of the speakers that say "Watch out for closing doors" and "Mind the gap between the platform and train." He turns to his uncle for attention, and soon they're playing peekaboo. My friend keeps talking about this or that. Outside the window my old subway station passes by, and I avert my eyes to avoid seeing the apartment building where we lived two years ago today. When I moved last year, I promised myself to never go back, and so far I haven't.

★　　★　　★

The air is raw and the sky gray when we arrive. For the first time in over a year, I find myself in the cemetery where you and I used to take walks in the evening, first without Ivan, then with him inside me, then later strapped to our stomachs. Today he's walking between me and your little brother. One hand in mine and one in his uncle's, he commands us to lift him up until he's flying in the air between us. We obey. He shouts in delight every time. This place doesn't mean anything special to Ivan. He doesn't remember your funeral in the big chapel to the left of the entrance, the 150 people who showed up to mourn the loss of you. He doesn't remember any of the slushy footpaths I forced his stroller down while the rest of Sweden watched Donald Duck on the first Christmas without you. Today it's still autumn, and snow won't arrive for a couple of months. I'm overcome by the uncanny feeling that this cemetery has been with us from the beginning, that it called to us even in the beginning, and now we are all here together. In different ways, in different forms, but we're here.

It's twilight when we arrive, and we're alone at the memorial slope. We take out our candles, and Ivan helps my friend place them in the grass. The wind is blowing up on the memorial slope, which sticks out as the single high hill in this rolling landscape. The trees offer no shelter, and the October wind is cold. My scarf flutters, and my hair whips in front of my eyes. The wind also finds its way to the candles. One keeps going out, and my friend tends to it, relighting it patiently again. Then a third time. She chats with the candle and Ivan and you in turn. Your brother and I stand silently behind her. I pull my coat more tightly around me, hide the lower half of my face behind my scarf until it's warm and damp from my breath. Your brother stands next to me, warming his hands in his jeans pockets, seems to be way too thinly dressed. He's aware of my situation on the home front, but we agreed over text not to talk about it with Ivan present. As for Ivan, he's soon bored with the candles, and his eyes rove over the lawn at the base of the slope. He wants to run down that steep hill rather than stare at some candle that won't burn. He comes over to us, takes your little brother by the hand, pulls impatiently on it, says, "Come on, come on now! Come with me!"

Your little brother seems relieved to have a reason to leave the grove and the awkward silence that has arisen in our group. My friend wants to stay a little longer. I stand, freezing, behind her, and she sits with the candle, her eyes glued to the flame. Without Ivan's persistent babbling, she now speaks without interruption directly to you. "Hello, dearest Aksel," she says. "We miss you and love you. You should know we think about you every day. Ivan is such a wonderful little guy. I hope you can see that from wherever you are." My friend seems both satisfied and unhampered to talk to you via a lit candle on the memorial slope. I suppose that's how this memorial grove is supposed to work. As for me, I can't get out a single sound. I can barely call you forth in my mind without focusing on myself instead. What should I say now? What should I do? Isn't it odd that I'm standing here in silence while my friend is there with the candles? Shouldn't it be the other way around? Should I go forward now? What should I say? How long should we stay here? Where did Ivan and your little brother go?

My gaze travels from the candles and out over the meadow, which stands between the memorial slope and the chapel. I see Ivan and your little brother running downward and away. They're headed toward the chapel and the big cross in front of it. Their silhouettes get tinier the farther away they go. Your brother is holding Ivan by the hand, and I can tell he's running slowly, carefully, as if in slow motion, so that Ivan has a chance of keeping up. Together they look like two little figures in an infinite landscape. The sound of them is getting fainter the farther away they go. The low sky and the huge cross outside the chapel seem to meet. It's a beautiful image. Fateful and symbolic. I see your brother tickling Ivan, who throws himself down onto the grass. Your little brother lifts him up in the air, holding him toward the sky, puts him on his shoulders. Ivan kicks his legs, his woolen hat tumbles down onto the grass, and even from this distance I can hear his joyous cry. I relax. Ivan is doing just fine.

My friend has quieted. She's still hunched down with her eyes on the candles. She runs her hand over the grass around them, seems to have finished talking to you for now. She lets out a puff of breath as she stands up. Puts her hands on her knees for support. Turns around. She comes over to me, puts her arms around me, holds me in her embrace for a moment. I pat her back and wonder who is comforting whom. Maybe we both are. I wait a moment, then gently disentangle myself from our hug, ask her if maybe we shouldn't get going. My friend pats my cheek—only she could get away with patting my cheek in that grandmotherly way—and says, "Yes. Let's go."

Arm in arm, we leave the memorial slope and the two candles that now flutter humbly in their cups in the wind on the hill. We make our way carefully down the steep steps. They're covered with clay and small stones. The grass is moist and the ground slippery. My friend keeps her arm linked with mine. Sometimes she loses her balance and leans against me. Sometimes I do the same. We make our way forward and downward at an easy pace. As we get closer to Ivan and your brother, their silhouettes become bigger and the contrasts in their faces more clear. I can see that Ivan is laughing. His blue hat is still lying on the grass. I think, I better buy him some new mittens soon. And rain pants. And autumn clothes in general. He's gone through a growth spurt lately, and almost everything he owns is too short. I should go shopping over my lunch break tomorrow. Better to do it before my procedure rather than after, I might not feel very good afterward. I decide to take care of it first thing tomorrow. There's no need to wait.

My friend breaks the silence and brings me back to the moment we're in. "Are you okay?" she asks and gently pats my arm as she says it. I don't know how to answer that so I don't say anything. Instead, we walk on in silence, her arm still linked with mine, my eyes still on Ivan and your brother. My friend seems to be content with my lack of an answer, so I take my time thinking about it.

I have no idea if I'm okay. Or rather: I guess I'm okay, depending on how one chooses to interpret the word. I'm breathing and alive. I'm healthy and have the strength to get us through the days in a way that makes them if not always enjoyable, at least bearable. I have friends and family who care about me and want the best for me. I have a job and a salary that we can live on. I still don't have a handle on my love life, and I'll probably need to mourn this lost love in secret for a while. But I'll get over it. Surely I'll get over it.

I watch Ivan laughing with his uncle, completely unaware that he's horsing around just meters from the chapel where his father's funeral was held less than two years ago. My Ivan, who still laughs every day and has an arsenal of people around him to keep him laughing. He'll probably miss the other halved family that's no longer with us. But he'll get over that too. I'll help him. As long as I live, I'll continue to fill his life with meaning and safety. Maybe I wasn't the best partner to you. Maybe I'm not the best friend to my friends. Maybe I'm not such a great sister or daughter or sister-in-law. I was definitely not the best girlfriend in my latest relationship. But in Ivan I've found my purpose, my reason for being. I'm not ashamed of that job. The rest will take care of itself. And if it doesn't, that's okay too. All in all, I guess I'm okay. In fact, maybe "okay" is the word that best describes it.

I clear my throat and answer my friend, a little late to really connect to her earlier question: "Yes, I am." She answers with a simple "Good" and then we stand there. My eyes are on Ivan. We're just a few meters from him, but he hasn't noticed us yet. He's busy playing with his uncle. I think, Life is so strange. In a few years, the memory of this day will feel remote, but perhaps this image of Ivan and your brother in front of the cross will remain. Maybe the thought that I almost, but only almost, became another child's mother will feel increasingly bizarre as the days go by. Or maybe it won't at all. I have no idea. I can only hope for the best.

Ivan has noticed me now. He storms over the grass, yelling, "Mama, mama, come look." He's found a leaf that looks like a ghost. He points to the eyes and the mouth. He stops, asks, "What should we do now?" I let go of my friend and crouch down. My knees become wet from the grass. My eyes are level with Ivan's. His cheeks are rosy, and pine needles and grass stick out all over his hair. I stroke his head and tell him it's time to go home and have dinner. He asks what we are going to eat and can his uncle come with us. I say, "Of course he can," and, "It's your choice what we eat." He says, "Poop dogs and butts," and laughs at his own joke, turns around to get his uncle's acknowledgment. He gets it. He gets mine too. Then he asks for meatballs and macaroni. I tell him that sounds good. Meatballs are the perfect choice for today. I pick up his hat from the grass next to him, put it on his head, and stand up. Stretch out my hand, and Ivan takes it. We start to go.

ABOUT THE AUTHO

Carolina Setterwall was born in 1978 in Sala, S
studying media and communication in Uppsala,
and London, she worked within the music and p
dustries as an editor and writer. Setterwall lives i
with her son.